JETTY CAT PALACE CAFÉ

Jetty Cat Palace Café

a novel

JUDY KEESLAR SANTAMARIA

LUMINARE PRESS

WWW.LUMINAREPRESS.COM

Jetty Cat Palace Café
Copyright ©2019 Judy Keeslar Santamaria

Jetty Cat Palace Café is a work of fiction. Apart from well-known actual people
and locales that figure in the narrative, all names, characters, places, and
incidents are the products of the author's imagination or are used fictitiously.
Any resemblance to actual persons, living or dead, is purely coincidental.

Printed in the United States of America

Cover Design: Claire Flint Last

Luminare Press
442 Charnelton St.
Eugene, OR 97401
www.luminarepress.com

LCCN: 2019917211
ISBN: 978-1-64388-223-9

This book is dedicated to Nick,
my beyond-amazing husband,
who makes the best cioppino on the planet;
who shares my insatiable love for all things coastal;
and who ignites the lights leading back to safe harbor
when my characters and I venture
where roof angels fear to tread.

Acknowledgements

Editing and Support

I'm deeply grateful to the incredibly gracious, creative, and talented staff of Luminare Press (luminarepress.com), who made my dream of publishing *Jetty Cat Palace Café* come true: Patricia, Claire, Kim, Melissa, Jamie, and Nina;

To Ronan Sadler (alembiceditorial.com), whose insightful editing and empathetic coaching gave wing to the spirit of this novel;

To Erin Brown (erinedits.com) and Meghan Ward (meghanward.com) for guidance during the earliest drafts;

And to Nick, who has read these pages umpteen times and still believes in me.

Inspiration

The people, marinas, and beaches of Washington's Cranberry Coast, especially Westport, Grayland, and Tokeland;

The jetty cats!
Please donate to Harbor Association of Volunteers for Animals (hava-heart.org) or at Sea Bird Gifts and Candy, 2563 Westhaven Dr., Westport, WA 98595;

San José State University Music Department staff
and students (1966-1970), especially
pianists Pamela Pyle Resch, Kathy Bullock, and
Sondra Wheeler;

Frédéric Chopin, Wolfgang Amadeus Mozart,
and Igor Stravinsky;

Stevie Nicks and Fleetwood Mac;

Adrienne (for thousands of reasons);

A nod to my music students, far and wide;

Individuals on the autism spectrum
 especially those with Asperger's syndrome;

And finally, Kai.
Wish I knew then what I know now.

With Gratitude and In Loving Memory

GEOFFREY FAIRWEATHER

ANNETTE LESIEGE

ANN MCCLELLAND

VERNON READ

BEANS, THE BEST ORANGE CAT EVER

MY PARENTS, OREON AND JULIA KEESLAR

*If a man does not keep pace with his companions,
perhaps it is because he hears a different drummer.
Let him step to the music which he hears,
however measured or far away.*

Henry David Thoreau
(1854)

1.

River Bridge Performing Arts
Boarding School for Girls, Redmond, Washington

Morgen hammered her way through the Fantasie for Piano, the scent of patchouli oil intensifying with every beat. As a vision in a tie-dyed dress danced closer to her grand piano, she heard a phrase from Stravinsky's Concerto for Piano and Wind Instruments, which was *not* the music she was playing, and a string exploded inside the piano, sending hundreds of pounds of energy surging through her fingers and into her arms. She recoiled, and her hands began to flap like featherless wings while she remained perched on the bench, eyes wide and every nerve on fire.

"Mom?" she whispered. She peered inside the piano, her fingers hovering above the keys, and another string burst with a flash like a snapped power line. "Poor old thing. I don't blame you. I'm approaching a breaking point too—"

"Dr. Marín?" the secretary interrupted over the intercom. "Headmistress Collier wants to see you. Shall I tell her you're on your way?"

"No, please tell her I'll see her tomorrow. I've been practicing since 5:37 this morning, and I'm going home to rest. Would you please send the tech to fix my piano again? The G above middle C and F# below just gave up the ghost. Thanks." She rubbed her tingling hands together. The dancing image had vanished, but her mother's scent wafted around the cramped office as though looking for a way out.

"You could come home with me," she murmured. She glanced at the collectables she'd arranged on the window-sill: an apothecary jar, jewelry dish, ceramic canister, and a colorful tin box. Each with a lid but empty. Together, a reminder of the cruelest theft.

Now this recently completed Fantasie was cruelly stealing her time. She pressed two fingers to her throat to check her pulse. *Moderato* ($\quarternote$ = 97 beats per minute, a medium pace). Fine for a metronome but rather high for a heartbeat, likely indicating anxiety. For the first time in her life, she'd been assigned a composition that was musically illogical and completely lacked emotion. Was Andras intentionally setting her up to fail, or was it her fault that his music didn't resonate with her? Why did practicing this particular piece make the healed fractures in her fingers ache as though they were cracking open? She blew warm breath into her cupped hands and studied the score. Something wasn't right, but she had to make it work. What if she changed a note or two? Would the Fantasie, or her entire life, unravel like a torn sweater? What if she tweaked the fingering again? As she erased the most recent sequence of numbers scribbled above an awkward phrase, she tore a small hole in the page. Maybe that was what Andras's Fantasie needed: to let some of his hot air escape.

She closed the sheet music and gazed at an announcement thumbtacked to her office wall amid a checkerboard of framed awards, diplomas, photographs, and programs.

You Are Cordially Invited to Attend
A Black-Tie Gala Concert Celebrating
the West Coast Premiere of Fantasie for Piano
Composed by Andras Bacon and Performed by
Morgen Marín

Monday, December 8, 2003, at 8 p.m.
Memorial Theater, River Bridge Performing Arts
Boarding School for Girls

Open Bar, Dinner to Follow

All Donations to Benefit the
River Bridge Scholarship Fund

She took her blue crystal star keepsake off the music stand and squeezed it. She'd written on the Fantasie cover an insightful quote attributed to Mozart: "The music is not in the notes but in the silence between." Evidently, she'd have to crack open that silence because the notes Andras had written made no sense to her, but who was she to question him?

THE CITY BUS WAS IRRITATINGLY JERKY AND SLOW, AND diesel smoke burned Morgen's sinuses. She slathered orange-ginger sanitizer on her hands. Her therapist had recommended that she apply lotions, because they were self-soothing in a socially acceptable way. She cupped her hands over her nose and mouth and gently rocked to avoid feeling nauseated.

Why did Andras's Fantasie threaten her senses of pitch, rhythm, and muscle memory? She could easily sight-read at tempo anything written for piano, but this twenty-four-page piece disturbed her on a visceral level. The much-anticipated work would complete his doctorate, but it sounded as though he'd written more notes than music. Was she fighting Andras himself, who might be trying to intrude into her life again? He'd often accused her of hiding secrets from him *inside* her hands. Maybe that was why he was trying to beat the crap out of them now.

Either way, she was committed. Headmistress Collier depended on her, as River Bridge's crown jewel, to deliver a performance for the ages. Andras Bacon, her former master teacher and worst nightmare, knew that her need for approval and acceptance guaranteed that she'd play his Fantasie perfectly.

Her fingers robotically tapped rhythms on her thighs as she stared at her reflection in the bus's rattling window: shoulder-length, golden-brown hair, lapis-blue eyes with flecks of gold, and a slight overbite but otherwise average features with a "subtle allure, a *je ne sais quoi*," as Andras had told her more than once. She still was unable to recognize her own face even after being examined by ophthalmologists and psychiatrists. It was as though by looking at her reflection, she was looking inward, and what she saw there was always in shadow.

ONCE INSIDE HER STUDIO APARTMENT, MORGEN BOLTED the door and dropped her backpack on the hardwood floor. When she flipped a switch, a pale-green limelight illuminated shelves of fragile collectables like the ones in her school office. A floor-to-ceiling beach scene she'd painted on the plaster wall also became bathed in light. Fanciful fish, gulls, sea stars, and hermit crabs greeted her with toothy

Cheshire-cat grins under a caption that read Mom's Pithy Advice: Correct Your Posture. Don't Chew Your Lips. Ask How Do You Do? Be NICE, and No Matter What, SMILE!

She crossed the room in a series of ballet leaps and pirouettes until she arrived in the kitchenette where she'd left her cell phone. Evidently, she'd missed two calls, so she checked her voicemail. "Darling, Gram here. I need to see you, so please come down on Saturday. I'll reimburse your bus fare and treat you to lunch."

She smiled and listened to the second message. "Hi, it's Violet, and guess what? I just found out that I get to learn the Stravinsky concerto for my baccalaureate concert. Dr. Byrd will conduct, and I wanted you to hear it from me. Can you believe it? Thank you for being my inspiration all these years."

Morgen's cheeks stung when she deleted the messages. That concerto had always been the foundation of *her* personal identity, and she had practically owned it after her own baccalaureate concert thirteen years, four months, and twenty-four days earlier when everybody had rhapsodized about her performance. "Why am I accepted only for what I do in the limelight and not for who I am offstage?" she whispered to the silent phone in her hand.

Why didn't they make Violet learn Andras's hideous composition instead? A bitter taste bubbled in the back of Morgen's throat as it often did when she thought about him. Sure, Violet had been her favorite piano student *ever*, and the two shared a peculiar history, because Violet was Andras's daughter.

She wound her metronome and set it at *allegro* ($\quarternote$ = 130, a quick and bright tempo), *tick, tick,* and started to pace around her apartment. Violet sounded giddy about winning the concerto, while she was stuck with the Fantasie, which was, in her opinion, the aesthetic antithesis of it. The U should have asked her permission for Violet to play the concerto. That would have been nice considering *she'd* sacrificed her youth to master the extended program. *She'd* endured Andras's passion for sensational theater complete with unprecedented wardrobe and makeup changes. By performing that concerto, *she'd* unwittingly cemented her estrangement from her mother for all eternity. "It's not fair," she yelled at the creatures painted on the wall. She silenced the metronome and rummaged through cupboards in her kitchenette until she found a plastic bag of "trio mix," aka trail mix to outsiders. "Three delectable ingredients in perfect harmony," her mother long-ago intoned like a saint or a witch while she assembled Morgen's medicinal M&M's, dried cranberries, and roasted almonds. "Trio mix restores equilibrium."

Thanks for the recipe, Mom. Morgen dumped half of a cup of trio mix onto the counter and sorted plain M&M's into rows by color and dried cranberries and roasted almonds into separate piles while considering her options: stay home and wallow in a foul mood, return to her office to practice, or enjoy a visit with Gram, who cherished her unconditionally but would want to discuss dying and her money. She popped five yellow M&M's into her mouth and swept the remaining trio mix into the plastic bag. For once, it was an easy choice.

She peeled off her faculty uniform, changed into her favorite white cable-knit sweater, jeans, and red sneakers, and shoved her blue crystal star keepsake and random essentials into her backpack. With a nod at her audience grinning at her from the mural on the wall, she grabbed her peacoat, turned off the limelight, and raced out the door to catch the next southbound bus.

THE WEATHER WAS CLEAR AND CRISP, AND FROM THE BUS window, Morgen could see the snowy summit of Mt. Rainier in the distance. Once in Kent, she walked twenty-three minutes until she reached a brick, ranch-style home. Mirrored glass balls on pedestals and whimsical rabbit topiaries surrounded a wood sign that read Water Street Eldercare. She crossed a lawn littered with maple leaves to a ramp leading to the front porch. After taking a deep breath, she knocked on the oversize yellow door and was met by a petite woman with jet-black bouffant hair and sporting lime-green scrubs.

"Hi, Pauline," Morgen said, offering her best smile to her grandmother's caregiver.

"Granddaughter, what a surprise. No school today?"

"Substitutes are covering my classes, because I'm on a performance assignment." She stepped into a roomy, yellow foyer smelling pleasantly of Pine-Sol cleaner. "Think house arrest with a grand piano." She followed Pauline down a wide corridor equipped with a handrail into an elegantly furnished assisted living suite.

"Please be positive," Pauline said over her shoulder. "Your granny is convinced that she's dying."

"Is that Morgen?" Grandma Eleanor was slumped in her wheelchair. As usual, she wore a pink velour pantsuit, fuzzy pink socks, and gold lamé slippers. Behind thick trifocal lenses, gray eye shadow accented her large blue eyes, and rouge warmed her otherwise-pallid cheeks.

"I've missed you." Morgen knelt to embrace Gram and breathe in her Chanel No. 5 perfume. At eighty-five years, four months, and twenty days, Gram was losing her battles against osteoporosis, congestive heart failure, and presumably dementia.

"I wasn't expecting you until Saturday, but since you're here now, let's not waste any time. With Pauline's help, I prepared a presentation for you." Gram coughed and cleared her throat. "I'll explain the three pet projects I want to finish before I die."

"I keep telling you that you're not dying." Morgen dropped her backpack and peacoat on the floor and shoved an armchair closer to Gram's chair.

Pauline returned with a tray. "This afternoon, it's Yankees-Red Sox, Marlins-Cubs," she said as she poured two cups of tea. "Yesterday, Mr. Moises tried to catch the baseball, but a fan got it instead, and my Cubbies lost their game." She hung Morgen's coat on a hook and left the room.

Morgen sat and sipped her tea. "Pet projects?"

Gram brightened. "First of all, I've made everything simple for you to manage. All my assets are in a trust with you as sole beneficiary."

"I love you with all my heart, but I don't need to hear about your assets again."

"Darling, I'm wearing out even though I take lots of medicine and have very loving help. Pauline's heart is in the right place, but she wants to save us all even when it's no longer possible. Anywho, I don't want you to go through what you did with your mother's estate. Good thing Andras Bacon took you under his wing back then."

"More like under his thumb." Morgen blushed and clasped her hands to keep them from flapping. She'd begged Andras to let her join marching band or glee club. She'd wanted to belong with her peers, but he had said no. She was a soloist; piano was her better voice.

Gram squinted at her. "In addition, I rented a unit in both our names at University Mini-Storage. Odds and ends, family heirlooms, and your red attaché case are in there along with a box of your mother's things."

Morgen patted her hand. "That's nice."

"I made it clear in my will that I don't want a service and that I want to be cremated. When you leave, take that fat envelope on the stand by the door, and keep it in a safe place. All my important documents are there along with my attorney's business card, a key to our storage, and a little spending money. Your only responsibility will be to scatter my ashes into the Pacific Ocean off Todos Santos on the Baja Peninsula in Mexico. That's where your mother's ashes were headed at her request before someone stole her urn from my guestroom a few years ago."

"I knew her urn had been stolen, but I didn't know anything about Mexico." Her fingers involuntarily twitched. She'd never told Gram about compulsively collecting substitute containers ever since.

"You also don't know that whoever snatched Charlie's urn left her silver necklace in its place, one that Grandpa Scott had given her but that I hadn't seen in many years. I thought she'd lost it, and then poof, there it was. I reported the theft, but the authorities wouldn't do anything because I'd gone next door to see the neighbor and left my doors unlocked. I keep my sanity by knowing your mother often disappears without telling me where she's going, who she's with, or when she'll be back. You know how your mother is."

Morgen touched Gram's arm. "It's was. I know how my mother *was*, past tense. Remember? We lost her more than thirteen years ago."

"Not entirely." Gram leaned forward in her chair, and her expression softened. "I know you better than anyone, darling. It looks like something's bothering you. Are you okay?"

Morgen's cell phone rang. "Hello? Oh, I was just going to call you, because there's been a family emergency, and I won't be back until Monday. No problem, I can practice here. Thanks. Bye." She exhaled through tight lips. "That was Headmistress. See, I'm scheduled to perform Andras Bacon's Fantasie from memory on December 8. Problem is, the piece knows that I hate it," she lowered her voice, "and it hates me. It's trying to break my poor fingers and then, surprise, surprise, I swear I saw Mom dancing in my office today while I practiced." She shoved the phone into her backpack and grabbed the bag of trio mix. "I think I'm losing what's left of my mind. Want some?"

Gram shook her head. "Family emergency? You just fibbed to your boss. Anywho, it's quite possible you did see your mother. She has a habit of dropping—"

"Really?" Morgen's eyes got big. "I wanted to hug her and tell her that I'm sorry, that it was my fault we were estranged, and now all of a sudden...I'm feeling sick or emotional. It's hard to tell which since I started therapy." She clenched her fists and tried not to cry. "I still miss her every day, but I missed her even when she was alive, because I loved her so much but never knew if she loved—"

"*Shh*, or Pauline will put us in time-out," Gram whispered. "Darling, I miss Charlie with all my heart too, and let's toss that evil Fantasie into the dumpster because it's upsetting—"

"What? I can't do that. I was *assigned* that piece, and the premiere is a big deal for everybody. Andras needs it to complete his doctorate, Headmistress wants the acclaim, and River Bridge desperately needs the money."

"Is it a big deal for you?" Gram raised her eyebrows.

"For *me*? I just told you, I was *assigned* the Fantasie by Andras and Headmistress, who have the authority to do so, and that's why it's a big deal to me. Although, come to think of it, that sounds controlling, doesn't it?" She half laughed. "All I do now is work on it, but I miss my students. I'm starting to feel even more disconnected than usual."

"Which might be part of their plan," Gram muttered under her breath. "Anywho, let's be grateful that the great continuum gave you music as a lifeline." She fumbled inside another pocket. "I planned to surprise you this weekend, but this is the perfect moment." She handed Morgen a necklace. "This is the keepsake that Grandpa Scott gave your mother, and I want you to have it."

"Mom wore this? Are you sure you want to give it away?" She held the silver necklace to the light. "Oh dear Lord, thank you. It's lovely and unusual." It felt oddly warm in her palm. "There's a tiny letter and treble clef sign on each bead."

"Did your mother ever tell you about your female ancestors?"

"No, she never talked about personal stuff. Were they witches? Because I was teased about being a—"

"No, more like witch-angels with wild dreams and daring raisons d'être. Four of the silver beads honor a female ancestor who prepared the way for you." Gram gestured at the first one on the chain. "*T* is for my Grandmother Therese, who would be your great-great-grandmother." She closed her eyes and smiled. "Therese was born in Avignon, France, immigrated to New York, and was a portrait painter who admired Mary Cassatt." She opened her eyes and tapped Morgen's arm. "Be forewarned. Therese was anything but a prude, and her racy self-portrait is in our storage unit. She also played the organ in a corner tavern and mortuary, and to be clear, those were two separate establishments. She never married and died a dreadful death giving birth to her only child—a daughter, Josette." She touched a bead on the chain. "See? The second one has a *J* for Josette. Legend has it that Josette's father was a sailor who soon abandoned her. The lure of the sea, you know? As well as the rum." As though that explained everything including abandoning a newborn baby.

"Did I get my middle name from your grandmother?"

"Along with your passion for music and art. Therese's tragic death inspired your mother to become a midwife. Anywho, Josette grew up to become a dancer and emulated Maria Tallchief but dabbled in striptease. You got your love of dance from her. She followed her fiancé to Seattle where she gave birth to her only child—a daughter, me, the letter *E* bead for Eleanor Rose. I gave ballet, flute, and harp lessons and played piano for dance rehearsals even after I married Scott and gave birth to my only child, Charlie, the letter *C* bead, who had only one child, you, the *M* bead for Morgen. I added that fifth bead after you were born." She caught her breath. "A complicated lineage but a significant one. Your mother was a natural healer, and you will be too in time." She squeezed Morgen's hand, imprinting the beads into the soft flesh of her palm. "There's strength in music and in the continuum and in the messiness of life too. Recognize what connects you, not just what separates you." She released her grip. "Find purpose in your offbeat instincts."

"Offbeat instincts? Somehow that makes me feel better about myself." Morgen draped the necklace around her neck and fastened the clasp. Gram was a great storyteller, but it would be nice if the part about the witch-angels was true. "I didn't know you used to be a musician and dancer. What magic did I inherit from you?"

"An offbeat imagination." Gram sipped her tea. "Is there anything else you want to know before I die?"

"Oh for God's sake." Morgen removed her manuscript journal from her backpack and wrote:

Therese (music and art), Josette (dance), Eleanor Rose (offbeat imagination), Charlie Josette (healing), and Morgen Therese (TBD).

She stared at the list and chewed her lips.

Gram watched her and waited. "Better spit it out, darling. I'm old and sick and living on borrowed time."

"I wish you wouldn't talk like that, but okay. One thing has haunted me for years." She bit her lip until it bled. "Did Mom love me?"

"Truth is, she *fiercely* loved you but didn't always understand you." She handed Morgen a tissue. "We thought you were gifted but difficult. Sadly, Charlie died before doctors understood the extent of autism, especially in girls."

Morgen blotted the blood on her lower lip. "In a way, finally getting the diagnosis was a relief. I may have perfect pitch, but I'm socially tone-deaf because of the way my brain works."

Gram interrupted with an audible sigh. "Now you can reframe your life in a fresh context and proceed with wisdom. It's like getting a second chance. That's more than most of us get."

"That's easier said than done, because nobody tries to understand or accept me unless I'm performing, and then they get all chummy and emotional. What am I supposed to do, tell them 'guess what, I have Asperger's syndrome'? They'll say, 'see, I *knew* something was wrong with you.' I know my disability doesn't make me inferior, but try—"

"Find purpose in your offbeat instincts *and* in your clever brain." Gram's eyes flashed. "Now back to business. My second pet project will be to design my own cremation urn."

"Oh dear Lord."

"Designing Charlie's meant a great deal, because it was my final gift to her, and I want to fashion my own so that I go out dressed to the nines. Give me my bag." She gestured at a quilted knitting bag hooked on the handle of her chair. "It's the only thing in my well-lived life that's off limits to Pauline and her feather duster." Morgen handed it to her, and Gram sorted through her treasures with tiny, arthritic hands before producing a photograph. "This was Charlie's aquamarine urn. Isn't it lovely?"

Morgen gasped. "You used the same design as her tattoo." Neither she nor Gram knew about this until after her mother died, and Morgen had it tattooed on her own tummy in remembrance. Cupped within the stars that formed the Big Dipper and North Star was a black treble clef sign with a bright-blue center like a spiraling wave and a red heart where the bottom line ended in a curl. She rubbed her breastbone and focused on the symbolism of the design, the rhythm and lure of the sea counterbalancing her mother's silenced heart.

"Charlie dreamed it up after you were born. Doodled it everywhere. Since it obviously was important to her, I had it engraved on the urn along with her name. You may keep that picture if you like." She coughed, and Pauline materialized with a glass of water and a box of tissues.

Gram clutched her bag, waved Pauline away, and continued in a hoarse voice. "I want you to take my ashes to Todos Santos where, according to legend, the saints live together in harmony. At least spiritually, your mother and I will be reunited."

"Okay, but please, not anytime soon." Morgen dried her palms on her jeans. "I feel sad when you talk about dying."

"I feel sad when you're unhappy about living."

"Touché." Morgen refreshed their teacups. "I hope your third pet project is about adopting kittens or a unicorn."

"It's more about you adopting a peculiar vehicle. I've kept your mother's Volkswagen in storage for decades and hired a man to fix it up. He called yesterday, it's ready, and now it's yours. Who knows...the thing's a relic and maybe worth something, and besides, you were born inside it on a beach near Todos Santos. That's why your hair is the color of sand, and your eyelashes and brows, the windswept freckles across the bridge of your nose. Conceived on a beach. Born on a beach."

"No, I was born in a commune in Wenatchee." Morgen's voice sounded shrill even to her own ears. "I have a birth certificate, and I'm getting uncomfortable with this conversation."

"Sorry, darling. We got that birth certificate after Charlie brought you back to Washington. Took some doing, but it's official. At the time, you didn't need a passport to cross the Mexican border, and babies were born at home or in the woods or wherever. Anywho, take a cab to European Auto Restoration. Pauline will call Herr Heinrich and tell him to expect you."

"Okay. Thanks for the peculiar vehicle, but I'm feeling anxious, because I *wasn't* born in Wenatchee, I have fifty-five days to perfect Andras's piece, and all I've eaten today is trio mix." She wrung her hands. "What time is it?"

"Why, it's *our* time until Monday, darling, when you have to be back at school." Gram blinked. "Trust me, you'll more than conquer that evil Fantasie. Think of it as a puzzle that only you can solve. Uh oh, I'm slipping out of my chair again."

Before Morgen could move, Pauline rushed in. "Okay, Miss Eleanor, it's time for a nap before supper. Let's give Granddaughter her nice warm coat. She has to get that old car from the German."

"Pauline, my granddaughter is staying for supper. Now please pour me another cup of tea, and then you may leave us alone." She yawned as Pauline left with a frown on her face. "Your mother may have had her problems, but she was a playfully spiritual woman. Do you know why she named you 'Morgen'?"

Morgen shook her head. Her mouth was dry, so she swished with tepid tea before swallowing.

"There's mouthwash in the bathroom. You're welcome to use it." Gram removed another photo from her knitting bag and handed it to Morgen. "Charlie was an activist in college. Like a hippie, only cleaner."

The girl in the picture had long bangs and wavy hair and wore a low-cut denim sundress. "We sure looked alike."

"Just like sisters. That's Charlie in 1968. She was such a pretty girl. My, how time goes by." She squinted at Morgen. "Put on some lipstick and blush. Don't let yourself go, dar-ling."

"She looks so young and innocent."

"Oh, she was and warm and full of life with great big dreams. She was also smart and idealistic, passionate about civil rights, women's equality, and the environment and vehemently against that brutal Vietnam War. Always in the middle of a protest or sit-in, sometimes getting teargassed or arrested."

Morgen nodded, her eyes on her mother's image. "May I keep this picture?"

"Yes, of course. Do you remember when you were preparing the Stravinsky concerto, she gave you a silk morning glory to pin on your gown? During college, Charlie called herself 'Morning Glory,' although I thought her given name was unique enough. Anywho, when you were born, she named you Morgen, which is German for morning. Long story short, you were named after your mother. She said she chose the name because she loved the three Bs: Bach, Beethoven, and Brahms. German composers suggested a German baby name. A bit far-fetched but, as usual, she didn't consult me." She leaned back. "I need to catch my breath."

"Me too, because I didn't know any of that." Morgen blushed.

"Daughters never know everything about their mothers, and that's why we're having this conversation. At twenty, your mother was a gifted music student at Northwest Coast University—"

"Not possible, Gram. She was probably in nursing school."

"Charlie was a piano major just like you were, and please don't raise your voice. Pauline will come flying in here with a fire extinguisher. Anywho, it was your mother's destiny to perform," her voice caught, "the Concerto for Piano and Wind Instruments by—"

"Igor Stravinsky? No, you're confusing us. Mom played piano well and was my first teacher, but you were there when *I* performed that concerto at the U."

"Charlie believed the concerto was her purpose, her reason for being." Gram fumbled for her lacy pink handkerchief. "We both called it her raison d'être."

Morgen recalled the scent of patchouli oil that morning and the vivid colors in her mother's tie-dyed dress. "Okay. Well, this is all very interesting, but let's not talk about—"

"Don't patronize me." Gram pulled a tattered piano score out of the seemingly bottomless knitting bag. "Pauline rescued this from storage so you and I could discuss it while I'm still alive."

"You're not dying." Morgen brushed away her tears, and her hands shook as she opened the cover. Beneath the concerto's title, her mother had doodled the treble clef/wave/heart design and written in art deco lettering:

Miss Charlie Marín
Student of Dr. Duane Kolvecky
Studio 212
Northwest Coast University
1968–1969

"Oh dear Lord, this can't be real." She touched the dates with her finger and felt the ink push back. Her mother would have been pregnant during the 1968–1969 academic year, because Morgen was born June 21, 1969. Why hadn't she said something like "Sweet Baby, funny story, you started learning the concerto in utero"? They could have laughed, hugged each other, and talked about the music they'd intimately shared, because that had been pretty darn intimate, Morgen swimming laps in amniotic fluid while her mother worked on fingering, phrases, and interpretation. Even more weird: studio 212 was Andras's years later when

Morgen was his student. *There are great life lessons in this concerto*, he told her more than once, *and in time, they may occur to you.* She paled as she slowly turned the pages. Sure enough, fingering had been penciled in, clusters of notes circled, reminders scribbled in the margins.

She looked at Gram. "I remember on the night before my concert, Mom said secrets were locked inside the piano concerto a long time ago, and they're going to come around and bite me on the derrière. I replied flippantly 'can't they simply kiss me on the cheek?'" Odd that both her mother and Andras had sensed something intangible hidden in the silence between the notes.

She turned to the second movement. As the music played in her mind's ear and the first exquisite piano solo was approaching, she felt a familiar ache from her wrists to fingertips. Without a doubt, Andras Bacon would always be in there—

"Oh no, the pages with the cadenza were torn out. It was my favorite part."

"I didn't do it. Anywho, your Grandpa Scott studied music in Paris during the 1920s, and his raison d'être was the bassoon. He performed that haunting introduction to *The Rite of Spring* ballet several times. So well, in fact, that he attracted Stravinsky's attention. Of course, all this was before my time. Anywho, it was during that time that Stravinsky composed this concerto. Scott told me that they discussed the challenging woodwind parts and, in the process, learned to enjoy each other's company." Gram's voice softened. "They liked the same cheese and, little known fact, the mandolin."

"Grandpa Scott was *friends* with Igor Stravinsky?" Morgen shoved a fistful of trio mix into her mouth. "That's amazing." She pictured her tall grandfather and the five-foot-three-inch composer sharing red wine, Brie, and baguettes, discussing mandolin music, and strolling the vibrant streets of Paris. "I wish I'd known."

"Your mother felt it would be a distraction." Gram paused. "She believed it was *her* destiny to perform that concerto. Scott encouraged her and gave her a Steinway upright, mahogany as I remember, just like her metronome. I don't know what happened to it, but happily, he lived long enough to know that she'd been awarded the opportunity. Look at the end."

Morgen flipped to the inside back cover and read,

> *It's your turn in the great continuum*
> *So take a leap of faith*
> *Let them hear your story in this music*
> *No words*
> *Only love.*

It was signed "Scott Charles Marín."

"The great continuum again. I think I'm going to call this my foremothers necklace." She touched the silver beads. "Was Mom named after Grandpa Scott Charles?"

Gram nodded. "I also engraved his verse on her urn."

Morgen's heart pounded as she turned to the last page of the piano score where her mother had doodled the seven stars of the Big Dipper beside the seven notes in the piano's final chord. "Mom told me to use the Dipper to find the North Star. That it would be my natural compass, and I'd never get lost. She also told me that when your life was over, you have to be ready when your personal star comes zipping by." She felt her mother's presence, behind her in a cloud of patchouli oil, looking over her shoulder and perusing the music.

"She was a radiant star and the most wonderful daughter a mother could dream of having, but she went through so much." Gram's voice shook, and her tea slopped as she set her cup on the saucer. "She never got to perform the concerto."

"Because she got pregnant with me?" Morgen sprang to her feet. "Is that why we were estranged? I'm good at calendar math, you know, and do you want to know something else? Even though we'd put on a good show for you, she and I had problems for years, presumably because *I* was different and difficult, and she couldn't understand me. Then out of the blue, she invited me for dinner the night before my baccalaureate concert. One thing led to another until I had a meltdown and accused her of being jealous because *she* wasn't good enough to perform the concerto. She slapped my face hard, I slapped her back, and she stormed out of the restaurant and out of my life forever." She buried her face in her hands and wept. "So help me God, between my autism diagnosis, dealing with Andras Bacon again and his evil Fantasie, and learning that Mom hid her fricking true life from me, I don't know who the hell I am anymore." She pounded both sides of her head with her fists. "She called me Sweet Baby, but she hated me. *I* hate me, and I'm sick of pretending to be normal, of knowing no one will ever love me including her because she's dead, or my mystery father, whoever the hell he is, just because of the way my stupid brain works."

"Your brain is not stupid," Gram cried as she lurched from her chair and embraced Morgen with her wasted arms. "Uh oh, I'm not supposed to do that," she whispered.

Morgen choked back tears as she eased Gram into her seat.

"Olly-olly-oxen-free. Now, where were we?" Gram trembled as she smoothed her velour jacket. "Oh yes. Because Charlie chose to disappear during her pregnancy, she didn't get the medical care or counseling she needed. After she came home with two-month-old you, she finished her music degree by writing a paper instead of performing while at the same time starting an accelerated nursing program. Kept you with her twenty-four hours a day, worked herself to death, and became a nurse caring for veterans of the Vietnam War that she'd so vehemently protested, and then a midwife in the spring of 1975." She cleared her throat. "I never talk this much."

"Me either." Morgen rubbed her forehead. "I gave myself a headache." She rolled her tongue into a U and began to rock.

"You may fidget and make faces to your clever heart's content, but I will not be deterred." Gram took a wheezy breath. "By then, you were an almost-six-year-old piano prodigy, and Charlie's legacy had become your destiny. Years later, as your baccalaureate concert approached, she became anxious and confused. What should have been fulfilling for her became threatening. I'm talking about that piano concerto."

Pauline bustled into the room. "It's time to go to the potty and take our medication." She glanced at her wristwatch. "Those damn Yankees are already winning the Red Sox, and Granddaughter was just leaving."

"No, she's not. Nothing, not even baseball, is more important to me right now than my time with Morgen. Now wheel me to the toilet, and then please bring my supper. I'll gladly share my ration with her."

"I brought dessert," Morgen said as she reached for the bag of trio mix.

After Pauline cleared their dinner dishes, Morgen was alone with Gram. "Maybe we should talk about baseball."

Gram squinted at her. "Maybe we shouldn't."

"Okay. Just remember that one of my offbeat instincts is to be blunt and invasive." She bit her lips. "Earlier you said that Mom disappeared during her pregnancy."

"She vanished for ten months, and I was terrified, because I didn't know if she was dead or alive." She dabbed at her tears with her pink handkerchief. "My beautiful daughter had been a loving, creative, and happy girl, and I knew she experimented with drugs but didn't know how much. She was high all the time, expanding her so-called consciousness before and during her pregnancy and afterward, even while she breastfed you. Thought a little marijuana smoke would help a fussy baby sleep."

"Mom told me I was different, because she'd been on medicine when she was pregnant with me, but now, given my diagnosis—"

"Medicine? Oh darling, your mother was high on drugs when she died."

"Please, don't—"

"Morgen Therese Marín, do you have ants in your pants?" Gram's eyes flashed. "Are you listening to me, child?"

"Yes, but I didn't bring my meds. My therapist has me on Zoloft and Ritalin."

"Oh poop, you don't need pills. Drugs were why Charlie was dancing like a prima ballerina in the street and made no attempt to get out of the way of that drunk driver."

"And I think *I'm* blunt." Morgen chewed a cuticle. "By the way, in addition to prescribing medication, my therapist is helping me understand why I feel and act the way I do around other individuals. I *pretend* to be normal and end up making an ass of myself and then look back and cringe at what I've said and done trying to make friends or fit in, kissing up or giving away stuff that's important to me and think that if I do, they'll like me. In the end, it never works, but I wake up the next morning and do the same old thing. I know I've unintentionally hurt others by what I say or do. Doesn't that sound like me?"

Gram shrugged. "Baked in the cake."

"Always was. My first- through third-grade teacher with dagger eyes said more than once that I was as conspicuous as a wrong note, and the other students would laugh. Didn't take much for her to banish me to the supply closet." She corrected her posture and attempted a well-rehearsed smile. "I feel validated to finally know why I've always felt like an outsider. I just wish I'd known earlier."

"Maybe you weren't ready to know." Gram polished her glasses with her pink handkerchief. "Maybe you're befriending the wrong people. Maybe it's more important that you accept yourself first, because you'll never control other people's opinions of you. Ever think about those things?"

"No." Morgen began to rock. "But I will."

Pauline floated into the room on silent bedroom slippers and closed the curtains against the night. When she spoke, her voice was hushed. "My Cubbies lost again, and it's over until next year. Miss Eleanor, let's get your medication, take you to the potty, and put on your flannel nightgown. Granddaughter can borrow the other one and sleep on the cot." She sniffled as she rolled Gram into the bedroom to get her settled for the night.

Morgen stayed behind, her fingers marking the missing pages in the concerto score on her lap. She and her mother had enjoyed hours together learning new pieces and playing "Chopsticks" and "Heart and Soul" duets. Why did she abandon the limelight, the raison d'être that could have bonded them like a normal daughter and mother? She licked her swollen lip where she'd bitten it and rubbed her aching temples. *I have to stop beating up on myself.*

MORGEN STRETCHED OUT ON THE COT. "WHY DO YOU SLEEP with the lights on?"

"So Pauline can prowl. Would you please bring me another serving of dessert?"

"Sure. Nothing like sugar at bedtime." Morgen went into the sitting area and returned with the bowl of trio mix.

"You have some too, and leave the rest on my bedside table."

Morgen lay down and covered her eyes with the crook of her elbow.

"I love you, Charlie Josette," Gram said, her mouth full of trio mix.

"You're confusing us. I'm Morgen, Charlie's daughter."

"Oh, right. I love you, Morgen Therese."

"I love you, too, Grandma Eleanor Rose."

"What are you going to do with your second chance?"

"I'm going to accept myself for who I am." Morgen sat up. "Which means I need to know the whole truth about my significant lineage. You said that Mom's legacy became my destiny, which means that her truth is also my truth. There are too many secrets and things left unsaid between us. I need resolution." *I need to find her urn. I need to bring her home.*

"Then quit isolating yourself." Gram yawned. "In life as in music, dissonance must resolve. You intuitively listen with your heart when you perform music with other instrumentalists, so listen to their words in a similar way. You might be surprised by what you hear. Hold on a minute." It sounded like Gram was whispering into her pillow. "Charlie says she'll help you get where you need to…" She began to snore.

"Storyteller," Morgen whispered. "I'm so lucky to have you in my life."

When she knew Gram was asleep, she returned to the sitting room and turned on a small lamp. She rummaged through the bottomless knitting bag for nothing in particular and, beneath a nest of tissues and expired grocery coupons, discovered a plastic bag that contained two cards in their envelopes and addressed to Eleanor Marín. The first, postmarked Seattle, read,

> *You have my deepest sympathy. Charlie meant the world to me, and I am devastated by her loss. Regards, Duane Kolvecky.*

Morgen remembered that her mother had listed him as her piano teacher.

Hand-painted morning glories in all shades of pink and purple decorated the second envelope from Issaquah, Washington, but only half of the street address remained. Inside, she found a message in gorgeous calligraphy:

> *I met Charlie years ago because we had friends in common in the School of Music, and she and I corresponded briefly while she traveled in 1968–9. Recently,*

I was delighted to read in the university newspaper that Morgen Marín, daughter of university graduate Charlie Marín, was presenting her baccalaureate concert. I attended hoping in vain to reunite with Charlie, and while I was deeply saddened to learn of her death, Morgen's performance proved to be an astonishing and inspiring celebration of life. I hope you find comfort in the music they both so fiercely loved. Affectionately, C. D. Hayes.

Morgen wrote the names and postmark information in her manuscript journal. After she made a wish on Pauline's twinkling nightlights, she grabbed her blue crystal star keepsake and curled up on the cot. Nobody knew where she was at that moment except Gram, Pauline, and maybe her mother, and their presence was as soothing as a cup of warm milk. She drifted off to sleep with curious rhythms beating like a pulse in her mind's ear.

2.

Thursday, October 16, 2003

"Good morning, Pauline," Morgen said as she entered the foyer. "Gram's still asleep. Please tell her that I'll call later."

"That's fine, Granddaughter. I have a yummy breakfast of pork lumpia packed for you. The German is expecting you, the taxi outside has his address down in Tacoma, and I already paid your fare." Pauline gave her a huge smile. "Keep the warm nightgown. Winter is coming."

"Thank you, and thanks for your hospitality." She shoved the nightgown and legal papers into her backpack. "You've been really good for her. She seems happy, and we had a great talk."

"Right. Talk." Pauline shook her head as she turned away. "Your old granny and her stories."

Morgen hugged her backpack. *I will help the universe hear our story in this music. No words. Only love.* She wasn't surprised to feel the necklace warm against her neck.

When Morgen arrived at European Auto Restoration, a white-haired, ruddy-faced man was waiting for her at the gate. "Fräulein Marín, I am Herr Heinrich, at your service." He bowed slightly.

"How do you do?" Her best smile came and went.

He led her into a tidy, well-equipped garage. "Here she is, ta dah," he said, extending both arms toward a Volkswagen bus. "1967 walk-through, roof rack, original dove-blue paint, and only 25,682 miles on the odometer. She's a good bus with a very old soul."

Morgen dropped her backpack on the concrete floor and stared.

"Come on, don't be shy. She's all yours now. Your *Oma* said she's rolling in strudel, her words, not mine, and gave me a generous budget to restore and modernize it for you and update the registration in your name." He handed Morgen a photograph. "This is what it looked like when it arrived."

Decades of grime and neglect had dulled the exterior. Peace signs and primitive flowers had been painted on the windows, and a sticker on the back bumper read Make Music Not War. All four tires were flat. "May I keep this?"

"Of course. Now take a look inside." He opened the cargo door on the passenger side. "We replaced the sleep cushions and eiderdown, and Fräu Heinrich happened to have a bolt of ticking that matched your paint. She sewed those new curtains all around. How about that?"

"It's amazing." More amazing was that her mother had gripped that same steering wheel and peered through that same windshield.

"She only has fifty-three horsepower and no power steering, so take it easy until you get used to her. I found a pair of binoculars in a compartment."

But they weren't binoculars; they were antique opera glasses—silver and ornate. Morgen put them on the passenger seat where they released the warm scent of patchouli oil.

"I also found this T-shirt that Fräu Heinrich handwashed for you."

She gasped at the shirt's bold lettering, Three Bs, as the silk-screened faces of Bach, Beethoven, and Brahms gazed back at her like a scene painted on a plaster wall. "Oh dear Lord, they are why Mom named me—"

"Of course, I know these three B composers, being German myself. Now a personal question. According to your *Oma*, this bus once belonged to your *mutter*. Might you be Sweet Baby?"

"Yes." Her eyes welled with tears. "How would you—"

"When I replaced the tattered headliner with new fabric," he gestured at the bus's ceiling, "I rescued some adhesive stars and found this letter tucked inside. For Sweet Baby's eyes only." He gave her the kindest smile as he handed her an envelope and a set of keys. "Safe travels, okay, Fräulein? *Auf Wiedersehen.*"

"Danke schön, Herr Heinrich." She dried her tears and sat on a driver's seat that had supported her mother's shoulder blades and spine, ferried her weight, and accommodated the length of her legs. No adjustments were necessary. Offering her best smile to a plastic statue of Our Lady of Guadalupe glued to the dashboard, she buckled her seatbelt and took a deep breath before turning on the engine. Gram had said that her mother would help her get where she needed to go. She placed both hands on the steering wheel and glanced in the rearview mirror at the cloudy silhouette of a woman's face. Maybe her mother would help her get her reflection back too.

AFTER DRIVING NORTH FOR FORTY-THREE MINUTES, Morgen developed a feel for her mother's peculiar vehicle but not for the personal direction she should go. She'd eaten all of Pauline's lumpia, so she stopped at a strip mall for bottled water and a few groceries. She returned to the bus, unlocked the cargo door, and climbed into the back.

When she closed the door, the air pressure changed, and she had to yawn to clear her ears. There was a table with bench seats and a small icebox. A platform bed extended beyond the rear bench to the back of the bus. She looked up at the headliner and saw eight fluorescent star-shaped stickers arranged in the shape of the Big Dipper and North Star. Tears filled her eyes again. Same as on every bedroom ceiling she'd had as a child. She rubbed her hands across the tabletop and felt the wood resonate under her fingertips.

Since she wasn't expected at school until Monday, what if she explored her old stomping ground? She could even use a practice room at the U to try to make some sense of Andras's Fantasie. After she organized her groceries, she slipped her mother's concerto music out of her backpack and, with it, the blue crystal star. When she set them on the tabletop, a violent shock surged through her hands and arms like when the string exploded inside her piano. She recoiled from the table and banged her head on the ceiling. "Piece of blue crap!"

She scrambled back into the driver's seat and sped away. A half-hour later, she pulled into NCU's parking lot, chose a space under a cedar tree, and turned off the engine. "No more hippie harmonics, okay?" she said to Dashboard Guadalupe.

Her fingers shook as she ripped open the envelope that Herr Heinrich had given her. Inside, she found a flat origami star made from binder paper and two Polaroid pictures. The first was of a young man with blond hair standing with his arm around a girl, her hair in loose braids, wearing a tie-dyed dress. They were looking at each other and laughing as ocean waves rushed in around their feet. Handwritten across the bottom of the photo were the words *Cranberry Coast. Summer 1968.* Morgen chewed her lips. That was the dress her mother was wearing when she visited Morgen's office the day before and had been wearing the night she was killed.

The second photo showed three college-aged, bare-footed couples posing on a wide porch and smiling with their arms around each other. The boys, long haired with moustaches and short beards, were dressed in loose, long-sleeved shirts and long pants, and two of the girls wore peasant blouses and ankle-length skirts. The third girl was wearing that same tie-dyed dress. The rear end of the VW bus on the right side of the photo had Make Music Not War on the bumper.

Morgen pressed her lips together as she shifted her attention to the porch and realized it belonged to a nearby old, caramel-colored house that had haunted her all her life. Memories washed over her, and she heard her mother's voice in her mind's ear. *Let's drive by the house on Ninth Street and look at the gardens. I want you to trick-or-treat and see who answers the door. I want to see if they got snow. It's almost spring, and the wild roses should be blooming. I wonder who lives there now.* Her mother would park their station wagon at the curb and stare at the house while a young Morgen crouched on the backseat and sucked on the ends of her pigtails.

She studied the girl in the tie-dyed dress. Long ago on rainy days, she and her mother dressed up in similar dresses, embroidered shawls, and elegant Victorian touring hats, turned up the music, and danced around the living room, pretending to be rocker Stevie Nicks of Fleetwood Mac. The last time they danced like that, Morgen tripped over her own feet, and her mother wept as though her heart were breaking.

Sorry, I just had a sad memory. Her mother had dried her tears on her shawl. *Sweet Baby, sometimes we don't understand certain things, and all we can do is give life our best and keep moving forward. Maybe someday we'll be able to look back, and it'll all make sense.*

Was Morgen the only one who sometimes wished she could go back in time to before the real world broke down the door? She dropped the origami star and photos on the passenger seat and turned on the engine.

She parked the bus at the curb in front of the old house on Ninth Street and let the engine idle. Was this where her mother had lived back in the patchouli oil days?

The neighborhood was beautifully tended and only three blocks from the university's concert hall. Mature fir, cedar, and maple trees framed endless acres of lawn. Wild rose bushes surrounded the house, which Morgen had never entered. Thick, square pillars supported the shingled roof extended to protect a full-length porch. Three sash windows looked out on the left side of the porch, and an entry door with glass brick sidelight windows was to the right. She remembered that her mother would stand for hours on the sidewalk, stare at the dormer windows, and occasionally sneak up five wood steps to sit in a chair on the porch. Once Morgen dared to press her childish nose against those glass bricks and wondered what it would be like to belong inside a home like that.

Directly across the street stood the house's mirror twin. Morgen always imagined that the two caramel-colored homes were estranged friends who chanced to meet, each at a loss for words but unable to move on.

She looked at the photo of the three couples, laughing and probably sharing secrets. She closed her eyes and visualized her own worst dark secret. A white pickup straddled the curb in front of that house, and two policemen knelt on either side of a bloodstained woman in a tie-dyed dress, her matted hair in two long braids. The woman held a glittering blue crystal star in her outstretched hand. Lurid details flowed in Morgen's mind's eye like wet paint: a college-age girl driving her mother's Subaru appeared to drive past the accident, because she was headed to her baccalaureate concert—

The sweet, simple "To a Wild Rose" by Edward MacDowell, presumably performed on Grandpa Scott's mahogany piano deep inside that house, replaced the chaos in Morgen's memory as hot tears burned her eyes. A drunk driver had struck her mother, but Morgen had been too dazed after her meltdown the night before to unscramble the commotion surging around her. Instead, when she noticed a bleeding woman staring at her in the rearview mirror, something deep inside *her* mind burst like an exploding piano string, and her own image blurred and disappeared forever. What had her mother been doing in front of that house on that particular night? Did it have something to do with secrets that threatened to bite Morgen on the derrière?

"To a Wild Rose" ended with an A major chord, *pianississimo*, very, very soft. She opened her eyes and brushed away her tears. How do you ask a dead mother for forgiveness? That question had haunted her for thirteen years, four months, and twenty-five days, especially when she looked at her reflection. *I can see features, but I don't know if it's me.* She paled. *My face was the last thing Mom saw, and she took it with her.*

As she shifted the bus into gear, the keys in the ignition jingled, reminding her of the key Gram had given her. Perhaps the answers to some of her questions were waiting in University Mini-Storage.

She opened the door to the storage unit and flipped on the wall switch, hoping her mother's urn was packed away with the other treasures. If only she could hold it and confess what she'd secreted away in her heart. Maybe then their estrangement would finally end.

As she ventured inside, she gasped when florescent light illuminated her great-great-grandmother's full-length self-portrait. "How do you do?" She curtsied to Therese from France who smiled demurely while wearing only a string of pearls. "*Comment-allez vous?*"

She surveyed the unlabeled boxes and random pieces of furniture piled around Therese and noticed her mother's precious conch shell, marooned on top of her own red attaché case. The heavy spiral shell had a drab, rough, knobby exterior but a remarkably glossy pink interior behind a thick, flared lip. As a child, she often held the large shell against her ear for an hour or more, hoping to hear her mystery father's voice.

She brushed dust off the attaché case, set the lock numbers at 1-8-8-2 for Stravinsky's birth year, and the latch popped open. She took out a leather-bound folder that she'd grabbed from Andras's studio, because she hadn't wanted little Violet to find it. She held her breath and opened the cover to a black-and-white photograph titled *Coitus Cadenza,* showing a couple seated on a bench in front of a grand piano. The woman was naked astride the man's lap with her back against his chest. Her skin glowed, her long hair floated as though weightless, and her legs were entwined in his. Her attention was on the printed music before her, and her fingers hovered above the piano keys. The man wore a tuxedo jacket with tails, but his pants were down around his ankles. Ornate mirrors around and behind the couple reflected their image from all angles. "Shocking back then," she whispered, "but rather blasé now."

She put the attaché case and conch shell on the concrete floor beside her backpack. Gram had unwittingly created a treasure trove of memories. She opened a cardboard carton and discovered her mother's favorite dishes. She rifled through weeks of wadded newspapers until she found the sugar bowl complete with a lid. "Oh, the perfect piece. You may have been Desert Rose to Franciscan Ceramics, but you always meant wild roses to Mom." She set it aside.

She unzipped a garment bag that hung from the neck of a floor lamp and removed the outfit she wore for the Stravinsky concerto portion of her baccalaureate concert. The midcalf-length, sleeveless black gown with a dropped waistline and daring V-neck had been fashionable in Paris in 1924 when Igor Stravinsky composed the concerto. With it, she'd worn black heels and a black headband with sequins, rhinestones, beads, and a bright blue ostrich feather. Her mother added the gorgeous electric blue morning glory at the hip, and Morgen had worn nothing else beneath the gown. "A morning glory from Morning Glory," she murmured, cupping the silk flower in her hand as though it were real. "I wish I'd known the significance at the time."

As she stripped off her T-shirt and jeans and slipped the dress over her head, she remembered strolling across the brightly lit stage toward the grand piano as the house lights dimmed and placing a black sequin clutch purse on the bench beside her as though she'd walked in off a Paris street. She'd held an elegant pose as Rylan Byrd in white tie, black tails and trousers, and patent leather shoes strode to the conductor's podium. When he cued the symphonic band and the introduction began, she heard the rhythm of her own name—*long, long, short, long, Mor-gen Ma-rín*—as though someone was calling to her.

When Andras Bacon first assigned Stravinsky's Concerto for Piano and Wind Instruments, he promised Morgen "a transformational experience." *The rhythms are playful and dark, the dissonances lovely and cruel,* he said. *This music is perfect for you.* It all came to fruition too soon.

When she turned around, she saw a paisley hatbox on top of a crate. She untied a faded, black ribbon and lifted the lid. A whiff of patchouli oil greeted her, and a wall as thin as a sigh between her and her mother vanished. "Oh," she cried when she saw her mother's Victorian touring hat decorated with silk morning glories, peacock feathers, and lavender tulle. As she put on the hat, the florescent light overhead softened. Two photographs and a packet of papers tied with a faded, blue ribbon lay at the bottom of the box.

The first photo showed Morgen as a grinning infant sitting on her mother's lap and facing an upright piano. The second was of toddler Morgen in her shiny swimsuit standing on a massive drift log at the beach, gazing out to sea through hands cupped binocular-style around her eyes as though she already felt that the rest of the world was far away from her. Meanwhile, her mother posed on the log at Morgen's feet, staring into the camera lens with an enigmatic expression.

She sat cross-legged on the concrete floor, put the photos beside her, and untied the ribbon around the packet of papers. The pages unfurled, and she recognized her mother's beautiful script:

Wednesday, July 30, 1969, Dear Sweet Baby, I know you'll always wonder who your father is, so I'm going to tell only you our story. Take a leap of faith, and listen with your heart.

"Oh dear Lord," Morgen whispered. On that date, she'd been only forty days old.

The pages that followed were the ones that had been ripped from her mother's concerto score, specifically that virtuoso solo cadenza, straining at and taunting the bar lines and daring you to listen.

MEASURES 1–3: Morgen stared at the opening notes and heard in her mind's ear the piano's booming octaves rising from deep in the bass. Her muscle memory awoke with a jolt, and her fingers involuntarily mimed playing the written notes.

MEASURE 4: Words and a familiar style of sketches on the tattered pages joined Stravinsky's phrases: *Friday, September 27, 1968.*

MEASURE 5: A colored-pencil doodle showed a blue VW bus on a beach beside a raging bonfire.

MEASURE 6: Musical notes transformed with pencil strokes into tiny individuals with flailing arms and legs, dancing and tussling beneath a starry sky.

MEASURE 7: She listened as her mother began to narrate her story. *Hundreds of friends, sky high on weed and drunk on Southern Comfort, shoved acid into my mouth, and I began to trip...*

MEASURE 8: He sawed off my right braid and attacked me. A doodle of a pink note with only one long braid lay squashed under a larger dark note.

MEASURE 9: I grabbed his pants and ran.

MEASURE 10: Past a drawing of a blue note, labeled "Riff," bleeding in the water under a jumble of drift logs.

MEASURE 11: Where does music go when it fades away? The pants flew like a ghost above a fleeing pink note.

MEASURE 12: Two bird-like notes, the ghostly pants, and pink note joined another note with a pointed hat and gold halo.

MEASURE 13: Saved by Bertie, the gardener, and the Widow Witch!

MEASURE 14: Pink note wept big blue tears inside a giant conch shell while jagged notes clawed at the exterior.

Morgen glanced at the marooned conch shell on her attaché case while cursive lyrics sang in her mind's ear. *My legacy is your destiny. Promise to come back and help me.*

MEASURE 15: The blue bus doodle resumed driving across the page. *Creak! Creak! I hear roof angels!*

MEASURE 16: Random musical notes, rests, and morning glories decorated the roadside, and presumably those were roof angels flying above the little blue bus.

"Tripping on acid?" Morgen frowned. "Nasty stuff."

MEASURE 17: After crossing a green, white, and red braid, the bus stopped at a sign that read *Bienvenidos a Todos Santos.* According to Gram, that was where Morgen had been born, so evidently her mother's prenatal care had been a road trip fueled by drugs.

MEASURE 18: The excerpt ended, and pink note reprised—*where does music go when it fades away*—as it wandered off and disappeared from the page.

Promise to come back and help me, her mother whispered in Morgen's mind's ear. Truth or hallucination? *Wait a minute.* She flipped back to the first page. Was pink note supposed to be her mother? The story in the torn cadenza pages began on September 27, 1968, which was eight months and twenty-six days before she was born—

"I do *not* want to know this!"

She scrambled back into her own clothing. When she hung up the concert dress, she discovered a sack in the bottom of the garment bag. The ghostly pants? A spider's nest? She tore it open, found her mother's tie-dyed dress, washed, folded with tissue paper, and complete with patchouli sachets.

Her cell phone rang from the depths of her backpack, and she counted sixty-seven seconds before checking her voicemail. "Chérie, I'll be in town tomorrow afternoon and fly back to New Jersey early Saturday. Why don't I pick you up for dinner around six? We have cause to celebrate, because you'll be performing the Fantasie in front of my doctoral committee in New York City's Carnegie Hall, December 15, instead of at the conservatory. I have some ideas about what you should wear. See you tomorrow night."

Damn Andras! With a sob, Morgen bit her lower lip, opening the day-old injury. "For the love of God, would you leave me alone?" *So many things are so horribly wrong.*

Tears flowed down her cheeks as she tenderly touched the sketched pink note, squashed under her attacker. "Somebody assaulted my mom, and she hid the pain for the rest of her life." She laid the touring hat back in its box and thought of those happy childhood dances—

I know you'll always wonder who your father is—

"Oh crap, or oh shit." She dialed her cell phone and began to pace the storage unit.

"Water Street Eldercare, Pauline speaking."

"Hi, this is Morgen, and I need to talk to Gram, please."

"Okay, Granddaughter. I'll pick up Granny's extension."

She pressed the crystal blue crystal star against her lips and continued pacing, left, right, left, right, *tick, tick.*

"Hi, darling." Gram wheezed.

"Hi, Gram. Hey, remember yesterday you asked me what I was going to do with my second chance, and I said I wanted to accept myself for who I am," her voice flew up an octave, "which meant that I need to know the whole truth about my significant lineage because Mom's truth was also my truth?" A sour taste flooded her mouth, and she spat on the floor. "Sorry, but here comes blunt and invasive again. Did Mom get pregnant with me because she was raped?"

Gram started to cry. "Charlie never got over the shock, and some people said she was a dirty hippie who deserved—"

"Time to hang up, Granddaughter," Pauline cut in, and the call ended.

"Gram? What happened to her damn urn?" Morgen screamed. She lowered the phone and fought to catch her breath. Come back and help her do what? Kick the larger dark note in his evil nuts?

Her father's identity was a big fat secret that she'd never understood, but the neighborhood bullies had known she was "different" and teased her that she was a witch, that she'd been adopted, or that her mother was a whore. After Morgen looked up "adopted" and "whore" in the dictionary, she quit talking to her mother for seventeen days. Meanwhile, she snooped through her mother's drawers for a keepsake and found a curious glass blue star that perfectly represented her: beautiful, mysterious, and distant.

She refashioned three of her Barbie dolls into father figures based on the television stars of the evening news: Howard K. was a draft dodger, Harry R. was MIA, and Walter C. was why she might be a love child from the Age of Aquarius. Because she was uncomfortable around and easily bored by children her age, the dolls were her best friends until she was thirteen and Andras Bacon entered her life as a surrogate father.

"I was anything but a love child," she said to Therese's portrait. At thirty-four years, three months, and twenty-six days old, she wasn't a child anymore.

It was dark when Morgen returned to the university's parking lot, parked under the same cedar tree as earlier, and turned off the engine. She got out and ran through the rain to the entrance of the concert hall. The doors had been locked and chained, so she slunk through the shrubbery to the double doors that led to the offices and classrooms to find them locked as well. She stepped back and peered up at the dark upstairs window of studio 212.

Her mother had often reminded her that although she was a piano prodigy, she was damned lucky to study with the much-celebrated Professor Andras Bacon, and she'd better do what he told her to do, because he was her only ticket to success. Success meant finally being accepted. Included. Appreciated. Because Morgen took everything literally and was blindly obedient, she tried to please him and did exactly as she was told: Andras blindfolding her with his necktie and having her spontaneously play a memorized piece in another key, in another meter, and even backward, which she easily did; Andras assigning her the Stravinsky concerto to prove how well he'd taught her; Andras composing the Fantasie, his magnum opus, which only Morgen would be capable of playing or humbly die trying.

Back inside the bus, she dried her hair on her peacoat, closed Fräu Heinrich's curtains against the dusk, and turned on the dome light. The stars on the headliner began to twinkle, which made Morgen think of tinkle, but, unfortunately, the bus lacked plumbing. She rummaged through the compartments until she found a plastic bowl that would make a fine chamber pot. If Gram was right and she'd been born inside the bus, she had every right to pee in it. When she had finished, she applied orange-ginger sanitizer on her hands and retrieved the origami star and old Polaroid photos from the passenger seat.

The girl in the tie-dyed dress smiled as though she didn't have a care in the world. "It's been an enlightening afternoon, Mom," Morgen said. As she carefully unfolded the grimy paper star, golden beach sand cascaded with a whispering sound onto the tabletop. "So there's more to the story?" She held the page to the light and read aloud as she followed her mother's colored-pencil sketches.

On the late afternoon before you were born, ocean waves roared like drums while you swam in your sleep. From the beach, I watched gray whales blow and play, the sound of their air exchange as arousing as music. A fisherman in an open panga waited just beyond the surf line until a big wave began to roll. He gunned his outboard motor, made a run for the beach on the crest of that wave, and slid up onto the sand to unload his catch.

That night as I dozed on my platform bed and listened to a distant, sad Mexican guitar, a wise-looking pelican walked toward our blue bus. Great brown wings cloaked its body like a priest's robe, and a red heart dangled outside its chest like a saint's medallion. Jeweled tears rained from its eyes and turned into tiny blue boats that sailed away on spiraling waves.

I went into labor with contractions that nearly cut me in half, so I gulped a shot of tequila, lit a fat joint, and sucked in the smoke until I floated away. My own screams wakened me at first light. Our Lady of Guadalupe pounded on the door, but you were already fighting your way out of me. You kicked and clawed, frantic to escape, and ripped my heart from my chest, pulling it down through my opening and into the light. There you were, squirming and mewing like a wet kitten between my legs with my miserable, bloody heart tethered to your cord. Where did you come from, and how did you begin? I still don't know, but I picked you up, fell in love forever, and that was that.

Morgen began to weep. "But you didn't have to. You could have just let me go, and no one would ever have known or cared." She wiped her face with both hands and struggled to read the remaining sentences floating in her tears.

I knew then that just like the pelican-priest, my heart would live outside my body in the form of you, my daughter. I am destined to die on the day that you finally leave me behind. Written and folded into a star on our beach, Todos Santos, Baja California Sur.

To top everything off, her mother had been all alone when she gave birth. Morgen sifted through her memories. The last time she saw her mother alive was the night before her baccalaureate concert. They had dinner in a restaurant on Lake Union and noticed a boat in the marina called *Epiphany*. Had her mother thought that the bizarre pelican figurehead on that boat was the same pelican-priest she'd encountered in Todos Santos and an omen that she was going to die? She frowned. *Evidently, I left Mom behind by performing the music that had been her raison d'être.* Morgen rubbed the ache behind her breastbone. Because her mother did die, as predicted, on the day of the performance.

She tugged her damp jeans down far enough to see a detail of her tattoo: the two-inch high treble clef sign in black ink with a blue center like a spiraling wave and a tiny, red heart where the bottom line ended in a curl. Her mother's hallucinating brain had transformed the silhouette of the pelican-priest into the treble clef sign they would both wear inked on their bellies for the rest of their lives.

The rest of the paper star was filled with "Char-lie Ma-rín Char-lie Ma-rín" on and on. She stared at those words and heard inside her mind's ear the rhythm of the opening phrase of the concerto: *long, long, short, long. Charlie Ma-rín. Mor-gen Ma-rín.* She carefully swept the beach sand onto the paper and refolded it into a star. All those years they heard each other talking but never listened to each other with their hearts.

She slipped on Gram's flannel nightgown and crawled under Fräu Heinrich's eiderdown on the platform bed. The bus roof creaked in the night air as she arranged her keepsakes at her side. "Hey, roof angels, do you remember me? I was born in this bus."

Friday, October 17, 2003

Morgen woke at six-thirty with the blue crystal star in her hand. What if her mother had been reaching for her own personal star as it went zipping by instead of offering that star to her? What if her mother had missed her celestial ride because Morgen had distracted her? Why had they consistently failed to connect? Was it because of her autism or her mother's secrecy?

She opened the cargo door for ventilation and looked up through the cedar branches. It was a comfort to know that stars shone even in the daytime. Three chattering college-age couples walked by, clearly present day but eerily reminiscent of the group in the porch photograph. "Cool bus," one of the young men said, and the girl with him smiled and flashed the peace sign.

Morgen returned the gesture and emptied her chamber pot under the tree as rain began to fall.

After stopping at the student union for a cup of decaf and a Northwest Coast University sweatshirt, Morgen headed to the library. She collected a dozen phonebooks from the greater Seattle area and searched each one for the two individuals who'd sent sympathy cards to Gram but found nothing listed for Duane Kolvecky or C. D. Hayes. She gathered armfuls of school newspaper archives and old yearbooks.

By ten o'clock, she'd learned that, on September 27, 1968, a twenty-year-old female student had been raped when a college beach party during the Cranberry Coast Festival escalated into a brawl, and the incident took place south of Westport near an unincorporated community known as Fish Camp. The victim's name and the names of the other students injured would not be released. Her mother's photo taken for the 1968–1969 school year had been deleted because she withdrew before the end of the term, and there wasn't anything about Charlie Josette Marín, aka Morning Glory, on the Internet. It was as though she'd never existed, and crap on whoever wrote the Internet anyway. "Wait," she cried out, and several young people turned to look at her. She already knew the names of two witnesses. She leafed through the torn cadenza pages until she located the bird-like note named Bertie-the-gardener. She raked her memory for similar names from her mother's past. Alberta, a nurse. Bertha, a phlebotomist. Roberta, a pharmacist. Could one of them also have been a gardener in 1968? Riff was the other witness depicted as the bleeding blue note under a jumble of drift logs, but in music, a riff is a phrase or rhythmic pattern that repeats throughout a composition, and that kept echoing inside her head.

She grabbed the old photo of her and her mother taken at the beach and stared at the jumble of drift logs. "Oh dear Lord, I know that beach. It's where I learned to surf."

MORGEN STUFFED HER THINGS INTO HER BACKPACK AND picked up a copy of the university's Chronicle. Thumbing through the paper, she saw an ad:

> *"Position Available: Director of Chamber Music, Spring Semester, February 1, 2004. See School of Music Office for details, requirements, and application."*

She corrected her posture. She needed a change of direction, and she'd always wanted to teach in a college. Why not her alma mater?

It was raining when she left the library. She hurried across campus to the music building, holding the newspaper over her head like an umbrella, and freshened up in the women's restroom although her reflection in the mirror remained ill-defined. Afterward, she wandered the familiar hallways before stopping to read a bulletin board. According to a concert hall rehearsal schedule, Arthur Ishikawa and Violet Bacon had reserved an hour starting at 12:30.

All things considered, it wasn't a good time or place for a reunion with Violet, but she'd love to watch part of the rehearsal, especially if it involved the Stravinsky concerto. She looked at a clock in a classroom. Why not work on Andras's Fantasie for forty minutes or so and then slip into the hall before Violet arrived? She found an empty practice room, yanked the Fantasie out of her backpack, and the battle was on.

Nine pages in, she stopped and dropped her hands to her lap. *I hate this. It's completely illogical.* According to Mozart, who knew how to spin light into his compositions, music lived between and all around, not simply in, the notes. She closed her eyes and visualized the shimmering chandelier of blue crystal stars and seemingly random notes that hung from the ceiling of studio 212. Those ornamental notes, mute as they were, were bathed in light and oxygen, unlike the notes Andras had written. She began again at the beginning, lunging through the ragged phrases, and soon a familiar umbrella of hope opened over her.

For eleven turbulent years, Andras's blue chandelier had been a witness to everything that happened to her, and its beauty alone reassured her that hope and enlightenment endured, but how, when, and why did her mother pilfer a star from that chandelier?

Years earlier while alone in the studio, Morgen had stared between the pendants and strings of crystal beads until she found the empty hook where her mother's star belonged. After a minor meltdown, she took a black felt-tipped pen from Andras's desk drawer, yanked thirteen music books off his shelf (Bach through Bartok), and drew on the wall a picture of her mother's star flying past the moon and falling down toward the old house on Ninth Street.

She closed Andras's music. Even "Chopsticks" had more heart and soul than his Fantasie. She began to play the classic duet, the treble with her right hand and the bass with her left, when she remembered being a child and teaching the piece to multiple individuals living in a mysterious old mansion who went delirious with joy when she played Scott Joplin's "Maple Leaf Rag," an organic piece that Andras could never play.

Morgen was mid-thought when a string, probably A-flat below middle C, snapped inside the battered upright with an undignified twang, and she leaped from the bench. "Sorry," she said to the old piano, "but you're not the only casualty in this war." She crammed the score into her backpack and left with A-flat still buzzing in her ears.

THE DOOR TO THE CONCERT HALL WAS OPEN, BUT NO ONE was around. Morgen sensed the warm presence of a long-ago audience and the twenty-four students in the symphonic band. She corrected her posture and strolled fifteen well-rehearsed steps across the dimly lit stage to where the concert grand crouched like a black onyx sculpture. "Remember me?" she whispered. After brushing the open lid with her fingers, she walked up an aisle to take a seat halfway back inside the cavernous hall and waited for the rehearsal to begin.

The lights brightened, and Violet, with her dazzling, kinky red hair, walked across the stage and sat at the grand piano. With her were Arthur Ishikawa, who'd been Andras's most competitive colleague, and Phoebe Keats, dressed identically to Violet in a white T-shirt, jeans, and black high-top sneakers. Phoebe moved a chair to the right of the bench where she could turn pages. Mr. Ishikawa murmured to the girls as Violet opened the score, presumably Stravinsky's Concerto for Piano and Wind Instruments.

Violet's signature fragrance of eucalyptus with a note of lime floated off the stage and into the seats. Morgen smiled as memories associated with the scent came to mind. All told, she'd been Violet's piano teacher for over eleven years, but off stage, they had a peculiar history.

Morgen closed her eyes and visualized her mother-the-midwife in Margot Bacon's elegant bedroom, coaching, reassuring, and welcoming Violet into the world, the fourth home delivery Morgen had witnessed. She'd cuddled baby Violet in her arms within an hour of her birth. Not a typical experience for a thirteen-year-old, but neither she nor her mother were typical. She dug the blue crystal star out of her backpack and squeezed it.

An equally vivid memory was when Violet's father, Andras Bacon, came home that afternoon from the university, reeking of mothballs and shoe polish. She'd been playing one of her mother's favorite pieces, the third movement of Mozart's Quintet for Piano, Oboe, Clarinet, Horn, and Bassoon in E Flat, by ear on his precious Bösendorfer grand when he scared her half to death with lavish praise and his fervent vow to retain her as his student. He brushed her cheek with his fingers and murmured "Chérie" before going upstairs to greet his newborn daughter. Afterward, her mother took her out for ice cream to celebrate her "musical apprenticeship." Sadly, she soon developed a lifelong aversion to ice cream.

Violet was stumbling through the allegro section of the first movement. Morgen winced and returned to her thoughts because, like Headmistress Collier often quipped, *tempus fugit*—time flies.

When Violet was admitted to River Bridge as a freshman in 1997, everything went well until her senior year when she was discovered having a romantic relationship with Phoebe. Headmistress notified Andras, cruelly outing Violet, and both girls were expelled. Livid, Morgen retreated to her office to have a meltdown. Headmistress followed and observed her. "Dr. Marín, compose yourself. This is a prestigious school of performing arts."

She remembered watching in horror as the raging Headmistress morphed in her mind's eye into old Dagger Eyes, chastising her for insubordination and banishing her to her office. From that moment, River Bridge was no longer a safe place, but she stayed anyway. She loved the curriculum and the girls, but the administration and faculty? Not really.

Mr. Ishikawa raised his hands and conducted the symphonic band parts to give Violet a sense of timing, and Morgen clearly heard in her mind's ear the other musicians playing, because Andras had made her sing one of their parts every time she practiced. Violet began to play where the piano joined in, and notes leaped and bounded off the pages with feline energy. Morgen was instantly engaged and sat on her hands to keep them from flapping as Violet powered through phrases with joy and confidence, but this had been *Morgen's* concerto, and no one had asked *her* permission...Involuntarily, her fingers mimed playing the notes, and her feet kept time with the ever-changing meter as the familiar umbrella of hope opened above her again.

From time to time, Mr. Ishikawa cut in, and Violet would repeat a phrase, correct fingering, or adjust tempo or dynamics. Morgen visualized her young mother, her hair in long braids and wearing the tie-dyed dress, rehearsing that same music on that same piano. How far had she gotten before it was snatched out of her hands forever? How could Morgen finally help her mother fulfill her dream?

Violet proceeded into the second movement with its lyrical opening phrases. When Andras introduced Morgen to this concerto, he cautioned her that it was as insanely difficult as it was exquisitely beautiful. He made her sight-read through the entire second movement while speaking softly, coaching her, and revealing how Igor Stravinsky peeled away layer after layer until you thought he couldn't go deeper, and then he did—

Violet arrived at the torn cadenza pages, and Morgen paled. *Please don't—*

Mr. Ishikawa interrupted Violet and mumbled while Phoebe searched through the score. Morgen relaxed, watched their discussion, and thought about teacher-student trust. About how it was a given. About how Andras brazenly violated—

She caught her breath when Violet ripped into the spirited third movement. She was still a fledgling and dependent on Phoebe to turn pages, but before long, she would leave the paper behind and soar.

The rehearsal ended, and the girls held hands and listened to Mr. Ishikawa's critique. Morgen clasped her hands too. Somehow, she, her mother, and Violet were connected by the concerto like fingers laced together. Mr. Ishikawa must have made a joke, because they giggled as they left the stage.

Andras never made me laugh. She took a deep breath and reread the job announcement. Grandpa Scott once wrote, *It's your turn in the great continuum, so take a leap of faith.* She shoved the blue crystal star into her pocket and patted a drum roll on her thighs. "Why not apply?" she whispered as the stage door closed and the lights dimmed.

A LIST OF FACULTY WAS POSTED OUTSIDE THE MUSIC office, and Morgen discovered that Rylan Byrd, conductor of the 1990 symphonic band, was now director of the School of Music. She corrected her posture and opened the door.

"Why, Morgen," Dr. Byrd said from behind the counter, "you've been on my mind recently, and here you are. Hannah," he said to the woman beside him, "I'd like you to meet Morgen Marín, my favorite alumna."

"How do you do?" Morgen pressed her lips together. *Restrain yourself.* Do not blurt that the name Hannah is a palindrome and that she knew many examples of palindromes or retrogrades in music like Bach's Crab Canon.

"What brings you here to brighten my Friday?" Although Dr. Byrd's hair had thinned, he was as dapper as ever.

"I want to apply for the chamber music directorship."

"Splendid idea. Hannah, let's give Morgen an application, and she can fill it out immediately."

Hannah, smelling like lavender and vanilla and wearing a silver-gray dress and stiletto heels, nodded at Morgen before assembling a stack of papers.

"Violet Bacon is our most outstanding soloist. Did you know that she won the baccalaureate competition?" Dr. Byrd asked. "We've agreed to her choice of performing Stravinsky's Concerto for Piano and Wind Instruments with the symphonic band."

"Yes. We're rarely in touch, but she left a voicemail." Morgen lowered her eyes. "Andras and Headmistress Collier told me to stay away from her, because I didn't dissuade her relationship with Phoebe."

Dr. Byrd frowned. "Nancy Collier did that?" He shook his head. "Violet's done well with Arthur Ishikawa, but I know she misses working with you." He forced a smile. "She's coveted the concerto ever since you played it."

"Ever since she was seven and a half years old." Morgen touched the beads on the foremothers necklace. "I just learned that my mother worked on that concerto when she was in college."

"Interesting." Dr. Byrd raised his eyebrows. "I just learned that you were invited to perform Andras's doctoral composition at River Bridge."

"He wanted a dress rehearsal far from East Cape Conservatory to see how it was received before he presents to his committee. By the way, I was coerced, not invited." Morgen blushed. "He said I owed him. Plus he promised me Carnegie Hall."

"I see." He crossed his arms. "Why not here?"

"Because he lives for sensational theater and wanted a black-tie gala with an open bar and dinner. Headmistress sees the performance as a lucrative fundraiser with increased celebrity for the school. Personally, I think Andras is making a statement to the River Bridge community by choosing me instead of Violet to perform it. He's never forgiven her for her sexual orientation as though it somehow reflects badly on him."

"How's it going for you?"

"The Fantasie? Technically, fine. I understand the math of it, but the art?" She shrugged. "Not really."

Hannah returned with a folder, and Dr. Byrd stepped aside while Morgen stood at the counter to complete the application. It concluded with a question: "What makes you uniquely qualified to be our director of chamber music?"

She thought a moment and wrote,

I have a Doctor of Musical Arts degree (summa cum laude), and my dissertation is titled "A History of Piano in Chamber Music." I mastered and analyzed nineteen compositions and toured with five different ensembles, some youth, some adult. Currently, I teach piano, theory, and music history, accompany student musicians, and direct six instrumental ensembles.

She chewed a cuticle and smiled.

I'm uniquely qualified because I'm wired differently in a special way.
When I listened to the third movement of Mozart's Quintet for Piano, Oboe, Clarinet, Horn, and Bassoon in E Flat. K. 452 (1784) for the first time as a child, I danced and wept with complete and unrestrained joy. My goal as a music teacher is to give my students everything they need to take a leap of faith, get off the written page, and experience music in a similarly uninhibited, perceptive, and offbeat way.

She put the pen down and handed Hannah the application.

As Hannah read the paperwork, her salt-and-pepper pageboy, perfectly parted on the right, moved slightly like an opening stage curtain. "Very impressive. We'll need an audition tape."

"We have several in our library," Dr. Byrd said, looking up from a file cabinet. He skimmed the application. "Everything seems to be in order. Ah, the Mozart. We'd started rehearsing…" He shook his head.

"Thank you, and could we please keep this private? Neither Headmistress nor Andras need to know at this point."

"Not a problem. Personnel issues are always confidential, and I'll happily present your application to the selection committee myself." He stepped into a side office and closed the door.

Morgen thanked Hannah and left, her eyes wide and pulse racing *allegro* ($\downarrow$ = 130). As she walked away, she heard a recording of Mozart's piano quintet coming from Dr. Byrd's office.

Back in the bus, Morgen practiced the Fantasie on the tabletop at half-speed and then double-time, shaking the bus with inaudible music. As she climbed back into the driver's seat, she thought about Gram and wished she were sitting in the passenger seat.

She dialed her cell phone and a woman who identified herself as Dorothy answered because Pauline was busy with another patient and Gram was napping.

"Oh, please don't wake her," Morgen said. "Just tell her that her granddaughter loves the blue bus and she's headed home." Only because Andras had told her that they had a date at six o'clock. However, for the first time in twenty years and eight months, he didn't know where she was at that moment.

She laced her fingers and turned her thoughts loose. Gram said that daughters never knew everything about their mothers. Had she sensed that they'd had similar experiences? Was that what this was all about? The oral history, the bus, the storage unit? Well, mothers never knew everything about their daughters either, but there came a time when you had to share something that was so horribly wrong. She rubbed her hands together while she mentally harmonized her own story with the one her mother divulged on the torn cadenza pages.

MEASURES 1–18: Tuesday, May 22, 1990. She'd been in shock after driving past her mother's horrific accident but performed her baccalaureate concert perfectly albeit robotically. Afterward, Andras had met her in studio 212 for a critique but never inquired why her mother had failed to attend. "I'm the only one who understands you, Chérie, and you were absolutely magnificent tonight," he said, shoving an audiotape of her performance into the stereo. While her beloved concerto played at high volume, he forced her down onto the hardwood floor and covered her face with his hand to muffle her cries before ripping open her exquisite black gown—

"He knew he was hurting me," she cried to Dashboard Guadalupe.

Alive or dead, estranged or not, she and her mother shared a similar history. Andras, like her mother's assailant at the beach, had not been a stranger. Now they shared the journey to figure out why neither of them had realized they were in danger.

After a short drive, she parked at the curb in front of the apartment he rented for her when she was a student. Sometimes you had to look back to understand how far you had come.

Rain began to hammer the roof, and the bus rocked with the wind gusts. Morgen listened for the roof angels and hoped they had slickers. She stared through the downpour, and in her mind's eye, a memory flowed down the windshield. Andras had chosen an adorable 1930s, hot-pink dress for her to wear for a performance. Not wanting to be upstaged, he wore a period, steel-blue suit. She blinked and saw herself as the pink note squashed on the floor under a larger dark note, its hand over her mouth. She touched the silver beads on the foremothers necklace and heard Gram's voice in her mind's ear: *Recognize what connects you, not just what separates you.*

It took fifty-four minutes for Morgen to drive the seventeen miles in rush-hour traffic to Redmond, but she amused herself by rhythmically changing lanes to the tick of her turn signal, which would have clocked *allegretto* ($\quarternote$ = 120, a lively tempo) on her mechanical metronome.

By the time she arrived at her apartment, she was grumbling to herself and trying to ignore a furious attack of prickly scalp. She grabbed her backpack and raced up the stairs. As soon as she stepped inside, she noticed a piece of paper shoved under the door. Andras had written, *Chérie, can't wait to see you tonight!*

She switched on the limelight and bolted the door. He would take her to a nice restaurant. He would take her back to his hotel room.

The recurring bitter taste crept up the back of her throat while she stared at the clock.

He would want her to shower. He would expect her to be appreciative and upbeat.

She wound her metronome and set it at *andante* ($\quarternote$ = 75, a moderately slow tempo). *Tick. Tick.* She crossed the hardwood floor in a sequence of leaps and pirouettes and turned off the limelight.

The last rays of natural light reached through the window and spotlighted the smiling sea creatures that she'd painted on the wall. Like her, they were captive participants in someone else's sensational theater. She'd always wanted to have smiling friends but lacked the intuition to know if they wanted her too or only wanted something *from* her. She tiptoed to the window and watched the Sammamish River roll along like she watched the rest of "normal" humanity, distant and separate from her. Maybe Gram had been right, that she'd tried to befriend the wrong individuals. Since she'd been given a second chance, what if she gave the *right* individuals a second chance to befriend her, nothing overwhelming, mind you, just something nice and casual? Something real and not pretend. Her perception shortened, and she saw a suggestion of her reflection in the glass. "I miss you," she whispered as her face began to dim.

Dusk arrived, but she didn't turn on the limelight. She wrapped her cell phone in three bath towels, placed it on the bathroom floor, and closed the door. She collected a few treasures and sat cross-legged on the floor. *From now on, I'm going to befriend the right individuals.* She rested the conch shell in a nest of torn cadenza pages on her lap, touched the foremothers necklace, and put the blue crystal star in front of her. The metronome wound down and fell silent.

At 6:03, she smelled Andras's signature scent of mothballs, shoe polish, and roses. She heard a knock on the door and visualized him smiling with a bouquet in hand, debonair like a young Leonard Bernstein with dramatic hair, an intense gaze, and immaculate dress. Her fingers trembled as she sorted trio mix on the floor. *I'm going to find the missing pieces of myself—*

Another knock. "Open the door," he said, dialing up his seductive Welsh accent.

She considered her options by eating M&M's one at a time. *Let him in. Keep him out. Let him in. Keep him out.* The muffled cell phone rang just as she knew it would, or was it coming from a different apartment? She stopped chewing and listened.

Andras was offering her a chance to play Carnegie Hall, but he often said that her success was entirely because of him. *It isn't right.* She shook her head. *I deserve better than this.*

The ringing stopped, and the bitter taste in her mouth vanished. Another knock on the door. "Chérie? Are you okay?" He tried the doorknob.

He'd been a phenomenal teacher and guaranteed access to the performance world she'd craved. Simultaneously, he'd used her curiosity and passion to satisfy his own dark fantasies. He often said that he loved her. He implied they might someday marry, and because she took everything literally, she believed him. She believed the wrong person, but from now on, she was going to accept and believe in herself.

Tears poured down her cheeks as she slammed her head with her fists, and trio mix skittered across the room like rice at a wedding. Her mother had walked away from music to be free of her nightmare. Because Morgen was the result of that nightmare, she'd have to walk away too.

She rose and crossed the room. It was quiet, but she could still smell him out there, less than three feet away. She pressed her palms against the door and waited. Seventeen minutes passed, and the odor faded. After another thirty-eight minutes, she dropped her hands and let them flutter at her sides. She corrected her posture. If her mother could escape the past and start a new life, so could she.

She shoved her cell phone into her backpack and fumbled around the dark apartment, stuffing a garbage bag with toiletries, her favorite books, dissertation, clothing, her passport, and a camera. Her therapist's medications? She shrugged and tossed them into the bag, but where could she go? She cradled the shell and nest of torn cadenza pages in her hands. Her mother had written *Promise to come back and help me* and then gave her the piece of blue crap that waited at the curb. What if she drove out to the drift logs beach and found the Widow Witch's giant conch shell?

She climbed on a chair, unscrewed the limelight bulb, and slipped it into the pocket of her peacoat. She stepped down, hoisted her backpack and the garbage bag, and nodded at the shadowy audience on the wall. Tucking the metronome under her arm, she grabbed her CD player, Fleetwood Mac's *Greatest Hits*, and a binder of her best performance CDs. She opened the door, stepped over Andras's bouquet of roses, and locked the door behind her.

FROM REDMOND, SHE DROVE SOUTH TO OLYMPIA AND then west toward Aberdeen. To stay alert, she began naming each of the bus's fifty-three horses but soon feared she'd fall asleep. She pulled off the highway, parked the bus at the edge of the forest, and stared into the darkness.

"I'm scared," she whispered into the conch shell. On impulse, she loaded "Gypsy," her favorite Fleetwood Mac song, into the CD player and remembered dancing to the magical rhythms and harmonizing with her mother so long ago, virtually levitating as though the song lifted them, weightless as roof angels, above the living room floor.

She bit her lip and fingered the silver beads on the foremothers necklace as the lyrics lingered in the air like patchouli oil. Was she getting a chance to redeem herself for having been a difficult daughter?

She closed Fräu Heinrich's curtains, curled up under the eiderdown on the platform bed, and was asleep before the music ended. In the deepest part of the night, she dreamed that the crystal chandelier above Andras's grand piano exploded. Shattered blue fragments cascaded down as she had sex with him on the cold, hard floor, but when she lifted her hands, shards of glass rose into the black sky to light the road ahead like brilliant blue stars.

Saturday, October 18, 2003

At first light, she awoke to clicks and squeaks. She flung open the cargo door and scrambled outside to investigate the sound. Something magical happened when diverse tones blended together, *tutti*, be they roof angel rhythms, Fleetwood Mac's voices, or individual instruments in the joyful Mozart quintet.

"That's it," she cried to the forest. In music, *tutti* indicated when the ensemble reunited after an extended solo passage. Well, *she'd* been the soloist long enough, and it was time take a leap of faith. "Piece of blue crap, I rechristen you Tutti." She climbed back inside, moved her mother's conch shell to the passenger seat, and nodded at Dashboard Guadalupe. "We are going where roof angels fear to tread."

3.

After a two-hour circuitous drive, Morgen arrived at the Walmart in Aberdeen. She loaded her shopping cart and had chosen a string of miniature white lights when her cell phone rang. She continued searching for a pendant cord that would accommodate the limelight bulb.

Back inside Tutti, she checked her voicemail. "Chérie, Nancy Collier told me you're having a family emergency. Can I help? I'll be back next week to iron out some concert details. Give me a call."

She brushed perspiration from her forehead and deleted Andras's message. She called Water Street Eldercare and left a message with Dorothy, because Gram was napping and Pauline was busy. "Please tell her that I'm headed to the drift logs beach south of Westport."

Forty-seven minutes later, Morgen took the first beach access road through the coastal dunes. By the time she reached an empty gravel lot, the rain had arrived, the tide was in, and the Pacific Ocean was deafening and immense. Seeing it again was like reuniting with an old and trusted relative. She turned on the wipers, leaned back, and watched as waves pummeled the sand.

Long ago on fair-weather trips to the beach, she would strip to her shiny, blue swimsuit and let her mother paint her nose with zinc oxide. She'd grab her inner tube and venture by herself into the chilly water. After a few shivering moments, she'd hop aboard, wedge her tiny derrière into the rubber ring, and let her arms and legs propel her like a blue jellyfish. She'd float so far from shore that her mother would be a speck on the empty expanse of sand.

At six, seven, eight, and nine, she had no fear of sharks or drowning or that if she had a problem, no one would be able to help her. She rejoiced in her buoyancy and belted out a verse she'd made up to the third movement of the Mozart quintet: *When I grow up, I will find my daddy out beyond the deep blue sea and bring him to my mom so we will be a fam-i-ly.* When she became a teenager, a surfboard replaced the inner tube, but she still continued to sing.

Pelicans flew low over Tutti and pulled Morgen back to the present. She heard Headmistress's catch-phrase jangling in her mind's ear like an alarm, *tempus fugit*, so she grabbed her mother's conch shell and ventured into the storm. With a whoop, she performed a perfect grand jeté off the dune scarp and landed in a puddle on the beach. A wavelet rolled up as she dunked the conch shell into the salty water. *Maybe this will activate magical hippie harmonics and get me some answers.*

She grabbed a handful of wet beach sand for her wild rose sugar bowl, raced back to Tutti, and scrambled inside with a gust of wind that sent a stack of her paperwork whirling toward the driver's seat. She locked the cargo door and caught her breath. After she filled the sugar bowl, she put the shell under the table, crawled between the front seats, and began gathering papers and photographs. On the floor by the gas pedal, she found a small envelope she hadn't seen before. The writing was faded and the postmark torn away, but she was able to make out the year: 1968. The note card inside was decorated with hand-painted flowers similar to those on a sympathy card.

Dear Charlie, I wanted you to know that your piano arrived safely here at my home. When the piano tuner had it all opened up, I simultaneously sensed great joy and equal agony and felt profound comfort realizing that music, and perhaps your piano as well, has some semblance of a soul. Please stay safe on your journey and come back to us soon. Sincerely, C. D. Hayes

This individual *owned* her mother's piano? Oh, if she could only get her hands on it. If she could practice the Fantasie on it, maybe her mother's hippie harmonics would release the elusive beauty imprisoned between the notes. She compared the partial return address to the one on the sympathy card that C. D. Hayes had sent to Gram. Voilà! Just enough from each to provide a complete address. She tore a blank page out of her manuscript journal and neatly printed,

Dear C. D. Hayes, My name is Morgen, and I am Charlie Marín's daughter. I just came across a card you wrote to my mother in 1968. I also found a sympathy card you sent to my grandmother, Eleanor Marín, after my mother died. As both had the same return address, I hope that this letter reaches you. I'm beginning to believe in leaps of faith. I'm writing because I'm very curious about my mother's piano. Do you still have it?

She looked at the deserted beach and shook her head. A good start, but where was C. D. Hayes supposed to send a reply?

She shoved the unfinished letter into her backpack and returned to the paved road driving south on Highway 105 along the Cranberry Coast through the seaside communities of Grayland and North Cove. Cranberry bogs and salt marsh lined the east side of the road, while to the west, endless ocean kept her company.

The highway split, and she chose the route through dense woods that would keep her near the water and lead her to the drift logs beach. A few picturesque homes lined the lane, and a half-mile farther, she came to the end of the road. A faded, blue sign read Fish Camp: Marina, Café, Lodging, Campground. Best Kept Secret in the Pacific Northwest.

A large propane tank stood to one side. Plastic pink flamingoes were stuck into the ground. In the adjacent marina, a dozen one-of-a-kind boats soaked in berths along two floating docks. Hundreds of chattering godwits and two stately herons hunkered down on the piers, while gulls perched on the pilings. A jetty made from boulders and concrete rubble stretched out into the water and protected the harbor from the rougher waters of the bay. A shingled building with a whale-shaped weathervane atop a red, gabled roof displayed a sign: Jetty Cat Palace Café. To one side, a man in jeans and a Seahawks sweatshirt was chopping firewood with an enormous Paul Bunyan ax.

Morgen rolled down the window a few inches. "Excuse me? Hello?"

The man dropped the ax and walked toward her. "Where the hell did you get this?" He lit a cigarette.

"From a German mechanic." She leaned away from his ashtray breath.

"Used to be a lot of them banging around in the sixties." He was nice enough looking in a tough-guy way with long-ish, dark hair and a five o'clock shadow. "Can I help you?"

"I'm looking for the road to the drift logs beach," she said, scratching her prickly scalp.

He rested his hand on the half-open window. "Long gone because of dune restoration. You have to walk from here or drive back the way you came."

She glanced in the sideview mirror and noticed that the pavement behind her had changed color. More hippie harmonics? Fatigue washed over her, and she wrinkled her nose at the stink of fish, fuel, wet wood, and bad breath.

"My name's Carlo Ricci, and if you want to stay, I have campsites available."

She was miles away from her comfort zone, and there was no cell phone service. She glanced at a flowery curtain in the building's only upstairs window and shivered as damp fog enveloped her. "Okay, I guess. Thank you."

She pulled on her peacoat, grabbed her backpack, and followed him toward the restaurant. Aging signs in the tall front windows proclaimed Free Fresh Crab Tomorrow, Trailers for Sail or Rent, and Be Kind! Spay and Neuter your Pets. She counted three cats lounging at the entry door. A fourth stood knee-deep in a nearby puddle, and another slunk under the boardwalk. A hefty yellow Lab ambled over, and she lifted her hands so he couldn't bite them.

"That's Salty Dog. He's a good old boy." Carlo led the way and held the door open for her. "You got a name?"

"Yes, I have a name, and it's Morgen. How do you do?" She stepped into the restaurant with Carlo on her heels, and the screen door slammed behind them.

"Hey, Shella, you have a customer." He turned to watch The Weather Channel on TV.

Morgen looked around the cheerfully lit café. It was nicely appointed but not the supersized conch shell she'd hoped to find. The entry door had tall windows on either side with shells and books arranged on the sills. Paintings of sailing ships were hung on pale-blue walls. Brass candle lanterns draped with red and green beads decorated four dining tables, a fire crackled in the fireplace, and a framed photograph of a woman hung on the wall over the mantelpiece. A pair of leaded glass doors showcased lacy white curtains, and a yellow kite hung on the wall above a couch. There had to be a piano somewhere, because she could feel vibrations echoing inside her bones. Or did the sensation come from an old boom box tucked in the corner?

On the right side of the room, a wood counter with black Naugahyde-and-chrome barstools separated the dining area from an open kitchen. She quietly crossed the scarred wood floor toward the kitchen area where a woman was scrubbing pots in the sink. She tripped on nothing and landed with a thud. "Oops, sorry."

"No problem." The woman dried her hands and walked to the counter. "Welcome to Fish Camp. I'm Shella." Her voice was warm with an Irish lilt despite braces on her teeth. She couldn't have been more than twenty years old and was tall and rather pretty. Her short, reddish-brown hair was tipped with black like the fur on something rare and wild. Most notably, her stomach stuck out in front of her like a big bass drum.

"How do you do? I'm Morgen. Are you pregnant?"

"Seriously?" Shella rolled her eyes and rested her hands on her belly. "Yes, and I only have about three weeks to go."

"Wow, congratulations. Is your husband a fisherman?"

"I'm not married."

"Oh. Well, something smells delicious in here."

"I'm baking sourdough bread. Dinner crowd will be rolling in soon. What can I do for you?"

"I'd like a campsite for three nights. I just need an electrical outlet and ice for the icebox. See, I'm looking for a beach my mom visited when she was about your age. What's your birth date?"

"May 2, 1983." Shella opened a receipt book. "You can have site six closest to the upper bathhouse. This time of year, you should have it all to yourself."

"You're three months and ten days older than Mom was back then." *And two months and fifteen days younger than Violet, which provides an interesting perspective.* "I'm here to find her drift logs beach." *Plus her cremation urn, a giant conch shell, and a Widow Witch.* "Your Palace Café is cozy, and I love hearing the foghorn." She corrected her posture. "In music, that tone is a G, you know. I have perfect pitch."

"Good for you, and they don't call it a palace for nothing. Stick around, and I'll tell you the history." Shella leaned closer. "Sometimes it's even haunted."

"Haunted?" Morgen whispered, raising her eyebrows.

"I'm serious." Shella uncapped a pen. "Campsites are eight dollars a night. If you want to include meals, it's sixteen a night, extra charge for beer. If you like, I'll show you the beach with the logs."

"That would be great. May I pay for three nights with meals, thank you, and a bag of ice?" Morgen rummaged through her backpack for her wallet.

After she paid, Shella wrote a receipt. "The freezer is to your left as you go out the door. Showers and laundry are located outside in the back. Anything else?"

"May I please use your phone? Mine doesn't work out here, and my grandmother is in poor health."

"Sure. It's at the other end of the counter. No extra charge." Shella lifted a cast-iron soup pot onto the stove and lit the burner. "Take the shoelace key in the drawer under the phone so you can get in after hours."

"Wow, thanks." After she left a message for Gram with Dorothy, she remembered the letter she started to C. D. Hayes. "Excuse me, do you have a stamp and an envelope I can buy? I'm not used to being away from—"

"Look under the counter next to the receipt book. Take what you need, and pay me later." Shella was busily chopping vegetables and didn't look up.

Morgen smiled to herself. It felt rather calming to be traveling incognito for a change. Nobody clamoring for her autograph or an encore. She grabbed a takeout menu, pulled her unfinished letter out of her backpack, and sat at the counter.

I'm at the coast, and my cell phone doesn't work out here, so please respond ASAP by overnight mail. Sorry for being so demanding, but this is urgent. I'm enclosing $10 to cover postage. I'm also including a menu from the Jetty Cat Palace Café with the café's mailing address. Thank you. Yours truly, Morgen Marín

She addressed a prepaid envelope and put it with the outgoing mail. Then she grabbed the shoelace key and followed Carlo outside. He lit a cigarette and called to a man in a Ron Jon Surf Shop cap who was repairing a section of the boardwalk while a calico cat scowled at him from underneath. "*Vamos,* Joe."

The man called Joe straightened up and tipped his cap, revealing raven-black hair. He brushed sawdust off his sweatshirt and gave her a shy smile.

"How do you do, Joe?" She climbed into Tutti and turned on the engine.

"Follow us," Carlo said as he and Joe walked up the dirt driveway.

She drove behind them and parked twenty-five feet from the bathhouse. Joe showed her where to plug in her extension cord, and he and Carlo left.

Quietude dropped like an embroidered shawl around her shoulders, and she audibly exhaled. In addition to campsites, there were three weathered travel trailers that looked relatively permanent with makeshift skirting, mold and rust streaks, and moss growing on the grimy sides and roofs. Draped crab pot buoys and boat fenders lent color and character to the exteriors. Two surfboards lay on a picnic table outside a trailer called Halibut. A woman with long, dark hair weeded a rose bed nearby. She waved, and Morgen waved back.

Her first stop was the bathhouse. After collecting five damp cigarette butts, she opened the metal door and looked around. Fortunately, soap and paper towels were provided, so she scrubbed the cigarette butt germs off her hands. The bathhouse appeared thoroughly sanitized. With a laugh of relief, she flapped her hands, extended her arms, and performed a pirouette without bumping into anything.

When she stepped outside, a roly-poly, orange tabby cat was waiting for her. She bent down to pet it, and the cat responded by licking her fingers. "How do you do? I rather like you, but please don't do that." She wiped her hand on her jeans and returned to Tutti. As soon as she opened the door, the cat leaped in and began to sniff around. "I too have a keen olfactory sense, and by the way, you're my first bus-guest." The cat watched her with an expression that resembled a smile. "Mom told me to smile, no matter what, so I did and got cast as the Cheshire cat in a school play based on *Alice in Wonderland*. But a bully drew a grotesque smile on my face with permanent marker. Mom tried soap, rubbing alcohol, toothpaste, and finally nail polish remover, and my cheeks were red and sore for a month."

She set her metronome at a relaxing *largo* ($\quarternote$ = 45, slow and dignified) and designated one compartment for her camera, clothes, and toiletries and another for books and sheet music in alphabetical order by author or composer. She placed the blue crystal star and wild rose sugar bowl on the tabletop. "I'm going to find your urn, Mom, and solve the mystery of the witch-in-the-conch. Maybe this nice kitty knows something about the Palace Café being haunted." The cat stared at the metronome with enormous hazel eyes as though hypnotized. Morgen shrugged and propped Gram's photo of the real urn behind the sugar bowl. *Why on earth would someone steal a cremation urn from a private home?* Very weird, but it had to be somewhere.

She spread out the torn cadenza pages on the tabletop. The giant conch shell had to be close enough to the drift logs beach for Bertie-the-gardener to get her mother to the Widow Witch. Was it a real place or a Southern-Comfort-and-acid hallucination?

The cat yowled and hopped on a bench seat when Morgen started draping the miniature white lights from stick-on hooks on the headliner. "There, as cheery as a dressing room, although I may have to leave the performance world behind." Tears filled her eyes. "I'm tired, I'm sad, and I'm pissed and don't know what I'm going to do. Oh dear Lord, you ask too many questions." The cat hopped to the floor, and she let it out.

After stowing her Walmart groceries with like things together and labels facing out, she made a peanut butter sandwich even though she'd prepaid for meals. She didn't have the energy for more chitchat, although Fish Camp did offer an interesting three-day social experiment. She poured half of a cup of trio mix onto the tabletop and began to sort and nibble as she dissected Andras's Fantasie one phrase at a time, one hand at a time. Each note was lovely and had just as much a right as the next one to be savored but, when thoughtlessly forced together, might be awful like trio mix in ketchup.

Social gaiety from inside the Palace Café interrupted her thoughts. She gazed out the window through the opera glasses. A boardwalk surrounded the Jetty Cat Palace Café with its main entrance on the lane facing the bay. According to irregular rooflines, the closet with lacy curtains as well as the laundry room and shower house at the side and rear must have been added on to the original building. Docks lay to the east, the harbormaster house was next to the boat launch, and the trailers and campsites were up a slight rise. What was she expecting to see? A literal super-sized kitschy conch shell? Fish Camp was anything but Coney Island. She peered through the gloom and saw four cats staring back, their eyes glowing.

Beyond the jetty, lights flickered on the horizon. She held her metronome in both hands and remembered how her mother would set it at a slow tempo and put it near her pillow to help her sleep. She set it at *grave* (♩ = 35, very slow and solemn). *Tick. Tick.* She brushed her teeth with bottled water, left Fräu Heinrich's curtains open, and unplugged the miniature lights. "It's okay," she whispered as she lay down on the platform bed under the eiderdown. "The door is locked, I'm in a safe place, I'm here to help Mom." *Tick. Tick.* Outside, Fish Camp pulled the fog up under its chin. When night eventually fell, everyone would sleep, secure under the weight of it.

Sunday, October 19, 2003

She slept in and awoke to fog so thick it looked like Tutti had parked inside a pillowcase. She scrambled into her new salmon-pink sweats, argyle socks, and damp sneakers, grabbed her bag of toiletries, and headed to the bathhouse, stopping to pick up another cigarette butt.

The orange tabby waited for her outside the metal door. "Good morning, kitty," she said. The cat followed her inside, and while Morgen went through her ritual, the cat sat on the floor grooming its fur. When they both had finished, they returned to Tutti. Morgen turned on the space heater while humming along with "O Sole Mio" blaring from the harbormaster house. The cat lay down on the eiderdown and purred.

"Normally, right now I'd be teaching my students, but I can't do that, which is a heartbreaking price to pay to end a nightmare." She glanced at her red attaché case where she kept Andras's *Coitus Cadenza.* "So why am I lugging that nightmare around with me? I should burn it." She remembered the afternoon when a flushed and, in hindsight, aroused Andras appeared at her side. He explained that the photograph was a parody of artist Maxfield Parrish's style and represented the quintessential union of man and music. As though that had meant something to a fifteen-year-old girl, yet for reasons known but to God, she never told her mother about incidents like that. Nor more recently had she confided in her therapist. She put her medications inside the attaché case and locked it.

She peeled a banana for breakfast and offered the cat a slice just as Shella tapped on the window. Morgen opened the door. "Good morning. Do you want to come in?"

"Sure, thanks. Doris, what are you doing in here?" Shella said to the cat. Shella wore a navy-blue *By-the-Wind Sailor Fishing Charters* sweatshirt and smelled like French fries. She handed a paper bag to Morgen and sat on the opposite bench. "When you didn't show up for meals, I thought I'd better check on you. I brought you some salmon chowder and sourdough."

"That's very thoughtful." Was Shella making a friendly overture? Morgen was a paying guest, and Shella was the host, and her therapist had pressed her about boundary issues and her inability to discriminate between strangers, familiar faces, acquaintances, friends, and foes, explaining that it was inappropriate to invite her dental hygienist, favorite barista, or parents of students to meet socially, which she'd already done in vain—

"It's a snack, not a feast," Shella said as though reading her mind.

Morgen nodded and petted Doris on the head. "Your sweet kitty has been keeping me company."

"Doris isn't my cat. She's one of the jetty cats, and they belong to no one but themselves. There're seventeen more of them, all fixed, twelve of whom are feral and stay out in the rocks away from everybody, surviving on fish parts, charity kibble, and TLC by our local vet. Watch out for One-Eyed Jack. He's a mean, big, blue-gray feral with long hair, one blue eye, and a nasty scar where his other eye had been. Can't miss him. Broken tail, left ear tipped, and an awful screechy voice, but he eliminates rats and intimidates the raccoons." She glanced around. "What a cozy little camper."

"Thank you. I named it Tutti."

"Tutti? Seriously? Cute!" Shella laughed again. "I better get back to work, that is *if* I can get out of here gracefully. Because of the baby, I've gotten fat, and now thanks to you, I'm craving tutti-frutti ice cream."

Doris yowled and followed Shella outside.

"I'll see you at breakfast tomorrow." After Morgen closed the cargo door, she imagined her very pregnant mother stuffed behind Tutti's steering wheel and fleeing like a fugitive across the Mexican border.

It was hard to believe that mom-to-be Shella was two months and two weeks *younger* than Violet Bacon. Morgen dug her manuscript journal out of the backpack. Violet, like a temperamental sibling, was always in the back of her mind. Gram had said to recognize what connected her, not just what separated her, and what connected her to Violet most at the moment was the arduous Stravinsky concerto, but evidently, Violet did not need her help.

She wrote the list she'd imagined on the drive, "Tutti's Fifty-Three Horses from Friday, October 17, 2003 to Present." Chronologically, not alphabetically, beginning with her female ancestors and ending with Shella and Doris. She studied the list and chewed her lips. She'd always wanted to belong but often felt uncomfortable or bored around others, resulting in a colorful history of social missteps that she didn't want to recur. Still, she might like to have coffee with Shella or salmon chowder if that was the tradition out there.

It sounded like the roof angels landed overhead while she ate. "It's about time you showed up," she muttered. She put the soup bowl into a plastic dishpan, bundled up, and ventured out to explore Fish Camp's marina.

An offshore wind kept the rain clouds at bay, and pampas grass rustled in the breeze. Crab pots were heaped like haystacks. Three weathered signs were nailed to a piling at the top of the ramp closest to the campground: Transient Moorage available—See Joe at the Fuel Dock, Tip Your Deckhand, and "Most boating accidents happen when the operator is not paying attention." She started down an incline following the sound of Dean Martin's "Volare." The music was coming from inside a bright-blue fishing boat moored perpendicular to the farthest dock. As she drew closer, the hair on the back of her neck stood up, and her hands began to flap.

A twelve-inch-high pelican figurehead on the bow of that boat had both wings stretched open as though to welcome her. A red heart was painted outside the pelican's chest, blue tears decorated its elongated face, and a spiraling ocean wave appeared to curl beneath its webbed feet. *Holy crap.* Before they slapped each other in the restaurant, her mother had seen that pelican-priest figurehead as an omen that she was going to die. Which she did. Morgen stared, mouth agape, until a deep, baritone voice called out, "Hey, baby, come on down."

"Is this your boat?" she squeaked, her throat tightening. She gestured at the transom. "*By-the-Wind Sailor?*"

"Yes, she is." The man was middle-aged, his sweatshirt and faded jeans were smeared with varnish, and dark curls tumbled from under a sweat-stained Cincinnati Reds baseball cap.

"I saw it almost thirteen and a half years ago on Lake Union, but it was called *Epiphany* back then." Her heart must have been beating at *vivace* (♩ = 144, quick and lively), and she faked a yawn to gather her breath.

"She's one and the same. I bought her five years ago and rechristened her." He gazed around his boat. His eyes, beneath thick eyebrows and eyelashes, were dark gunmetal gray, and he reeked of Old Spice. "I'm Captain Angelo Vincenzo Bordacelli, a gentleman fisherman, and that," he said, pointing at a seal swimming in the water nearby, "is Jim the Harbor Seal." He dropped a piece of sandpaper and stepped closer. "What brings you out on north float? Boat ride? Fishing? Whale watching?"

"None of those activities, and how do you do? I'm Morgen Marín."

"You can come aboard if you like."

She shook her head. "I just want to know more about this boat and that pelican, thank you." She glanced past him at the aft deck. Fishing nets and poles stood upright in racks. Buckets and tackle boxes were piled nearby. Cans of varnish and thinner, brushes, and sandpaper littered the deck.

"Suit yourself, pretty lady. The boat's a 1989 thirty-six-foot Grand Banks Europa, and she's my true love. As for that pelican, it looks like a mortician to me, but it came with the boat, so it stays. Want the tour? See what lurks in the bowels of my grand ship?"

"No, thank you." He was probably Andras's age, and that alone made him dangerous.

The recording of "Volare" ended, and "Everybody Loves Somebody" blared across the water.

"I like Dean Martin too, but he's dead." She wanted to flee back to Tutti, but she also wanted to interrogate this Angelo individual. "Is he your favorite singer?"

"Is the Pope Catholic?" He raised his eyebrows. "Truth be told, he died on Christmas Day 1995. Ruined Christmas for me forever, but he was a real romantic, a song and dance man, and a comedian too, as well as my hero, and he sure sounds better than Carlo's opera singers. I'll let you decide. We both tend to crank up the volume." He chuckled. "All in all, my boat's compact yet comfortable enough for a bachelor. I live on board. Never wanted a destroyer or a yacht. Just a trusty trawler, although her radio quit working, and the electronics have been acting up. I'll have Joe check them out. He's Mexican. He can fix anything." He tapped the ship's bell mounted near the door. "No disrespect."

"Why did you change the name?" She shoved her hands into her pockets and was delighted to find an M&M.

"*Epiphany* sounded too New Age for me. *By-the-Wind Sailor* works better. You know the little blue jellyfish *Velella velella*? It stays afloat on the surface of the sea, can right itself when capsized, and always makes it to shore. Now that's a lucky namesake."

"I know those jellies. I used to pick them up and throw them back into the water." She popped the linty M&M into her mouth and leaned over to study the figurehead. "So why *that* pelican?"

"Come to think of it, when I moved in, I found a poem tucked away. Hang on." He went inside, returned with a scrap of paper, and read aloud.

A pelican bird is a humble disguise
For a fallen angel to be

While earning absolution
Ferrying poor souls lost at sea.
Blue tears they weep while heaven bound
Plunge alive to the surging sea
And sail the waves to distant shores
To comfort those who grieve.

"Brown pelicans dive face first like falling angels, so I suppose it makes sense, although God knows I'm no poet." He shoved the paper into his pocket. "Is that your blue minivan? Reminds me of the good old days, if you know what I mean."

"It's a 1967 VW bus."

"Funny. You strike me as more of a Beemer girl." He appeared to be amused or condescending.

She didn't know which, so she corrected her posture. "I'm not a beemer. I'm a teacher and too old to be called a girl."

"Want to share a beer and talk baseball? Game two of the World Series tonight. We can listen on my radio."

"Some other time." In addition to Old Spice, he also smelled like alcohol, just like Andras, and she knew where that inevitably led.

"Beemer girl or not, you're in safe harbor now, but suit yourself." He went inside and started the engine.

She noticed he had a limp. "What's wrong with your leg?"

"Trick knee." He smiled. "Don't worry about me, Morgen Marín. I'm going fishin'. Ciao, baby!"

She watched as he cast off and motored away. Her mother had gone into labor after a real-life pelican-priest approached Tutti. Twenty years and eleven months later on the day before she was killed, she'd encountered it again in the form of an ominous figurehead. Now the bow of Angelo's boat, bearing that same figurehead, was carving through the water setting in motion ripples that raced back to rock the dock where she stood. She shivered and shoved her hands deeper into the pockets of her peacoat.

SHE CLOSED THE CARGO DOOR AND SAT DOWN AT THE table. "Okay, Mom," she whispered into the conch shell, "I'm in the right place, I found our pelican-priest, and I'm befriending the right individuals." She opened her manuscript journal, turned to a fresh page, and printed *My Social Experiment Wisdom.*

1. *The individuals in Fish Camp don't know me and won't judge me by my job or diagnosis, and I don't need to pretend to be normal.*
2. *Usually after "how do you do" and a mental cataloging of a few interesting details, I lose interest, but now? I'm actually more interested.*
3. *I don't have to do anything I don't want to do just to be accepted.*

Her fingers spasmed, and she stared at her hands. Were they overly tired or trying to solve the Fantasie conundrum?

She looked down the hill through the opera glasses and noticed an older individual climbing off an ATV in front of the café. Carlo leaned against an old red pickup and lit a cigarette. Salty Dog trotted across the boardwalk and paused to look in her direction. He wagged his tail and offered a bark. She sent a sincere smile his way and closed the curtains.

LATER THAT EVENING, WHILE SHE WAS ALPHABETIZING HER repertoire list in her manuscript journal, a prompt for two missed calls appeared on her cell phone. When she tried to pick up her voicemail, all she got was "Call Failed." Maybe Violet needed help with the concerto. She grabbed her flashlight and the shoelace key that Shella had loaned her and hurried through the night to the darkened café. Once inside, she hung the key around her neck and tiptoed to the phone to retrieve her voicemail. "Dr. Marín, this is Headmistress Collier. Time flies, *tempus fugit*, my dear. I hope your grandmother is feeling better. I look forward to seeing you bright and early Monday morning." She deleted the message. "Chérie? About this family emergency of yours. You only have one grandmother who appears to be fine, so what's going on?"

Her prickly scalp flared up, and she deleted his message too. *How would he know Gram was fine?* She dialed Headmistress's number, and luckily the call went to voicemail. "This is Morgen. I'm sorry. I won't be in this week." She caught herself making eye contact with the woman in the photo above the mantelpiece. "It's gotten complicated here, but I'll keep in touch. Thanks." She hung up, and as she waited for her pulse to return to normal, her gaze wandered through the semidarkness and paused where thin, white light seeped up around the baseboard nearest the leaded glass closet doors.

Armed with her flashlight, she tiptoed between the tables dressed for breakfast and approached the closet. Her flashlight beam reflected back at her like a spotlight, and she caught a glimpse of her wide eyes in an otherwise unfamiliar face. She slowly opened the glass door and saw rain gear and two folding chairs. A laundry basket full of Christmas decorations and jars of poster paint had been shoved against the wall closest to the mystery light. She shone the beam at the back wall. The closet wasn't as deep as it appeared from the outside.

She knelt and put the flashlight on the floor. With both hands, she slid the basket out of the way. The flashlight flickered and dimmed, and she caught her breath. Shella had said the Palace was haunted. She waited for her eyes to adjust and, on hands and knees, resumed her exploration of the closet. Because she couldn't see clearly, she used her fingertips to feel the floor and inside wall for any irregularity.

A spiked club raked her back. She turned to fight for her life, and the Palace's haunter scrambled back and yowled. The blue-gray cat that Shella called One-Eyed Jack glared at her with his good eye before pushing past her into the closet. "Go away," she hissed. Jack flicked his broken tail, pressed his forepaws against the wall, and stretched. As soon as he dug in his claws, a piece of wallboard broke away, light increased behind it, and he leaped through the opening.

Evidently, the piece of paneling had been Velcroed to the wall with a handle on the inside. Morgen peered down after Jack and saw narrow, steep steps descending into a dim chamber that unfortunately conjured up Dagger Eyes' supply closet. As she leaned through the opening, she found the source of the eerie light: a dusty, old incandescent light bulb suspended from a frayed wire on the ceiling had enough energy to glow but not illuminate. When she aimed her light into the spooky abyss, she found a dangling electrical cord with a plug hanging near a rusty outlet just inside the opening. Didn't individuals often get electrocuted or lockjaw? Her fingers shook as she reached inside and pushed the plug into the outlet. A grimy string of white lights lit the cellar. What if there were spiders or dead things down there? She squeezed feet first through the opening and gingerly descended five tiled steps. Jack purred and sidled around and between her knees while she stared at the walls. The cellar looked like a jeweled grotto from a childhood fairy tale. "Could this be Mom's conch shell?" she whispered.

One-Eyed Jack gave her a look that said *Oh yes, it is.*

Tears filled Morgen's eyes. On the torn cadenza pages, her mother had sketched a weeping pink note (evidently herself) taking refuge inside a giant conch shell that was located near the drift logs beach. "It's real," she whispered, rubbing her hands across the shimmering walls. "Mom was actually in here. Thank you, Jack." He nuzzled her leg in reply. But it meant that her mother really had been attacked by some creepy jerk "friend" while sky high on weed and drunk on Southern Comfort. *Oh dear Lord, Mom, I'm so sorry about what happened to you.* She sat on a low glass brick bench, the only object in the room. *This is now about more than just finding your urn.*

It was obvious from the damp muck on the tiled floor that no one had been in there for a long time, and presumably, the space was vented to the outdoors, because she could smell cool ocean air and hear the foghorn and roar of the distant surf. Fish Camp itself, however, felt light years away. The cellar resembled the inside of a giant conch shell and was about the size of her office at River Bridge. The steps she navigated had been built into the shell's broad flared lip. The curving whorled walls and floor were covered with swirls of all shapes and sizes of mirror pieces and mosaic glass, stone, and ceramic tiles ranging from the palest to the darkest shades of pink. The effect of the twinkly white lights, reflected in the mirror fragments and warmed by a broad spectrum of pinks, made her dizzy and then oddly calm. She focused on her fractured reflection in the tiny mirrors as though she'd entered a giant kaleidoscope. Her breath caught in her throat. *Fractured* reflection? Her mother had seen her own battered reflection in these walls on September 27, 1968. Had she also seen her bleeding reflection in the white pickup's fractured windshield twenty-one years and almost eight months later?

Morgen glanced up and saw a plywood panel nailed to the outside wall just left of the top step. The night before, she noticed that in addition to the curtained closet, the laundry room had been added on to the original structure just above her. Her heart skittered. Did that piece of plywood seal off the opening her mother had accessed? According to the doodled story, her mother hadn't been alone in there. Evidently, the Widow Witch had helped her. More hippie harmonics, or somebody real?

She gazed around her mother's conch grotto and saw an eighteen-inch-tall statue of Our Lady of Guadalupe keeping watch from a nest of dried kelp and soiled fake flowers on a ledge at the top of the shell's lip. Like the pelican-priest on Angelo's boat, Guadalupe's tears were as blue as sapphires.

She was awarded with an exquisite sense of purpose. *Mom, I promise I will find and fix the missing pieces of our lives.* Her mother's truth was her truth too, the evidence of that was likely within reach, and they both had a right to own it. Jack nudged her, and they scrambled up the steps. Before she closed the panel in the closet wall, she unplugged the lights, leaving the conch grotto in darkness.

Monday, October 20, 2003

Morgen hung her damp peacoat on a hook by the door and noticed eleven chewing strangers and Carlo Ricci watching her, but it was okay, because she had a delicious secret: she alone knew about the pink-tiled secret wonderland inches beneath her sneakers.

"Good morning." Shella bustled around the café, cheeks pink and braces gleaming. "Coffee?"

"Yes, thank you. Decaf, please." But first she needed to choose a comfortable place to sit on the perimeter, not in the middle of the dining room, because she was feeling conspicuous. "May I please give out your phone number? My cell phone doesn't work."

"Sure, use the phone whenever you want."

"Do you have D batteries I can buy? Mine burned out last—"

"Second drawer with the duct tape and screwdrivers."

"Thank you." She eased onto a barstool beside the elderly ATV man.

Shella poured a mug of decaf and set it on the counter. "Sweet rolls are just out of the oven."

"Scrumptious," ATV man said. His denim jacket was shabby but clean over a red flannel shirt and denim bib overalls, and he smelled sweet like smoked salmon. "They call me Grumpy John."

"I call him Grampy John. He's the least grumpy person I know." Shella gave her a large pastry on a plate, topped off their mugs, and made the rounds.

"How do you do? I'm Morgen." She took a bite. "This is delicious."

"Sourdough. My family's recipe," John said. "Went up the Chilkoot Trail to the Yukon goldfields in 1898." His face was supple as soft leather, and his smile came easily.

"Good morning, Morgen," said a voice behind her.

She blushed and turned at the sound of her name. "Good morning, Angelo."

"I see you two have met," Shella said. "Breakfast?"

"Women! I'd prefer a fancy brunch, but the usual is fine even though there's cause for celebration. Thanks to Andy Pettitte, the Yankees tied up the World Series last night. Good morning, Grumpy John." He gave the older man a rub on the back.

"Skipper." John nodded.

Angelo took a mug out from behind the counter and filled it with coffee. "I see you're meeting the fine citizens of Fish Camp." He sat at one of the tables.

By sitting at the counter, her back was to the dining tables, which made conversing with Angelo awkward. She turned on the barstool so her knees were facing but not impinging on John's personal space. "Yes, everyone's friendly."

"Right, and some can be overly friendly like Carlo, so watch out."

"You're the fool she needs to watch out for, since you're drunk half the time." Carlo headed for the door.

"Chrissake, for once in your unfortunate life, will you please think before you speak?" Angelo winked at Morgen. "What are you gonna do?"

She frowned. It was rather awkward navigating between the conversation and her breakfast. She speared a piece of sweet roll with her fork and ate it. The woman from Halibut trailer gave her a quick, infectious smile as she set scrambled eggs, smoked salmon, and a scoop of spaghetti in front of

Angelo. She was barely five feet tall with a gentle face the color of a latte, and her long, black hair was contained under a white chef beanie.

"*Gracias*, Mia," Angelo said. "And just so you know, Morgen Marín. Mia only speaks Spanish and is married to Joe the boat mechanic who speaks *un poco* English. Hey, Shella, give me the granulated garlic, doll. Can't have too much garlic. What's cooking tonight?"

"Steamed whole or half crab," Shella said. "Clam or smoked salmon chowder. Fish, chips, and slaw. Smoked oyster tortellini. Zucchini frittata, and Mia's specialty, fish tacos with cranberry salsa."

"You attract a crowd with your cooking," Morgen said, swiveling on her barstool. "It's rather hectic in here at the moment."

"They come in before and after work and sometimes instead of." Shella turned away and continued serving her customers.

Morgen wiped perspiration from her brow. "What's your birth date?" she asked John. "That is, if you don't mind."

"August 21, 1930. Not just mine neither—"

"See? It's the best of having company and family all at once." Shella reappeared out of nowhere and was wiping the counter. "I get paid and have a place to live." She gestured toward the stairs. "This is my world."

A raucous one at that. Morgen turned to John. Her therapist had recommended that she navigate chitchat by asking insightful questions. "Do you fish?"

John continued eating his breakfast. Morgen took another bite. Must have been a stupid question, but since he was seventy-three years and two months old, he might know the Palace Café's history such as the origin of the conch grotto and whether a Widow Witch really rescued her mother—

"*Catchalot*," he said.

"I beg your pardon?" She grabbed her napkin. "Sorry, my mouth is full."

"Name of my boat. Old but sound." He wiped his plate with his roll. "Out end of south float. Double end salmon troller. Forty-foot. All wood. Built in 1935." He slapped a Nelson Crab cap on his head. "Have a nice day," he said as he left.

Mia, the Spanish speaker from Halibut trailer, collected John's dishes and topped off Morgen's mug. She began sweeping, her broom whispering *whish-whish-whish* across the wood floor.

"Muchas gracias, Mia," Morgen whispered. She struggled with nonverbal cues, but Mia, who reportedly spoke no English, seemed intuitive and communicated kindness with her eyes and facial expressions. Perhaps being kind in return wouldn't violate a boundary.

"What brings you out here?" Shella asked from the kitchen.

Morgan had told Shella about looking for her mother's beach, but evidently, she'd forgotten. "I needed a couple days of peace and quiet and a change of scenery before—"

"Gray whales migrate past here between Mexico and the Bering Sea. Folks go out whale watching. Is that the kind of scenery you're looking for?" She applied pale-pink lip gloss.

Before Morgen could answer, Angelo said, "What's the schoolteacher up to today?"

"I teach music." She was beginning to feel agitated and short of breath. Everybody interrupted each other. Maybe she'd gotten regular coffee by mistake, because her eyebrows were starting to itch. "Excuse me." She stumbled to the windowsill and read the book titles: *Moby Dick, The Old Man and the Sea, Treasure Island,* and *Gift from the Sea.* Oh the temptation to reestablish routine and order. She took four deep breaths while she rearranged them alphabetically by author: Hemingway, Lindbergh, Melville, and Stevenson.

"My old man used to write stories about Italy and Atlantis. I don't write," he patted his chest, "although I have a story, but enough about me. You didn't tell me you taught music."

"I'm a pianist and I chair the music program at a performing arts boarding school for girls." She didn't want to talk about work, but he seemed to be making a friendly overture, and she might want to get a closer look at that pelican-priest. "Exclusive college prep, highly competitive, only a hundred students, and girls and faculty wear uniforms—"

"I'm impressed, Morgen Marín." He studied her face. "You enjoy all that, do you?"

She smiled at him. "In the thin morning light when my students arrive smelling of shampoo and breakfast and are eager to make music, that's what I enjoy. That and listening to their dreams and problems and sharing late-night hot chocolate. The rest?" She shrugged. "I'm job hunting."

"Do you play boogie-woogie? We could put a piano in here, and folks would come from miles around to hear you tickle the old ivories."

"Sorry, I'm not a lounge act."

"What kind of an act are you?"

"I was a concert pianist in college and soloed in a Stravinsky concerto."

"Stravinsky? Didn't he play hockey?" Angelo poured his cold coffee back into the pot to reheat it and refilled his mug.

Shella rolled her eyes. "Gosh, would you please quit doing that?"

"Hey, we're all friends here."

Morgen stared into her mug, grateful that he didn't drink decaf. She glanced out the window as a white van pulled up in front.

"That's my appointment." Shella smiled broadly. "I got *chosen* to be in a special program paid for by a foundation. Every week, baby and braces. Pretty cool, huh? If you want to go to the drift logs beach today, meet me here at ten-thirty." She hurried toward the door.

"That'd be great, thanks." Morgen watched her go. "Shella's been very accommodating."

"She learned how to cook cioppino just because I like it. You know, Italian fish stew? I'll tell her to make a pot for you." Angelo looked out the window at the van. "Got off the local bus all by herself last winter. A fish out of water with dyed black hair, black clothing, and a bunch of black shit on her eyes. Bit of a wild child, but that all changed. She's a sweet kid and a hard worker."

Morgen's shoulders dropped. It seemed that everyone out there had a story if not a screenplay or miniseries. She wanted to ask Angelo about Shella being pregnant with no partner in sight but had reached her chitchat limit, although she was learning it was easier to listen to individuals she found interesting. "Excuse me. I need to use the phone."

"Good timing, because I have to see a man about a boat." He headed for the door.

She rinsed her mug in the sink and grabbed two flashlight batteries out of the drawer. She called the School of Music and left the café's number for Hannah. Just in case.

"Thanks for showing me the way," Morgen said. "I vaguely remember an access road, but Carlo said it's gone." She buttoned her peacoat and hung her camera strap around her neck. "I used to surf out here, but it's been at least fifteen years."

"I don't go in the water, but I love to walk the beach. My doctor says exercise and fresh air are good for me and my baby." Shella wore a trendy black raincoat that couldn't zip over her belly, and she carried the café's yellow kite.

As they strolled along, an offshore breeze tossed gray clouds on the ocean like rumpled bedding on a lumpy, blue mattress. Salty Dog yipped with joy and galloped toward a flock of tiny sandpipers feeding at the edge of the surf.

Shella held a spool of string in one hand and tossed the kite into the wind with the other. A gust sent it whirling into the sky.

Morgen focused her camera and snapped a picture. "I've never seen that technique before."

"It was just a decoration, but now it can fly."

The kite wheeled higher and higher. Morgen felt a battle escalate as the kite fought the string. She understood that there was security in being tethered to something but oh, the temptation to break free and soar to new heights.

Shella laughed as she maneuvered the kite through spirals and figure eights, the yellow fabric snapping in the wind like sheets on a clothesline.

While Morgen watched, she replayed in her mind Gram saying that the great continuum had given her music as a lifeline. Had she meant that *Morgen* was like a kite and that music was the string that kept her tethered? If so, tethered to what? And who held the string? She tugged her sleeves down over her hands.

After a while, Shella brought the kite down, and they wandered down the beach. Salty Dog galloped ahead of them, tongue flapping and paws kicking up sand.

"Look." Morgen pointed at the sun's reflection on the glimmering sand. "When the beach is wet, it's like walking on the sky." She did a pirouette. "When I was little, my mom and I came out here, and I searched for glass fishing floats. There was nothing I wanted more than one of those glass balls. It would have been like holding my own world in my hands."

"Angelo said that on his way here in his boat, he saw one that had been bobbing along for thousands of miles."

Morgen looked out to sea as two pelicans dove into the surf at once. "Did you know that pelicans can live for twenty-five years and feed forty miles offshore? That they have a wingspan up to seven feet and have been around for forty million years? That their bones are hollow? Did you know all that?"

"Nope." Shella squatted and picked up a beached jellyfish. "But I know that by-the-wind sailors don't sting. Angelo calls me Shella Bella Velella velella. Says it rolls so sweetly off the tongue. Isn't that cute?" She dropped the jellyfish. "*Velella velella* is the scientific name for by-the-wind sailors, in case you didn't know."

Morgen enjoyed marine life chitchat. "Did you know that gray whales are born head first?"

"Are you insinuating that I'm as big as a whale?"

"No, not at all," Morgen cried. "I'm so sorry."

"No, I'm too sensitive. I'm trying to do the right things. I even took out my belly button ring and quit dying my hair because it might poison my baby." She picked at a blemish on her chin. "Under the circumstances, you'd think I'd at least outgrow zits. When I moved out here, all I wanted was cute surfer boys, but I've grown up, and I'm ready to be a mother. My mom had me when she was seventeen and the same for her mom. For both of them, it only took a couple of contractions and a sneeze to pop out the baby."

Probably stretching the truth, but Shella would find out soon enough. "Your baby's lucky to have you for a mom."

"I hope so." Shella pouted. "I don't think my mom ever felt lucky to have me, especially after my real dad died."

Morgen chewed a fingernail. Shella's candor was disconcerting, especially since *she* avoided discussing her family, and if it came up, she artfully redirected the conversation.

"Her boyfriend, Ronnie, had been around since I was a kid, and he was a *creep*." Shella's cheeks turned bright red.

"That's sad." Morgen wanted to be empathetic, but this was getting rather awkward.

"When Mom wasn't home, he hurt me." Tears spilled down Shella's cheeks. "You know, smacked me around, so a couple of times, I peed on his toothbrush. Hers too. Sorry, freaking emotional hormones." She sniffled and tried to laugh. "We used to do girly things together like shop for clothes, get our hair, makeup, and nails done, and then go out to lunch. People thought we were *sisters*. Then Ronnie stole her away from me. I miss her so much." She rubbed her belly. "She doesn't know I'm pregnant."

"Oh no. Really? I miss my mom too. She died in an accident." Morgen felt her own tears rising. "I think your hormones are contagious, because now I'm feeling very emotional."

"That's okay, because we girls are outnumbered in Fish Camp and have to stick together."

Morgen's thoughts raced. Maybe Ronnie was the possessive and controlling type like Andras, but why didn't Shella's mom protect their relationship? Along those lines, Morgen had been annoyed when her mother had been overly protective but more so when she hadn't, especially when it came to Dagger Eyes and Andras. *Oh dear Lord, it's so complicated.* She shoved the memory out of the way. "When is your baby due?"

"Middle of November. Is this the place you're looking for?"

Morgen had been so caught up in the chitchat that she failed to notice the vast piles of weathered drift logs looming ahead.

"You explore." Shella sat down on a log and rubbed her lower back. "I'll wait here."

Morgen continued as though entering a dreamscape. Most of the logs were shiny and bleached like dinosaur bones, and many had probably witnessed her mother's attack. In her mind's eye, a little girl stood on the biggest one with hands cupped binocular-style around her eyes; a young mother with an enigmatic expression sat at the girl's feet; a blue note named Riff lay crushed under a jumble of logs at the edge of the surf. Swallowing a sob, Morgen dropped to her knees and rolled onto her back where, on Friday, September 27, 1968, a pink note lay squashed under a larger dark note—

"Are you making a sand angel?" Shella yelled from her perch.

"No, but my mom—"

Salty Dog barked and flopped at her side, panting and drooling on her arm.

"I rather like you, but please don't do that."

"Let's go. I've got to get back to work."

Morgen put a pinch of sand in her pocket for the sugar bowl and jogged back to Shella's side. "I want to take your picture, right here with these logs." She focused the camera.

"Oh, my baby's dancing again." Shella laughed, and Morgen pushed the shutter button just as a long high wave curled in the background and an undulating string of pelicans flew overhead looking like rags on a kite tail. Salty Dog took off ahead of them, yipping and chasing the waves.

Morgen walked with Shella who continued chattering about babies, cravings, and hormones. She tried to pay attention but sensed her young and very pregnant mother dancing alone among the drift logs to the saddest Mexican guitar. When she glanced over her shoulder, she glimpsed the hem of a tie-dyed dress vanishing into the fog.

Morgen chewed her lips. Something odd was happening, because her defenses had softened in the salt air. Had she crossed the boundary that should exist between host, aka Shella, and guest, aka her? She couldn't read nonverbal feedback, and now things would probably feel awkward going forward. She arrived at Tutti just as Carlo was leaving the upper bathhouse with a toolbox in his hand.

"I had to change the fill valve in the toilet," he said, chipping a gull dropping off the bus roof. "I'd like to take a look inside your bus. It's a classic—"

"Carlo Russo Ricci, quit showing off your tools, and come give me a hand," Angelo hollered from the dock.

"Look, Angelo needs my help and he pays the bills. Maybe later?" Carlo lit the cigarette he'd tucked above his ear and sauntered down the hill toward the marina.

Sorry, probably *not* later. Now Morgen was highly mindful about boundaries between guests (her) and hosts (aka those who worked in Fish Camp like Carlo).

She unlocked the cargo door, plugged in the space heater, and sat at the table. Shella had been frank about her troubled relationship with her mother. In contrast, she'd never been able to put her finger on what had instigated her estrangement with her mother. She unlocked the attaché case and took out the photo of her mother in the denim sundress circa 1968. She picked up her blue crystal star and reflected while touching each of the five points. One: Shella said that she and her mother had been girly like sisters. Two: Gram said Morgen and her mother had only *looked* like sisters. Three: Could Morgen *not* being girly or sisterly enough be the cause of their estrangement? Four: Shella felt Ronnie stole her mother away from her, and Morgen felt Andras stole her hard-earned repertoire and replaced it with his Fantasie. Five: She would recover her repertoire, but how could she retrieve the mother-daughter love that was lost? She stared at her manuscript journal. How can you turn a page before the truth has been written?

She shrugged, opened the journal, and named seven more of Tutti's horses after the individuals who had been helpful with the social interaction part of her experiment. Why was she still calling them horses? To depersonalize them? She frowned. To experiment meant to try new ways of thinking, so she added a column to assign her therapist's delineations: strangers, familiar faces, acquaintances, friends, and foes. In pencil, in case she had to change them later. When she came to the end of the list, she added Andras's name. Friend or foe? She chewed the eraser and added *Never be alone with him again.*

She stood, hung the pendant cord from the headliner, and carefully screwed in the limelight bulb. Perhaps Fish

Camp was a good venue in which she could explore new ways of thinking. Perhaps the time had come to "right the ship" as Fish Campers might say. With a smile, she turned on the switch and watched as pale-green light illuminated the Big Dipper and North Star stickers on the headliner. "There. Now Tutti's wired differently," she said to Dashboard Guadalupe, "just like me." She began to practice the Fantasie on the tabletop, even though her right hand didn't know what the left hand was doing and vice versa.

AFTER ANALYZING AND PRACTICING THE LAST FIVE PAGES of the Fantasie for three hours, she returned to the café to ask Shella if she could stay another day or two.

"No problem. Stay as long as you want, and we'll settle your bill when you check out."

"Hey, Morgen." Angelo waved her over to his table. "And Shella Bella Velella velella, fetch us some beers."

"Oh my gosh." Shella rolled her eyes. "That sounds so impertinent. Can you at least say please?"

"Sure, doll. Fetch us some beers, *per favore*. That's Italian for please."

"I'd prefer a diet cola, please." Morgen took a seat at Angelo's table, and Shella served them before taking an order from another customer. "Think it's going to rain?" Fishing and weather. Always safe topics.

"Hey, it's October. How goes your day?" Angelo opened his beer and raised it. "Salute. That's also Italian, just like per favore. Just like me."

"I had a good day, thank you, and you?" A sensible follow-up question.

"Busy. Worked on the boat. Avoided Carlo."

"Carlo Russo Ricci? Doesn't he own all this?"

"He'd like to think so, especially since he lives in the harbormaster house. He has a drug problem but tries to keep his shit together. He can also be a pain in the ass, but I owe him big time. He saved my ass more than once."

"Do you mean in the war?"

"Not in the war you're thinking of. Anyway, he drives into town twice a week with Shella's shopping list. Enough about him. Then I talked to Grumpy John and Jim the Harbor Seal and played catch with Joe and Salty Dog. All in all, a busy day at the office."

She scrambled to harmonize her questions with his train of thought. "Did you ever work in an office?"

"Back in the day. Family business. Got my captain's license." He set his beer down and picked at the label. "And then?" He sniffed and looked away. "Joined the Navy. Got shipped over to Vietnam. Wanted to protect my country from godlessness and communism. Fucking war. Not as much fun as the recruiter promised, and I was underage but manly looking and, hell, they were desperate for warm bodies. Went on river patrol and got shot in the knee and belly. Came home like a gutted fish, but all in all, I liked the Navy. They let me drive the boat." He downed his beer. "Over thirty years ago now. Shella Bella, fetch me another beer, per favore." He leaned forward, a tear or two in his eye. "A music teacher. Fancy that."

Shella banged another bottle of beer on the table in front of him.

"On the sea, you have to keep your Bering Strait." He took a drink. "That's Alaska boat humor. How are your navigation skills?"

"I have trouble navigating one-way streets as well as most social situations, and FYI, my mother protested the

Vietnam War. What's your birth date?"

"Right. Half protested, half fought in it, half didn't give a shit. July 17, 1950. Why? You an astrologer?"

"No, I'm just curious." That made him one year, ten months, and twenty days older than Andras but didn't make them even remotely alike. Andras was pretentious, whereas Angelo seemed more down to earth—

"I'm taking the boat back to Alaska one of these days," he said to her and everyone in earshot, "maybe all the way back to the Bering Sea. Fell in love with it years ago, and it tried to kill me. Storm came out of nowhere. Blowing seventy with freezing fog and spray. Forty-foot rollers breaking over us. Lost most of the pots and a deckhand overboard. Threw up what guts I had left. Scared the ever-loving shit out of me."

"Are you two ready to order?" Shella asked. "I have other fish to fry."

Morgen hid a smile behind her fingers, but it faded. She was light years away from her adoring students, sagging bookshelves, and familiar seclusion. Tutti was an extension of her mother, but she missed her studio apartment with its goofy mural and views of the Sammamish River. Tears blurred her eyes, and she saw Gram frying fish in the kitchen and Violet sweeping the floor, her kinky, red hair stuffed under a chef beanie, stopping to reassure her with a quick, infectious smile.

SHE SAT ON TUTTI'S BENCH SEAT AND FOLDED HER HANDS. The lights of Fish Camp went off for the night, and she pinched the silver beads around her neck. Her mother had asked her to come back and help, but she got sidetracked by trying to befriend the right individuals, which was going pretty well. She rocked, rubbing her temples. What did her mother want her to do all these years later?

She skimmed the torn cadenza pages for the umpteenth time and made notes in her manuscript journal.

Mom had been high and drunk at the beach before taking acid (can't help you there); one of her hundred friends raped her and cut off her braid (who was he because, presumably, he was my mystery father, so follow up); someone named Riff got hurt (and had been a witness, so follow up); Mom had been rescued by Bertie-the-gardener (another witness?) and the Widow Witch. (How to ask John?)

"Almost bingo. I found the beach and Widow Witch's conch grotto. Even though I rarely see the forest for the trees, if I follow enough branches, I'll get my hands on the jerk who raped you, excuse the language."

She pulled on her peacoat, grabbed her flashlight, and slipped out of Tutti. The only sound was Pavarotti singing "Donna è Mobile" inside the harbormaster house.

The sky was clear and black, and the Big Dipper was coming into view in the northern sky. When she reached the drift logs beach, she turned off the flashlight, faced the ocean, and dug her toes into the sand. She stripped off her clothing and stood naked, waiting to conjure up the friend-turned-rapist's face. Nothing happened. She took a deep breath of briny air and waded into the surf. The water was colder than cold and made her bones ache. She pushed against turbulent waves into deeper water, shut her eyes, and abruptly turned her head, hoping to ignite an inherited visual image as one might strike a match.

Sand vanished from under her feet, she tumbled backward, and waves smashed into her face. She struggled and fought the riptide as it pulled her away from shore until the current unexpectedly released her. She dog-paddled through inky, black surf and crawled back onto the beach, gasping. Sand smothered her ears, nose, and mouth as subsequent waves attacked. She choked and fought as more sand penetrated deep between her legs as it must have done to her mother that awful night, and fleeting images surfaced before drowning in her tears.

4.

Morgen heard the roof angels pacing entirely too early on Tutti's roof but didn't open her eyes. It had taken an hour-long hot shower, a space heater, and Fräu Heinrich's eiderdown to warm her up. Who knew the ocean could be so cold? No wonder her mother and a hundred of her friends had built a bonfire before diving in.

She'd arrived in Fish Camp just four days earlier but felt that she too had amassed a hundred friends or, rather, acquaintances. Between the interesting individuals, the affectionate animals, and the great outdoors, she was becoming distracted. She rolled over, opened her manuscript journal, and wrote *What do I want/need from this place before I leave it?*

1. *I want to resolve my estrangement with Mom.*
2. *I want to accept myself so that others, including the Fish Campers, will accept me for who I really am and I, them.*
3. *I want to respect myself so that I NEVER beat up on myself again.*
4. *The best way for me to do that is…*

Her fingers read the beads on the silver foremothers necklace and paused when they found the one with the letter C for Charlie.

*…to find and fix the missing pieces of OUR lives,
including Mom's urn, and to be brave in dealing with
Andras and his Fantasie so that I can walk away
from him and reframe my life in a fresh context.*

She put her head on the pillow, but before long, her fingers resumed practicing a series of particularly troublesome Fantasie phrases. "If that's what you want to do, go right ahead," she whispered, "but I'm going back to sleep."

When Morgen walked into the Palace Café, Mia gave her a big smile as Angelo brushed his lunch crumbs off the tablecloth and onto the floor. Morgen shot him an exasperated look, but Mia responded with an almost imperceptible shake of her head and continued sweeping with her straw broom.

"Good afternoon, Morgen," Shella said, glancing at a clock above the sink.

"You can sit here," Angelo said, raising his beer bottle. "Quick before Carlo—"

Carlo barged in singing "Funiculì, Funiculà."

"Never mind, too late," Angelo said to Morgen, "but that's a great T-shirt. The Three Bs, huh? Bagwell, Biggio, and Berkman, the Houston Astros Killer Bs from the nineties?"

"No, sorry. Bach, Beethoven, and Brahms." Morgen sat at the counter, and Shella poured her a cup of decaf.

"Music history? Hell, I can elaborate on that." Carlo flopped into a chair at Angelo's table. "Bach, 1685 to 1750, Baroque period. Beethoven, 1770 to 1827, Classical period along with Haydn and Mozart, and Brahms, 1833 to 1897, Romantic period."

"Excuse me, we're talking baseball here," Angelo said, staring at the national forecast on The Weather Channel. "It's raining on Cincinnati, home of the Reds. Finished sixty-nine and ninety-three and second to last in their division this season, but never forget they used to have Johnny Bench, greatest catcher of all time."

"Part of the Big Red Machine." Carlo mimed swinging a bat but seemed to be taking aim at the portrait over the mantelpiece.

"Whoa, you're smarter than you look. Hell, I could have been Johnny Bench. Fourteen-time All Star and enshrined in the Hall of Fame in '89, for Chrissake."

"Right, and I could have been Pavarotti or Casanova. Excuse me." Carlo tripped over Mia's broom as he headed to the phone. "I'm overdue for a rendezvous with naughty Natasha."

That sounded rather disrespectful. Morgen stared into her coffee mug. It'd be fun to discuss music with Carlo, but he seemed rough around the edges. Mia was murmuring something about him in Spanish, and it sounded negative, but since Morgan had had to pass only reading proficiency in French and German, that was conjecture. She swiveled on her barstool and met Angelo's red-rimmed eyes. "Are you unhappy?"

"I'm happy as a clam at high tide considering I'm hung over." He rubbed his ears. "Damn helicopters roaring inside my head again all night long. You like baseball? See, growing up, I had two dreams about my future: catching fish and catching baseballs. After the Vietcong shattered my right knee, I couldn't get in a squat anymore." He took a drink. "You married?"

"The roaring in your ears could be tinnitus." She frowned at him. "Exacerbated by alcohol."

"It's just beer. So are you married? Carlo wants to know."

"No, I've never married." She stood. "I'm feeling uncomfortable."

"Me, I'm twice married, twice divorced. First to a little blonde, gold-digging stewardess post-Vietnam. Second to a redheaded, gum-snapping, knuckle-cracking bartender in Kenai, Alaska." He finished his beer. "Carlo has never married for several reasons—"

"Listen," Morgen cried, motioning at The Weather Channel. "Rachmaninoff's Prelude in C# Minor. I played that."

"I'm impressed." He got up, turned off the TV, and switched on the boom box. "Back in the day, I played this on my accordion. Salute." He opened another beer and hummed along with "Gentle on My Mind."

She listened a moment. "That doesn't sound like Glenn Campbell."

"That's because it's Dean Martin. Catchy little tune, huh? Topped the charts in '69."

"That's the year I was born." She couldn't help swaying to the music.

"Oh my gosh, were you a hippie love baby from the Age of Aquarius?" Shella said, teasing her.

"Hardly, although my late mother was called Morning Glory."

"Ease up on the throttle there, woman." Angelo set his beer on the counter with a thud. "Your *late* mother was called Morning Glory?" He paled as he stared at Morgen. "Sweet Jesus, Mary, and Joseph—"

"Morgen, I have a record collection I'd love to share with you," Carlo said as he walked past them. "Right now, I'm headed to Aberdeen because naughty Natasha is ready, willing, and able."

"Great. Ciao." Angelo watched Carlo until the door closed and the song ended. When he looked at Morgen again, his expression had lost its bravado. "Was Charlie Marín your mother?"

"What?" Morgen felt tears well up in her eyes. How would he know?

"Sorry if I upset you." Angelo's voice came from far away. "Fetch me a beer, Shella Bella."

Morgen rubbed her ears, trying to erase what she'd just heard.

"Do you have an earache?" Shella asked her, handing Angelo another beer.

"No, I just wasn't expecting to hear my mom's name."

"Yeah. Sorry, neither was I," Angelo mumbled, "and besides, I'm not known for my timing, for Chrissake. This is getting personal. Let's sit at a table."

Morgen joined him and folded her flapping hands in her lap.

Angelo cleared his throat. "You said 'late mother.' What happened to her, and when did she die?"

"Run down by a drunk driver. May 22, 1990." She wrung her hands. "She was only forty-one years, ten months, and two days old."

"My deepest condolences, Morgen Marín. What about your old man?"

She stiffened. "I have no idea who he is."

"That's a damn shame, but I imagine he'd be proud of you."

Morgen leaned forward. "Tell me how you knew her."

"Want to share my beer?" Angelo asked.

"No, thank you. I don't drink, but okay, sure, you mean right out of the bottle? That's unsanitary." She took a long drink. The Palace Café quieted and seemed to shrink. "Okay, I'm listening."

"It's not like I *knew* her." He shifted a little in his chair. "But back in the day, she lived on my block."

"And?" Morgen took another sip.

"Yeah, so she lived with a bunch of students, you know, miles out of my league, but yeah, I noticed her. Hell, I grew up cloistered on an estate in Puget Sound. You want me to describe what she looked like?"

She watched him closely and nodded.

"She was a pretty girl, if you don't mind my saying so. Long colorful dresses, flowers in her hair, fancy hats, and shawls, sandals."

"That's a lot of personal detail about someone who was two years older than you as well as out of your league."

"More like a lot of personal pain. Hell, it was 1968. Dr. King and Bobby Kennedy were assassinated. Vietnam War escalated." His voice wavered. "Got my draft notice. Enlisted in the Navy. Got sent over, but I already told you that." He stood. "Excuse me, game three of the World Series is on."

Evidently, he'd connected the memory of her mother to his personal pain, so there had to be more to the story. Morgen swallowed her emotions and concentrated on the bottoms of her feet as the darkness in the conch grotto pushed up from under the floorboards.

Wednesday, October 22, 2003

AT FIRST LIGHT, MORGEN STOOD BAREFOOT ON THE DUNE scarp down the road from the café. As she stared across the ocean, the beach in front of her began to glitter in the sunshine. "Jellies?" She grabbed her wet sneakers and scrambled over the drift logs stranded on the sand.

Thousands of by-the-wind sailors had washed ashore during the night. Why did those odd jellies glide like little blue sailboats across open ocean only to beach themselves on a random shore?

A pelican flew in off the water, landed nearby, and eyed her. She rolled up her pant legs. With the pelican waddling behind her, she trudged down the beach gathering jelly after jelly by the sail and gently tossing them back into the surf. *Leave, stay, leave, stay, flowers in her hair, fancy hats and shawls.* What else did Angelo know? She stopped in her tracks. She *had* to stay, because she was discovering clues about her mother. She *would* continue her social experiment and practice any music she wanted on the tabletop, because neither Headmistress nor Andras would find her out there. If it all went bad, she'd drive away in Tutti all the way to Todos Santos.

The rain returned, strafing the beach and churning up frothy surf. She whooped, stepped into her sopping red sneakers, and raced back to Fish Camp, refreshed and ready for breakfast.

By the time she reached the road, the squall had passed. Sleepy gulls squatted on their designated pilings. *By-the-Wind Sailor* rocked in her slip. Angelo stood on the aft deck in his sweatshirt, boxer shorts, and rubber knee boots, surveying a clutter of cans and brushes. John had parked his ATV along the boardwalk. She collected a record seven cigarette butts before hurrying up the hill. After towel-drying her hair, she grabbed a bag of trio mix and headed down to the café.

"Good morning," Shella said. "What can I get you for breakfast?"

"A raison d'être?"

"We have raisin bran."

"How about a cup of decaf?"

"Coming up."

"Hi, John. May I join you?" It was time for a local history lesson.

"Please do." John sat at a table eating a bowl of oatmeal. He motioned to the chair next to his, and she sat down with her decaf. "Say, I was telling you about my sourdough starter."

"Yes, but that was day before yesterday." She took a sip and watched Mia smile to herself while sweeping the floor.

"I just add flour and warm water, let it ferment overnight, put a cupful back to save, and give the rest to Shella to make bread or pancakes."

She put her bag of trio mix on the table. John grabbed a handful and stirred it into his oatmeal.

She counted to ten while she chose her words. "I need to know the history of Fish Camp and the Palace Café."

He grabbed a biscuit from a basket. "When I was a boy, I worked. Logging, fishing, cranberries. Speaking of, I like your gorp." He kept chewing. "I remember Nanny baking during the war. Dad had joined the Navy, and the rest of us stayed out here. Me, my mother and brother, and Nanny and Gramp. Our civilian duty was to help protect the coast. After Pearl Harbor, it looked like the West Coast would be attacked next, and the sad thing is, we was taught to fear our own Japanese neighbors who had been here for generations. Bunch of bunk." He shook his head. "American soldiers was patrolling everywhere with foxholes dug into the beach. We had blackout curtains, rationing, and curfews. Couple times, they talked about evacuating us. That sourdough starter kept my Nanny and her women friends busy baking and feeding everybody." He squirted honey onto his biscuit. "Something good that come out of the war. That and our victory garden."

"What's a victory garden?" It was a sincere as well as an insightful question.

"Right. You wanted history. Victory gardens helped keep folks fed during the war. Across the road, that was the old road that washed away, and back a ways was the cranberry bog. Up the hill farther back and out of sight is our garden. Still there. Facing south, more sun. Even has an apple tree. Always too much zucchini." He leaned closer. "There's something magic about our garden," he whispered. "We have a natural spring with water that bubbles up from the heart of the ocean." He leaned back. "There's more, but that's enough for now."

"You should write a story about your life." She glanced around the café. "Did you ever meet the original owners of the Palace Café?"

"Marty and Lydia? Sure, I helped them build it. Over fifty years ago now." He wiped his mouth. "Marty Cooper was my twin brother, but I lost him out on a tug in a hell of a storm." He cleared his throat. "After Marty perished, I took care of Lydia until she got the cancer and died."

Hot tears welled in Morgen's eyes. "That's so sad," she whispered.

"Lydia refused treatment. Did everything I could for her. Tried to help her feel connected to Marty and, at the same time, look inside herself. That's her picture over the fireplace." He pushed his bowl away. "Now you must know some history too, seeing as how you asked."

Mia's sweeping grew louder, and Morgen's heart rate spiked to *presto* (♩ = 160, very quick). "Maybe. I'm not sure yet." Except that her mother evidently took refuge down in that conch grotto.

"When you're sure, will you let me know?" He raised his eyebrows.

She nodded as she stared across the room at Lydia Cooper's picture.

"Then it's a promise, sure as the tide." John stood. "Let's have Shella take you up to my garden. You need to look into that spring."

"Okay. Thanks." *What a gift you are.* She walked over to take a closer look at the picture. Lydia was sitting on a massive drift log and petting a presumably orange cat curled up on her lap. She appeared to be in her fifties, hair pulled back, barefoot in jeans and a fisherman's sweater. Morgen was transfixed by the expression in her eyes. "Who are you looking at?" she whispered, "and what do you know?"

Morgen offered some trio mix to Shella. "It'll give you instant energy for the hike."

"Thanks." Shella popped a handful into her mouth, slung a cloth sack over her arm, and led the way up a rutted logging road that led from Fish Camp. Near the top of a hill, they abandoned the road and walked a hundred steps through the woods before entering a small clearing.

"This is Grampy's victory garden. Pretty cool, huh? Ever since World War II. The spring he wanted you to see is over there."

Morgen stood still, mesmerized by the spiritual ambience. A gnarly old apple tree draped with lichen and moss loomed in front of them, and a rich, fertile scent hung in the mist. Nearby, zucchini, rhubarb, blackberries, and strawberries flourished in wild grass that stood ten inches tall and waved in the offshore breeze. Crickets chirped and songbirds sang.

"Wasn't your mom named Morning Glory?" Shella said. "There's a bunch of them growing by the spring." She rubbed her huge belly and sat down on a weathered bench fashioned from glass bricks. "God, I'm getting so fat."

"You're not fat. You're pregnant," Morgen mumbled, staring at the bench in disbelief. It looked exactly like the one in the conch grotto. "That's a rather unusual garden seat." She peeked sideways at Shella. "Have you ever seen one like that before?"

"Nope, and it's hard as a rock under my butt." Shella got up and, using her pocketknife, began to pick zucchinis and drop them into her sack.

Morgen sighed with relief. Evidently, Shella hadn't been in the conch grotto, or she would have noticed the twin glass brick bench. Morgen walked over to the spring, and when she looked past the tangle of morning glories and into the water, the reflection of a yellow-eyed pelican stared back at her. Startled, she glanced around but couldn't see a pelican anywhere. *Very strange.* She sampled the water, and it tasted peculiar. Maybe it was a secret portal to the sea.

"I have a million recipes for these." Shella continued working. "Did you know that a zucchini is a fruit?"

"News to me." It was interesting that the morning glories were the same vibrant blue as by-the-wind sailor jellies and the hull of Angelo's boat. She collected a pinch of dirt for the sugar bowl before picking a perfect blossom to press in her manuscript journal. "Thanks for bringing me up here. It's pretty special." *And somehow more significant than an abandoned garden.* "Sorry, I'm not used to all this hiking, and my feet hurt." She sat on the bench and splayed her fingers on the weathered glass bricks.

"I can give you a massage when we get back," Shella said. "I've been told I'm a natural."

"Thanks for offering." She gripped the bricks with her fingertips and remembered being a teenager with Andras massaging her fingers, hands, wrists, forearms, neck, and shoulders because she needed to be suppler. Putting lotion on his hands and lacing his fingers with hers. *Now*, he'd whispered, *mime playing the Bach.* She did while fighting her fears and aversion to touch. She shuddered. All those years, she never touched him with affection. Only Gram and, on rarer occasions, her mother—the glass began to melt under her hands, and she jumped to her feet. "I'm okay now. Let's go."

When Shella turned away, Morgen tasted her palm. *Salty as the heart of the ocean.*

She was on her way back to Tutti when she heard Carlo whistle at her from outside the harbormaster house.

"Come on down," he hollered. "Got something to show you."

"Maybe later," she yelled back.

"Look at this." He held up a record album. "Why the hell are we yelling at each other? Hang on." He jogged in her direction. "I just got *Best of the Three Tenors*," he gasped. "Haven't even opened it yet. God, if I were stranded on a desert island, all I'd want is this collection and fresh water. And a carton of Camels. Want to attend the inaugural spin? I'll make popcorn."

"I'm sorry." She rubbed her forehead. "I've had a long day."

"Come on. You're the only one out here who understands real music. There's so much more to life than fishing, weather, and baseball." He did that squinty thing with his left eye. "I'm not a bad guy, honest. Ask Luciano Pavarotti." He put the record against his ear and pretended to listen. "He says he likes me." He raised his eyebrows and grinned at her. "What do you say?"

"Thanks for the invitation, but I need my solitude right now."

His smile faded. "Rain check?"

"First tell me your birth date."

"June 17, 1947. Why? To enlightened people like us, age doesn't matter, does it?"

By saying "us," Carlo was attempting to scale her well-fortified personal boundary. What to do? Equivocate as usual and keep the peace. She shrugged. "Okay, maybe." He was a year and a month older than her mother, three years and a month older than Angelo, and almost five years older than Andras. Unlikely that enlightenment had anything to do with his interest in her.

Thursday, October 23, 2003

Morgen snuggled under the eiderdown with a handful of old photos and reread the letter Shella brought her.

Dear Morgen, It was a pleasant surprise to hear from you, and out of respect for your mother, I'm returning your money for postage. Many years ago, I corresponded with her because she needed a place to store her piano. I wanted a piano, and we were brought together by a mutual acquaintance. However, your mother never came back to get it. So, to answer your question, yes, I still have her piano and will be happy to pass it on to you. However, I have several short trips planned, so I'll have to contact you again next month. Sincerely, C. D. Hayes.

She looked at the picture of her mother's urn. "I'd sure like to get my hands on your piano, but I don't know where I'll be tomorrow, let alone next month." She petted Doris, who rolled over and yawned. A prompt for a missed call appeared on her cell phone. When she tried to pick up the voicemail, she got "Call Failed." She dressed and dashed down to the café where Shella and Mia were prepping for breakfast. She waved at them and headed to the phone.

Violet had left a message that she was panicking about the two concerto cadenzas and *desperately* needed Morgen's help. Between hiccupping sobs, she said that she wanted to die.

Morgen's fingers shook as she dialed Violet's number. *You are NOT going to die like Mom did just because of that concerto—*

"Hi, Violet? Sorry, I just got your message. Slow down, I can't understand you." She stared at Lydia Cooper's picture while she calmed her breathing to *largo* ($\quarternote$ = 45, slow and dignified). "Have you asked Dr. Byrd or your father for help? No? Now, Violet, please relax, take a deep breath, and hang on a minute. I need to compose myself too."

She closed her eyes as a comforting warmth rose up through her feet and into her legs from the conch grotto where her shattered mother had taken refuge. She saw the twinkly lights and pink glittering walls, heard music in the roar of the surf, and felt sweet One-Eyed Jack sidling between her knees. Gram said that the concerto had been her mother's reason for being aka her raison d'être, and her mother had written, *My legacy is your destiny. Promise to come back and help me.*

"Okay, how can I help you?" Morgen opened her eyes and listened. "I'm glad you called, and I'll be there as soon as I can. We probably just need to tweak the fingering. No, I know where they live."

After hanging up, she noticed that One-Eyed Jack literally had appeared out of nowhere and was nuzzling her leg, his good eye on her face and broken tail keeping time with the beat of her heart. "You're a good kitty, Jack," she whispered. Grabbing the smoked salmon and fried egg sandwich that Shella had wrapped in a paper towel, Morgen headed for the door. "Thanks for breakfast. Sorry, family emergency, but I'll be back. Sure as the tide." She raced up to Tutti to break camp.

IT WAS A TEDIOUS NONSTOP DRIVE, BUT MORGEN WAS expected at Phoebe Keats's parents' home in Auburn ASAP. She'd always liked Phoebe who, like Grandpa Scott, was a woodwind specialist, made her own reeds, and had mastered so many instruments that she probably could play most of the Stravinsky concerto all by herself.

She already missed the satisfying conversations with Fish Camp's interesting individuals. The great social experiment had been a success, because Shella, Mia, John, and Doris had been upgraded from acquaintances to friends. Maybe it was time she tested her improved social skills in the real world, although the Widow Witch's conch grotto might be as real a world as anywhere.

A deer and fawn dashed into the road, and she slammed on the brakes. The fawn disappeared into the woods, but the doe stopped to glare at her. "You're going to get killed, and your baby will have to grow up all by herself," Morgen yelled. The deer flicked its tail and sashayed away, chewing its cud. "That was anything but subtle, Mom, and okay, I won't let you down this time. First, we have to help Violet Bacon who, because *we* delivered her, transposed my simple life forever into a discordant key." She glanced at the rearview mirror as she returned to the highway. "By the way, I'd appreciate it if you'd return my face, because I hate looking in mirrors."

Before Andras had even held his newborn daughter, he had adopted Morgen as his protégée and a member of the family, and sometimes she pretended her mother was Mrs. Andras Bacon instead of Margot.

Tutti stalled, and Morgen wrestled the steering wheel, coasting to a stop off the roadway. She turned the key, but nothing happened. "Okay, Mom, I'm sorry, and you know as well as I do that I've always loved you *fiercely*. It's just that except for you and Gram, I was shunned as a child, so when anyone else paid attention to me, I was hopelessly infatuated with them. As you also know, I've paid dearly for that weakness." She raised her voice. "I grew up with undiagnosed autism, but now that I know, it's not going to happen again, so will you please restart Tutti?" She held her breath, turned the key, and all fifty-three horses came back to life, eager to run.

Morgen parked in front of the Keats's home and felt her heart rate increase to *presto* ($\quad$ = 168, an unhealthy pace that indicated elevated anxiety). She'd last seen Violet rehearsing with Arthur Ishikawa at the U a week earlier, but they hadn't met face to face since Violet had been expelled from River Bridge.

She rocked in the driver's seat. She loved Violet like a little sister even though they were thirteen years, seven months, and twenty-nine days apart, but there'd been tension between them because of Morgen's clandestine relationship with Andras. Now, she and Violet were adults, and she made the trip specifically to help Violet with the concerto—the composition that had launched Morgen's performance career while breaking her mother's heart. She pulled her mother's torn cadenza pages out of her backpack and committed the notations to memory.

As she grabbed her backpack and climbed out of Tutti, she was overwhelmed by a cloud of Violet's signature scent of eucalyptus with a note of lime.

"Oh my God, it's great to see you," Violet squealed as she barreled through a bed of red marigolds and tackled Morgen. "Sorry, I know you don't like hugging, but thanks so much for coming. I'm having a crisis."

"You're fine and the music's fine. We just need to get you both on the same page."

Morgen accompanied chattering Violet into the house. Phoebe had gone shopping with her mother, so Morgen sat beside Violet on the piano bench.

"There are nine elastic measures in the first cadenza and ten in the second." Violet said. "The entire concerto's a bitch, and I love it but need your help. You're so analytical."

"Why, thank you." Morgen had never noticed how much Violet resembled Andras in temperament and appearance. She had his hazel eyes, his intonation, and something indescribable about his carriage. Morgen had buried him in the past, but Violet conjured up memories of the teasing expression in his eyes, the hair on his wrists below French cuffs, and his manner at once erotic and cruel.

"Like here." Violet attempted the eighth measure. "My fingers keep tripping over each other."

Morgen nodded. "I remember your father made me transpose that phrase into another key, play it backward aka retrograde, and then cross hands and play. Said it would make me one with the music." Her words turned into nails in her mouth. *And make me one with him.*

"He used to do that to me too." Violet laughed. "Parlor tricks." She returned to the music and Morgen, to her thoughts.

Andras always had chosen her repertoire for her—the dazzling, the difficult, and the dramatic—so *he* would receive praise as her master teacher. What about all the other music? She scrolled through a list of pieces she'd squirreled away like assorted chocolates to savor in private: Joplin's *Complete Piano Works* (1899), MacDowell's *Woodland Sketches* (1896), Mozart's *Variations on Ah, Vous Dirai-Je, Maman* aka the Twinkle Little Star variations (1782), and Mussorgsky's *Pictures at an Exhibition* (1874). But the Fantasie had hijacked her life.

True, there was a certain elasticity in music, but you could stretch it only so far before it broke. She tapped into her memorized notations, and as she and Violet debated and took turns with each phrase, she realized that her mother's markings were far superior to Andras's and Arthur Ishikawa's. Her mother had been beyond brilliant enough to perform this concerto, contrary to what Morgen accused her of the night before Morgen's baccalaureate concert.

"Son of a bitch." Violet hit three wrong notes in a row. "I can't—"

"Yes, you can. Start here."

Morgen pointed at the page but continued reminiscing. When Andras coerced her into learning his Fantasie (and, in the process, publicly rejecting Violet), he claimed that it was because he didn't want to upstage his students. He noted that if she were to play it as his former protégée, his credibility as a teacher would increase. On completion of his doctoral program in composition, he would be promoted to department chair at East Cape Conservatory. *I'm giving you Carnegie Hall,* he said. *Besides, you owe me.* But considering their personal history, did she owe him?

She penciled in an alternate fingering on Violet's score. "Try that, and see if it feels better."

She had asked for a recording to help her make sense of the Fantasie, and he told her that part of the artistic discovery was for her to hear it first under her own hands. But she knew it was because he wasn't capable of performing his own composition.

She heard him play other pieces on several occasions when he was unaware of her, and he'd never been as good as she thought he should be. The music always sounded mechanical. How could he be a doctoral candidate when he had no sense of rhythm? When he noticed that she was watching him, she couldn't read his expression. *I like that one,* she'd said, letting him off the hook. She had discovered his truth and greatest fear. He was a pretender too, just as she was in her own offbeat way. She felt a weird connection to and compassion for him. *But not anymore.*

"I think I've got it. I just need to practice, practice, practice." Violet yawned and closed the score. "By the way, how's life at old River Bridge?"

"Fine, I guess. I'm off-site on a performance assignment."

"Daddy's doctoral piece?"

Morgen nodded.

"Super." Violet headed into the kitchen. "Want some ice cream or a milkshake? They have a blender."

"No, thank you." Morgen followed her, but her throat closed up as she flashed back to the last time she ate ice cream: when her mother took her out to celebrate Andras's laying claim to her.

Violet filled a bowl with rocky road. "Do you like the music he wrote?"

"I'm still…" Morgen's deodorant failed. "It's challenging. Like you said, I just need to practice, practice, practice."

Violet's spoon clanked against her teeth. "Do you like Phoebe?"

"I've always liked Phoebe. You know that." Morgen visualized the girls holding hands and listening to Mr. Ishikawa's critique.

"Does it bother you that we're in love?"

"No. I told you that three years ago."

"Right, when River Bridge expelled us. Shit, Daddy was livid and humiliated, said I was going through a stage and Phoebe was corrupting me. He proceeded to invite male students to the house, one by one, to *woo* me. He even said that he wished I was more like you." Her scent morphed from eucalyptus with a note of lime into kerosene as her temper heated up. "Daddy always liked you better than me, and I had to compete with everything you did, because you were perfect and I would never be as talented as you."

"I'm far from perfect. In fact, I was just diagnosed with—"

"He knew that you were my first crush! Jesus, I wrote poems and songs."

"What? Violet, I'm sorry. I never knew, because I'm socially tone-deaf and was just diag—"

"Daddy's going to be blown away when he hears me play *your* concerto."

"Is that why you want to learn it?" Morgen's illusions shattered like ice cubes in a blender. "To prove something to him?"

Violet's face reddened. "He never even asked me if I wanted to learn his fucking Fantasie—"

"I thought you've loved that concerto since you were seven and a half."

Violet began to cry. "I've *always* loved it. Besides Phoebe, it's all I've ever had to live for. Mom left me forever, Daddy dated your mother while you babysat me, and then he married Chloe, the slut who told River Bridge about—"

"Violet, stop it. What are we even arguing about?" Morgen wiped her face with her sleeve. "Crap, the master of sensational theater won another round, because he has us fighting each other."

"It's sick." Violet's kinky curls trembled like red marigolds in the wind. "What has he done to us?"

"I'm not sure, but I think it's more about the *why* than the *what*." Morgen corrected her posture. "May I please have some ice cream?"

"He never says he loves me anymore, but I don't care." Violet sniffled as she took another bowl out of the cupboard. "Vanilla, rocky road, or peppermint?"

"One scoop of each, thank you." Morgen was spent but had to go where roof angels feared to tread. "Did my mom really date your father?"

"Only once that I know of." Violet's spoon clattered as she devoured her ice cream. "You know, I've never understood your relationship with him." Her eyes narrowed. "Whose side are you on anyway?"

The kitchen lights flared, and Morgen winced. She put the bowl on the sink, picked up her backpack, and left.

THREE BLOCKS FROM PHOEBE'S PARENTS' HOUSE, MORGEN pulled over and parked. She always restrained her emotions and buried her feelings to protect herself. She always *pretended* to feel what she thought *they* wanted her to feel, but Violet broke through her defenses as harshly as Dagger Eyes smacking her flapping hands with a flyswatter.

All she'd wanted to do was help Violet with the concerto. Instead, she'd been ambushed by how her relationship with Andras had disturbed Violet. How much did she know? "I don't get it," she whispered to Dashboard Guadalupe, "but I don't get a lot of things." She rubbed her temples, and tears filled her eyes. Was it true that her mother had dated Andras? The bitter taste crept up the back of her throat.

She'd always hoped that *she* and Andras would marry and that *she'd* become a proper mother to Violet. Surprise, surprise. After she performed the four Chopin ballades for her master's concert (with "thrilling artistic ferocity" according to reviews), he introduced her to his seven-months-pregnant second wife, Chloe. She charged into a practice room to have a meltdown. Andras had followed, insisting that Violet must have told her, which she hadn't. Then he expected their relationship to continue, which it did because sex had nothing to do with love, a premise that still flummoxed her.

No wonder Violet was a wreck. She asked, "What have they done to us," indicating that she and Morgen were friends. She'd followed with "Whose side are you on anyway," suggesting they were adversaries.

"No wonder I'm a wreck too." So much had gone so horribly wrong, yet she'd gone along with it, gone along with *him*, oblivious that ripples went out and affected other individuals too, like wavelets from the pelican-priest on Angelo's boat. She'd have to figure out how to help Violet with more than just a concerto cadenza.

She played a Chopin étude on the steering wheel while her mind wandered back to a therapy session she'd had about empathy, about analyzing a situation when she may have been insensitive, about imagining how the other person might have felt. Her mind hadn't been on her side at all, and she'd *become* Andras's wife Chloe, arriving at *their* home with *their* brand-new baby boy to find that Andras and Morgen had cruelly left *their* bedding rumpled. She'd *become* her mother, unable to move and slowly dying while Sweet Baby stared at her through the car window, turned her face, and drove away—

"Crap." Her fingers shook as she dialed her cell phone. "Hi, Gram. I'm just checking in."

"Darling, your voice is trembly. What are you up to?"

"Oh, I'm enjoying a much-needed vacation in Mom's bus, and I've met some interesting individuals." She grabbed hold of the beaded silver lifeline tucked inside her shirt. "You told me to find purpose in my offbeat instincts, and that's what I'm trying to do." *But it's so hard.*

"Do you remember what I told you? Quit isolating yourself." Gram's voice sounded gravelly. "You intuitively listen with your heart when you perform music with other instrumentalists, so listen to their words in a similar way. You might be surprised by what you hear."

"Thanks, Gram. I miss and love you."

"Me too, darling. Be patient. In life as in music, dissonance must resolve. Bye now."

Morgen put the phone down and looked at her mother's torn cadenza pages annotated with doodles on the passenger seat. In an attempt to identify Bertie-the-gardener who'd guided her mother to safety, she recalled three names from her mother's past. One had been her friend Alberta, a nurse who worked at a residential care facility. She rubbed her temples to stimulate her memory. When she and her mother visited Alberta at work, Morgen had been told that special individuals lived there because they had disabilities and needed extra help. Wanting to befriend them, Morgen plopped herself onto the piano bench and played fun pieces for them like "Chopsticks," Mozart's "Twinkle, Twinkle, Little Star" variations, and Scott Joplin's "Maple Leaf Rag," and they loved her.

She gazed through the windshield. She didn't know Alberta's last name, if she still worked there, or even the name of the facility, but she remembered it was in Fall City, such a curious name, which was only an hour away.

WITH THE MEMORY OF A MOUSE IN A MAZE, MORGEN drove past several exclusive residences in Fall City before finding Red Cedar Haven at the top of a hill. An eight-foot wrought iron fence surrounded the wooded and gated facility. After she parked Tutti at the curb, she pocketed her blue crystal star, took a pinch of sand out of the wild rose sugar bowl, and put a sprinkle in each sneaker. *Because you used to bring me here, you can come in with me now.*

She approached a tall entry gate where she rang a buzzer with an attached speaker. She was admitted after identifying herself and her wish to see Alberta. Once inside the Victorian-style mansion, she followed the receptionist through a wide archway into a solarium at the rear of the building where several individuals were visiting or milling about. The room smelled fresh and clean, the lighting was subdued, and the atmosphere relaxed. "Alberta is busy with a resident but will be with you shortly."

Morgen took off her peacoat and settled into an armchair. If she couldn't visit her mother, maybe she could befriend one of her mother's friends who might remember the attack.

"Morgen? Hello, I'm Alberta," a woman exclaimed. Her graying hair was in a ponytail, and she wore an off-white artist's smock, black slacks, and cute red ballet slippers. "The years go by, don't they? It's wonderful to see you again."

"Yes, and how do you do again?" Morgen stood. "I remember you in a starched white dress."

Alberta laughed. "Our residents respond better if we look like we're part of the same community, which we are." A suntanned man, smiling broadly and wearing jeans and a tropical print shirt, approached. "I'd like you to meet Spencer, our music therapist," Alberta said. "His program focuses on promoting wellness and quality of life."

"How do you do?" Morgen shook his hand. "Have we met?"

"Possibly," Spencer said. "I've worked here for thirty-some years. Alberta told me that you're a pianist, and as soon as word got out that you were here, several residents assumed you were performing a recital like you used to do. I hate to put you on the spot, but if you'd play something for them, they'd be thrilled."

"Of course." Morgen walked over to the familiar upright piano shoved up against a wall while Alberta helped several individuals choose their seats. She turned to face her audience. Four staff. Thirteen residents. Several looked vaguely familiar. Most smiled at her, their faces flushed with excitement. One rocked while juggling a Nerf ball. Another sat with a service dog curled up at her feet. Two held hands and whispered to each other. A few names came back to her: Sally, Mrs. Withers, Clifford, Timmy O, Brady, and Charlotte BG. *Funny what the offbeat brain remembers.*

"Come on, do piano for us, please," Timmy hollered. "Thank you."

"I would love to."

Morgen sat, and as she played, some individuals swayed with the music, and some got up and danced. She heard her mother's voice coaching in her mind's ear. *Everyone struggles with something and sometimes needs an especially safe place… extra help…kindness…respect…acceptance. Everyone has a story…has feelings…loves life.*

Thirty-three minutes later, she turned to acknowledge her cheering and applauding audience. "Thank you," she said, tears filling her eyes.

Timmy O saluted her with a big smile. Sally walked up and kissed her hand just as she had decades earlier. Clifford approached with his walker and Nerf ball, nodding to a lingering beat. Without looking at her, he began to play the bass part of "Chopsticks" on the piano. Morgen laughed. "I remember now. We played this when I was a little girl." She joined him while Sally and Timmy O waltzed around the room. When the song ended, they all drifted away.

"Music heals in so many ways," Spencer said, "including social interaction, rhythm and movement, and pain and stress management. Some who had difficulty speaking have found that they can sing words and phrases. In addition, most residents create performance goals because we produce talent shows." He looked at her as though trying to remember something. "Please come visit us any time." He walked away.

"You made our day," Alberta said. "What brings you here after all these years?"

"I wanted to know if you like gardening. I miss my mom, and I wanted to talk to you about stuff that happened to her, but maybe we could meet another time, maybe for coffee or chowder?"

"Whichever you prefer. This is long overdue." Alberta smiled. "May I have your number?" She handed Morgen a scratch pad and pen.

Mom would be so pleased. "I'll give you two because sometimes my cell doesn't work."

"Wonderful." Alberta nodded at Clifford, who waited at the doorway with his Nerf ball and walker. "Time to bring closure to our day. Goodnight, Morgen."

"Good night," Morgen echoed as Alberta and Clifford left the room together. Without a care in the world, she curtsied and crossed the empty solarium in a series of ballet leaps and pirouettes, the memory of a goofy little girl dancing beside her, thrilled that she'd just played a rousing Scott Joplin for her best friends.

Morgen closed the entry gate and heard it lock behind her. She'd lost all track of time. Night had fallen, and the sky looked threatening. The neighborhood was quiet except for a few birdcalls and the distant barking of a dog.

She turned back and peered through the fence. From the outside, Red Cedar Haven looked like a castle, albeit one without a good dungeon like the conch grotto or a punishing one like Dagger Eyes' supply closet. As a child, she'd explored every room and turret, even testing the elevators to see which one transported her up and down the quickest. She stared up at the lit windows hoping to catch a glimpse of someone. Hoping someone would see her and wave.

She buried her face in her hands. Was it raining again, or was she crying because she'd been broadsided by emotions and revelations? She always felt like she was on the outside looking in at how life was supposed to be lived. Her therapist said that home was a metaphor for mother and that her longing meant that she had unresolved issues with her mother. Oh, if her therapist only knew. She had also insisted that Morgen "come out of her shell" as though she were a hermit crab. Okay, she was a bit of a hermit, but the symbolism of wanting to *return* to her shell was not lost on her.

To celebrate that clever metaphor, she wiggled her fingers like a hermit crab might with its pincers and scuttled sideways through the downpour and back to Tutti, her current shell of choice where she felt safe and comfortable.

She scooted into the driver's seat, hair, clothing, and red sneakers sopping wet. She turned on the engine and heater and watched the wipers battle the squall. "I want to go home," she told Dashboard Guadalupe. It was too late to disturb Gram and too far to drive to her apartment, and she couldn't stay with Violet who had been so furious at her.

Violet was right about one thing though: Morgen's relationship with Violet's father had been suspect. Like how he'd deliberately left *Coitus Cadenza* for Morgen to find and then catch her looking at it. *Chérie, do you find this image erotic?* He'd rested his hands on her shoulders. He was always touching her—

She shivered, turned up the heater, and applied orange-ginger sanitizer. Alberta had agreed that they would meet for coffee or chowder but sometimes individuals said "I'll call you, we'll do lunch" when they had no intention of following through. She kept falling for it though.

She nibbled the remnants of Shella's smoked salmon and fried egg sandwich while, using her opera glasses, surveying Red Cedar Haven's windows, which overflowed with yellow light. Everyone struggled with something and sometimes needed an especially safe place. Everyone had feelings. Everyone loved life.

Night deepened as she tootled west toward Fish Camp, still highly aware of the lights on inside other people's homes. What if someone was looking back at her from one of those windows and wondering about the individual motoring by in a little blue bus? She reached up and turned on the dome light for a few minutes, illuminating Tutti's interior like a theater in the round, and her golden-brown hair glowed like a sunrise in the rearview mirror.

She stopped in Olympia to buy gas and a pocket English/Spanish dictionary, then continued on, staying awake by singing through her repertoire and pounding syncopated rhythms on the steering wheel in counterpoint with the ticking of her turn indicator and metronome, *allegretto* (♩ = 120, a lively tempo).

When she reached the coast, she located the access road through the dunes. Breathing a sigh of relief, she turned off the dark highway and drove out to the gravel lot. She couldn't see the ocean but knew it was out there, because Tutti shuddered as tons of water crashed against the shore just yards from the front bumper.

She picked up her mother's conch shell and pressed it against her right ear while listening to the deeper roar of the unceasing surf outside with her left. The two sounds resonated in harmony deep inside her bones. "Guess what?" she whispered into the conch shell. "I'm not scared anymore."

She rested the shell in the nest of torn cadenza pages on the passenger seat and fingered the silver beads on her necklace. Her eyes welled up as she turned Tutti around and headed south to Fish Camp.

Friday, October 24, 2003

She arrived before dawn, parked in the site nearest the upper bathhouse, and listened as the roof angels arrived via parachutes of fog. Famished and thirsty, she grabbed the shoelace key and her flashlight and hurried down to the Palace Café. After patting One-Eyed Jack on the head, she let herself in, took a beer and a sandwich from the fridge, and headed to the conch grotto.

As soon as she plugged in the string of white lights, she sensed her mother's voice greeting her in her mind's ear. There was something healing about Fish Camp. Was it the sourdough bread, the prevalence of hippie harmonics, aka her mother's playful spirituality, or simply the kindness of strangers or "acquaintances"? Maybe these individuals resonated with her because they were struggling with life too.

Maybe she resonated with them for the same reason. *In Fish Camp, I'm allowed to have feelings, to experience kindness and respect.* A hungry sob rose from her gut. She collapsed onto the glass brick bench, opened the beer, and tore into a crab, Swiss, and shredded zucchini sandwich. As she chewed, she imagined sitting on a piano bench and recalled how at the end of almost every school day, Andras would lock his studio door, sip a glass of vodka, and watch her undress. With a flourish, he'd put a white linen napkin on the piano bench, blindfold her, and demand that she play from memory anything he requested from her expanding repertoire. Afterward, she'd lie on the cold floor with Andras on top of her, stinking, grunting, and hurting her because she was bad, because she'd let her mother die.

"Stop beating up on myself!" She guzzled the rest of the beer to the rhythm of Gram's words: *Your mother was a natural healer, and you will be too, in time.*

The time was now, and she was healing herself in an especially safe place because Guadalupe perched on her ledge while Lydia Cooper kept watch upstairs. She unplugged the lights and curled up on the floor in her peacoat. In her sleepy mind's ear, she heard the distant ocean, Shella murmuring in her sleep, and Luciano Pavarotti singing "Santa Lucia." She sensed her mother's arms around her, Gram's unintelligible words of wisdom in her ear, and, oddly, Headmistress Collier playing a clarinet in the distance. She drifted off to sleep while her fingers involuntarily practiced Violet's troublesome concerto phrases forward and backward, upside down, and in fragments like trio mix tossed into the wind. At one point, she was grateful when a purring jetty cat or two curled up on her feet to keep her warm.

5.

Friday, October 24, 2003, continued

She awakened in a shivering panic, desperately need-ing to pee. Had she been banished to the supply closet because she'd been bad again? *Restraint is your friend,* Dagger Eyes droned. *Wait here, be silent, and think about your behavior.* Too many times, Morgen had been chastised in front of her peers and shut inside that closet with no chair, just cold, hard floor. Because she took everything literally and was blindly obedient, she did exactly as she was told even when the school day ended and Dagger Eyes went home. Even when she had to pee so badly that she wet her pants.

Light threaded between the floorboards overhead, allowing her to distinguish the conch grotto from the prison of her childhood. As she squatted to relieve herself, she caught the scent of mothballs and shoe polish along with a muffled exchange between Shella, Angelo, and Andras Bacon.

What was he doing there? How did he find her? She'd only told Dorothy so that she would tell Gram. Plus C. D. Hayes. *Well, crap.* She felt her way back to the bench and sat, wringing her hands and rocking to Carlo singing "Funiculì, Funiculà" fifteen feet away while he split firewood, presumably with his Paul Bunyan ax. The entry door slammed, Andras's scent faded, and she heard Angelo's resonant voice. "Must have got back late…sleeping in…"

She waited, suffering to the smell of sizzling bacon and rummaging through her pockets in vain for trio mix leftovers. While her stomach growled, she practiced everything in her repertoire on the glass bench except for the Fantasie. The breakfast crowd came and went. She felt her way around the conch grotto, performing ballet steps to calm her anxiety, and found a tile fragment for the sugar bowl. She strained her ears and heard footfalls and kitchen noises. Was it already time for lunch? She scratched her prickly scalp, flapped and wiggled in the darkness to her heart's content, and practiced rolling her tongue, which was likely connected to her mystery genetics. It was beginning to look like she'd be imprisoned until she died of thirst, her body rotted, and they discovered poor tragic her.

The entry door slammed again, and she listened to footfalls on the stairs. Shella's afternoon naptime? After counting to one thousand, she crept up the steps and into the closet. As she slowly opened the glass door, she came face to face with a terrified Mia, poised to strike with her broom. When Mia recognized Morgen, she let loose a whispered rant in rapid Spanish.

"Sorry." Morgen blinked in the bright light before rifling through her new dictionary. "*Lo siento.*"

Mia peered past her, mouth open, eyes wide, her perfectly arched eyebrows twitching a variety of emotions.

"Okay, I'll show you, but promise not to tell. *Promesa.*" She pressed her finger to her lips, and Mia nodded. She plugged in the conch grotto lights and helped Mia navigate the hole in the closet wall. Once inside, Mia gazed at the pink tiled and mirrored walls, put her hands on her hips, and glared at her.

Morgen shrugged and smiled. The Fish Camp social experiment just leaped into a higher orbit. She was stymied by intonation, subtext, and innuendo, but Mia, lacking English, could communicate only with facial expressions and hand gestures, which was helpful because miming was easier to interpret than words. Too often with normal individuals, words and nonverbal cues such as body language didn't match.

Mia dropped to her knees and crossed herself beneath the statue of Our Lady of Guadalupe. As she whispered her prayers in Spanish, Morgen knelt beside her and listened to the music in her voice.

Morgen had just unlocked Tutti when Carlo came trotting up. "Glad you're back." He gasped. "Now may I take a quick look?"

She chewed her lips. "First promise to quit throwing your cigarette butts on the ground. They're disgusting and toxic to wildlife. Second, tell me what's with you and Pavarotti."

"I'll elaborate." A lock of dark hair fell across his forehead as he began to sing "Funiculì, Funiculà" at full volume but, a few measures in, he began to cough.

"You're not half bad, but you'd do better if you quit smoking. And you're a little flat. I know, because I have perfect pitch."

"I studied opera." He blinked as though something was irritating his eyes. "Destined to be the next famous Italian tenor, but like you said, I fell flat and didn't make the cut." He snickered. "I still like classical music though."

She shifted her weight from one foot to the other. "Who's your favorite composer?"

"Beethoven. I know a lot about Beethoven. Spent his life composing, and now he's decomposing."

She flinched. "If that was a joke, it was in poor taste."

"No, it's not. Beethoven will never die. He's too great."

"Do you believe in ghosts?" She watched him, and the words *con artist* came to mind.

"Absolutely." He smirked. "The Palace Café is haunted by the little old lady who built it, and for some reason, she has it in for me. The place gives me the creeps." He rested his hands on Tutti's roof and closed his eyes. "I sense this bus is haunted too—"

"Ghosts can be nice, too, you know. Like I have roof angels—"

"Maybe by Beethoven himself." He began to belt out "Ode to Joy" in German.

After a few bars, she interrupted him. "Okay. Do you know the name of his only opera?"

"*Fidelio*. Vienna. 1805."

She opened Tutti's door and remained outside while Carlo stepped in and slid across the bench.

"Confining but efficient. You've fixed it up real nice. My dad liked to camp but was more interested in gambling. Ended up with colossal debt." He looked at her with sad eyes. "And committed suicide two days before I caught my fiancée two-timing me. To top things off, I got my draft notice. I like your old bus though. Haunted or not, it's got a happy vibe." He put a cigarette in his mouth and fished for a match. "The wood metronome is a classy touch—"

"You can't smoke in there, but if my bus makes you feel better, you can come by again." *Shouldn't have said that.* She began to itch all over.

"Appreciate the invitation." He did that squinty thing again with his left eye. "I've got nothing but the best stuff, so let me know when you want to get high and listen to some real music."

After he left, she wiped the tabletop and seat with orange-ginger sanitizer. She found him interesting when he talked about music and ghosts but not when he assumed she'd want his "best stuff." She addressed Dashboard Guadalupe, "I don't think I understood the subtext of that social interaction." She opened her manuscript journal, turned to the *My Social Experiment Wisdom* page, and wrote:

Regardless of how others present themselves, you never know what's going on with them or how they feel about you.

She added Alberta to Tutti's horses list as a friend, upgraded Carlo to a friend, and downgraded Violet from friend to acquaintance.

She dumped half of a cup of trio mix on the table and sorted the pieces into separate piles: plain M&M's, dried cranberries, and roasted whole almonds. She was adept at sorting and making lists. If only finding and fixing the missing pieces of her life could be so easy. For example, locating her mother's stolen cremation urn, getting out from under Andras's thumb, and feeling good about herself.

Everything fluctuated day by day like the tide, but "finding and fixing" sounded like a good raison d'être. She popped a handful of trio mix into her mouth and lay down on the platform bed. As with Gram only ten days earlier, there was nothing like a little sugar at bedtime. While she chewed first at half speed and then at double time, her fingers resumed practicing the Fantasie on the eiderdown, changing the meter, transposing into another key, crossing hands, and playing while cigarette smoke mingled with Fish Camp's ubiquitous fog.

Saturday, October 25, 2003

MORGEN HUNG HER PEACOAT ON A HOOK IN THE CAFÉ AND headed to the phone to call Gram.

"Hi, Pauline. She has a cold? What, a head cold or a chest cold? Laryngitis? Has she seen a doctor? She's eighty-five and a half. Should I come?" She felt her heart rate spike to *allegretto* ($\quarternote$ = 120). "Okay, if you're sure, but please tell her that I love her. Thanks." Now Gram had a little cold like she had a little autism and Shella had a little pregnancy. Those weren't little conditions. Either you had one or you didn't. She took a seat at the end of the crowded counter because all four tables were full with cheerful regulars.

Shella scowled while she shoveled sourdough pancakes onto Carlo's plate.

"May I please order some too?" Morgen's question fluttered in the air.

"Mia," Shella said rather loudly, "all of a sudden, everyone has to have pancakes. Can you quit sweeping for a minute and help me out?"

"Panqueques por favor," Morgen whispered after consulting her pocket dictionary. Shella was edgy again and had forgotten that Mia couldn't speak English. Morgen rested her chin in the palm of her hand. Pauline had told her not to worry about Gram, but she was worried.

"What smells so good?" Carlo asked, his cheeks bulging with breakfast.

"Cioppino." Shella put a plate of pancakes in front of Morgen without looking at her. "Maple or cranberry syrup?"

"Cranberry, thank you. Is something wrong? You seem—"

"Coffee?" Shella made the rounds.

"Yes, please." Carlo held out his mug. "Cioppino for Angelo, again?"

"Oh whatever. There's always enough for everybody. Mia, I need to go upstairs." She put the pot on the burner and stomped up the stairs. The café fell silent except for The Weather Channel reporting a cold front homing in on the Pacific Northwest.

"Welcome home, stranger." Angelo burst in. "Since you're not a tourist anymore, this is for you." He handed Morgen a *By-the-Wind Sailor* hooded sweatshirt.

"Thank you very much." She pulled it on. "I am deeply touched."

"That's great, but you need to know that a guy with a funny accent was here yesterday looking for you. Even asked if Fish Camp had a piano. We played dumb, so he gave up and left. You in trouble?"

"Who, me?"

"Good. You're in safe harbor here. We don't rat on anybody, even when we should. Now finish your breakfast but leave room for cioppino tonight." He strode over to a crowded table and joined the conversation.

It was interesting that Angelo had noticed Andras's accent. She remembered how he would reward her for mastering a piece by reciting her favorite poem, "Fern Hill" by Dylan Thomas, in his Welsh accent while lightly stroking her face and giving her those first chaste, dry kisses that should have come from a boy her own age.

Shella clomped down the stairs, her cheeks glowing and her belly preceding her like a huge glass float. She threaded her way through the crowd to the front door to greet a FedEx driver. "Morgen," she said, turning around, "would you please take the truck and run this out to Grampy John? It's his medication, and asking Carlo is more trouble than it's worth."

Once again, Morgen was flummoxed by subtext and innuendo because Shella's words and nonverbal cues didn't match. She'd asked Morgen for a simple favor and had said "please," but the timbre of her voice and her flushed complexion signaled irritation. At whom? John? Carlo? *Me?* She put down her fork and rubbed her temples. "Sure, I'll get my license." As she headed to the door, she heard her mother's gentle words in her mind's ear. *Sometimes we don't understand certain things, and all we can do is give life our best and keep moving forward. Maybe someday we'll look back, and it'll all make sense.*

A squall blew ashore, and the sky grew dark and heavy with rain. Morgen followed Shella's directions and steered the old red pickup onto a narrow mud and gravel lane and parked in front of a lopsided shingled cabin. The foundation was moored with heavy ropes to a stand of shore pines, the rain gutters choked on bushels of moss, and white paint peeled off the trim in streamers around the only window.

"Hi, John. It's Morgen," she called out. He opened the door and shyly invited her in. "This package just came, and Shella thought you'd want it."

"That's nice." Even in rubber knee boots and red flannel pajamas, John smelled like sweet smoke and machinery that had purpose, worked hard, and endured. "Make yourself at home. Nothing fancy, just my old cabin."

After she gave him the package, she glanced around his tidy little house. A wood table held a wash basin, toiletries, and a mirror along with a hot plate with a coffee pot. In the corner, a fish smoker doubled as a nightstand beside a single bed. The floor listed slightly, and one wall leaned a little off square, which upset her equilibrium. She walked over to read a framed cross-stitch hanging on the wall by a doorway at the rear of the cabin.

*The Lord is my Shepherd...He leadeth me beside the
still waters...He restoreth my soul...Amen.*

The windows on either side were boarded over.

John had opened the box and was sorting through the contents. "It looks like they got my order right this time. Say, I was telling you about my cabin. Only one room now. Didn't used to be, but it's big enough. Mind your step though. I've moved this house three times. Won't be moving it—"

"Is this the bathroom?" she asked, but as soon as she opened the door, the wind slapped her back. The rest of the house was gone, and twenty feet below, surf gnawed at the eroding cliff.

John rushed over to steady her. "I should have warned you." He gestured at the ocean. "Used to be miles of land out there. My hometown. Pastures. Roads. It's washing away, and there's no saving it."

She stared into the face of the storm and began to cry. "We have to evacuate!" She grabbed his washbasin and toiletries and headed toward the front door. "Load the truck! We're going to fall into the sea and drown—"

The rear door yanked and thrashed against its rusty hinges like a chained beast.

"Please calm down and put my things back on the table."

"May I at least please shut that door?" Morgen clenched her fists. "It's annoying and I'm feeling rather chilled."

He helped her secure the door. "This is nothing new," he said in a tired voice.

"You mean hanging by a thread over the fricking Pacific Ocean, largest geographic feature on earth that averages thirteen thousand feet deep?" She fought to catch her breath. "John, you're not going to win this one."

"That's common knowledge." He turned on his hot plate. "Would you like a cup of coffee?"

"Decaf?" she sniffled. "Thank you. Where should I sit?"

"Regular coffee, and I have sugar but no milk. You can sit on the bed."

"Okay. And black's fine." She cradled the mug in her hands.

He sat beside her and sipped his coffee. "What are you really afraid of?"

"I'm not afraid of anything—" The damn door bucked against the jamb again as though threatening to escape, and she almost slopped her coffee.

John chuckled. "Take your time."

"You're nice, and I don't want you to get hurt." She sniffed.

"Me neither." He shrugged. "What else?"

"Delicious coffee, but I won't sleep for a year, and my eyebrows are already starting to itch. Caffeine, you know?" She took another sip. "I need to tell you something, and please swear you won't tell another soul."

A wave slammed against the cliff and the old house shook. "Promise?" she cried.

John nodded.

"My mom was raped and got pregnant with me on the drift logs beach, and a Widow Witch saved her life in the conch grotto!" She felt her life would explode. "Was that Lydia Cooper? Promise you won't—"

"A 'conch grotto,' you call it? Say, I remember a nice lady named Charlie brought her baby out here from time to time, and the baby made Lydia happy, because she never had one of her own." He stared at Morgen and brightened. "Miss Charlie was your mother, and you was that baby in the photo."

Morgen corrected her posture. "What photo?"

SHE WALKED THROUGH THE CROWDED PALACE CAFÉ AND headed to Lydia Cooper's photo over the mantelpiece. In the soft evening light, she could tell that parts of the black-and-white photograph had been subtly colorized: a shiny, blue swimsuit on a little girl kneeling at Lydia's feet, a blue jellyfish stranded on the sand, a brown pelican standing behind the drift log, and something else seemed vaguely familiar.

"Hey, Morgen Marín," Angelo said. "Come sit down and have some cioppino."

Shella stood beside him, his right hand resting on her beach ball belly. "Angelo likes to feel the baby move." She giggled.

The word *awkward* came to mind as Morgen pulled off her wet sweatshirt and peacoat. She noticed Mia, her back to the crowd, scrubbing a mountain of dishes and excluded from the banter because she couldn't communicate in English. "*Buenas tardes*, Mia."

Mia turned and smiled at her.

"Sorry I was snippy earlier," Shella said. "Freaking emotional hormones again." She returned to the kitchen. "It's soup night, and we've got all-you-can-eat cioppino, salmon noodle, and chicken salsa soup."

"I'd like a scoop of spaghetti too if you don't mind," Angelo said.

"May I try a cup of each, please?" Morgen sat at Angelo's table. Her hands twitched, and she wanted to play scales, études, anything familiar and secure. "I'm feeling agitated. I was just out at John's, and we're all going to fall into the sea and drown." *Although he fondly remembered Mom and me—*

"We keep telling him that he ought to move up here, but his family has lived out there for generations." Shella had returned with a bowl of spaghetti for Angelo and three ramekins of soup for Morgen. "Mind if I join you? My feet are killing me."

"First, get me some garlic, per favore."

Shella rubbed her lower back and returned to the kitchen.

"I love the ocean," Morgen said, "but out at John's, roads fall off cliffs, and homes, yards, gardens, and even part of a cemetery have washed away. Very unsettling." *He actually remembered me as a baby.*

Shella banged a shaker of granulated garlic and another bowl of cioppino on the table.

"Thanks, doll." Angelo dumped a quarter cup of garlic powder into his soup. "He used to have acres of cranberry bogs but sold most of it along the way. Long time ago, there was good land with farms, businesses, homes, a school, but it's pretty much gone now. The currents or something changed, maybe because of dredging or the jetties. Anyway, the coastline has been eroding for years and has receded by at least a couple miles."

Shella sat with a grunt. "All that erosion makes you respect the power of the ocean."

"Hey, the ocean washed away Atlantis, and it's washing away the Pacific Northwest. Old Mother Nature can knock your socks off." Angelo took a drink. "Most sock-knocking water I've been on was the Bering Sea north of the Aleutians. Scared the ever-loving hell out of me, and I loved every minute." He finished his spaghetti.

Morgen couldn't let it go. "Can't John build a place up in his victory garden?"

"Great idea. Hey, game six of the World Series is on the radio if you care to join me. It's a must win."

"No, thanks," Shella said. "I'm exhausted." She headed up the stairs.

Angelo stood. "A couple things, Morgen Marín. Grumpy John was born in that house. My Uncle Vic, the lawyer, brought me out here when I was a boy so I could learn how to fish. *Catchalot* was the first boat I got to drive, and Fish Camp has always been a safe harbor." He stared at her a moment before nodding at Lydia's portrait. "That sweet lady loved me like the son she never had. Goodnight." He bent and picked up a penny before heading to the door.

"Goodnight, Angelo." She carried the rest of the dishes to the sink. *He said, "welcome home" and that I wasn't a tourist anymore.* Was she about to overstep the boundary between guest and host again? She shrugged and grabbed a dishtowel.

When Mia began shaking a mayonnaise jar full of soapy water to wash it, Morgen grabbed a jar of granulated garlic, matched her rhythm, and began to sing, "*La cucaracha, la cucaracha, ya no puede caminar—*"

Mia grinned and sang, "*Porque no tiene, porque le falta, marihuana que fumar—*"

"Knock it off," Shella hollered from her room upstairs. "I'm trying to sleep."

Morgen pressed her finger to her lips, Mia mirrored her, and they silently laughed so hard that tears ran down their cheeks.

Sunday, October 26, 2003

Morgen waited until the last of the breakfast diners had bussed their dishes, overpaid their bills, and departed. She returned to the fireplace to resume her contemplation of Lydia Cooper's photograph. As she met Lydia's eyes, she caught a trace of a peculiar buttery sweet aroma from her childhood. "Shella, what are you doing?" she asked.

"Baking biscotti."

More like baking déjà vu. Morgen's olfactory memory kicked into overdrive as she gazed at Lydia. "Where'd you get the recipe?"

"It was stuck in the back of a drawer, but I'm enhancing it. Why?"

"Just curious." A smile bloomed on her face. "I remember now," she whispered. "You used to let me lick the bowl." The Palace Café was silent, but like on the day she arrived, she sensed the vibrations from a piano inside her bones. She refilled her mug and sat on a barstool. "You said you'd tell me the history of the Palace Café."

"Okay, sure," Shella said. "Local legend is that it was built around 1950 by a tugboat captain named Marty Cooper and his wife, Lydia, an eccentric cat lady. They were very young and extremely devoted to each other, and they celebrated their love by adopting stray cats. He went missing out there, apparently lost in a storm, but she wouldn't accept his death and lost her mind with grief. Some people thought she turned into a witch. She held vigils and séances and added secret entrances so her husband's spirit could come home. These were boarded over later when they remodeled. For years, Lydia even draped twinkly white lights all over the building and kept them burning every night like a beacon."

Morgen knew for a fact that not all the entrances were boarded over and that some of those lights still burned. "What happened to her?"

"Got sick and died, but she still haunts the Palace in a good way." Shella lowered her voice. "I've only seen her in that picture on the wall, but I *feel* that she's here, but more protective than scary, you know? I don't usually talk about it, because people would think I'm nuts."

"I don't think you're nuts. I think it's entirely possible."

"Okay, good. After Lydia died, all the cats went feral. Supposedly Doris was her favorite. She must be sixty years old by now. Crazy, right? The building was vacant for years before becoming a restaurant."

"Why'd they call it a palace?"

"Because she was his princess, and he was her prince, and they were supposed to live happily ever after here by the sea." Shella pulled a cookie sheet out of the oven.

Interesting that Shella didn't mention that Marty Cooper was John's brother. Maybe she didn't know or hadn't connected the surnames. Morgen herself often had issues with language. She turned away from the kitchen and glanced out the window as a battered, sea-green car with a convertible top pulled up and parked. She looked at the make and model on the grill. "Do you know what a heteronym is?"

"No idea. Is it important?"

"Could be. Otherwise someone might confuse a 'bass fish' for a 'bass drum.' Heteronyms are words that are spelled the same but are pronounced differently and have different meanings. See, a Geo Tracker just pulled up. What's interesting about the Geo part of the name is that it's pronounced gee-oh, whereas the Pacific geoduck, the clam with an obscenely long siphon, is also spelled g-e-o but pronounced gooey, so Geo can be gee-oh or gooey depending on the situation. That is another example of a heteronym."

"I keep forgetting that you're a schoolteacher. All I know is that geoducks make great chowder."

Morgen resumed watching the "Gooey" Tracker. After a moment, the driver emerged. He locked the door, gazed around Fish Camp, and, after crossing the boardwalk, entered the café. Four jetty cats followed him in, clearly excited and all meowing at once. "Hello?" He approached the counter. "You have lodging available?"

The quiet rhythm and melody of his accent startled Morgen, and his physical presence sent a shockwave that instantly corrected her posture. British, Caribbean, or Australian? He couldn't have been much taller than she was, maybe five foot seven, but interesting looking with the powerful build of a much taller man. He obviously wasn't from around there.

"The trailers in the RV park are for rent. Morgen, please shoo the cats out of here. I don't want fur in the food."

Morgen studied the man as she hurried the cats to the door. Tousled dark hair. Gray parka. Faded jeans. Running shoes and no socks. *What an unexpected turn of events.*

"What are your rates?"

"Twenty dollars a night or a hundred a week with a twenty-five-dollar cleaning deposit. Add eight dollars a day for the meal plan, extra charge for beer, and you have to provide your own bedding and towels. I'm Shella. Welcome to Fish Camp."

The floor rolled beneath Morgen's feet as she headed back to her barstool.

"My name's Fetu, and I'd like to stay a week. Maybe longer, but I'll pay for a week now." He smiled slightly. "Something smells good in here."

"I'm making biscotti. Let's see." Shella lifted a binder from under the counter and flipped through the pages. "Joe and Mia live in Halibut, and Tuna's last tenant cleaned razor clams in the toilet, which created a mess in the waste tank. Carlo's supposed to take care of that. Give me a minute. I thought Salmon had a reservation coming in."

Morgen focused her attention on Fetu and felt a warm, glad feeling in her core. He was about her age. His hands were large and strong, skin and nails clean. He probably didn't fish. "Coffee?" She caught her breath.

"I'd love a cup, thank you." He sat on a barstool and looked at her with warm, bittersweet chocolate eyes. A smile crossed his face and faded. He glanced at her eyes, mouth, and back to her eyes with an expression that could be interpreted as bold or guarded.

She poured a mug of coffee, set it in front of him, and collapsed onto her barstool. "How do you do? I'm Morgen, and I like your Gooey Tracker." She pressed her hands against her hot cheeks, and the word *crimson* came to mind. "Geo is a heteronym, because g-e-o is a car but pronounced gooey when it's a clam—"

"Let's put you in Salmon," Shella said. "The trailers are old but well maintained. Here's the key if you want to check it out first."

"No worries. I'll take it with the meal plan." He took a sip of coffee before pulling a wad of bills out of his back pocket. "Cash okay?"

"Cash works fine." Shella counted his money. "It has a single berth, coffee pot, a sink, and a head. Showers and laundry are located out back. Now what's your full name, and where are you from?"

"Fetu Lemalu. I'll spell my first name for you—F-E-T-U. It's Samoan, but I'm from Auckland, New Zealand."

"Oh, have you seen *Finding Nemo*?" Morgen asked. "It takes place down there."

He laughed. "Yes, I have."

"Have you been to the Great Barrier Reef?" Her eyes brightened.

"Not yet. That's in the Australia part of New Zealand." He picked up the key. "Shall I move the Gooey up?"

"Sure." Shella laughed and handed him a receipt.

He pointed at their sweatshirts. "What's a *By-the-Wind Sailor*?"

"It's the common name for a jellyfish," Shella said, "and the name of our friend's charter boat."

He nodded, set his coffee mug on the counter, and left with Salty Dog leading the way.

"Oh dear Lord, I could listen to that accent all day long." Morgen combed her fingers through her hair and decided that she needed a shampoo and clean outfit ASAP.

"He's kind of cute, don't you think?" Shella said.

"Maybe." She refilled her mug. "Probably."

"Are you ready to try my new recipe?" Shella set a plate of biscotti on the counter. "I made them in your honor with M&M's, dried cranberries, and slivered almonds." She took one for herself. "I call them raison d'être biscotti but without the raisin part. Out here cranberries are much more apropos."

"That's brilliant, and they're so colorful." And made with Lydia Cooper's magic cookie dough recipe. She closed her eyes and took a bite, and memories flooded her mind's eye: Mom playing the piano; stairs descending into the grotto; hot dogs roasting at sunset; sandcastles rising out of the beach.

"I have a dozen wrapped up for you to take home. Come on, I need to get off my feet for a few minutes." Shella picked up the plate of biscotti.

They'd just settled at a table when Fetu returned. "May I join you?"

"Sure," Shella said. "Will Salmon be okay?"

"More than adequate." He sat down. "*Kia ora.*"

Salty Dog sniffed Fetu's shoes and collapsed with a sigh against his legs.

"Push him away if he gets too lovey-dovey." Shella got up, refilled Fetu's mug, and returned to the kitchen.

"What does *kia ora* mean?" Morgen brushed crumbs off her chin.

"It's a Māori greeting that means both hello and be well."

"Great. Okay, *kia ora.* What do you do in New Zealand?"

"I owned a production company and recording studio. Mostly music and film, some artwork and computer graphics. Also a thousand-seat performance venue. It was creative, fun, and lucrative and gave me a lot of freedom, but I recently sold it to a longtime client. Are you on holiday also?"

"I'm on a short leave from my teaching job." She shoved her hands under her thighs. "What brings you out here?"

"My father was born near here, in Ocosta, and directed that when he died, his ashes should be poured into the Pacific, specifically off this coast. Hell of a long way for me to come, but as his only child, I felt I should grant his last wish." He patted Salty Dog on the head, and Salty licked his hand.

Morgen studied the remarkable geometry of his face: high cheekbones, dark, wide-set eyes with thick eyelashes, and the largest white teeth she'd ever seen. She saw no indication of grief or loss.

"Sorry, I've got jet lag." He rubbed his face with both hands. "I need to hire someone with a boat to take Dad's ashes out for me. Unfortunately, I'm terrified of the ocean, which must seem odd considering my ancestry, but I had a close call as a kid." He took a biscotti and broke it in half. "The ocean is so awfully deep."

"Yes, it is." Morgen caught herself rocking as the rhythm of Fetu's accent resonated inside her bones and made her heart pound, or was it the sugar in Lydia's cookie dough recipe?

Later that afternoon, Fetu returned with Salty Dog at his side, and Morgen gestured to an empty chair at the table she shared with John. "Please join us. John, this is Fetu from New Zealand." She noticed a half-inch-wide, wavy blue band tattooed around Fetu's left forearm.

John shook Fetu's hand, and Salty Dog lay down by the fireplace, crossed his wrists, and grinned.

Shella brought Fetu a bottle of beer.

"You can fetch me one, too, per favore, Shella Bella Velella velella," Angelo said as he entered the café. "I have a wicked thirst, because the damn Yankees lost the World Series last night, and Roger Clemens is retiring. Still, Pudge and Posada, good guys, great match up, and who the hell are you?" he asked Fetu.

Morgen blushed. "This is Fetu from New Zealand. He's renting Salmon trailer." A fake yawn disguised her sigh.

"Fetu, huh? Sounds like a fancy cheese." He raised his beer. "Salute. How long are you staying?"

"A week or so. I'm taking care of some family business. Cheers to you."

"Just a week, huh?" Angelo looked at the blue band around Fetu's forearm and positioned his own arm to show off his *Famiglia per Sempre* tattoo. "I started this in Vietnam and finished it years later on a snowy night in Anchorage when I was drunk and miserable."

"'Family is forever'?" Fetu watched Angelo's face. "Is that a threat or a promise?"

"Long, sad story for another day." Angelo frowned as he stood. "Come on, everybody. Let's show the Kiwi my boat."

There it was again, innuendo and subtext. They'd just communicated that they had something significant in common concerning family, but as Morgen watched Angelo, the word *vulnerable* came to mind. She followed them out of the Palace Café and down to north float.

"You know, Kiwi," Angelo said to everyone in earshot, "I ran a charter in Alaska back in '89 when *Exxon Valdez* dumped eleven million gallons of crude into Prince William Sound. Incidentally, I helped with the cleanup. Long story short, channel markers! Follow the green lights to starboard going out and the red lights to starboard coming in. The old adage is 'green going, red right returning.'" He clambered aboard and turned on the cabin lights. "Welcome, me hearties," he roared. "Do any of you landlubbers know how much it costs for a pirate to get his ears pierced? A buccaneer! Get it? Hardy har har! Now everyone muster to starboard. I need to explain PFDs, lifeboats, and emergency procedures while I steer methodically, deliberately, and vigilantly like the good skipper I am."

Her therapist would say Angelo was overcompensating for his display of vulnerability. Morgen followed Shella into the cabin, but Fetu hung back a moment before stepping on board.

"You need to find your sea legs, Kiwi. I myself can never get the hang of land legs." Angelo opened the refrigerator. "Beer for the bros, sodas for the ladies." He turned on his tape deck and began to sing along with Dean Martin's "Everybody Loves Somebody." Then he paused. "Okay, it's time for the tour. You too, Morgen Marín. Shella already knows the ropes." He patted the cabinet he was leaning against. "Liquor locker. Very important feature. This entire area is called the salon." He beckoned them forward. "This is the helm, and the galley's over there."

"I love your Dashboard Guadalupe. She's even wearing a life jacket." Morgen touched the wood wheel. "So many instruments."

"Yes, except they've been acting up." He smacked his hand on the control panel. "Otto is my autopilot, and I'm about to give auto Otto the old heave ho. Without accurate working instruments, it's a whole different ballgame out there."

"Where's your life jacket?"

Angelo laughed. "That's a PFD, Miss Schoolteacher, a personal flotation device. I never wear one, because all they'd do is prolong the agony."

"I read that most coastal villages in Mexico don't have marinas. When the fishermen are done fishing, they wait in their pangas beyond the surf line until a big wave starts to roll. Then they gun the outboard, catch that wave, and ride it up onto the beach."

"Has to be hard on the hull, but those people are very resourceful. Joe's Mexican, and he can fix anything except Otto the autopilot." *By-the-Wind Sailor* rolled. "Oh, feel that? My boat must have heard your exciting panga story. Easy now." He patted the wheel. "You like boats, Kiwi? They say no matter how big the boat, the wake eventually disappears. That's a metaphor, or, long story short, my legacy." He gestured toward a narrow stairway. "Come on and try to keep up with your tour guide."

As they stepped below, Morgen followed. Distracted by Fetu's curious scent of petrichor and lemon grass, she stumbled off the bottom step. "Oops. Sorry. Oh, what a cute room." Water lapped against the hull, and she remembered that four feet away, the pelican-priest figurehead kept watch.

"Glad you approve. This is the captain's stateroom, my private quarters. V-style berth, storage all around, head to starboard and shower to port."

There was a pile of dog-eared boating magazines on a built-in desk. A catcher's mitt and shabby missal lay on the bunk, and a black-and-white POW/MIA flag bandana was tacked to the wall. A Purple Heart medal and a tiny green purse dangled from a crucifix above the head of the bed. Angelo took a Mason jar half filled with pennies off the desk and set it on the floor. "Always have to stow the treasure before casting off. Don't need a catastrophe down here in steerage."

They followed him back to the salon where Shella waited in an armchair. Morgen slid onto the settee. Fetu joined her, and he glanced at the rods hung from the ceiling. "Have you always fished?"

"Even in Vietnam, back in the day. We'd patrol the river with that insane war all around us. I'd look at the water and wonder what kind of tackle and bait to use." He forced a laugh before downing his beer. "Hell, even Kiwis fought in Vietnam, and see what happens when I drink? I brood about that fucking war, the pain and guilt, damned if you went, damned if you didn't, like Carlo the draft dodger. What a dick." He rubbed his eyes with the heels of his hands.

Shella struggled but couldn't get out of her chair. "Angelo? Please stop—"

"Me coming home shot to hell with my million-dollar wound and getting shit on by protesters when fifty-eight thousand good people couldn't come back, and their names are etched forever on the Memorial Wall." He shot a direct look at Morgen. "Except for one pretty nurse who saved my soul and, shit, I've got to quit drinking." His hand shook as he opened another beer. "Sorry, yes, I've always fished. What's it to you?"

Shella moaned and grabbed her belly. "I need to move." She gripped the arms of her chair, breathing long and deep, and perspiration beaded on her forehead. "Braxton Hicks contractions. I'm okay. It's normal."

"You're having a dress rehearsal for the big event." Morgen handed her a linty tissue and helped her up. "Fetu, you may answer Angelo's question about 'what's it to you,' while we take a few steps." She whispered to Shella, "Because we girls are outnumbered in Fish Camp and have to stick together, remember?" She tried not to flinch when Shella clutched her arm.

"Would you do me a favor when you go out again?" Fetu asked Angelo.

"You want to go fishing?"

Fetu shook his head. "My father passed away, and I'm supposed to have his ashes scattered into the Pacific. I can't go, but I'd gladly pay you."

"Sure, Kiwi, no charge. Don't like boats?

"I almost drowned when I was a kid."

"Clearly you didn't, so lighten up. Shit happens." He downed the last of his beer. "Be a man, learn to read the water, the ocean is in our souls, to quote my old man, Vincenzo Bordacelli, may he rest in peace." He thumped Fetu on the arm. "I'd be honored. Just bring him by. You Catholic? You want a prayer said?"

"I didn't even think about that. What would you want?"

"Me? I say my prayers to the sunset every night, and that's good enough for me, but I'll come up with something. Sure you don't want to take the plunge? Sail across the bounding main in a big boy boat and all that? It'd make a man out of you."

"Excuse me, but I need to get back to work," Shella whispered.

"I'll go with you." Morgen stood up. "Angelo—"

"Don't worry about the Kiwi. I'll loan him a flashlight if he needs one. Wouldn't want him to fall in, for Chrissake." He winked at her.

Had Angelo been trying to tell her though innuendo that *her* mother had been his nurse? She would have to compose an appropriate follow-up question. She followed Shella as *By-the-Wind Sailor* settled against her ropes and bumpers, and the offshore breeze whistled in her ear before running away to sea.

Monday, October 27, 2003

MORGEN SAT AT A TABLE WITH HER MANUSCRIPT JOURNAL and watched as Mia and Shella de-veined a mountain of shrimp, aka *camarones*, and put them in a bowl of marinade. "Does Angelo often get emotional like he did last night?"

"Whenever he talks about the war," Shella said, "and about his family, although he likes Uncle Vic. That's his dad's brother and some sort of a lawyer or accountant. It seems to me that he's hurting pretty deep, which must be why he drinks so much, but I don't ask him personal questions. I just try to take care of him without riling him up."

"He's lucky to have a friend like you." But was *Famiglia per Sempre* a threat, a promise like Fetu had asked, or just a biological fact? Look at *her* vicious conception. Nothing sentimental there. Fetu lingered in her thoughts. She'd blurted "Gooey Tracker," which sounded stupid, but he'd taken her by surprise. She turned to a new page in her journal and wrote:

Fetu Lemalu. Exotic. Pleasant face, great hair, brown eyes, muscular body, lovely accent, music connection, well-mannered, and kind.

The antithesis of Andras for whom she'd sacrificed her entire life to secure a career. Not to get ahead of herself, but what would she have to give up to have a relationship with Fetu? She felt something curiously visceral for him, but then her brain bounced back to Andras who, as usual, demanded her undivided attention. She still had to deal with his Fantasie, because the concert at River Bridge was only forty-three days away.

Cooking aromas beckoned everyone back to the Palace Café, and Angelo was the first individual through the door, leading a swarm of hungry regulars. "What's for dinner, Shella Bella Velella velella?"

"Fish, chips, and slaw. Shrimp and cranberry quesadillas. Zucchini frittata. Sourdough pizza with Alfredo sauce, Dungeness crab, pineapple chunks, and extra cheese." Shella loaded baskets with sourdough rolls.

Morgen closed her manuscript journal and watched Mia lean her broom against the wall and begin taking orders. It was likely that she understood more English than she could speak, aka receptive versus expressive language.

Just as Angelo grabbed a bottle of beer and sat down beside Morgen, the phone rang, and Shella answered. "Who? *Dr.* Marín? You mean Morgen? Hang on. It's for you." She returned to the kitchen and tossed a chunk of halibut into the fryer.

Morgen grabbed her journal and pen. "Hello?" She listened for several moments. "As associate professor and director of chamber music? Wow, Dr. Byrd, yes, of course I accept, thank you. The Mozart piano quintet by special request? Fantastic!" Her hand shook as she wrote down the required repertoire. "Oh sure, no problem. Teach keyboard and mallet lessons and advanced piano collegium plus mentor student composers. Great, but I'll take care of notifying Headmistress Collier. Thank you again very much." She hung up and grinned at Angelo. "I just landed a dream job at NCU, and Dr. Byrd said my applying made the selection process easy for them." She collapsed into her chair and drummed her hands on the table. "The U School of Music is my alma mater, and I have to sign a contract and pick up the music by December 1."

"NCU? I almost went there. Long before your old buddy Mozart though. Hey, you didn't tell me you were a doctor, for Chrissake."

"I have a Doctor of Musical Arts degree, *summa cum laude*. I'm *not* a medical doctor but speaking of medical, were you implying that my mother had been your nurse?"

"Yes, she was, and it's a long story for another day. Now about your new job. You should be very proud of yourself, and I am too." He beamed and crossed his arms over his chest. "This calls for a celebration. Shella? Fetch, me a beer, per favore."

Fetu burst in wearing a cap embroidered Trailer Trash.

"That hat goes great with your sexy Kiwi swagger." Angelo opened his beer. "Salute."

"I found it in Salmon trailer." Fetu smiled at Morgen. "What do you think?"

"*We* think," Angelo interrupted, "that Morgen Marín just got offered the job of a lifetime."

"I want to hear all about this." Fetu's gaze searched her face. "When do you start?"

He was too raw, too bold. She flushed and clenched her teeth. What she wanted to hear about was her mother the nurse and Angelo with the Purple Heart.

MORGEN RETURNED TO TUTTI TO CONTEMPLATE THE LIST of compositions she had to learn. Imagine, someone in the department especially requested Mozart's Quintet for Piano,

Oboe, Clarinet, Horn, and Bassoon in E Flat. "I finally get to perform it," she whispered into her mother's conch shell. "A lifelong dream come true." She mimed playing from memory the third movement on the tabletop while singing her childhood rhyme, "*When I grow up, I will find my daddy out beyond the deep blue sea and bring him to my mom so we will be a fam-i-ly.*" After she closed Fräu Heinrich's curtains, she plugged her cell phone into the extension cord and noticed that she'd missed another call.

At midnight, she peered through her opera glasses and was confident that Fish Camp had shut down for the night. She took her blue crystal star out from under her pillow and slipped it into her pocket. She hung her camera and the shoelace key around her neck, grabbed her flashlight, chamber pot, and shopping bag, and stepped outside onto Doris's plump orange paw. Doris screeched, and Morgen stumbled. "I'm sorry, but what are you doing out here anyway?" Doris yowled a reply and licked her paw. "Oh come on, but you're sworn to secrecy."

After a visit to the bathhouse to fill the chamber pot with soapy water, she crept through drippy fog down to the café with Doris on her heels. She quietly unlocked the door and tiptoed to the phone to pick up her voicemail. "Dr. Marín, I need to let you know that Andras Bacon dropped by this morning and told the attendance clerk that he needed to pick up a book he'd loaned you. Regrettably, she gave him a key, and by the time I was informed, he'd been alone in your private office for nearly an hour." Headmistress Collier hesitated for four seconds. "Your gala fundraiser in December is an opportunity for us to showcase River Bridge, but I'm disturbed by Andras's cavalier intrusion into our school. I feel he overstepped a boundary, and I'm very sorry. Please let me hear from you soon. *Tempus fugit.*"

Morgen's hand was steady when she hung up the phone. Well, crap on Andras for being such a sneak and touching her personal things. Of course, in the past, he'd touched more than just her belongings. *And I didn't know how to defend myself.* She shuddered, and tears filled her eyes. He shouldn't have taken advantage of her innocence. He shouldn't have come out to Fish Camp. He shouldn't have gone into her private office.

How would her life have been different if Arthur Ishikawa had been her teacher? If her mother had lived? If Fetu Lemalu had been her first lover? *Just imagine.* She glanced at Lydia Cooper's photo above the mantelpiece, and a curious phrase came to mind: *The tide is about to turn.*

She borrowed Shella's roll of duct tape and managed to get everything down the tiled steps and into the conch grotto without mishap. She eliminated light leaks between the overhead boards with duct tape and washed the glass bench and tiled walls, stopping from time to time to take photographs.

She sat back on her heels and stared at the glistening walls. What if her mother had been *celebrating* Morgen finally bringing the concerto to fruition by dancing in her tie-dyed dress as they used to do together? Right there in front of the old house on Ninth Street where she'd likely happily lived while preparing for her own concerto concert? Or what if… *Oh Mom, I wish we could talk.*

As she scrubbed the floor on her hands and knees, she hummed the distinctive opening rhythm of the concerto, *long, long, short, long, Mor-gen Ma-rín,* harmonizing with the call of the waves and foghorn and whispering *solfège* to Doris's contented purr. "I enjoy your company too, you with your Cheshire cat grin and me like Alice tumbling down Fish Camp's secret rabbit hole, but that's been my lifelong problem. I've always been an actor in someone else's sensational theater." She started to stand but slipped on the soapy floor and fell, smacking her forehead on the glass brick bench. She grabbed her head with both hands as memories welled in her eyes like kaleidoscopic tears. "Mom's forehead was *bleeding,* because she hit the windshield, but I couldn't help her." Lightheaded, she collapsed onto the bench. "She lay *bleeding* in the street while Andras held me down under the piano and hurt me." She rocked, and her words came in stinging little puffs, *crescendo.* "She should have protected me," she yelled at Guadalupe on the ledge. "She should have seen what he was doing, because when I didn't want to have sex with him, he raped me." She slapped her hands over her mouth and began to cry. "*Shh, shh, shh,* because I still love my mom."

Doris hopped onto her lap, and Morgen petted her. Doris responded by licking her fingers with her velvety tongue.

"Sweet kitty," she sniffled.

Sweet Baby.

"Mom?" Morgen corrected her posture as her mother's written words came to her: *Promise to come back and help me.* "I'm here, and I'm trying, and I'm sorry that I let you down, but I was so screwed up that I didn't recognize you." She buried her face in her hands and breathed in the scent of her mother's patchouli oil.

Far away, the rhythm of the ocean delivered her mother's response. *My legacy is your destiny, which includes the concerto that I would never play yet keeps on playing.*

Tears ran down Morgen's cheeks. "Will you ever forgive me?"

I already did, a very long time ago, and now you need to forgive yourself.

She sniffled. "Did you date Andras, because my skull is going to explode—"

He just wanted to know my history with the concerto, but I didn't tell him.

Outside, the surf surged and ebbed.

"Why did you take my face?"

I didn't, Charlie whispered. *You've always been a stranger to yourself, and although I often didn't understand you, I've always loved you.*

"When do I get my face back?"

When you unlock your music and your heart. Everything you need is right there under your fingertips, and I don't mean that cat.

A wave crashed against the jetty as, sure enough, the tide began to turn.

"But Mom, we've been trapped in a painful legacy for over thirteen years, and I want to find your beautiful, long-lost urn and fix the missing pieces of our—"

She flinched as Doris kneaded her lap with claws extended. "I rather like you, but please don't do that." She petted Doris, but in her mind's eye, saw herself pressing her childish nose against the glass bricks in the old house on Ninth Street. It was as though she'd always lived inside an igloo of thick glass bricks, longing to be like the individuals on the other side. What if she'd been making romanticized assumptions about what it was like to *not* have autism? Everybody in Fish Camp had troubles too but had included her, and come to think of it, she hadn't had to pretend to be someone else since she got there. What if she continued to melt her insecurities little by little like she did with the glass bricks up in John's victory garden?

Recognize what connects you, not just what separates you. Gram's words rushed into her ears. *There's strength in music and in the continuum.*

She was now part of Gram's continuum, which meant that she was strong too. "Baked in the cake," she whispered. What if the missing pieces of her life were also baked into that cake like trio mix in raison d'être biscotti? She stared at her distorted reflection on the conch wall as she touched each of the five beads on the foremothers necklace. "I want to heal. I want to be whole again."

Proceed with wisdom.

Andras had long chipped away at her wobbly sense of self. What if she pushed back and used the Fantasie to beat him at his own demented game? Performed it beyond his wildest dreams and then strolled off his stage forever? "I would be free of my not-a-stranger-rapist, and by reverse legacy, Mom would be set free too." She gazed around the grotto. "Hello? Mom?" she whispered. "I love you. Good night."

Doris blinked her huge hazel eyes, hopped down onto the damp tile floor, and shook water from her paws as she bounded toward the steps.

Morgen took the blue glass star out of her pocket, gave it a kiss before tossing it up at Dashboard Guadalupe's feet, and heard a tinging when it landed. She shoved her things into the shopping bag and followed Doris out of the conch grotto.

6.

Tuesday, October 28, 2003

Morgen woke at 5:17 a.m. to rain pelting Tutti's roof and Doris licking her bruised forehead. "Thanks, but please don't do that." She crawled off the platform bed and looked at her stack of music. What was for breakfast? Andras's evil Fantasie? The robust Stravinsky concerto? The full-bodied Chopin ballades? She sat, turned on the limelight, and began to play Chopin from memory on the tabletop with rich parallel octaves rising in her mind's ear from deep below middle C, *lento* (♩ = 58, slowly).

Doris purred, and a chorus of secrets and memories sang along in time. Morgen had tackled the ballades shortly after her mother was killed, and after Andras took her under his wing, aka thumb. Only Chopin could have understood the chaos in her soul because he'd composed it, and frankly, she hadn't known or cared who the master was: she, the piano, or Frédéric Chopin himself from the grave. She'd blissfully lose herself in the music for hours until it flowed through her and she was only a channeler.

Andras never knew any of that. She'd catch him with tears in his eyes while she played, because her artistry moved him. Bewitched him. Tormented him. That's when he'd loved her the most, but it didn't matter anymore. He was part of her former life, while her repertoire was perennial.

Thirty-five minutes later, she thanked Chopin and put Andras's Fantasie on the tabletop. The time had come for her to stop trying to like it and just do the work. All she had to do was approach it objectively like a puzzle only she could solve. Keep it simple. Not expect too much. Break it down logically. Learn the notes. Complete the assignment. Reframe her life in a fresh context at the U and proceed with wisdom.

AFTER ALMOST FOUR HOURS OF PRACTICING, SHE NEEDED a break. She raced through the rain and into the Palace Café desperate for decaf and conversation but stopped short when she saw a shirtless Fetu on a barstool, his head cradled in his tattooed arms and Shella giving him a massage. "Excuse me, but what are you two doing?"

"Fetu has sore trapeziuses. If you're looking for coffee, decaf is in the second pot." Shella didn't look her way. She continued kneading Fetu's broad, muscular shoulders while her giant belly rhythmically nudged his lower back.

"Hi, Morgen," he said, unable to make eye contact. "I'm awfully stiff from so much travel, and Shella's a natural masseuse. Oh, that feels so good. Do it harder."

"Hi, Fetu." Morgen's cheeks burned as she inched toward the coffee pot while stealing glances. He had the prettiest skin. A fake yawn disguised her sigh. She could have given him a massage even though she had a mild aversion to touch. She had strong hands and arms from years of piano training. "Never mind, I don't want coffee." She fought back tears and headed to the door. "I came in to tell you that I have to leave now, or I'm going to lose my job, so bye-bye, but don't worry, I'll pay my bill before I go."

"Seriously?" Shella hollered. "Don't you even think about leaving."

As soon as Morgen got outside, she smacked both sides of her head and sprinted up the hill to the bathhouse. "Oh, that feels so good, do it harder," she mimicked Fetu's accent in a song-song voice while she collected an armful of toiletries.

"What are you doing?" Fetu stood in the doorway of the bathhouse, drenched from the rain but fully clothed.

"Packing. I have to leave, or I'm going to lose my job."

"Your new job at the university? When does it start?"

She put her things back on the counter and scratched her prickly scalp. "February 1," she whispered.

He gathered his breath. "I can see that you're upset. Tell me what happened."

"What difference does it make?" Her voice flew up an octave. "In a couple of days, we'll never see each other again."

"Maybe, but right now, it matters to me. You were full of good energy when you came into the dining room, but you saw that Shella was giving me a massage, and it upset you. Please help me understand, and then I'll leave you alone."

"Listen, I'm a concert pianist and teacher. I work all the time and don't have much of a social life, but when I see how normal individuals relate," she began to cry, "like massaging each other, I fear that I've missed the boat."

"Did you just break up with someone?" He raised his eyebrows. "Is that why you're hiding out here?"

"I beg your pardon." She clenched her teeth and her fists. "I'm not hiding, I'm trying to find and fix the missing pieces of…oh, never mind." Her shoulders dropped. "Crap."

"Morgen, the concert pianist, I'm not used to hanging out in women's washrooms. Is there someplace else we can talk?"

"Maybe." She glanced outside. "Okay, sure."

AN OFFSHORE BREEZE SWEPT THE RAIN CLOUDS AWAY AS she led Fetu to the dune scarp. It was close enough to the Palace Café for personal safety but far enough away to have a private conversation, and it was scenic. They could hear pebbles rattle and click in the gently rolling waves and watch Joe out surfing all by himself.

"I like it here," Fetu said. "There's more nature than civilization."

Morgen pulled her sleeves down over her hands and bit her lips. What should she say? "I was born on a beach in Mexico. Were you born here or in New Zealand?"

"Westport, New Zealand. Story goes I was conceived under the North Star and born under the Southern Cross. My mum's family moved from the Cook Islands to New Zealand in the 1950s. Years later, her church sent her to Seattle where she met my dad, a garden-variety American. When she was pregnant with me, they decided to start fresh, and because he grew up near Westport, they decided on Westport, New Zealand."

"Oh. I haven't been to New Zealand, but I get to play Carnegie Hall in December. It's in New York City and was built in 1891."

"That's great." His eyes got big, and he smiled. "What are you going to play?"

Her mood dipped. "A composition written by my master teacher. Hey, look at Joe. He's a good surfer." She wrung her hands. "Maybe we should go back."

"Not yet." He appeared to be studying her. "I want to tell you a music story. When I was about twelve years old, my friend's grandfather came to live with him. He was bent over with age and often stumbled when he walked, but when he sat in a straight-backed chair with a guitar in his arms, he was a master. He'd play for hours and never utter a word. I was mesmerized. I began to imagine that someday I would play music like that, that I would be more like him and less like my father. One day when I visited him, he had two guitars, and he said, 'That one's yours.' It was the only time I heard him speak. Even as he taught me chords, finger picking, rhythms, note reading, tablature, he never said a word. It was all in his hands and his eyes. Ultimately, music took me to another level where life had meaning. After he passed, the family gave his guitar to me, and I still have both of them. I designed my production company based on that experience by creating an artist collective where people could develop, share, and market their talents."

"Your elderly friend sounds nice. I like that he inspired your entire life."

"Speaking of inspiration, if you could learn anything new, what would it be? By the way, that is a conversation starter, or in this case, a conversation continuer."

"My therapist gives me worksheets on those. Okay, I'd like to learn to play the mandolin like my Grandpa Scott. You?"

"I've helped hundreds of people produce their work, but I want to write my own song."

"Wow, I like that answer. What's your birth date?"

He smiled. "April 28, 1969."

"Mine's June 21, 1969, in case you wanted to know." That made him one month and twenty-five days older than she was. Her hands began to flap.

His expression darkened, and he altered his stance. "Why are you doing that?"

"What? This? I don't know." She shoved her hands in her pockets. "Why?"

"My brother used to do that."

His voice and face had squinched, but Morgen couldn't interpret why. Pain? Anger? Sorrow?

"He was my best friend. He loved music, and I always knew when he was happy, because he'd flap his arms like that and wave his yellow paper fan." He stared at the horizon. "He had Down syndrome and drowned when we were kids."

"He *drowned*?" The words flew from Morgen's gut, and she began to cry. "What was his name?"

"Some kids called him Bozo the Clown. Pretty mean, huh? His real name was George. He was a year and a half older than me. Hey, I'm sorry. This is real personal shit, and I have no right to take advantage of your kindness."

"No, I want to know everything about you, but this is sad and overwhelming, and I don't know how to respond." She massaged her hands together.

"No, you're very caring." He cleared his throat. Was he going to redirect the conversation? "You have a bruise on your forehead." He reached out to touch her but wisely seemed to check himself. "How'd you do that?"

"I hit my head." She scratched her prickly scalp. "I should go practice. I have a deadline." She swallowed a sob.

"Fine, but please don't leave Fish Camp yet. I enjoy your company."

"Okay, sure." She walked as close as she could to him without touching as they headed back to the Palace Café.

After Morgen agreed to meet him later, she returned to Tutti just as Carlo was leaving the upper bathhouse carrying a toolbox in one hand and his Paul Bunyan ax in the other.

"I hung a full-length mirror for you. Sure brightens up the place." He did that squinty thing with his left eye. "Fetu's kind of short, but Beethoven was only five feet three inches tall. Just saying." He laughed. "Look, there's a brass choir concert in Olympia on Saturday night. You and me could go, have dinner before. Think about it." He sang "Donna è Mobile" as he ambled down to the woodpile.

Olympia was too far away for a one-day roundtrip with dinner and an evening event, although it would be fun to talk to him about spiritual things like his aversion to ghosts and her love of Widow Witch roof angels. Besides, she'd rather go out with Fetu Lemalu. When she started to open Tutti's door, she discovered that Carlo had wedged a baggie with a fat joint in it under the handle. Rather presumptuous. She climbed inside, tossed the baggie into the trash, and resumed practicing the middle section of the Fantasie on the tabletop.

Hours later, she put her hands in her lap and smiled. *Wow. I've memorized more than half of this.* She pulled on her peacoat and dashed down to the Palace Café to call Headmistress. Because *tempus fugit.*

"It's a slow night," Shella said as Morgen loped across the dining room. "We just ate leftovers and chowder. If you're hungry, there're sandwiches in the fridge."

"Thanks. Maybe later, and hello everybody. I need to use the phone." She flopped on a barstool and dialed, but luckily, the call went to voicemail. "This is Morgen. Since I'm committed to perform the Fantasie fundraiser in forty-two days, I've found a place to practice in seclusion away from distractions and interference. Please inform Andras Bacon and respect my request for complete privacy."

She bit her lip. Headmistress had a right to know. "Also, I want you to know that you'll be receiving my letter of resignation. As much as I've enjoyed teaching at River Bridge, I've decided to accept a position at NCU." Because she needed to reframe her life and unlock her music and her heart. Because she wanted to work in a college community that celebrated diversity and growth, one that wouldn't shame girls like Violet or manipulate women like *her*. Because she'd earned Dr. Byrd's repertoire and *that* concert hall. Unsure if she'd ended the call, she said, "Okay, goodbye." She dialed Water Street Eldercare, and after a pleasant exchange with Pauline, she heard Gram's voice and nearly wept. "Hi. I think about you all the time. Are you over your cold?"

"Pauline wants to call the fire brigade every time someone sneezes." Gram sounded tired and far away. "I'm just dandy, darling. You?"

"I'm practicing hard for the December concert, I've met some nice individuals, I've accepted a teaching job at the U starting in February so I'll be closer to you, and I love Mom's bus. Remember Grandpa Scott's quote in Mom's score? I think he meant that music is actually a facet of love. I like that."

She heard Gram gather her breath. "Ultimately love is our raison d'être. Your mother was just beginning to understand, before she got hurt, that no matter how dark life gets, love perseveres. I'm happy to report she's doing better. Now tell me about your new boyfriend. He sounds exotic."

"*Mom's* doing better? What new boyfriend?" Morgen blushed.

Pauline's muffled voice interrupted in the background.

"Oh, poop, it's time for potty, medication, and a nap even though I just ate breakfast. Darling, often a leap of faith takes the scenic route. Be brave and strong." The line went dead.

"Gram? Hello?" Morgen felt a chill and redialed, but the line was busy. She turned around and was surprised to see Fetu and the Fish Campers watching her.

"Clam tide tonight and no rain," John said. "I'm going."

"I'll pass," Angelo said. "Call me when they're cleaned and fried in butter." He shoved his chair under the table. "Anyway, I have to see a man about a boat."

Morgen hung up the phone. Why did he keep seeing a man about a boat? He already had one.

"Razor clams? Count me in." Shella dried her hands on a dishtowel.

Morgen slid off the barstool. "I don't have a license, but I'd like to come along if I don't have to clean them."

"This is new to me, John," Fetu said. "Will you explain what you're doing?"

"Sure as the tide, son. I'll teach you how to read the beach," John said, carrying his chowder bowl to the sink.

"Oh, what the hell, give me fifteen minutes," Angelo said. "Dress warm, folks, and bring a flashlight if you have one."

"Morgen," Shella said, "will you go up and get my raincoat? It's on a hook behind the door."

"Of course and I want to get my camera, so don't leave without me."

Morgen raced up the stairs and into Shella's attic bedroom. Dwindling orange sunlight reached between the flowery curtains and warmed a wicker chair. She remembered looking up at that window when she arrived eleven days earlier. So incredibly much had happened since. *Tempus fugit.* A colorful quilted bedspread covered the double bed. A postcard print of Van Gogh's *Starry Night* was thumb-tacked to an otherwise bare wall next to the wrought iron headboard. She straightened the few items on the dresser and picked up a gold pocket watch with the name Seamus Maloney engraved on the back. She polished it with her sweatshirt and put it back.

MORGEN WATCHED ANGELO DIVIDE UP SHOVELS, BUCKETS, clam tubes, and lanterns just as the sun began its descent. "Why didn't you invite Carlo too? He's nice and has a remark-able voice. He even asked me to go to a concert."

"Nice as a dog fart," Angelo mumbled. "Carlo may be my cousin but he's not your friend, got it? Repeat after me: he's a sick bastard, because his brains are fried."

"Okay, that's graphic. What do you suggest I tell him?"

"Women usually reject me by telling me they have cramps." He unzipped a gym bag and handed Fetu a *By-the-Wind Sailor* hooded sweatshirt. "It's an extra if you want it, especially since you foolishly forgot to bring a jacket."

"Thanks." Fetu pulled the shirt on over his head.

A Coast Guard helicopter flew by, and Angelo waved.

"Do you know them?" Morgen asked.

"Coast Guard's a good bunch of guys, and a big old helicopter carried me, half-butchered, out of Vietnam." He sniffed. "Now why don't you sweet ladies run along and play. We virile men can manage all this cumbersome clamming equipment in spite of our unfortunate war wounds."

Salty Dog nodded and broke into a run toward the drift logs beach. John knelt to light the lanterns, handed one to Morgen, and she and Shella walked on ahead.

Shella glanced back over her shoulder. "I think Fetu has a crush on you. He watches you all the time."

Morgen flushed. "All I know is that I love what he does to his vowels and phrasing."

"Maybe you should try flirting with him instead of with Angelo."

"What? I don't flirt with Angelo. I'm just trying to get along with everybody, but I have difficulty socializing in general, so if I did or said something inappropriate, I'm embarrassed and sorry."

"No, I'm sorry for being snippy. Being pregnant is stressing me out." Shella pouted. "I like you, but you're skinny, and I'm fat."

"You're not fat, you're pregnant. It's temporary, and you're still pretty, okay?"

The others caught up. Shella joined them, but Morgen stopped short and stared at a massive and oddly familiar drift log, one she hadn't noticed when she and Shella—

"What a crowd," Fetu said.

She turned and looked at the beach. The tide had retreated, exposing acres of fresh wet sand, and dozens of clammers were already at work, walking, kneeling, and digging. Waves that once begged for attention now broke a hundred yards farther out. Tiny sandpipers ran in circles, visiting and poking the sand in search of food. Children shone flashlights at each other and played chase. Gulls watched and laughed to themselves.

The Fish Campers, which included Morgen, gathered around while John pointed out tracks left by various birds, crabs, and snails. "See that dimple? Razor clam." He tapped the wet beach with his boot toe, the clam spurted some water, and he began to dig.

Morgen stepped back to take pictures while in the distance lanterns twinkled along the shore like freshly bathed stars.

THE MOON ROSE, AND FAMILIAR CONSTELLATIONS BLAZED above the drift logs. Morgen watched the clamming activity in awe, and before long, John and Angelo had caught their limit. John gathered some driftwood, lit a bonfire, and picked up his bucket. "I'll clean the clams." He took a lantern and headed back to Fish Camp.

"Here we are, the Fish Camp singles club," Fetu said while feeding the flames with pieces of driftwood.

"I brought everybody a present." Angelo reached into his gym bag and pulled out three navy-blue knit beanies. "Now you can all look like me."

Morgen and Shella pulled theirs on, and Fetu slipped his over the Trailer Trash cap.

"Great. Hold that pose." Morgen balanced her camera on another drift log and set the timer. Everyone smiled, and Salty Dog wagged his tail. When the flash faded away, she retrieved her camera, pocketed a little sand for the sugar bowl, and sat on the beach beside Fetu. Angelo squeezed himself between her and Shella and stretched out his bad leg.

While they visited, wooly, dank fog crept ashore and surrounded them, the temperature dropped, and frogs croaked from their hiding places in the dune grass. Salty Dog perked up his ears and held his breath.

Morgen crossed her fingers. *Please don't break the spell.*

"Let's share secrets," Shella said. "You know, something about yourself that you've never told anyone. Like, I want to get my GED and go to massage school." She looked at her hands. "I've been told I'm a natural, probably from kneading all that sourdough, and people always feel better when I'm done with them. Angelo, it's your turn."

"Sure, Shella Bella, but you can't get a hit until you start swinging the bat, so you better get going on that before you miss the proverbial boat." He cleared his throat. "My secret is I hate clowns and monkeys. Always did. My old man knew that but still invited seven clowns with monkeys to entertain at my seventh birthday party, which messed me up for a long time. Anyway, that's my secret. I hate clowns and monkeys. Your turn, Morgen Marín."

"Hard to top clowns and monkeys." She glanced at Fetu. Was he thinking about his brother George, cruelly nicknamed Bozo the Clown? She considered the secrets she could share: she wanted to find purpose in her offbeat instincts, find her mother's urn, outfox Andras, and discover who her biological father was—

"We're waiting with bated breath."

"Okay. Sometimes when I'm alone, I dance to certain rock and roll classics."

"Sung by whom?" Fetu held his hands toward the fire.

She blushed. "Mostly Fleetwood Mac."

He grinned. "When I was a child, I wanted to be a rock star. Learned a little guitar. Played a few gigs. I've thought about buying another guitar to play while I'm traveling. I did bring along my favorite pick though." He pulled it out of his pocket and held it in the firelight.

"May I look at that?" Morgen's fingers twitched.

Fetu handed it to her, and she rubbed it between her fingers until it warmed. "A pick is also called a plectrum, even on a harpsichord."

"You can keep it if you want. Save it for when you get that mandolin—"

Angelo cleared his throat. "I suppose you want to know another secret about me. I took tap lessons when I was a kid. Is that what you want to hear? The dirt?" He got up, did a soft-shoe routine on the sand, and everyone laughed and applauded. "There's more. I took accordion lessons too. Could've been a song and dance man, just like Dean Martin. So there." He took a shaker of garlic powder from his pocket and tossed a handful of granules into the flames. "You never can have too much garlic." The particles exploded with fragrance and rose like crushed gold shards into the black sky. "Now enough of these secrets." He eased himself down.

"Party pooper," Shella sighed. She gestured toward the water. "Did you know that there used to be one huge super-continent and one ocean? Imagine what it must have been like when it split apart."

"It didn't happen all at once like Atlantis," Angelo said.

"You mentioned Atlantis before," Morgen said. "Is that because you like the old song by Donovan?"

"More than that. According to the great Vincenzo Bordacelli, it's the land of my ancestors."

Morgen frowned. "If it sank and all the inhabitants perished, how could you be a descendent?"

Angelo laughed. "Because my people were out fishing that day, what do you think? Hail, Atlantis." He nudged her shoulder. "That was a joke."

"Oh." She sat on her hands to keep them from flapping. "That's rather disappointing."

"You guys are fooling around and not taking me seriously." Shella had tears in her eyes.

"I'm sorry," Morgen said, flicking sand off her fingers, "but I take everything literally. It's how my brain—"

Fetu squeezed her hand before looking at Shella. "We're listening."

Shella wiped her nose and took several deep breaths. "I'm scared of being a mom. I'm scared that something will be wrong with the baby or that I'll drop it. I want it to be happy, but I'm afraid it won't like me. I never even babysat. Sometimes people aren't nice to little kids. They hurt them and make fun of them." She gazed at the fire. "How do you protect a child from this world?"

Evidently, you can't. Morgen swallowed a sob. "I honestly believe that you and this baby will love each other *fiercely* and forever. No matter what happens, you'll always have that love."

Fetu took her hand again. She looked at him and couldn't read the expression in his eyes, but the word *compassion* came to mind. She waited five seconds before pulling her hand away.

"Oh, Shella Bella." Angelo sniffled. "Fish Camp is your home now and forever if that's what you want, and everybody loves you, and they're going to love your kid too."

"Everybody?" She sniffed.

"Yes, everybody, and now I'm getting all emotional here, but since you insist we spill our guts and get our miseries off our chests, once I took a boat through the Narrows when I was blind drunk. Bad idea. Too much liquor makes me piss constantly and aggravates my vertigo, which can be deadly in heavy seas. I timed the tide wrong. Pushed against it, full throttle, went nowhere, and if I'd tried to turn the boat around, we would have capsized for sure. The weather and water got rougher, and it was raining so damn hard you could hardly catch your breath. I desperately needed to pee *again*, so I grabbed an empty coffee can, let go of the wheel just for a second, the damn boat lurched, and one of my deckhands lost his balance and fell overboard." His voice wavered, and he rubbed his face. "Left a young wife and a new baby."

"Does it help you to talk about it?" Fetu sifted sand through his fingers.

"I guess. Better than talking to a bored priest." Angelo shrugged. "Truth be told, Mama Gianna wanted me to go to the seminary."

"Motherhood seems to be a theme tonight." Fetu shook his head. "Sometimes I can't remember what my mum looked like. All I had was my father. He was a chain-smoker, and there was always cigarette ash everywhere, even in our food. One night, he was angry about something, knocked me down, and I started crying, so he took his lit cigarette and flicked ashes and embers into my mouth." His jaw muscle twitched. "Ironic, isn't it? Now I'm here with *his* ashes."

Oh Fetu. Tears filled Morgen's eyes. She sniffled, corrected her posture, and took a deep breath. "I've always been afraid to talk about *anything* to anybody, but it's time to let the jetty cat out of the bag." She looked at Angelo. "That last part is supposed to be a joke."

He nodded and smiled at her.

"Right, okay. Motherhood. Even loving mothers never know everything about their daughters." She laced her fingers together so tightly that her knuckles cracked while the foghorn thrummed a warning across the dark water. "I had a lengthy affair with my professor, Andras Bacon, because I believed I had no other choice. He's seventeen years and seventeen days older than me and had been my master piano teacher and an odd kind of father figure since I was thirteen and a half. When I was fifteen, he left a photograph in the studio for me to find. It was a side view of a man and woman having sex on a piano bench. Some would call it art, others porn, but it was clearly an inappropriate image for a child to see." She vigorously petted Salty Dog, who had curled up at her feet. "Now, fast-forward ten years. He decided that we should resurrect the concerto that I played in college in an arrangement for two pianos, which he never would have been capable of playing. I went to his studio for a rehearsal and found a bunch of mirrors set up, a camera on a tripod, and him in his tux." She slammed her fists against her forehead, and Fetu grabbed her wrists to restrain her. "He wanted to replicate the scene depicted in that photograph. He ordered me to undress, and I did and sat astride him, impaled for lack of a better word, with my fingers on the keys. I drew a blank and couldn't play, so he got mad, grabbed the keyboard lid, and slammed it on my hands. Yanking himself out from between my legs, he sat down with his bare derrière on the lid and my hands crushed inside. It was so painful that I couldn't utter a sound, and he stared into my eyes the whole time." She pulled her hands away from Fetu and shoved them inside her sweatshirt pocket. "How do you protect a child?" she whispered to Shella. "Or yourself for that matter? I guess you believe in love and wisely choose the individuals you invite into your world."

"I'll drink to that," Angelo mumbled. "God, I need a—"

"No, you don't," Shella said. "If anything, you need a bowl of cioppino to warm you up." She tried to stand but couldn't get her feet under her.

"Hey, before we go," Fetu said, "I just found these in the sand." He held five snail shells in his palm. "I hope they can remind each of us to be smart like a hermit crab and carefully choose our best world." Everybody picked one. "The fifth shell is for the baby."

"Hermit crabs?" After Morgen put the shell in her pocket, she wiggled her fingers in Fetu's face like hermit crab pincers.

A sneaker wave engulfed the drift logs and drowned the bonfire embers. Salty Dog yipped and scrambled to his feet as Angelo lifted Shella to her feet, grabbed his bag, and yelled, "Man the lifeboats! Women and children first!"

Morgen laughed and wept with relief when Fetu pulled her onto that massive and oddly familiar drift log.

Wednesday, October 29, 2003

At two in the morning, Morgen crawled out from under Fräu Heinrich's eiderdown. She couldn't sleep because she kept seeing that drift log in her mind's eye. She switched on the dome light, opened her attaché case, and rummaged around until she found one of the pictures from the paisley hatbox. "That's it," she whispered. She grabbed her flashlight, camera, and shoelace key and slipped out into the night.

No one was around, not even a jetty cat. She let herself into the Palace Café and tiptoed up to the mantelpiece. "Hi, Lydia," she whispered. "It's just me."

She turned on the flashlight and positioned it on one of the tables. With the portrait illuminated, she was able to take it off the wall and turn it over but was disappointed to find that there wasn't an inscription on the back. She rehung it, rubbed her temples to sharpen her focus, and held the snapshot from the hatbox beside Lydia's photograph. In one, her mother sat on that massive and oddly familiar drift log, staring into the camera lens with an enigmatic expression. Toddler Morgen, in a shiny swimsuit, stood beside her on the log and gazed out to sea through hands cupped binocular-style around her eyes. In the other, Lydia Cooper posed on the same log, petting a cat curled up on her lap, and toddler Morgen, wearing the same shiny, blue swimsuit, knelt at her feet. Morgen's eyes darted from one to the other, *allegro* ($\quarternote$ = 130, a quick and bright tempo). Some thirty years ago during a lovely day at the beach, two remarkable friends had taken each other's picture. She smiled and took a photo of the portrait.

"Good night, Lydia," she whispered, turning off her flashlight. She headed to the door but froze when she smelled cigarette smoke. *Oh crap.* She ducked behind the counter. Had she locked the entry door from the inside? Did Carlo have a key?

He had a flashlight, because she could see ropes of light slither over the threshold like hungry eels. He tried the doorknob, but she'd locked it. She exhaled and waited. Angelo had said that Carlo was a sick bastard and his brains were fried, which was an off-putting image, but she was inclined to trust Angelo as a friend and demote Carlo to the "never be alone with him again" delineation along with Andras.

"Fucking bitch-ghost, you're dead," Carlo shouted through the door. "Leave me alone, or I'll have the pastor do an exorcism."

She heard Carlo stomp down the boardwalk and waited, sipping cold coffee and counting to something astronomical before slipping out of the Palace and sneaking back to Tutti.

SHE WAS DEEP INTO PRACTICING UNDER THE LIMELIGHT bulb when Doris hopped off the stack of music and bumped the cell phone in her direction.

"Go back to sleep, sweet kitty. I've just about got this, because I have reframed my attitude about this composition, and I am brave and strong."

Hours later, she opened Fräu Heinrich's curtains and saw Fetu headed her way. She still wore Gram's flannel nightgown and hadn't combed her hair or brushed her teeth, but she opened the cargo door after he knocked. "Sorry, I haven't reported to hair and makeup yet." She turned on her CD player.

"No worries. You look lovely." Fetu kicked off his shoes and sat. "Your bus is cute and suits you. Arty, very cool, good energy. Imagine the tales it would tell if it could talk."

"Right. Just imagine. FYI, her name is Tutti, which is a musical term that indicates when all musicians are to perform together, usually after a solo passage. I've always been a soloist in more ways than one but always loved harmony. I'm babbling because I drank cold coffee in the middle of the night, and evidently, it was caffeinated." She bobbed her head to the music. "Like I started to say at the bonfire, I used to dress up like Stevie Nicks and dance with my mom around the house, harmonizing to Fleetwood Mac, and guess what? Lindsey Buckingham was my first crush. Want some?" She offered trio mix to Fetu.

"Thanks." He popped a handful into his mouth. "The talented Mr. Buckingham was my second hero," he said while he chewed. "Very wild and creative guitarist."

"Speaking of wild." Her shoulders slumped, "About last night? I've never talked about any of that before, and once I started, I couldn't stop. And about your father burning you—"

"It was a cathartic evening for all of us. Must have been those magic drift logs, but you retreated into your shell again." He pulled his hermit crab shell out of a pocket and rolled it between his fingers like a coin.

Morgen clenched her fists. "In grad school, Andras became my manager as well as my teacher and wanted me on birth control so my performance career wouldn't be interrupted. But the pill made me sick, my body rejected devices, and he refused to use condoms, so on his recommendation, blindly obedient me had my fallopian tubes 'tied.' And as my fricking manager, he made me sign a consent form that I hadn't read. He drove me to a clinic, paid for the procedure, and drove me back to my apartment. I thought that someday I could simply untie them like shoelaces. I didn't realize they had been cauterized and that the effects were permanent." She gnawed a cuticle until it bled. "He and I continued on for another year until my world came crashing down in the guise of that keyboard lid. I ruin everything because I rarely think about the consequences of my actions. My brain isn't wired that way."

"In your defense, he'd ruined quite a bit before your poor hands were crushed. At some point, we're all collateral damage." He flipped the shell into the air, caught it, and smiled. "Heads," he said. "We both win." He gestured at her mother's copy of the concerto. "Is this the piece you talked about last night?"

"Yes. The composition is musically perfect, although my favorite part was torn out of this copy." She flipped through the pages. "See how the rhythm here imitates this other part? And look, the meters keep changing, and when you hit this measure in 3/8 time, it's like a sudden freefall." She turned the page. "This part's jazzy, then immediately tender, and here the piano provides an intricate texture behind the other instruments. After I memorized the first movement, my teacher—" She blushed.

"The infamous Andras Bacon?"

She nodded. "He made me play the right-hand part at tempo on the grand while he played the left on a second piano, then we'd switch, and I played the left-hand part against his right. It bent my brain. Next he had me play certain phrases and, at the same time, sing one of the instrumental parts. I thought he was overchallenging me until he explained that although the piano is the primary solo instrument, it's only one voice among many, and I needed to understand where I fit in."

"That part seems reasonable. Now, in one sentence, tell me what this music means to you."

"It's a portrait of my family." She bit her lip. "Rather impulsive answer—"

Shouts erupted from the docks. She grabbed the opera glasses and peered through the windshield. "There are tools and boat pieces all over the place plus Angelo, Joe, John, and Carlo. Do you want to go help them?"

"I guess I should since Angelo offered to take out Dad's ashes."

"Okay. Thank you for visiting me." She studied his face. "You're always welcome here."

Morgen saw a closed sign hanging in a window, and the door to the Palace Café was locked. Shella and Mia must have taken a break, so she had to run back to Tutti to get the shoelace key and a bag of trio mix. Finally, she was able to access her voicemail. "Nancy Collier told me you are in seclusion and want complete privacy. What kind of a sophomoric stunt is this? Chérie, cut the diva crap, and call me."

Morgen listened to her second message. "Headmistress Collier here. Congratulations on your new job at the university. You'll be deeply missed at River Bridge, but I'm very proud of your accomplishments. I will personally oversee the packing of your personal items and hold them as long as necessary. I phoned Rylan Byrd, and we agreed that you are the perfect candidate. A letter of resignation isn't necessary, and I would like to keep you listed in our directory as emerita. I look forward to visiting with you over coffee after your December performance."

Over coffee? She replayed the message. *Keep me in the directory? No, sorry, you may NOT continue to use me to recruit students.* She slipped off the barstool. Nothing like a solitary walk on the beach to decompress.

She followed two sets of bare footprints in the sand: the smaller ones presumably belonging to Mia and the deeper ones to Shella. Before reaching the drift logs, she came across Mia sitting on a dune, watching Joe surf. Mia turned, smiled, and beckoned her.

Morgen settled into the sand, comforted by Mia's companionship and the absence of expectations. A squadron of pelicans flew single file through thin midday fog looking like musical notes in a chromatic scale. "It's like they're on their morning commute deep in troughs between walls of water billions of years old." She caught Mia's eye, pointed at herself, and wrote "06-21-69" in the sand.

Mia laughed and wrote, "27-11-75."

"Wow. Okay, you'll be twenty-eight in thirty days. Want some?"

Mia took a handful of trio mix. "Gracias." Her voice was airy and sweet.

"*Yo* surf *muy bien.*" Morgen pointed at Joe and then at herself. "I learned right here at this beach." She pulled her dictionary out of her back pocket. "*Aprendí aquí.*"

Mia nodded and smiled, arms waving, miming riding on a board.

"I rarely talk about this, but I have a form of autism called Asperger's syndrome, and the reason I'm bringing it up is because you and Joe seem so happy together, and I'm envious." She flipped though the dictionary. "*Envidioso. Usted y Joe.*"

Mia said several sentences in Spanish.

"Whereas *I* have always struggled with relationships. In fact, I've only had one partner in my whole life, although it was never a love affair or *amorío.* His name is Andras, and he became my teacher when I was a little girl. Pretty sick, huh?"

Mia replied in Spanish while she sorted trio mix in her palm.

"That's called *mezcla trio* and I sort it too because sorting things helps me think. But because of Andras, I've always struggled with shame and confusion, lousy self-esteem, and sexual dysfunction, but I think I'm finally getting a second chance. I think I'm attracted to Fetu."

"Fetu?" Mia raised her perfect eyebrows. She said quite a bit in Spanish and then took Morgen's dictionary. "Nice," she read. "Handsome. Intelligent. He. Love. You." She grinned. "Sexy."

"Oh, do you think so?" Morgen grabbed the dictionary. "*De verdad piensas eso*? See, I had to pass proficiency in German and French but not Spanish, which irritates me on a practical level, although I'm highly motivated now because of you. I've always had a communication deficit, even with English speakers, and wonder why we have to have so many languages on this planet when relationships are already difficult to navigate." She put the dictionary on the sand between them. "Mia, *usted mi amiga*, do you think—?"

Somebody sneezed violently in the distance, possibly from the drift logs beach. Morgen and Mia looked at each other. Then they heard a scream.

"Oh, crap, is that Shella?"

They leaped to their feet and began to run, sand flying from their heels. Startled, great flocks of gulls and tiny sandpipers took flight. They found Shella lying in a heap on top of her yellow kite, her pink overalls soaked and her chest heaving.

"I saw you guys but was afraid you wouldn't see me." Tears poured down her cheeks, and she groaned and grabbed her belly.

"We sure *heard* you." Morgen mimed driving a car, and Mia took off running back toward Fish Camp. "You're probably going into—"

"I went for a walk, because I thought I'd barf if I cooked breakfast. My stomach was squeezing hard all night, the bed was wet." She groaned and grabbed her belly again. "Shit!"

"*Shh*, baby can hear you."

"Oh God, it's coming, I can't help it. I want to push!"

Oh dear Lord. Mom, help me help her. Morgen wrestled Shella out of her stained, wet overalls. "My mom was a midwife. I've attended six births although never outdoors, but we don't have a choice now, do we? There, good, let's see, wow, okay, this baby is definitely crowning, and you're doing great, Shella, gentle pushes, keep going, you are so brave, so strong, just a little bit more…" Shella cried out, so did the baby, and Morgen felt her own tears rise. "Here comes your beautiful new baby at last!

"Good thing you had kite string and a pocketknife." Morgen pulled off her sweatshirt and draped it over Shella and her baby. "She's absolutely gorgeous albeit a little sandy."

Shella giggled through her tears. "No, silly, not Sandy. I'm naming her Pearl. Apropos, don't you think, a beautiful gift found on the beach? It was almost like my mom said. A big old contraction knocked me down, I had a giant sneeze, and I started to deliver. But it hurt real bad and was more violent and fast than I expected." She opened her top, and Pearl nuzzled her breast and began to nurse. "I'm so glad you're here. Sorry, we're a big sloppy stinky mess."

"Don't worry about it." She helped Shella slip her legs into her overalls. "Sorry, I have to massage your tummy to help your uterus contract. By the way, the medical term for the sloppy mess is *placenta*, and the one for Pearl's first cry is *vagitus*. I know because of my mom."

"And because you're a schoolteacher. Thanks for…" Shella's face went white, and she closed her eyes. "I'm freezing cold and kind of woozy."

"Keep your eyes open and stay awake." Morgen kept rubbing. "They'll be here any minute to get us." She studied Pearl, who gazed back at her with clear, blue-gray eyes, unafraid and snug in her mother's arms. A tangle of damp, dark curls covered her head like a little cloche hat. Her skin was rosy and flawless, and her toes and fingers plump and perfect. Tears filled Morgen's eyes again. "How do you do, baby Pearl?" she whispered, pocketing a pinch of sand. "Come on, Shella Bella, you need to stay awake."

The wind calmed, and they rested and waited together. Mewling gulls swooped, and tiny sandpipers chased away the tide. A pelican landed nearby, eyes blazing in its long, antediluvian face, and etched lacy messages into the sand. Morgen continued massaging Shella's stomach with her left hand but reached out and flapped her right hand in reply.

Thursday, October 30, 2003

MORGEN SPREAD NEWSPAPERS ON SHELLA'S BEDROOM floor and organized the poster paints and brushes she'd found in the glass door closet. She sat back on her heels, touched the silver necklace around her neck, and turned her imagination loose on the bare walls. As fanciful images flowed like wet paint in her mind's eye, she picked up a brush and began to work.

"What'd you do with the Kiwi?" Angelo sat in the wicker chair and watched her.

"He went shopping in Aberdeen. You know, diapers and baby gifts." She changed colors. "I can't believe you drove to the hospital without telling anyone. Do you have a driver's license?"

"Hey, I kept the truck between the buoys. Green going, red right returning. Remember? Anyway, someone had to give a teddy bear to Pearl and flowers to Shella. Although I must complain, the parking lot was a mile away, and my bum knee is still in a bad mood."

She continued painting. "Do you know who Pearl's father is?" She heard the wicker chair creak behind her.

"She never said. Maybe she was pregnant when she got here, but I wouldn't know."

She rinsed her brush and climbed up on a step stool. "Amazing what you can do with six colors."

"You're a pretty good painter, Morgen Marín. Pearl's going to love this."

"Thanks." She worked on the pelican's face. Not a pelican-priest's face, rather a cheerful pelican. "Tell me about my mom being your nurse."

Angelo coughed, and the wicker chair scraped on the floor. "I was being treated for complications from my war wounds. I'll spare you the gory details, but she was real nice, gentle, not squeamish. She even remembered me, you know, from before."

Morgen continued painting the sky. It had to be a pretty and happy sky, a daytime sky but with stars.

"Yeah, we had a real good talk about Vietnam, about her protesting the war and me fighting in it." He blew his nose. "Great lady. There's more, but I can only handle so much. Want a beer? I'm buying."

"Maybe later, okay?"

"Suit yourself."

She heard him thud down the stairs. *Maybe you're rather great yourself.*

Three hours later, the mural extended from Shella's postcard print of Van Gogh's *Starry Night*, up the walls, and across the ceiling with similar swirls of color and design. Gray whales, salmon, and by-the-wind sailor jellies swam in spiraling waves. Grinning hermit crabs played castanets as they scuttled among the drift logs. Gulls, herons, and pelicans performed aerial acrobatics on puffy, violet clouds across powder-blue skies. The whale-shaped weathervane danced with a flock of pink flamingoes on the red roof of a quirky, stylized Jetty Cat Palace Café, a garland of Mia's red roses framed Shella's upstairs window, and Salty Dog and the jetty cats jauntily posed on hind feet along the boardwalk. In the upper north corner of the room, she'd painted the North Star and Big Dipper. Opposite, in the south corner, she'd added Fetu's Southern Cross.

"Welcome to your world, baby Pearl," she whispered. "Welcome home."

Friday, October 31, 2003

Morgen spent an hour helping Mia clean and decorate the Palace Café. She returned to Tutti and, with time to spare before the baby shower, sat at the tabletop and surprised herself by playing the entire Fantasie. "Well, crap, that wasn't so bad. All I have to do now is memorize it," she said to her mother's conch shell. Like shining a flashlight on a ghost under the bed. In reality, the Fantasie was no more threatening than a dust bunny.

Fetu knocked on the window before opening the cargo door. He climbed in with a box in his arms and an envelope in his hand. "Here's the gift certificate you wanted. Are you ready for the big homecoming?"

"Absolutely. Is that a baby gift?"

"No, I got *you* a present." He looked rather pleased with himself.

"Me?" The word *awkward* came to mind, and her scalp began to prickle. Why would he buy her a present? They'd only known each other for six days. Did he assume they had a relationship? She jumped at the sound of packing tape being ripped off cardboard.

"Surprise!" He opened a leather case and showed her a brand-new mandolin.

"Oh dear Lord, it's beautiful, but you shouldn't have. It's too much, too expensive."

"You're worth it, and you already have my guitar pick or plectrum. Please accept this and promise me and your grandfather that you'll take lessons when you get to the university."

His smile melted her unease. "Okay. For Grandpa Scott." She latched the case. "A long time ago, he wrote a verse that I like:

It's your turn in the great continuum, so take a leap
of faith. Let them hear your story in this music.
No words. Only love."

She shrugged. "Generally speaking, I'm better at music better than words, but thank you. We'd better go." She unplugged the string of lights.

They moved toward the cargo door, got tangled up, and laughed as Angelo leaned in. "How are you dune? Get it? Dune instead of doing? It's a little beach joke, and Happy Halloween. What are you doing in here, Kiwi? Following me again? Now hustle. Shella's going to be home in time for dinner and Pearl too."

"I'm moving as fast as I can." She'd never seen him so giddy.

When she got to the Palace Café, she called to pay her rent and utilities. Her apartment manager said she reported a frazzled man to the police after he inquired about her whereabouts. Based on the description, it could only be Andras, and the words *harassment* and *stalking* came to mind. She considered giving notice but didn't want to get ahead of herself.

As soon as she hung up, the white van pulled up. Everyone scrambled out the entry door and yelled "Surprise" while Shella stepped out of the van with Pearl in her arms, wrapped in a pink blanket. Shella grinned and introduced her driver and a nurse practitioner to the crowd. Fetu gave her a hug and unloaded her things. Doris rolled on her back and swooned. The other cats yowled and offered to help, and Salty Dog danced like a pup.

Inside the Palace Café, the Weather Channel promised "sunshine and mild temperatures." Everybody vied for attention while piling presents on the counter and merrily clipping money with clothespins to a crab pot decorated with hundreds of pink satin ribbons. Joe tended bar, and Mia served crab enchiladas and Mexican wedding cookies.

Angelo stuck a yellow Baby on Board sign in one of the entry windows and pulled Morgen aside to introduce her to an older gentleman dressed in a dark suit and white shirt, bow tie, and polished shoes. "This is Uncle Vic, the lawyer. Gray as a pelican's armpit but a hell of a good man."

"Hello, Morgen." Vic bowed slightly. "Angie's told me all about you, and I'm glad we finally met."

"How do you do?" She offered her best smile. But what on earth was there to tell?

"Let's grab some chow before it's all gone." Angelo steered Vic away.

Morgen stepped back to watch the festivities, and Fetu joined her.

"That's for you, Shella," Carlo announced, pointing to a rocking chair with an enormous pink bow. "I already put the matching dresser upstairs."

"Angelo also buy two crib, one for up the stair and one for *cocina*," Joe said. "Mia buy little *ropa* for Perla."

Mia smiled broadly and dabbed her eyes with a tissue.

"Thank you. I never expected a party." Shella sat down in her new chair and began to rock Pearl. Salty Dog curled up at her feet and crossed his wrists, and Doris settled beside him with her head resting on Angelo's teddy bear.

Carlo sidled over to Morgen. "Can you feel it?" he whispered. "The old lady is floating around."

"You don't need to be afraid of her," she whispered.

"Afraid of whom?" Fetu asked.

"Not important," Morgen said. "It's a long ghost story for another day."

"Is Carlo bothering you?" Angelo walked up, his mouth full of enchiladas. "I swear, Carlo, you're as useful as tits on a squid."

Carlo glowered at him and left in a huff, stomping on Doris's paw. She slunk away and hid under the couch. Angelo tossed a piece of crab in her direction. "Poor old cat."

"He hurt her on purpose for no reason, and she's so sweet," Morgen said. "I think she should be Shella's au purr. Get it? Au pair? Au purr?" She laughed.

"That was pretty good. You're catching on." He turned so that everyone could hear him. "We also ordered an electric dishwasher for you girls." He pulled a navy-blue knit beanie out of his pocket. "This is for Pearl so she can look like a Fish Camper."

"A baby beanie?" Shella's eyes filled with tears as she pulled the cap on Pearl's head.

"Aw, shucks," Angelo said. "Women!"

The crowd drifted away. "What a wonderful party," Shella said, stifling a yawn.

"You have to be exhausted," Morgen said.

"A little, but my doctor said I was hale and hearty and ready to come home. Besides, the nurse practitioner will be out here twice a week for a while. Pretty cool, huh? It's the post-partum care part of my special program. Mia is going to help me full time now too, like take over the prep and do more of the cooking."

"Good plan." Morgen handed her an envelope. "This is a gift certificate for a year of diaper service."

"Oh my gosh, thanks. What a perfect present. For such a tiny little person, she sure can make a mess." She began to unbutton her top. "Now it's time for her supper."

"Come on, Kiwi, party's over. Goodnight, ladies." Angelo headed to the door.

"You can stay. I don't mind," Shella said.

"No, we'd better go. Goodnight." Fetu closed the door behind him, leaving Morgen alone with Shella and Pearl.

"You two are absolutely gorgeous," Morgen said. She remembered Violet as a newborn, as a cute child, as her student and protégée. *Tempus fugit.* "May I take a picture?"

"Yes, please do. She *is* the most beautiful baby in the world."

Pearl grew drowsy, and Morgen helped get Shella and some of the gifts upstairs. As soon as Shella opened the door, the whimsical mural of Fish Camp reached out to welcome her.

"Oh my gosh, it's beautiful. Did you paint this for us?"

"Yes." Morgen blushed. *So that Pearl will grow up believing in love and being careful about who she invites into her magical world.*

Sometime after midnight, Morgen's cell phone rang, which it had never done in Fish Camp. Half asleep, she scrambled out from under Fräu Heinrich's eiderdown and tumbled off the platform bed. She switched on the dome light and cleared her throat. "Hello?"

"Granddaughter? It's Pauline at Water Street Eldercare. I have bad news. Your granny passed away an hour ago. The last thing she said was that she loved you. Doctor said it was heart failure."

"Oh God, please no." Her heart rate spiked to *presto* ($\quad$ = 168), and her vision blurred. "Please not Gram." She collapsed onto the bench seat.

"I'm so sorry." Pauline's voice broke. "Ambulance took Miss Eleanor to the mortuary, and they won't let us see her anymore. I promise to take special care of her precious treasures and put everything in your storage unit."

Morgen began to tingle all over and fought to catch her breath. "Please, no, please tell me—"

"I'm very sorry for your grief. Miss Eleanor was truly a light in this world. You may come see me in a week or so. Her cremation urn will be waiting for you." Pauline hung up.

Morgen sat frozen to the bench seat, swaddled in Gram's flannel nightgown and listening to the rain batter Tutti's roof. "I love you so much," she wept. She buried her face in her hands while words and images flashed like auras behind her eyes: sharing secrets as friends are supposed to do; honoring family treasure; laughing and crying over the messiness of life; sharing how her mother had been a playfully spiritual woman. She gazed at Dashboard Guadalupe as she touched the beads on the silver foremothers necklace. *Continuum, female ancestry, witch-angels.*

She caught the scent of Gram's signature Chanel No. 5 and remembered Carlo's fat joint. Maybe, just maybe, she could catch up with Gram's spirit by using some of her mother's hippie harmonics. She found the joint in the trash, plugged in the hot plate, and used the glowing coil like a lighter. The twisted paper tip ignited, and she inhaled the smoke. "Gram? Mom? Can you hear me?"

As she smoked, her fingers numbed, and she absent-mindedly braided the hair on the right side of her head while singing, "*La cucaracha, la cucaracha, ya no puede caminar.*" She blotted her tears with her flannel sleeve and held her breath. Smoke permeated her offbeat brain. "*Porque no tiene, porque le falta, marihuana que fumar...*"

Soon she discerned secret rhythmic patterns hidden within the drumming raindrops overhead, musical, yes, but also like Morse code, perhaps a cry for help against an assailant. "If you so much as touch my roof angels, I'll cut off your evil nuts." She flung open a compartment and grabbed a knife.

She stumbled barefooted out the cargo door and into the storm, and the wind met her like a slap across the face. "Somebody help us," she screamed, scrambling up to the roof rack. Her knees buckled when a gust of black wind slammed against her. One by one, she rescued the trembling wet roof angels and dropped them down the neck of her sopping flannel nightgown. *Therese, Josette, Eleanor,* and *Charlie*—their names spilled out of her mouth like broken teeth. She stretched out her arms like the wings on the pelican-priest, flapped her feathered fingers, and when a monster touched the nape of her neck, she grabbed its short, hairy finger and severed it with her knife.

A claw loomed from the shadows, clutched her ankle, and dragged her off the roof while hissing *shh, shh, shh* like hot steam escaping. She slashed at the sound with her dagger, but it stole her knife, shoved her back inside Tutti, and slammed the door. *My brain's in a blender, and I'm going to die—*

"What the hell are you doing?" Something caged her in its arms. "Why did you cut off your hair, hair, hair?" A male voice reverberated in Morgen's brain. "Shit, you're smoking *weed*?"

Morgen cried and fought, hitting and kicking, but he covered her mouth with his hot hand like he always did, *shh, shh, shh.* "I'm having a nightmare, my eyes are open, but I can't wake up, I'm spinning, I'm snapping—"

"Morgen, it's Fetu." Evidently, he was rolling her up in Fräu Heinrich's eiderdown, because she was snug as a hermit crab in a—

"Where did you get this shit?"

"It was a present. Oh dear Lord, I can't stop shaking. My sweet Gram and my hippie mom died, and my face was the last thing she saw, and she took it with her, because I was bad." She yanked her arms free of the cocoon.

"*Shh,* you're not bad." Fetu smoothed her hair. "You have a beautiful face, and I'm touching it now." His eyes were flat and black like onyx buttons, and his fingers were gentle and kind.

Morgen mirrored him, exploring his face. "You have Cheshire cat teeth, huge like sugar cubes." She traced his lips with her tongue. "You taste, alphabetically, like cayenne, chocolate, cinnamon, coffee, and smoked paprika." She began to cry. "Pauline just called, my grandmother died, and her body is still warm. I've only smoked marijuana secondhand before. Can you tell?" She cupped her hands over her ears like seashells. "I can't even tolerate caffeine. My heart gets agitated, and my eyebrows itch."

Fetu sniffed the roach. "This is laced with something."

"You can take a hit if you want," Morgen whispered, her eyes wide as pancakes.

"No thanks." He unplugged the hot plate and opened a window. "It's a bad trip, but it'll eventually end."

"No, it'll never end!" she shrieked. "You don't understand. He hurt my mother and groomed me to be his mistress. It wasn't my fault, honest. I was just a kid."

"No, it wasn't your fault."

"It's *always* my fault." She grabbed the knife, and he yanked it out of her hand. "Super-duper-party-pooper." She buried her face in his neck and licked his skin. "Can you do this?" She rolled her tongue. "It's my favorite personal quirk and probably genetic."

"No, sorry, I can't, and you're chilled. You need to get out of this wet gown."

"What?" Morgen's eyes ballooned.

"I'll close my eyes and won't look."

"Oh, sure you won't. I wasn't born yesterday, mister." She watched him as she unwrapped the damp eiderdown and pulled Gram's flannel nightgown over her head. "Why are these wet leaves stuck to my chest?" She picked them off, placed each one on the tabletop, and pulled on her sweats. A torrent of rain startled her, and she looked at the headliner. "Did you know that the Big Dipper is up there even though it's raining? Did you know that after Andras crushed my hands, he left me bleeding and alone in the studio, so I stole his porno picture with my broken fingers so little Violet Bacon would never find it?" She corrected her posture. "Retribution is important. My secret is that I still have that picture in my attaché case."

Fetu smiled at her. "That wasn't your momma's flower-child weed, and in my humble opinion, you shouldn't do drugs."

"Oh, that's a promise, honest, and really, I'm fine now. I just need to sleep, because I feel a headache coming on. You can go, but I'm so hungry. Have you ever had a grilled peanut butter-honey-and-Oreo sandwich?" She opened a compartment door, peered inside, and closed it again. "If this is how my mother felt all the time, it sure explains a lot."

"I'm going to stay with you for a while, okay?"

"Maybe, okay, but don't tell anyone anything." She climbed up on the platform bed and began to cry again. "Poor Gram."

Over and over Fetu whispered, "*Kia ora*, you're fine now, it's safe to go to sleep. I love you, and I'm going to stay with you." She floated, dozed, slept, wakened with a start, and dozed off again as he repeated his kind words. *Kia ora, you're fine now, it's safe to go to sleep. I love you, and I'm going to stay with you.*

There was a knock on the door followed by Fetu's muffled conversation with Carlo. Before first light, Fetu whispered, "I'm going to go now lest your reputation be tarnished. I'm sorry about your grandmother. Go back to sleep."

After he left, she took a pair of scissors out of a compartment and, without a mirror, cut her hair until she'd evened it out rather nicely. She looked at the twinkling stars on the headliner. "Goodnight, roof angels. Goodnight, Gram."

7.

Saturday, November 1, 2003

When Morgen finally got up at ten, she dressed and pulled on her navy-blue knit beanie, heading to the bathhouse to hang up her nightgown to dry and then to the Palace Café for something to eat. She found Angelo standing on the boardwalk holding his gym bag and conversing with a huge brown pelican.

"Why the long face?" he said to the bird. "Got troubles on your mind?" The pelican took flight when she approached. "It's about time you got up, Morgen Marín." He dumped a ball, bat, and glove out of his bag. "We're going to do warm-ups for fifteen minutes or so and then go eat." Salty Dog barked in agreement.

She rubbed her aching forehead. "I've never played baseball, because I can't risk hurting my hands."

"For Chrissake, this is a softball. I'm not going to hurt you. Just easy throws, I promise." He limped thirty feet away, turned to face her, and hollered, "Play ball! Here it comes, you ready? Move your feet, and use both hands."

Morgen closed her eyes, reached out with stiff arms, and caught the ball.

"Great," Angelo cheered. "Now throw it back to me."

The ball floated back and forth between them seven times before Angelo said, "You got a good eye, strong arms, and quick thinking. I'm recruiting you for second base."

Fetu jogged down the hill and joined them.

"Glad you showed up, Kiwi, because Morgen Marín needs some batting practice. I'll pitch, you can catch, and Salty and the pelican will shag balls." He swatted Fetu on the derrière as he trotted by. "Now hustle. You're no Johnny Bench, but with a little coaching, you could be reasonably mediocre." The jetty cats strolled to their positions in the outfield. "Here's the deal. It's the bottom of the ninth, bases are loaded, two out, and we're down one run. You're up, and the count is three and two. Got the picture?"

"But I've never—"

"No problem. Weight on your back foot. Keep your back shoulder up. Eye on the ball. Here it comes."

Morgen bit her lip and swung and, with a crack of the bat, launched the softball into the marina. "Well, that's baseball." Angelo shrugged. "Or, truth be told, my only softball." He collected his gear. "Let's eat."

"Wait." She corrected her posture. "Wasn't that a walk-off grand slam?"

"That was rather fun," she said while the three of them entered the Palace Café.

"You were lucky Jim the Harbor Seal wasn't paying attention." Angelo caught the screen door before it slammed. "He catches fly balls better than he catches fish."

"Good morning, Shella," Fetu said. "What smells so good in here?"

"Joe and Mia are doing most of the cooking while I get to sit here and make my special kiwi lime sauce for tonight's halibut. Want to taste? It's good enough to drink." Shella licked the spoon.

Fetu blew a kiss at Pearl in her crib. "*Kia ora*, baby Pearl." He poured three mugs of coffee and gave one to Angelo and one to Morgen. "No worries. It's decaf."

Shella continued stirring the sauce. "Did you know a halibut begins life with eyes on either side of its head like most fish? Then one eye migrates over near the other one, and it lies down to become a flat fish. Just thinking about it gives me a headache."

Fetu took his coffee and headed to the door. "I'm doing laundry this afternoon. Later."

"Well, 'bye." Morgen's shoulders slumped, and she pulled off her knit beanie.

Shella squealed. "Oh my gosh, what happened to your hair?"

"Right. Surprise!" Morgen faked a glamorous pose. "I needed a new look, and you inspired me with your cute, perky hairdo."

Shella stared at her. "I did *not* inspire that." She patted Pearl's back. "We're going upstairs to change our diaper."

"*Me gusta*," Mia said from the kitchen, pointing at Morgen's hair.

Angelo studied Morgen before passing judgment. "You look like a fancy, modern college professor to me. Now sit down and keep me company, Morgen Marín."

She poured herself a fresh mug of decaf, topped off Angelo's mug, and sat at the table across from him.

"I noticed that you closed your eyes. Here's a tip from a seasoned catcher. In baseball, you can't flinch. Keep your eyes open, and see everything happening around you. Next, you need to learn how to care for your baseball glove. Watch." He took a can of shaving cream out of his bag, squirted some onto a soft rag, and worked it into the leather. "Important to take care of your gear."

As she sipped her decaf, tears rolled down her face.

"You paying attention?" He looked at her. "What? Don't have a glove? Hell, I'll buy one for you."

She shook her head and began to cry.

"What'd I do?"

"My grandmother died last night. She was the sweetest, smartest woman in the whole wide world, just like my mom was, and I'll never see either one of them again." She wiped her tears with the back of her hand.

"Oh, Morgen Marín, you have my deepest sympathy." He pulled off his Reds ball cap. "You know, their legacies will live on in you, because *you're* the sweetest and smartest young woman in the world. Here, dry your tears, and your nose is running." He handed her his handkerchief. "Speaking of your mother, you know how it's nice to have something to remind you of an important person you lost? I want you to have this."

He took the tiny purse that had hung in his stateroom out of his pocket and handed it to her.

Morgen let it rest in her palm: faded green brocade with silver threads and a silver clasp. "Why?"

He stared at the purse while he sipped his coffee. "Back in the day, I helped your mom. Later, she became my nurse when my world was going to hell. My guts weren't healing right, and I'd given up on life." His eyes reddened. "You know what your mother did? She reached into her pocket and handed me a penny. 'Now you're worth something, now you've got a future,' she said." He suppressed a sob. "God, I get so emotional."

Morgen opened the purse and found a shiny copper penny dated 1972.

"Then she gave me the peace sign and went to help another vet, but I never forgot it. It's like she saved my life."

Morgen touched the penny to her lips. "Tell me about the jar of pennies on your boat."

"Very observant. Afterward, I kept every penny I got." He half laughed. "I lost track of how many jars I've filled, but the point is that every time I get a new penny, I remember *wanting* to get well, because a very special person thought I was worth saving."

Morgen dabbed at her nose and folded his handkerchief. "You're a good friend and a very special man, Angelo Vincenzo Bordacelli." She put the penny back in the purse and fastened the clasp.

"I don't know." He took her hands in his. "Sometimes my capacity for imperfection astounds me, but remember, I'll always be here when you need me."

Notwithstanding her aversion to touch, it was a lovely gesture, and she enjoyed it.

SHE FURIOUSLY PRACTICED THE FANTASIE UNTIL MID-night when her cell phone alerted her to a missed call. *Violet?*

It wasn't raining, so she slipped on her damp sneakers, grabbed the shoelace key, and, wearing only her flannel nightgown, stepped outside Tutti. The night was so silent that she was reluctant to shut the door and disturb the calm. A translucent moon floated through the mist like a milk bubble, the Big Dipper reached between the stars like a chowder ladle, and all around her Fish Camp slept. She nodded drowsily with the rhythm of the ocean's mantra. Something moved, and she ducked back inside Tutti and turned off the limelight. She grabbed her opera glasses and peered between Fräu Heinrich's curtains. Joe and Mia were walking toward the road with Doris and One-Eyed Jack trotting along behind them. Where were they going in the dead of night?

She followed, and as she crept past Halibut trailer, she discovered that they were strewing rose petals behind them as they headed toward the beach. She followed at a safe distance until the procession reached the dune scarp.

She tiptoed as close as she dared, watching them take five cream-colored pillar candles from a sack, place them in a row on the sand, and arrange the roses around them. Joe lit the wicks, and five tall yellow flames reached into the night sky like sacred fingers.

"Hola," Morgen whispered.

Joe, Mia, Jack, and Doris turned to look at her. Mia beckoned her to join them.

She approached and knelt in the sand, fearful that none of it existed and that she was stoned out of her mind all over again. They smiled at her, and the cats purred and rubbed against her. "Sorry, I didn't bring my dictionary, *mi libro*."

"No problema. Is night, la noche, between Día de Todos los Santos y Día de los Muertos," Joe said. "You say 'Day of the Dead.' We think of dead family, talk stories, love them, eat, and drink."

Mia offered Morgen a warm tamale and a thick beverage in a mug.

"Is atole," Joe said. "Special Mexican drink. Warm and delicioso."

Morgen wrapped her nightgown around her legs and settled deeper into the sand to sip atole and watch the flickering candles. Presumably five candles for five dead family members. Jack and Doris cuddled on her feet while Mia and Joe murmured in Spanish, probably about memories of their dearly departed.

She only had four dearly departeds. She bit into the tamale while the roof angels addressed each other by name, *Therese, Josette, Eleanor, Charlie.* Morgan felt comforted by their serene, immortal voices. She searched through scraps of memories, sipped her atole, and recalled her mother's story about the Widow Witch who saved her life. In reality, she must have been Lydia Cooper. "Lydia," Morgen whispered, embracing the woman above the mantelpiece as her fifth Widow Witch roof angel.

She accepted another tamale and stayed until the candles burned down and the moon set. Everyone stood and shook off the sand. Morgen helped Joe and Mia gather their things, and they returned to Halibut trailer following the rose petal path. "Muchas gracias," Morgen whispered as Joe and Mia hugged her, smelling sweet like chilies, cinnamon, and pineapple.

"Goodnight," Mia said with a sweet smile. "Joe teach me goodnight."

"Buenas noches, mis amigos."

With Jack and Doris on her heels, Morgen went to the Palace Café to retrieve her voicemail. "Chérie, kudos on your new job. This is the perfect time for us to finally tie the knot and maximize our talents on both coasts. Let's meet soon. I'm thrilled about this prospect." Andras's voice sounded oddly off-key.

How did he know about her new job? What did he not understand about seclusion away from distractions and interference?

Sunday, November 2, 2003

SHE RACED THROUGH THE PALACE CAFÉ, SMILING AND waving at the breakfast crowd. This method of accessing her voicemail was getting annoying, but she couldn't ignore a prompt for a missed call. She dialed, listened, and cringed when Violet screamed, "My asshole father went ballistic and cut me off because of *you,* and I *loathe* this concerto!" End of message. *Click.*

"Oh dear Lord." Morgen poured a mug of decaf and sat quietly to gather her thoughts. Eleven days earlier when she drove in to help with the concerto, Violet had been, well, "bitchy," and while listening to the voicemail, Morgen had visualized a field of red marigolds in flames. Gram's mantra came to mind: *In life as in music, dissonance must resolve.* She and Violet might survive this, but it would take time. Obviously Violet didn't loathe the concerto, but she did hate Morgen's relationship with her father, which was understandable.

She sipped her decaf. Likewise, maybe she didn't hate the Fantasie as much as she hated how Andras had treated her. Maybe she wasn't as much looking for her mother's cremation urn as she was looking to discover a greater truth. She put down her mug, dried her palms on her jeans, and returned Violet's call.

After listening to Violet for twenty-three minutes, she learned that Andras had berated Violet again for loving Phoebe, demanded information about Morgen's where-abouts, and threatened to cut off Violet's allowance if she continued working on the Stravinsky concerto, which came out of the blue and made no sense at all. Violet had countered that her love life was none of his damn business and that she wouldn't give up the concerto for *anything*. He said he was going to quit paying the rent and have her locked out of her apartment immediately, which was shitty, because she and Phoebe would have no place to live. Phoebe's parents had just put their house on the market.

"Okay, now it's my turn to talk," Morgen said. "First, you must never, *ever* sacrifice your music because of abusive individuals who want to control your life. You must beat them at their own demented game, perform your music beyond their wildest dreams, and walk off the stage with your head held high. Second, in case you haven't heard, I accepted a job at the U starting in February. I want to move closer to campus, so I won't be needing my apartment in Redmond. Rent and utilities are paid through November, and although it lacks a piano and is seventeen miles from campus, you're welcome to stay there. If you accept, I'll call my landlord, and she can give you a key."

"Thanks, Morgen." Violet was weeping while Phoebe cheered the news in the background. "You've always been here for me even when I'm a bitch."

"Ever since the moment you were born." Morgen smiled. "Now you and Phoebe get packing so you can continue preparing for your baccalaureate concert, because *tempus fugit*." She hung up and bit her lip. They needed to sit down together and calmly talk over coffee or chowder.

As she left the Palace Café, she saw Fetu up at Salmon trailer washing Gooey. He waved at her, and she headed his way. He turned off the hose. "I like your haircut. Did you finish styling it yourself?"

She blushed. "I had to. Evidently, I made a mess of it."

"Yes, you did." He picked up a chamois and began drying the hood. "What else do you remember?"

"That you stayed with me. That I was terrified that I was going to die." She clasped her hands. "I live a very tidy albeit narrow life, but I saw and felt things." She shuddered.

He hung the chamois on the sideview mirror. "You mumbled several names while you slept, like Gram and Mom."

She felt tears rising. "Anybody else?"

"I wrote a list." He went inside Salmon and returned with a notepad. "This is where I write down ideas for my songs." He leafed through the pages. "Therese, Josette, Lydia, Violet, and I think you said roof angels."

She nodded. "I have roof angels."

"I'm sure you do." He smiled. "Then you said Carlo. More than once, and each time you sounded anxious."

"Carlo Ricci has a magnificent tenor voice, and he's harmless. He's just afraid of ghosts."

"So I gathered during the baby party. He said something about an old lady floating around although I didn't see her."

"That would be Lydia, the woman in the portrait," she said. "Do you believe in ghosts?"

"I believe that we're all haunted by something or somebody." He swallowed hard. "Not a day goes by that I don't think about my brother, George. So I guess, he stays with me like a—"

"Right, I know, like my mom and Gram. They're good and loving spirits."

"Are they your roof angels?"

"Yes." She counted on her fingers. "Plus Therese, Josette, and Lydia."

He stared at her for a moment. "I like you, Morgen."

She blushed. "That's what you said when I was stoned out of my mind after Gram died."

"No," he lowered his voice, "that night, I said that I love you."

She corrected her posture but had no words.

"No worries. I love your energy. I love the world you inhabit."

She shifted her weight from one foot to the other.

"I love being with you. It's comfortable."

"Thanks, I understand that better now." *Rather platonic. Well, crap.*

"Good. So is Carlo right? Is the Palace Café haunted?"

She shrugged. "It's more spiritual than haunted and a little magical."

He crossed his arms. "I sense you have a deeper story." He leaned closer. "I'll tell you mine if you tell me yours. We could share secrets again. Remember? Like at the bonfire?"

"Oh dear Lord. I shared way too much that night." The phrase *take a leap of faith* came to mind, and she pinched the hermit crab shell in her pocket. "Okay, but deeper stories deserve a deeper venue. Can I meet you here tonight, like a couple of hours after the Palace Café closes? We'll have to be secretive, because what I'm going to show you isn't part of Shella's world."

THE WIND CHANGED, AND MORGEN AWOKE WITH A START. She sat up and peeked through the window. Under the inky night sky, Fish Camp looked fixed in time like a black-and-white photograph, but a light burned inside Salmon trailer. Fetu must be waiting for her.

She quietly opened the cargo door and listened. Nothing but wind and surf, and the offshore flow was pleasantly mild. She grabbed her flashlight, put on her damp sneakers, and tiptoed down to Salmon. She tapped on the window, waited, and tapped again.

Fetu opened the door wearing a T-shirt and gray sweatpants. He put on his flip-flops, stepped outside, and closed the door. "This plan seems complicated."

"Nothing's complicated if you have the right key." She reached into her sweatshirt.

THEY STOOD ON THE TILED FLOOR OF THE CONCH GROTTO in complete darkness. "That was a tight squeeze," she whispered. "I thought your shoulders were going to get stuck." She plugged in the string of lights, and they were awash in soft, white light. The conch grotto gleamed and smelled fresh. Even the acoustics were perfect. *Please, after it went so terribly wrong for Mom, let her love finally heal me.*

"What the fuck?" Fetu's eyes opened wide as he looked around.

"I read about this place in an old diary, but I had no idea it existed. Late one night soon after I arrived, I was using the phone and saw a light flicker between the floor and the closet door, so I investigated."

He rubbed his hands across the curving tiled wall. "Amazing. The Palace Café has a dungeon. A trifle surreal, but it has a spiritual feel. Do you know the story behind it?"

"Part of it. Long ago, this was the home of Marty and Lydia Cooper, and that's her picture over the fireplace. He was a tugboat captain who was lost at sea. She was desperately in love with him and went mad with grief." Her voice softened. "I call it the conch grotto."

The mirrors reflected pinkish-white light like stars dancing across their skin, and a cool puff of air passed over them. "Ghosts? Really? You weren't kidding," he whispered. "It's extremely feminine with the curving pink glistening walls and all. A bit erotic, especially in the middle of the night."

Erotic? Her scalp began to prickle. Was it a mistake to bring him down there? Time to redirect the chitchat. "What do your tattoos mean?"

He extended his arm. "This wave band represents the Pacific's horizon." He turned so she could see the four blue stars on his upper arm. "Rising above that horizon is the Southern Cross constellation. I know this sounds weird, but I saw it once in broad daylight, and it saved my life." He took her hands, but she pulled away from him.

"Sorry, you startled me." Her voice shook. "Remember? My hands were crushed under a grand piano lid. That's when I learned that there are twenty-seven bones in the human hand and that fingertips have some of the densest areas of nerve endings. That's why I jumped just then." She tried to swallow but coughed instead. "All of a sudden I'm experiencing immense social anxiety."

"No worries. We came down here to share secrets, not terrify each other."

I want to love you. She gazed past his shoulder at her fractured reflection within the pink tiles and perceived her image more clearly. A sparkle in her eyes. A rosy tint on her cheeks. A suggestion of a smile at the corners of her mouth. For years, she'd trained herself to feel nothing with Andras, so what if she felt nothing with Fetu? She had an aversion to touch and wasn't a cat lady princess who could live happily ever after with just a kiss from a tugboat prince. Although she might tolerate one kiss. She sat on the glass brick bench and motioned for him to join her. "You said you'd tell me your deeper story if I told you mine."

"Sure. I only rehearsed this for you a hundred times this afternoon." He stared at the floor. "Here it goes. When I was five years old, Mum left us, and I haven't heard from her since. The day after she left, I stole the neighbor's skiff so George and I could row to America to find her, but it capsized, and George went under like a rock." His voice wavered. "I swam deeper and deeper trying to save him, but he kept going down. Right before he sank out of sight, he let go of his yellow paper fan as though he wanted me to have it." Tears ran down his cheeks, and he pointed at his Southern Cross tattoo. "I watched that stupid fan float past me toward the surface and was losing consciousness when I saw these four stars shining in broad daylight down through the water above me. That's when I decided to live."

"I'm so sorry." Morgen watched him, tears welling.

He took several deep breaths. "After we got home, Dad told me that although George was better off dead, it was all *my* fault, and in a way, it was. In addition, he had to pay for the boat, which pissed him off. To punish me, he burned the palm of my hand with his cigarette, and when I cried, he threw me down and flicked embers in my mouth." His color deepened. "As soon as I could, I changed my name to Lemalu, after the old grandfather who taught me guitar. My putting Dad's ashes to sea is symbolic of *me* finally drowning *him*."

"That's awful." Morgen's hands began to flap, and she leaped to her feet. "Oh crap, not now." She shoved them under her arms. "I'm so stupid."

"No, you're fine, really." Fetu stood up. "George did that when he was happy."

With a groan, Morgen embraced him, but images shot up her spine like electric shocks, and she recoiled in fear of being exposed, not only the most private parts of her body but the pain caged in her bones and the rot in her DNA. She pushed him away. "I don't know if I want to like you. I don't know if I'm pretending emotions or not. I don't know what to think anymore." She slapped her hands over her ears against memories that yelled in her mind's ear. Andras had said that his *erotic* photograph represented the quintessential union of man and music, and she'd said, *Fine, but what about the girl on his lap and* her *feelings?* He'd laughed and said that she, like Morgen, was a muse, an illusion, and didn't really matter. Then he'd dropped his pants and sat on the bench. Because she was innately bad, she sat on him but couldn't play that beautiful music, so he crushed her hands—

"Don't do this to yourself." Fetu tried to restrain her, so she slapped his face with all her might. The blow echoed throughout the conch grotto like a gunshot, but he held his ground. "Hitting me doesn't change how I feel about you, but I must say, it's been a bloody hell of a week getting to know you."

She slapped her own face and head. "I hate him, I hate what he did!" She stared at the fractured images of herself in the mirror fragments on the walls until the edges dissolved. "Please understand me," she whispered, dropping her shoulders, dropping her guard.

"I do. I think I always have." He gave her the first chaste kiss she'd ever received from a man her own age.

"Why, thank you," she hiccupped. "I rather liked that." In

her mind's eye, she saw Andras Bacon frown and leave the stage, because to certain other individuals, she *did* matter. Maybe moment by moment, she was beginning to matter to herself, too. She caught a faint but familiar scent. "I smell Carlo," she whispered, pointing up at the floorboards of the café. She dashed over and pulled the plug on the miniature lights. "I didn't lock the door."

"Stupid old ghost," Carlo growled overhead. "I know you're in here."

Morgen heard footfalls and flinched when a table screeched across the floor.

"I was about to get laid real good," Carlo said, "and you had to start spooking around. I'm going to cremate your fucking soul once and for all."

She jumped when she heard a crash followed by the entry door slamming. "Oh no, now I smell—" A smoke detector began to blare.

"Go," Fetu yelled, and they scrambled up the steps and into the dining room.

Clouds of black smoke billowed from the fireplace. "Oh no," Morgen cried. "Lydia's portrait!" The fire screen was wide open, and Lydia's burning frame had fallen out onto the hearth, sending live coals skittering across the hardwood floor. Fetu grabbed the fire poker and shovel and pushed the smoldering mess back into the firebox while Morgen waved a tablecloth until the smoke detector stopped wailing.

Shella stumbled down the stairs with Pearl in her arms. "What's going on?"

"Just a minor disaster." Morgen grabbed a chair to steady herself. "Are we okay now?" she asked Fetu.

"Fire's out if that means we're okay." His voice shook. "Let's open the entry door and some windows."

"The fire was down to embers, and I swear I closed the screen." Shella was still half asleep. "What are you two doing in here?"

"I smelled smoke. You see, Fetu and I were conversing—"

"Oh no, what happened to the picture? I bet it was stupid Carlo. He's so afraid of her. Could have burned the place down with us in it. It stinks in here. I'll open my window too." Shella headed up the stairs. "Thanks, guys. Goodnight."

Morgen waited until she heard Shella's door latch. "I don't think she knows, but Lydia was John's sister-in-law, and he's going to be crushed." She looked at the hearth. "Let's clean this up as best we can. Funny, after our bonfire on the beach, I took a picture of that portrait, because I liked it. Will you please drive me into town tomorrow? I want to get a replacement made ASAP."

Monday, November 3, 2003

MORGEN DIDN'T SLEEP WELL BECAUSE CARLO-THE-ARSON-ist kept the *Best of the Three Tenors* album cranked up all night. She dearly loved listening to "Nessun Dorma" aka "None Shall Sleep" and trying to match the tempo with her metronome, but by the time the tenors sang "You'll Never Walk Alone" from *Carousel* for the fourth time, she buried her head under the pillow while somewhere in the marina Salty Dog yipped and howled like a coyote.

At first light, she peered between Fräu Heinrich's curtains. The red pickup was parked outside the harbormaster house, and a strange woman appeared to be reeling toward the upper bathhouse. Morgen pulled on her jeans and cable-knit sweater and went out to investigate.

"How do you do?" She approached the woman whose face was ashen and clothing disheveled. Her purse swung from her neck like a cowbell. "I'm Morgen. Are you okay?"

"I don't have my car." The woman's voice was toneless, and the word *zombie* came to mind. "I want to go home, but I don't have my car." She fixed her purse strap so it hung from her shoulder.

Morgen glanced at the harbormaster house. "Are you a friend of Carlo? Because I can get him."

"No, no." Her hands shook as she rubbed her face. "Dear God."

Morgen wrung her hands. "It's cold out here." She gestured over her shoulder. "That's my blue bus. Her name's Tutti. Would you like to come inside and sit down?"

"I watched what he was doing but I couldn't move," the woman whispered.

Morgen's scalp began to prickle. "Come on." They walked side by side to Tutti. When she opened the cargo door, the woman peered inside. "You may sit on either bench seat. What's your name?"

"Natasha." She sat at the table and touched the wild roses on the sugar bowl as though testing for wet paint.

Naughty Natasha from Aberdeen? Morgen closed the door. "Natasha's a pretty name." She opened a bottle of water. "Drink this."

"Gave me a glass of wine. Said it would relax me." She coughed and spilled the water on the table.

Morgen grabbed a paper towel. *Well, crap, I know where this is going.*

"Something. I don't know. Out of body." Natasha drank again. "Just a glass of cheap wine."

Morgen watched her. Carlo had said, *I've got nothing but the best stuff, so let me know when you want to get high.* On the other hand, Gram had said that her mother was a natural healer and that she would be too in time. Angelo had said that he'd helped her mother and then she helped him. Now it was time for her to step up to the plate, so to speak. She dumped a cup of trio mix onto the tabletop. "Try some. It's my mom's recipe. Trio mix. Raison d'être. *Mezcla trio.* Depending on your choice of language." She began to sort and munch but kept an eye on Natasha, who stared at nothing. "You see, sorting trio mix helps me think—"

"He's still asleep." Natasha ate an almond. A couple of cranberries. She swept up a generous handful and popped it in her mouth.

There was a knock on Tutti's window, Natasha jumped, and the cargo door opened.

"Sorry," Fetu said, sitting beside Morgen. "I didn't know you had company."

"This is Natasha," Morgen said in a steady voice, "and this is my friend, Fetu. We have to go to Aberdeen now. Do you want a ride?"

"Yes." Natasha stood up but hit her head on the ceiling and sat again with a groan. She grabbed another handful of trio mix and wolfed it down.

"That's okay. I hit my head all the time." Morgen half laughed. "Do you have a doctor there because I think you should—"

"Yes." Natasha looked at Morgen, and her face crumpled. "He didn't need to do it like that. I liked him—"

"Hey, Angelo, you seen Natasha?" Carlo yelled across the marina.

Morgen looked at Natasha and pressed her finger to her lips.

"Who the hell is Natasha?" Angelo shouted back.

Fetu lined up M&M's for a tic-tac-toe game with Natasha. "You go first," he whispered. She ate a blue M&M, Fetu made his move, and she countered by eating a yellow one.

Morgen smiled. *He can be so kind.*

"Hey, Carlo," Angelo yelled, "I'm taking old man Kiwi's ashes out, and then I'm fishing if you want to come along. No? Fine, suite yourself. There's a late run of silvers coming, and we're throwing a big old wake for him tonight, but first I need coffee."

Morgen watched through her opera glasses until she saw Carlo go inside the harbormaster house and Angelo head toward the Palace Café. Fetu ate another M&M, and Natasha made her move. "I win," she said.

"We all win, because Angelo doesn't know about the fire yet," Morgen said. She grabbed her peacoat and camera. "Let's go before it hits the fan."

On the way to Aberdeen, Morgen sat in front with Fetu, and Natasha squeezed into the backseat. "Do you want to stop for breakfast? I'll buy."

"No thanks, but you know, he asked me if I wanted to get high. I said, oh, sure, so he sang to me and then played a Three Tenors album. God, Carlo has such a beautiful voice, like Pavarotti, but by then, I was half anesthetized." Natasha paused. "I'm still numb."

Morgen measured her breath. Although the sun was unseasonably bright, there was a cold reality to this day. Natasha's story was her mother's story, and it was *her* story.

Beautiful music. Beautiful bait. She chewed her cuticle and thought about Andras. It wasn't about the Fantasie; it was the way he'd deceived her. She clawed at her scalp, but it wouldn't stop itching. In Carlo's case, it likely wasn't so much about Lydia's ghost as it was about something else.

"I met him in the music store, we talked, met for lunch a couple of times, then drinks, and he invited me here to see his record collection." Natasha began to cry. "I feel so dirty, so ashamed—"

"No," Morgen cried. "This wasn't your fault, and if you feel ashamed, he gets away with it."

Fetu reached over and tapped Morgen's clenched fists with one finger. He waited, and with a quiet sob, she grasped his hand. By the time they came to the Westport turnoff, Natasha was asleep.

"She's stuck, you know," Fetu said. "She said she went out there knowing there'd be drugs and sex. Carlo could argue that it was consensual."

"It's so wrong." She clenched her hands. "I'm speaking broadly and historically." Maybe Angelo was right. Maybe Carlo wasn't her friend.

When they came to the drawbridge over the Chehalis River, Natasha woke up and said, "Go through the next stoplight, turn left, and keep going. The clinic is up the hill near the hospital."

"I'll go in with you if you want," Morgen said.

Natasha said nothing, even when they dropped her off.

"I SHOULD HAVE BOUGHT YOU LUNCH FOR DRIVING ME IN." Morgen rummaged through the grocery bag for a snack. "Let's share a kiwi. Do you have a knife?"

"Look in the glove box." Fetu kept his eyes on the road. "Angelo said he'd host a wake for my father tonight, so dinner should be ready when we get back. By the way, a kiwi is a bird. That's a kiwifruit. The bird is native to New Zealand. The fruit is not."

"News to me." Morgen ate half and put the other half in Fetu's mouth. "Thanks for taking me to the frame shop. Amazing that they can replicate Lydia's portrait from just a memory card and deliver it in less than a week. Thanks for taking me to the music store too."

"I wanted to hear you play, and you exceeded my expectations. Chopin rocks."

She laughed. "It was also fun playing 'Chopsticks' and 'Heart and Soul' duets with you." As was sitting beside him on the piano bench. "Are you sad that you weren't with Angelo when he spread your father's ashes?"

"Not at all. You know how I feel about boats."

Morgen stared through the windshield. "I don't know who my father is."

Fetu let her comment hang there.

"I know who my mother was, and I miss her." She took a breath. "Someone stole her cremation urn, and I feel like it's waiting for me to find it."

"What difference would it make?"

"It's symbolic of my finally helping her. She reached out to me so many times, and I missed it. She even reached out to me when she was dying, and I missed it." She heard Gram's voice in her mind's ear. *There's strength in music and in the continuum and in the messiness of life too.* She seemed to whisper softly like wind under a locked door. *Recognize what connects you, not just what separates you.* Morgen cleared her throat. "Do you want to hear my deeper story? Because I want to tell you."

"Yes, I do." He pulled onto the side of the road and turned off the engine. "I'm listening." He turned to face her.

She bit her lip and pulled her sleeves down over her hands. "Oh, my fingers look like hermit crab pincers. That's a joke." Tears streamed down her face. "Thirty-five years, one month, and eight days ago, my mother was raped on the drift logs beach, and I was the result of that rape."

Fetu mumbled something and slammed the steering wheel with his hands.

Morgen began to hyperventilate. "I never, talk about, this, but it makes me so sick." A bitter foam rose in the back of her throat. "Thirteen years, five months, and thirteen days ago, I played my heart and soul out and performed the Stravinsky concerto perfectly. My reward? Andras Bacon complimented me and then forced me to have intercourse on the floor of his studio on the U campus." Her hands began to flap, and she let them go wild. "I was a virgin. I didn't expect it. I didn't consent to it. He just did it." Her heart rate must have hit *prestissimo* ($\quarternote$ = 200, as quickly as possible) because her body shook. "Consensual sex? An *affair*? Bullshit! He raped me as though he were patting me on the back for doing a good job! Because he was my *master* teacher. *Master?* No big deal, right? Because he'd groomed me since I was thirteen years old to be not only his protégée but also his fricking partner. Excuse me, please." She opened the car door and vomited until she had nothing left inside. A cool breeze carried away the stink, and her pulse slowed, *ritardando*, from *vivace* to *allegretto* to *andante*. She closed the door. "All better," she whispered.

Fetu's cheeks were wet. "Andras Bacon is a disgusting prick, but he'll get his." His voice quavered. "You, of all people, deserve to be loved and respected." He handed her a wad of tissues. "I am sickened by what you've been through. And about what happened to your mum."

She burped and wiped her mouth. "I'm craving something clean and bubbly. May I please have one of your beers?"

He pulled one out of the grocery bag and opened it. "How much longer are you staying in Fish Camp?"

"I'm thinking about leaving soon. Gram wanted her ashes spread in the Pacific off Todos Santos. I need to get to Baja so that I'm back in Seattle in time to move and get ready for spring semester." She drank the beer and gazed out Gooey's window. "I think I'll buy a little keyboard. Rent a room in the pueblo and hang out on the beach. Watch the baby whales. Feast on mangoes and fresh lobster. Get my chops back in shape, learn all that new music, and slow dance to the saddest Mexican guitar." Her thoughts drifted like crumbling autumn leaves. "Want to come along?"

"Absolutely."

Fetu turned on Gooey and returned to the highway. They rode along in silence. Black clouds rolled in, and rain began to pummel Gooey's roof. Morgen kept her eyes on the road. The scenery was familiar yet strange, because it seemed every parking lot, side street, and driveway had a boat on a trailer. She remembered seeing *Epiphany* on Lake Union with her mother. Eventually *Epiphany* became *By-the-Wind Sailor*. She fingered her foremothers necklace and frowned at the weather.

8.

Morgen knew there was trouble the instant she crossed the threshold. "Sorry, are we late for the wake?" As she glanced around the Palace Café, she began to perspire, and her palms itched. Nobody was cooking. "What's going on?"

"Angelo went out by fishing himself and should be back by now." Shella's face was white. "The storm came up so fast."

"Everybody needs to calm down." John's voice boomed, but his face had lost its color. "He's a good skipper." He glanced at the blank wall where Lydia's portrait had hung. "Hell of a storm though."

Morgen's scalp began to crawl. Was John thinking about twin Marty, lost on a tug in a "hell of a storm"?

"Did you call him?" Fetu asked.

"Yeah, but he don't answer. We worked on that damn radio for hours, you, me, and everybody, but we never got it to work right, and we all know Skipper. To hell with life jackets and radios and telling anybody what he's up to."

Shella held Pearl against her chest as she looked through the window. The wind accelerated, bending the glass. Sand blasted the door, and pampas grass clawed the weathered siding.

Morgen joined her. She heard feral cats out on the jetty wailing in misery. She clenched her teeth against her own cry for help, turned her face, and stared at Angelo's empty chair.

MORGEN POURED ANOTHER ROUND OF COFFEE FOR EVERY-body. Because she didn't know what else to do, she walked through the Palace Café reestablishing routine and order by straightening every ship picture that hung on the walls. Fetu, John, Joe, and Mia sat at the counter while Shella nursed Pearl in the rocking chair.

"I'm not scared to be a mom anymore," she said to Morgen, "but I'm scared to death about Angelo. My real father used to fish for Dungeness out there, always by himself. They think a buoy line tangled in his prop and he fell in trying to clear it. Found his boat but never found him." Tears rolled down her cheeks.

"Angelo will be home any minute," Morgen said, rubbing the ache behind her breastbone.

Fetu put his hand on Shella's shoulder. "We're all here for you. We're all in this together."

"I'm in this more than you think." Shella began to cry in earnest. "I thought everything was finally going to work out between him and me."

"Between you and Angelo?" Morgen thought she'd faint. "Is Angelo Pearl's father?" she whispered.

Pearl began to wail, and Shella walked around the dining room, patting Pearl on the back. "Don't cry," she said. "It's going to be—"

"Oh dear Lord, why did I not see this coming?" Morgen's hands started to flap, and she didn't care.

Shella shot her a desperate look. "Please don't do that hand thing. It's weird."

"It's just a dance move called jazz hands—"

The entry door crashed open, and three wet men stomped in. "Hell of a storm. What's cooking, Shella?"

Shella shook her head and collapsed into the rocking chair, and Morgen watched the men's faces. John evidently murmured the news because the word *crestfallen* came to mind. With a nod to each other, Morgen and Mia went into the kitchen to brew more coffee, thaw frittata, and heat pots of chowder and cioppino.

After everyone settled in with coffee, soup, and sourdough, Morgen excused herself. "I have to go up to Tutti," she told Fetu. "I won't be long."

She grabbed her peacoat and ventured into the storm. *How could Angelo be Pearl's father?* She swallowed a sob without knowing why.

Ropes whipped and clanged against the masts, and sour, flabby fog suffocated the marina in spite of the wind that had picked up, moaning and whistling through the harbored boats' rigging. She fought her way toward the campground through sideways rain and ankle-deep puddles but stopped short when she saw something heaped on Tutti's roof. Marooned jetty cats? Raccoons?

"Angelo?" she whispered.

As she ventured closer, she saw an enormous pelican with glowing yellow eyes huddled on the roof rack, dark feathers waterlogged, and jeweled blue tears streaming down its long face. "No, dammit, go away!" She began to cry. "Please don't let him die."

The bird blinked its mournful eyes at her. If this was the pelican-priest from *By-the-Wind Sailor*'s bow, it was too late.

She touched the rough-hewn feathers on one great wing, partly to communicate empathy and partly to confirm that the bird was real. "You've come a long way, haven't you, and you must be very tired." She tried to control her tears. "Please stay and rest as long as you want, but with all due respect, I'm not giving up on him yet."

She climbed into Tutti, shoved her manuscript journal, cell phone, and an extra toothbrush into her backpack, and said a prayer into her mother's conch shell. She saw the wild rose sugar bowl on the table and thought of Natasha. "I hope she's okay," she whispered. "I hope she's got friends too." She stared at Angelo's little purse with her mother's penny of hope inside. She grabbed it and Fetu's hermit crab shell for good luck along with a handful of Doris's cat kibble.

After nodding at the shivering pelican-priest, she hurried down to check on Salty Dog. Poor old pup was slouched on the float by Angelo's empty slip and, in one afternoon, had become an old dog. His wet coat had lost its luster and seemed sizes too large for the bony frame beneath. He licked her hand but refused to eat the kibble. She tried to reassure him, but rain scrubbed the words out of her mouth.

As soon as she entered the dining room, she put her hermit crab shell on a windowsill.

Fetu placed his beside it. "Come home, come home," they whispered. Shella dug hers and Pearl's out of a pocket and added them, creating a path of tiny stepping stones.

Mia appeared at her side. "*Diccionario*, por favor."

Morgen handed it to her and waited while Mia searched for a word. "Hope," she said.

Morgen looked at the page. "*Esperanza*," she whispered. "Gracias, Mia. Hope is fine, but I'm calling the Coast Guard anyway." She put the dictionary on the counter and peeled off the list of telephone numbers taped to the side of the cash register.

The small crowd stirred and mumbled. Finally, a lone fisherman spoke. "Better not yet. He'll be pissed. Likely waiting for the tide."

"No, I'm going to call now, because I'm more concerned about Angelo's safety than his pride." Her hands shook, and she bit her lip hard to keep from blurting about the pelican-priest. "I'm also going to call Uncle Vic, the lawyer."

MORGEN KEPT WATCH FROM A WINDOW AND SAW CARLO emerge in his yellow rain gear from the harbormaster house long enough to change the flags on the pole from small craft warning to gale warning. Then she gasped when the seven plastic pink flamingos took flight. Horizontal rain and wind kicked the door, cracked the glass, and throttled the whale weathervane overhead. How much water could one sky hold?

Her fingers cramped while she fidgeted with the cuffs on her cable-knit sweater. What was happening out there on the deep blue sea? Would Angelo ever come home to Pearl's mom so they could be a fam-i-ly?

A prompt for a missed call appeared on her cell phone. She frowned and went to the Palace's phone to access her voicemail. "Chérie, it's vitally important that you call me immediately. I'm standing here with a New York fashion designer to order your gown for the gala, and she needs to talk to you. Right now. Call me."

She deleted the message. All those years, she could have walked away from him but didn't because of the limelight and his lavish sensational theater. What he did to her was wrong, and she wasn't going to let him off the hook this time. *He'll get his, Fetu promised.* She took her manuscript journal out of her backpack and scribbled on the cover, *I deserve to play any music I choose simply because I have the ability to do so.* She squeezed the penny purse and heard Angelo's voice in her mind's ear. *You know what your mother did? She reached into her pocket and handed me a penny. Now you're worth something, she said. Now you've got a future.*

"I have a future too," she whispered, but at that moment, she'd trade her entire repertoire for Angelo's safe return.

The door opened, and a man blew in, his ginger beard dripping and clear plastic raincoat snug as a sausage casing over a brown sweater and jeans. John greeted him. "Pastor Tim, good of you to come." Everyone but Morgen knew Pastor Tim. He made his way toward her.

"I'm Tim Olsen, and it's truly an honor. John speaks highly of you."

"I'm Morgen. How do you do?" she said, her chin quivering.

He lowered his voice. "I fished with Angelo many times in Alaska, and if anyone can get that boat home, it's him. Meanwhile, we have to stay strong and positive for Shella."

Morgen bit her lip to keep from blurting about the pelican-priest on Tutti's roof. "I grew up never knowing my father. I hope and pray Pearl doesn't have to go through that."

Pastor Tim nodded and turned away. Morgen noticed he had a small book shoved into his back pocket, and she remembered seeing Angelo's shabby missal tossed on his bunk.

MORGEN SAW A SILVER PORSCHE PULL INTO THE LAST available parking spot at the end of the road. Moments later, an icy gust of wet wind shoved Uncle Vic through the entry door, bow tie askew and raincoat drenched. "Any news?"

She shook her head, and Mia handed him a mug of coffee.

Vic rubbed his forehead and turned away to listen to the Weather Channel report. "Gale warning. High surf advisory. Seas are severe. Waves fourteen feet with breakers. Near zero visibility. Coastal flood warning is in effect."

He walked to the telephone and dialed. "Louise?" His voice ripped through the quiet like a cry for help. "I'm staying. Angie's boat is still missing." He turned away to finish his conversation.

A murky light through the tall windows cast the longest shadows. Morgen watched Fetu bury his face in his hands. *The ocean is so awfully deep*, he'd said. She stared at him and couldn't see the bottom.

MORGEN WAITED WITH EVERYBODY ELSE IN THE DINING room, dozing off intermittently and waking with a start. Pastor Tim rocked a sleepy Pearl while Shella stood facing the window as frozen and transparent as a glass brick bench.

Evidently, in waterfront communities, news of a missing boat spread quickly, so Joe and Mia scrambled to keep coffee and snacks available. Locals, fishermen, and surfers came and went and returned again offering support, hope, and prayers, and Morgen watched in awe. *They're like family. They love him. They believe he's coming home.*

Fetu came in wearing an ankle-length yellow raincoat. "John just lit a huge bonfire at the entrance to the bay, not far from the drift logs beach. It took a truckload of firewood and a couple of gallons of kerosene to get it going. The storm is nasty out there, so we should each take a shift." Murmurs of agreement rippled across the room.

Morgen handed Fetu a mug of coffee. "I'll make a couple of sandwiches for him." She went into the kitchen.

Vic followed her. "Never been on this side of the counter before." He stared at the sink. "Never been through anything like this before either." His voice sounded unsteady. "Angie is like a son to me, and I'm very proud of him. My brother, Vincenzo, Angie's father, was a wealthy man but unnecessarily strict." Vic shook his head. "Demanded loyalty to family no matter what."

"Like Angelo's tattoo, *Famiglia per Sempre*?"

"Exactly." He watched Morgen assemble a variety of snacks.

She offered him a sandwich. "Beverages are in the fridge. Help yourself."

"Thank you. The beauty is that Angie's loyalty has often been to those in need. He may live on an old boat, but he manages a generous foundation." He opened a cola and wandered away with his sandwich.

Morgen recalled Shella's statement, *I got chosen to be in a special program paid for by a foundation. Every week, baby and braces. Pretty cool, huh?* "Pretty cool," she murmured.

Tuesday, November 4, 2003

Morgen massaged the aching muscles in the back of her neck. Angelo had been gone for twenty-four hours, and the storm had raged nonstop. All the individuals remained though, clinging to *esperanza* for the simplest and most logical reason: because Angelo hadn't returned didn't mean that he wouldn't. Fish Camp had been her base for eighteen days, and there was no turning back now except she could turn back to what she'd written in her manuscript journal. She pulled it out of her backpack. *Tuesday, October 21: What do I want/need from this place before I leave it?*

1. *I want to resolve my estrangement with Mom.*
2. *I want to accept myself so that others, including the Fish Campers, will accept me for who I really am. And me, them.*
3. *I want to respect myself so that I NEVER beat up on myself again.*

She reread the list, and it seemed like the best way to accomplish those things was to find the urn, fix the missing pieces of her life and her mother's life, and be brave in dealing with Andras and his Fantasie. But what about her life *now*? About not agonizing about the past or worrying about the future but being mindful in that moment? She chewed her lip while she gazed around the dining room.

Mia closed the oven door to bake a batch of thawed sourdough sweet rolls. Someone turned down the volume on the TV, and the jetty cats disappeared one by one. Rain flowed down the windowpane like the tears on Shella's cheeks. The only sound other than the storm was Mia in her lopsided white beanie starting to sweep the hardwood floor for the umpteenth irritating time. Joe was out foraging for firewood, John tended the signal fire, and Salty Dog kept vigil at Angelo's slip. Everybody else, and there were many, sprawled around like bedding on the floor of a cheap hotel.

Evidently, Fish Camp had taught her one big life lesson that had *not* been on her want/need list: that there was an amazing, huge world outside of Andras Bacon's twenty-four-page Fantasie. Each of these individuals had a life as full and complicated as hers. She felt reassured by their warmth and stubborn hope as they chitchatted about fishing, weather, and Angelo, and that they'd acknowledged her as part of their tribe with their smiles and offers to help. She added Fetu, Lydia Cooper, Pearl, Uncle Vic, Natasha, and Pastor Tim Olsen to Tutti's horses list.

"Scared?" Mia whispered, dictionary in hand.

"Sí," Morgen said. "*Muy asustada.*"

Mia returned to the kitchen, and Morgen sat on the couch beside Fetu. "I'm scared for Angelo."

"Uh huh." He continued writing on his notepad.

"Did you cry when your father died?"

"Nope. Only with George." He kept writing. "The upside is that my song lyrics are making me like you even more."

Morgen felt a chill. That could become a problem, because as her therapist had said, she had trust issues. She sighed and turned to the page where she'd written, *Fetu Lemalu. Exotic. Pleasant face,* and wrote:

1. *Fetu always wants to be near me, but I don't want to be under his thumb.*
2. *Fetu says he likes and loves me, but so did Andras.*
3. *Fetu gave me an expensive mandolin, so what does he expect in return?*
4. *Fetu's musical, nice looking, and is from a part of the world that interests me.*

The phone rang, and everybody jumped. Morgen hurried over to answer it. "Jetty Cat Palace Café. Oh, Natasha, hi. This is Morgen. I was wondering how you're doing."

Fetu walked over and leaned close enough so he could hear both sides of the conversation. Natasha thanked

Morgen, said she was doing better, unhappy but wiser, and that she'd opted not to tell the police because in he said, she said cases, the woman always lost. "Carlo took pictures of what he was doing to me," she said, "and he has a huge cache of drugs. Could you tell somebody so what happened to me doesn't happen to other women?"

"Sure." Morgen exhaled through tight lips. "Give me your number." A moment later, she hung up. "I'll tell Angelo or Vic but not today."

"Great, but in the meantime, stay away from him." Fetu returned to his pencil and notepad.

"No worries. I wasn't born yesterday."

"Everything's wet," Shella said to no one in particular. She sat in shadow in the rocking chair with Pearl in her arms and stared through the window at the bruised and swollen water in the bay. "I hear boats, but I can't see them." She handed Pearl to Pastor Tim and, with trembling hands, folded paper napkins into little lifeboats and lined them up on the windowsills with the hermit crab shells and model ships in an armada pushing west toward the horizon.

The rain froze to hail and crashed against the windows like shovelfuls of gravel.

I have to do something. With a burst of energy, Morgen crossed the room and opened the doors of the curtained closet. A startled One-Eyed Jack dashed past her with three other jetty cats hot on his heels. She ignored them and rummaged through the basket of Christmas decorations. She pulled out two strings of multicolored lights and sat cross-legged on the hardwood floor with four cats crouched around her. Her fingers shook while she unscrewed and sorted the bulbs. The finished product included one string of red lights and another of only green.

She went behind the counter and grabbed the duct tape. With an entourage of jittery cats at her ankles, she taped the red lights to the tall window on the left of the entry door and outlined the window on the right with the green lights.

After glancing around the dining room, she collected the brass candle lanterns off the tables. She arranged the lanterns draped with green glass beads among the model ships and paper napkin boats in the window to the right of the door and the other two with red beads on the sill to the left. Starboard and port. Green going, red right returning. After plugging in the lights and lighting the candles, she put her arm around Shella's shoulders, stared at the entry door, and waited.

Morgen poured two mugs of coffee and sat at the counter with Vic. "I don't know what to say except I'm so very sorry."

"You're a fine young woman. You don't need to say anything. You just need to indulge a sad old man." He took a sip. "*Famiglia per Sempre*. God knows, you don't get to choose your family. Oh, Vincenzo and Gianna built an empire, and the estate still owns their private island home on Puget Sound where Angie grew up an only child and too secluded. I've always loved him like a son. Taught him to fish." Vic paused and rubbed his eyes. "Right here in Fish Camp."

Morgen felt sick to her stomach as his words sunk in. She pulled her sleeves down over her hands and noticed that the grimy cuffs had begun to fray.

"Let's amend the Bordacelli axiom from 'family is forever' to 'blood alone does not a family make.'" Vic stood. "We'll see how it all plays out, won't we?" He offered her a halfhearted smile, put his mug in the sink, and headed to the door. "I'll be in the harbormaster house."

Morgen covered her face and cried.

"Sad?" Mia asked, tears in her eyes.

"Sí," Morgen said, "*muy triste.*"

"Are you okay?" Fetu whispered, gently patting her perky haircut.

"No, thank you, I'm not okay—"

The entry door banged opened, and a FedEx driver staggered in. "Hell of a storm, but we got diapers for Shella. Your dirty pickup is delayed due to the weather, but at least they sent you something. Also a package for Morgen Marín. Looks like art to me. Sign here."

Morgen ripped into the box before the door closed. "Lydia, you're back," she cried, and everyone cheered.

Fetu helped her hang the portrait over the mantelpiece, better than ever in a spectacular frame and beautifully colorized. Restraining her tears, she grabbed her manuscript journal and hurried out the door. By the time she reached Tutti, the pelican-priest had gone on its merry way. She tossed her manuscript journal on the table so Fetu couldn't read what she'd written about him. She ripped the string of lights from the headliner and sloshed through the deluge to the Palace Café.

Shella had told her that, for years, Lydia draped twinkly white lights all over the building and had kept them burning every night like a beacon so that Marty could find his way home. Maybe, just maybe, similar lights would help Angelo find his way.

Halfway through hanging the miniature lights around the entry door, Morgen watched as the signal-fire shift change delivered John back for a break. "Good evening,

Morgen," he said in a weary voice as he tromped through the door.

"Good evening, John."

Eight seconds passed before he cried out, "Well, I'll be. Lydia's come home."

Yes, she has. Morgen finished hanging the Lydia lights, and the power went off.

Wednesday, November 5, 2003

MORGEN WAS HALF ASLEEP WHEN THE POWER AND EVERY light in the Jetty Cat Palace Café came back on. On the roof, the weathervane buzzed hysterically like a blade on a helicopter. "Angelo?" she mumbled. Those damn helicopters had roared in his head all night, probably tinnitus aggravated by drinking, but thankfully, a helicopter had carried him, half butchered, out of Vietnam.

"Angelo!" She sat up on the couch with a start and stared at the penny purse she'd clenched in her hand. The Fish Camper crowd had thinned, and the fire in the fireplace was reduced to embers. She got up and looked out the kitchen window. According to the whipping flags straining at the ropes, the weather advisory had upgraded from gale warning to storm warning. Salty Dog fought to keep his footing on Angelo's dock while he gazed into the rotting water, soaked to the bones and shoulders drooping.

She turned to look at the TV where the Weather Channel meteorologist, who in her anxious mind's eye resembled Jim the Harbor Seal, was frowning at the camera. "The Pacific Northwest is experiencing winds in excess of sixty knots, heavy rain, and damaging surf. Creeks and rivers are approaching flood stage, and water is over the roadways in many areas. Power outages are widespread. All travel is discouraged."

Shella remained bolted to her chair with Pearl in her arms, rocking furiously. The cats crouched, curled up on her feet, their eyes fierce and unblinking, except for Doris, who'd always coveted the upstairs crib. She was probably up there sleeping like a baby while everyone else worried. Joe and Mia slept slumped in the chairs at Angelo's table. Carlo remained out of sight for whatever reason.

Fetu woke up and groggily looked around. Morgen gave him a tired smile. She poured a mug of decaf and walked over to the tall window decorated with twinkling, red Christmas lights and candle lanterns. *Channel markers,* Angelo had said. *Follow the green lights to starboard going out and the red lights to starboard coming in. Green going, red right returning.* She stared at the bay and squeezed the penny purse until the clasp pierced her palm.

"I hate to go against Coast Guard orders," John said, "but I'm going out looking for him. Pastor Tim's minding the fire."

"I'll go with you." Fetu sounded half asleep.

"Bad idea, son. You're pale as clam meat. Better if you help tend the fire."

Morgen heard John top off his thermos with coffee. "Come home," she whispered through the glass. The wind changed direction, and a blade of brassy sunlight appeared followed by a patch of blue sky. She set her mug on the sill, dropped the penny purse, and placed her palms on the exterior wall. "Listen!"

Shella leaped out of her rocking chair with Pearl in her arms, threw open the entry door, and stepped outside. Morgen grabbed the penny purse and hermit crab shell and shoved them into her pocket. Everyone rushed out to the boardwalk. A ship's bell rang in the onshore wind followed by the sound of a boat engine growing louder in the dense fog.

"Angelo?" Shella raced toward the beach with Morgen and Fetu chasing behind. Salty Dog bayed and rocketed past all three of them. When Shella reached the sand, she kicked off her flip-flops and ran barefoot with Pearl's blanket flying like a sail in the wind.

As the sound of a boat grew louder, a shadow appeared out of the fog.

"Skipper!" John shouted and waved.

But *By-the-Wind Sailor* veered away from the channel markers and entrance to the harbor and staggered through soupy brown swells toward the drift logs beach.

"Something must be wrong with the boat," Fetu cried. "It could swamp or run aground. Come on, we may have to go in after him." He grabbed Morgen's hand, and they sprinted down the rain-pocked beach, John chasing behind them.

Meanwhile, the boat pushed on, methodically, deliberately, and vigilantly like a Mexican panga on the incoming tide, idling just beyond the breakers, seeming to wait until the perfect swell approached from behind. When it did, the boat accelerated, careening high on the crest of that wave. With a screeching roar, it hit the shore full throttle. The keel cleaved through wet sand until it beached with the jellies near the drift logs, and the engine died.

Shella clambered over the gunwale with astonishing agility. Fetu gave Morgen and John a boost into the boat before climbing over the transom. They hurried into the salon.

John headed down the steps to Angelo's stateroom while Morgen went to the helm and found Doris sitting in the captain's chair, damp and trembling with a mournful expression.

"Doris?" Shella cried, "What are you doing in here?"

An empty beer bottle wobbled in the cup holder.

Morgen felt a chill. "Where's Angelo?" She peered down the stairway and saw several inches of water on the floor. Broken glass and thousands of pennies littered the stairs, bunk, and floor, and anxiety ballooned inside her chest.

"Angelo?" Shella screamed. "Where did he go?" The boat's control panel began to smoke, and an acrid odor filled the salon. "Fire!" She hugged Pearl to her chest and jumped to the beach. Doris yowled and leaped behind them. When the control panel burst into flames, Fetu grabbed Morgen's arm. "Let's go!"

Morgen choked on the black smoke and shook him off. "No, where's Angelo?" She grabbed a coffee-sodden dish towel from the galley sink and beat at the burning panel.

"Where's the fire extinguisher?" Fetu yelled.

"Skipper don't bother with fire extinguishers, son." John staggered up from the stateroom. "Say, you did a job there, Morgen."

She coughed and pressed the damp towel against the blackened instruments and melted wiring. "Where is he?" She tried to go below, but John restrained her.

"There's shattered glass all over. Nobody there anyway."

"But how did the boat—?" Her eyes searched the horizon. "Listen to me. Angelo could be out there floating in a life jacket."

"Never wore one." John surveyed the fire-damaged instruments.

Morgen glanced at Dashboard Guadalupe calmly praying in her life jacket, grabbed John, and spun him around.

"We have to try. Maybe he caught hold of a drift log. John? Angelo's strong, and he's my friend."

She turned to Fetu for help, but he was on the aft deck picking up the splintered remains of the box that had held his father's ashes. She gazed down the beach through her tears and saw Vic standing alone fifty yards away, shoulders slumped, head bowed, his polished shoes buried in the sand. Beyond him, Mia carried Pearl and helped a weeping Shella walk toward Fish Camp while Doris trotted daintily behind them.

"Fuel tank dry," Joe said. He looked at the trench carved in the beach, crossed himself, and gazed out across the ocean.

Morgen eased herself off the boat and examined the bow. As expected, the pelican-priest figurehead was gone. She stumbled to the transom.

BY-THE-WIND SAILOR
FISH CAMP, WA

The boat's bright-blue hull faded to gray before her eyes like a dying jellyfish. She dried her tears on her sleeve with an ironic smile. Angelo had explained his boat's name with such pride: *it stays afloat on the surface of the sea, can right itself when capsized, and always makes it to shore.* "Of course you'd come home," she whispered. She tucked a pinch of sand into her pocket and climbed back onto the boat.

Fetu had picked up the broken tape deck and was rewinding a Dean Martin cassette tape with shaking fingers. Was he thinking about what had happened to Angelo or about how George had drowned after letting go of his yellow fan?

She stepped into the salon and saw John weeping while he grasped the scorched ship's wheel. She pocketed a few of the pennies of hope from the top stair while Salty Dog looked around the cabin as though in disbelief.

"Oh, Salty," Morgen whispered, petting his head. "I'm sorry, pup. I'm so sorry for all of us." She sat on the settee with her head in her hands. All that remained was a wrecked, smoldering trawler. *By-the-Wind Sailor* was no more.

MORGEN WADED IN THE SHALLOW SURF CARRYING A BOTTLE of cranberry wine she'd taken from the kitchen. Evidently, *Catchalot*, crewed by Fish Campers in orange life jackets, had coaxed *By-the-Wind Sailor* into the rising tide because the two old boats appeared to be roped together and heading back to safe harbor. Bonfire coals and ash ebbed away from the lifeless drift logs, and fresh by-the-wind sailor jellies floated ashore and tickled her ankles. Angelo's verse came to mind, the part about poor souls lost at sea: *Blue tears they weep while heaven-bound plunge alive to the surging sea and sail the waves to distant shores to comfort those who grieve.* She picked up blue jellies by their sails and gently returned them to the surf. "Are these the tears you cried when you knew you were leaving this world behind?" She gulped the cranberry wine. "You told us your deckhand fell overboard and drowned, leaving behind a young wife and baby." She stared at the horizon. "I'll help look after Shella and Pearl for you, because like Uncle Vic says, blood alone does not a family make."

She'd ripped the cuff of her favorite white cable-knit sweater while climbing into the boat, and when she pulled on the snag, it began to unravel. With the bottle of cranberry wine tucked under her arm, she rhythmically flapped her smarting hands and spun the yarn into a snarl while she stumbled down the beach. Pelting rain and wind gusts rolled in off the ocean. She huddled down and tugged on the yarn until nothing was left but a damp, dirty tangle and she was wearing only her sopping wet, white bra and jeans. With a shrug, she guzzled the wine. "To Mom. To Gram. To Angelo."

Swinging the bottle like Angelo's baseball bat, she climbed up on the familiar massive drift log, but something in the strandline caught her eye. Could it be a missing piece of their lives? She performed a grand jeté onto the beach.

Nestled in kelp and debris, a glass fishing float glistened like a shiny blue baseball. It probably had been bobbing along for thousands of miles before washing up during the storm. When she cupped it in her numb fingers, it felt like she was finally holding her own world in her hands. "Perfect throw," she whispered. "You could have been Johnny Bench." She closed her eyes and listened as icy, wet shards fell from the umbrella of stars.

Thursday, November 6, 2003

Morgen shivered inside the lair she'd dug into the dune scarp as the night sky lightened and stars disappeared one by one. Gulls stood sentry on a silent beach. Clams slept under the glossy ebb tide. A lone pelican flew high enough to reflect the first rays of dawn. She inhaled the kelpy fresh air and watched the morning sun illuminate white satin ruffles on the blue rolling surf. *This is where I was conceived, and this is where I'll die from hypothermia if I don't get going.*

Mia appeared before her in a halo of fluffy gray fog, looking like Our Lady of Guadalupe in a celestial blue shawl, serene and sweet with the scent of roses. She crossed herself, knelt on the sand, and helped Morgen crawl out of the collapsing dune.

"I feel sick," Morgen whispered. She blinked in the harsh light and stared at the ocean. "I don't understand. Angelo was a good man."

"Sí, amiga." Mia wrapped her shawl around Morgen and kissed her hair. "*Siempre un hombre muy bueno* and now in heaven."

Morgen struggled to her feet and brushed the sand from her jeans. "Oh dear Lord, I got a halibut headache, and my favorite sweater seems to have unraveled just like I have." She picked up the glass fishing float and blew across the mouth of the empty wine bottle like a flute. "That's an F. I have perfect pitch."

Mia took Morgen by the arm. "Your long worry is very soon over," she said in pocket dictionary English. "Be brave and strong. Come, mi amiga, I help you go home."

Morgen looked over her shoulder at the ocean in time to see a brown pelican dive face first like a falling angel.

AT 11:20 P.M., ANOTHER STORM CAREENED INTO THE coast, and the power went off again. Morgen crouched on the bench seat in her flannel nightgown, cradling the glass fishing float in her hands like a crystal ball. She always felt safe in Tutti, but now? Not really. She peered between Fräu Heinrich's curtains. Nonstop lightning illuminated rivers of storm water cascading down the campground hill. Tree branches littered the boardwalk, and Fish Camp

perched like an ancient ruin on a sinking continent. She turned on her flashlight and then her metronome, last set at *grave* (♩ = 35, very slow and solemn), the perfect tempo for bedtime. *Tick-tick-tick-tick—* "What?" She stopped the pendulum. "I did *not* set this at *presto* (♩ = 160, very quick)." Her scalp began to prickle as she shone the light around Tutti's interior. She always set the numbers on her locked attaché case at 1-9-1-8 for Gram's birth year, but they'd been rolled to 1-2-3-4. "What the—" She reached for her manuscript journal. "Where's my—?"

A gust smashed against Tutti's side, and she was afraid the bus would blow over. She yanked off her nightgown, pulled on her sweats, and stepped into her chronically wet red sneakers. Wrapped in a slicker she'd borrowed from the curtained closet, she grabbed her flashlight and the shoelace key and left to take shelter in the Palace Café.

She took matches out of a drawer behind the bar, stoked up the fire in the fireplace, and lit the candle lanterns that had been returned to the tables. She couldn't take much more tragedy, and now her manuscript journal was missing.

A scuffling commotion on the front porch interrupted her thoughts. She opened the door and found John bruised and trembling in his sopping red flannel pajamas. His old cross-stitch drizzled water on his bare feet.

"Storm's pretty wild," he whispered.

Morgen pulled him inside. "What happened?" She took a blanket off the couch and draped it over his shoulders.

"My house is gone." His face was white with shock.

"Oh no, that's terrible!"

"I woke up when lightning flashed through my window, and wind and rain poured in. Wood and nails screeched, everything I own slammed against the back wall, and my poor cabin screamed and slid twenty feet into the sea with me inside riding my mattress like a toboggan." He shivered and stepped closer to the hearth. "Say, you made us a nice fire."

"Morgen? Is that you? The power's off again." Shella tiptoed downstairs in her pajamas. "Oh, Grampy, what happened?" Her voice was hoarse and her eyes pink and swollen.

"It's gone, Missy." His eyes were wide and red rimmed. "My house is gone." He plucked bottles of pills from his pockets with his shaking hands and put them on the table next to his soaked cross-stitch.

"Oh no," Shella cried. She grabbed a dishtowel from a cupboard and dried John's hair. "I'm so sorry." She hugged him to absorb the chill, while outside the wind howled in victory.

When Shella went into the kitchen to warm some milk, the entry door flew open, and Fetu hurried in, dressed in his parka and rumpled gray sweats. "Power's off again. Is everything okay?"

"Grampy John lost his house." Shella was shaking all over.

"Oh no." Fetu looked at John. "I'll grab some clean sweats for you." He headed for the door.

"Socks too," Shella called out. She filled a mug with hot milk and marched over to John. "Drink this."

"Seventy knot winds out there." John sipped the milk.

"There are too many tragedies happening all at once." Morgen chewed a cuticle until it bled. "And now I can't find my manuscript journal—"

"I can't find my daddy's watch." Shella covered her face with her hands and began to cry. "It was all I had of his to give Pearl someday—"

"What's going on in here?" Vic burst in armed with a flashlight and accompanied by Salty Dog. He closed the door behind him.

"Victor," John whispered, "my house is gone."

"Oh for Godsakes. Are you hurt?" He rushed over and put his hand on John's shoulder.

John appeared to take inventory. "No, not too bad."

"That's a blessing." Vic turned to Shella. "Did Carlo fix Tuna trailer?"

"Yes, it's fine now. I'll get the key."

Overhead, Pearl began to fuss in her crib, and Doris, the au purr, bounded up the stairs.

Shella gave a key to John. "Tuna's all yours. I better check on Pearl. May I?" She grabbed Morgen's flashlight and dashed up the stairs.

Fetu returned with an armful of clothing. "I lit the propane heater in the shower house and put a couple clean towels in there for you."

Vic glanced at the entry where the storm pummeled the door. "Take a hot shower, and get some sleep, John. Tomorrow, we'll see what we can salvage, and try not to worry. You'll be well taken care of. All of you need to rest. I'm Angie's executor, and those are my orders."

After Vic left with Salty Dog on his heels, John held his cross-stitch up to the firelight and read,

"'The Lord is my Shepherd...He leadeth me beside the still waters...He restoreth my soul...Amen.'

Trouble is, they've been anything but still waters."

Morgen watched him. *Bless his sweet, fearless, old heart.*

A peculiar blast of wind exploded underneath their feet

followed by the sound of crashing water. The Palace Café shuddered and lifted slightly as seawater foamed up between the floorboards.

John stiffened. "Say, this isn't good."

"What was that noise?" Shella scrambled down from her room with a wailing Pearl in one arm, and Doris tripping along behind them. "What's going on?"

A cat screeched for help, its yowls gurgling up from below as though it were drowning.

Shella ran toward John, her eyes as big as cioppino pots. "We've got to get out. This place is haunted by Lydia, the cat lady, and her jetty cats."

"No, wait," Morgen cried as more seawater flooded up through the floor, soaking their feet. "That sounds like Jack, and he must be down in the, like, crawlspace."

"Everybody needs to calm down." John looked at Lydia's portrait while he hugged Shella and Pearl against his damp red flannel nightshirt. "There's nobody haunting nothing. I ought to know, but sometimes we get a storm surge."

Jack howled again under the scarred floor as the old building trembled.

"Crap, Shella, you took my light!" Morgen grabbed the waterproof flashlight from the drawer and ran to the curtained closet.

Fetu grabbed her arm, but she shook him off and flung open the closet door. She ripped off her slicker and sneakers, popped off the panel, and squeezed through the opening into inky black water. Jack let out a desperate, five-second-long growl. "Hang on," she said. She quasi-dog-paddled toward him, waving the light and trying to keep her head above water. Jack cowered on the ledge with Our Lady of Guada-lupe, pressed against the ceiling and pleading for help, his teeth bared and his good eye red with terror. She reached him and treaded water. "Come on, Jackie, come to Mama, water's damn cold, come on, nice kitty."

"You okay?" Fetu called from the closet.

"Oh, sure," she hollered.

Poor Jack wrapped his trembling, bony forelegs around her neck and buried his face in the matted, wet hair behind her ear, uttering weird and un-cat-like complaints. "Great, now hang on, but please pull in your claws."

As she turned to paddle back, she glimpsed an object she hadn't noticed before. She grabbed hold of the ledge and shone her light on the statue of Guadalupe. Behind it in a pool of water, kelp, and sodden silk flowers lay a shiny object that looked oddly familiar. She would have fainted had Jack not nipped her earlobe. "Ouch, quit it!" Wave action sucked them down and threw them up against the ceiling. "Oh no, you don't. We are *not* going to drown tonight." With Jack trying mightily to crawl on top of her head, she managed to reach the submerged steps.

Jack scrambled up through the opening, and Fetu helped Morgen climb out. "Completely flooded down there. Maybe we should get out." Her foremothers necklace was wrapped around the shoelace key and hooked over her right ear.

"You saved his life." Shella sniffed, wrapping Jack in a dish towel and handing Morgen a blanket.

The power came on, and the Palace Café filled with light. Morgen saw John sitting in the rocking chair with Pearl in his arms, and when he looked at Morgen, his expression paled. "That your necklace?"

Morgen shivered. "Yes, but I don't usually wear it over my ear." She tucked it inside her shirt, and Fetu wrapped the blanket tighter around her shoulders.

Jack glowered and sneezed while Doris and the other jetty cats groomed and comforted him.

Vic burst in, and Carlo pushed him aside. "I've got this," he snapped. "Who turned on all these lights, why are these damn cats in here, and why is the floor wet?" He saw Lydia's new portrait glaring at him from the wall and screamed loud and long enough to, well, wake the dead.

Nobody cared, and it occurred to Morgen that she'd never heard a man scream before. It was rather disturbing, and after Carlo bolted for the entry door, she pulled Vic aside. "If he's so afraid of her, why does he stay?"

"Because Angie let him live here for free, but that's going to change."

She told Vic about what Natasha had reported seeing in the harbormaster house, and about the poisoned joint Carlo had left for her. As Vic listened, his expression blackened like the heavens before a squall. "I will take care of this."

Morgen felt more chilled than she had while treading water in the conch grotto.

Friday, November 7, 2003

Morgen sat in Tutti, munching trio mix and methodically rearranging photographs face down on the tabletop like a shell game, a calming activity after hours of helping plan Angelo's memorial service and helping Mia get a heart-broken Shella upstairs to rest. She'd hoped to find her manuscript journal in her attaché case but, sadly, had not.

She selected a picture and turned it face up. "Finally, a good omen," she whispered, staring at Gram's photograph of her mother's cremation urn. Something about it was eerily similar to the object she'd seen at Guadalupe's feet. But why on earth would her mother's stolen urn end up in Lydia Cooper's conch grotto? Maybe Lydia was a ghost witch as Shella said, with telekinetic magical powers.

The foremothers necklace grew exceedingly warmer against her collarbone. Some sort of hippie harmonics? There was only one way to find out. She looked out the window through her opera glasses and watched Vic, John, Joe, and Fetu pile into the red pickup. Probably going to salvage what they could of John's possessions. She surveyed the shuttered Palace Café and waited ten minutes before stuffing a towel into her shopping bag and grabbing the shoelace key.

She unlocked the door and, after finding the waterproof flashlight, crept through the dining room to the curtained closet. She stripped off her sneakers and jeans and slipped through the opening. John had been pumping out seawater, but she knew the grotto was still flooded.

Once inside, she left the shopping bag on the top step and, knee deep in cold water, shone the light across the hundreds of sparkling tiles and mirrors on walls cut into the ancient sea floor. She saw a drain hose trailing out toward the jetty through the airshaft in the conch's whorl. It seemed as though the rhythm of John's sump pump was trying to coax something from deep in her memory while the curving conch wall, like a cochlea, resonated with dreams, bones, and lives once shattered but now reassembling and healing.

She hoped the mysterious item was still up on the ledge. She waded to the back of the grotto and tossed the flashlight up into the nest of kelp and fake flowers. Our Lady of Guadalupe had survived the flood and maintained her vigil. With a grunt, Morgen lunged, grabbed the cornice, and pulled herself up by hooking her left leg on the conch's lip. Behind the statue, the flashlight illuminated a shiny, aquamarine object partially rolled up in a shroud, and the blue crystal star keepsake that she'd tossed up at Guadalupe's feet twelve days earlier was resting on top of it. With a sob, she grabbed the shrouded bundle, blue crystal star, and flashlight and dropped feet first into the water.

She sloshed back to the entrance, collapsed on the top step, and propped the light so she could see the task at hand. Her labored breathing overwhelmed her hearing, but when she uttered, "Mom," the conch grotto softened to the sound of water gently washing the walls. With the reverence of a young nurse, she loosened the shroud, which fell away, exposing a cremation urn.

It was about ten inches tall, heavy for its size, made of dense metal, and coated with thick, aquamarine paint. She wasn't surprised to find a musical staff with the opening phrase of Stravinsky's Concerto for Piano and Winds—*long, long, short, long, Char-lie Ma-rín, Mor-gen Ma-rín*—etched around the base in a never-ending band. Eight gold stars representing the Big Dipper and North Star surrounded an oversized treble clef sign stretching from cap to base with the centermost curl resembling an ocean wave right before it toppled. There was a small red heart where the bottom line ended in a curl. It was the same design as her tattoo and her mother's. *Charlie Josette Marín* was engraved on it, followed by Grandpa Scott's "great continuum" verse.

Morgen hugged the urn against her heart like Shella would cuddle Pearl and began to rock and weep for thirteen years, five months, and seventeen days of loss. Her sobs ripped her insides to ribbons, and she cried until she was too weak to breathe. She started to rewrap the urn in its shroud, but her fingernail got caught on a zipper and tore down to the quick. She sucked on her finger—

Zipper? She took a closer look, and what she thought was a shroud turned out to be a pair of dirty, tan pants. Doodles flashed through her memory like sets of waves approaching a beach and toppling over one another: her mother-the-pink-note on the drift logs beach, grabbing the attacker's pants to cover herself, escaping through the night, pants flying like a ghost overhead until she was saved by Lydia, the Widow Witch.

Morgen shivered. Was it from being in the cold water or from the reality of the moment? She wrapped the towel around her shoulders. The zipper was down because the assailant had taken off his pants to...Her fingers shook as she reached into the left-front pocket and found a fragile piece of paper and a wadded cigarette wrapper, faded but clearly labeled Camel Turkish & Domestic Blend Cigarettes. She unfolded the paper and read: *Order to Report for Induction. To Carlo Russo Ricci. Greeting: You are hereby ordered for induction into the Armed Forces of the United States...*Her pulse crescendoed like kettledrums pounding in her skull.

She felt the other pocket. A soft lump inside didn't move at her touch. Dead rat? Dirty handkerchief? Biting her lip, she reached in and pulled out a thick braid of golden-brown hair, tied with a pale-blue ribbon. Tangled with it was a rusty switchblade knife engraved with the initials CRR. *Carlo? You shit.*

She heard footfalls and the refrigerator door opening. Carlo's signature stink of sweat and nicotine drifted into the closet like toxic gas. She pulled on her jeans, gathered her things, and peeked between the curtained doors.

Carlo stood in the kitchen with his back to her, raiding the refrigerator while singing "Santa Lucia."

With the shopping bag on her shoulder and tan pants over her arm, she slipped between the doors, crossed the dining room floor as silently as One-Eyed Jack stalking a rat, and positioned herself halfway between Lydia's portrait and Carlo. *My father?* She retched into her palm.

"Hey, Morgen," Fetu said as he burst in. "We turned back to follow the sheriff—"

"What?" Carlo spun around, dropping a sandwich.

"I hate you!" Morgen screamed as she waved the pants like a matador's cape. "You're afraid of Lydia Cooper, because she caught you with your pants down!" She heard Vic mutter as John groaned and dropped into a chair, but her eyes stayed locked on Carlo while she yanked the urn and braid out of the bag. "This is Morning Glory's braid. You hacked off my mother's hair, it was my mother you raped, and *I* am the result of that attack!" She gasped for breath. "These are her ashes." She gripped the urn like she did Angelo's baseball bat and charged, smashing Carlo across the face and bloodying his lips and nose. Then she kicked him in his evil nuts, and he fell to his knees. "You're nothing but shit, and Pavarotti would spit in your face!"

"What's going on?" Shella clomped down the stairs with Doris bounding behind her.

Carlo scrambled to his feet while Salty Dog growled and bared his teeth. He kicked at Salty, grabbed the truck keys from Fetu's hand, and raced out the door.

Vic gripped Fetu's arm. "Don't worry. He won't get far."

Morgen stared through the tall window lined with green lights as though watching a nightmare unfold. She dropped onto a barstool and cradled the urn in her arms. "I promised

I'd come back to help her, and I finally did." She handed Carlo's knife and draft notice to Vic and dissolved into tears.

Nobody moved except Doris who sidled up, sniffed Carlo's pants, and sneezed. She hopped onto Morgen's lap and began to lick her hand.

"Sweet au purr," Morgen whispered. "Sweet kitty."

Sweet Baby.

9.

As soon as Morgen found a comfortable spot for the urn to reside and unplugged the limelight, she heard a vehicle pull up. The engine was left running. She started to peek between Fräu Heinrich's curtains but smelled Carlo's telltale odor and froze when she heard him singing Pavarotti's "*Jamme, jamme 'ncoppa, jamme jà, Jamme, jamme 'ncoppa, jamme jà—*"

An explosion shoved Tutti sideways, and Morgen screamed and grabbed the table—

"*Funiculì, funiculà, funiculì, funiculà—*"

A second blast near the front bumper dropped Tutti to her knees like a wounded animal. Morgen heard footfalls outside on the gravel, circling Tutti like a predator moving in for the kill, and then a deafening concussion shook the right rear corner of the bus.

"*'Ncoppa, jamme jà, funiculì, funiculà—*"

A siren wailed in the distance. Fetu yelled at Carlo to stop as a fourth blow struck the left rear corner, and Tutti slumped to the ground.

Morgen flung open the cargo door in time to see Salty Dog, illuminated by security lights, torpedo up the hill toward Tutti like a great white shark, horrendous fangs bared and eyes red with hate. He launched into Carlo, knocking him off his feet and sending the Paul Bunyan ax flying.

Flashing lights strafed Fish Camp, and Fetu grabbed the ax like a baseball bat and glared at Carlo. "Don't move—"

Carlo scrambled into the truck with Salty Dog's teeth shredding his pant leg and started down the hill, but a patrol car blocked his escape.

Fetu dropped the ax and hurried to Morgen's side. "Are you okay?"

She watched the officer handcuff Carlo and shove him into the back seat. "I thought he was going to kill me." She pressed two fingers to her throat to check her pulse: *allegro* ($\quarternote$ = 135). "You risked your life—"

"No worries." Fetu walked around Tutti, his flashlight revealing the damage. "Except Carlo slashed all four tires and bent the rims."

"This was my mom's bus," she cried. Shella, John, Joe, Mia, and seven jetty cats rushed up the hill to comfort her. Salty Dog galloped back, and she knelt to pet him. After Vic talked to the officer, he told everyone to go back to bed.

"Do you want to sleep in Salmon?" Fetu asked.

"No, I'm not leaving Tutti." She shivered. "I know it's over, but please stay. That's all. Just be here?"

"Anything," he whispered. "Anything." He opened the cargo door, and Salty Dog leaped inside first, panting and wagging his tail. "Since Salty's here to chaperone, may I please lie down too? I'm exhausted."

"Sure, but Salty sleeps on the floor." She climbed onto the platform bed, and Fetu kicked off his shoes and followed, hitting his head twice on the ceiling.

"Very cozy. Glad you found your mum's urn. Goodnight." He rolled over and fell asleep.

Although they were fully dressed, Morgen pulled the eiderdown over them. "Sleep well, Fetu Lemalu," she whispered. Sure, she had major trust issues, but he'd always been nice to her and treated her with respect. She liked his looks, his natural scent, and that he too was a musician. Also, like Mia had said, he was sexy. She moved her knee against his leg so that they were barely touching. "I like you so much that it terrifies me," she whispered.

She closed her eyes, and as she dozed off to Salty Dog's snoring and Fetu's soft breathing, she heard Pavarotti singing "Funiculì, Funiculà" in her mind's ear as tire after tire exploded like cannon fire.

Deep in the night, she awoke with a start. Her mother must have thought Carlo was going to kill her too, brandishing a switchblade, hacking off her hair.

Tears filled her eyes as she imagined her helpless mother pinned to the beach and fighting for her life against Carlo. *Goddamn him forever.* But her mother prevailed by living the rest of her life as a caring, brave, strong woman. That too was part of her legacy. She dried her face on the eiderdown, reached under her pillow for her blue crystal star, and squeezed it in her palm. Fetu mumbled and took her other hand. She held onto him as the glad feeling warmed her heart, and she went back to sleep.

Saturday, November 8, 2003

Morgen and Shella waited behind several rows of chairs set up on the beach for Angelo's memorial service. Both wore *By-the-Wind Sailor* sweatshirts, and Shella had a rope of garlic bulbs dangling over one arm. She pulled the knit beanie down over Pearl's ears. "How did you know about that crawl space and I didn't?"

"The curtained closet always intrigued me, and I snooped," Morgen said. "I'm glad, because that's where I found the paint for your mural. I'm also glad because One-Eyed Jack was down there barely hanging onto his ninth life."

"What are you going to do about your camper?"

"I don't know. Get her fixed somehow."

Fetu joined them and took Morgen's hand, and they contemplated the growing audience of Palace Café regulars and members of the Coast Guard. Beyond the chairs, bleached drift logs reflected sunlight onto the crowd. Gentle waves washed the beach. A large brown pelican glided by, blessing the water with the tips of his wings. Joe had lashed two pieces of driftwood together to form a cross and had stuck it in the sand between the crowd and the surf. Mia arranged red roses at the base. Vic added a small Italian flag, Salty Dog dropped a well-chewed baseball among the roses, and Shella draped the rope of garlic around the neck of the cross.

The group gathered closer together. Vic, dressed in a suit plus a Cincinnati Reds bow tie, briefly introduced his wife, Louise, to everyone.

"Welcome, friends. Please be seated," Pastor Tim said. He wore a long brown cassock and hiking boots. "We are here today to celebrate the life of Angelo Vincenzo Bordacelli." Everyone settled, and the ocean calmed. "Angelo always said that his legacy was like the wake behind his boat, that his significance would fade, vanish, and be forgotten, but Angelo's wake stretches out, and the ripples keep on rolling."

Morgen's thoughts drifted. She'd spent only sixteen days with him, but it seemed like forever. Old Spice. Baseball. Beer. Corny jokes. Pennies-of-hope. Such a complicated and caring man. She gazed at the crowd and joined in as the Mariners' Hymn ended:

> *"Oh, hear us when we cry to Thee,*
> *For those in peril on the sea. Amen."*

"And now, a moment of silence," Pastor Tim said, and the crowd hushed.

Shella began to cry, and Morgen put an arm around her shoulder.

John stepped forward and opened a Bible. "My name's John Cooper. Skipper was my friend." He straightened his worn denim jacket and cleared his throat. "I will read to you my favorite parts of Psalm 107.

> *They that go down to the sea in ships,*
> *These see the works of the Lord,*
> *and his wonders in the deep.*
> *He maketh the storm a calm, He bringeth*
> *them unto their desired haven."*

He closed the Bible and whispered, "Amen."

Vic walked up and stood beside him. "Angie was my nephew, my godson, and my dearest friend," he said, his voice wavering, as he raised a brass bell to shoulder height. "This is the bell from *By-the-Wind Sailor*, and this is for Angelo Vincenzo Bordacelli." He slowly struck the bell eight times, signifying the death of a sailor.

Morgen took a deep breath and stepped forward. "Thank you, everybody, for coming today. Please join us at the marina for the placing of the plaque. Afterward, brunch will be served in the Jetty Cat Palace Café. We made a huge pot of cioppino and extra loaves of sourdough bread. We'd love to see all of you there."

Down on north float, Morgen turned on the boom box, and while Dean Martin sang "That's Amore," Joe nailed a brass plaque to the piling.

In Loving Memory
Angelo Vincenzo Bordacelli
Skipper, By-the-Wind Sailor
July 17, 1950 - November 3, 2003
"Don't worry about me. I'm going fishin'! Ciao, folks!"

She saw Jim the Harbor Seal pop to the surface and stepped aside when Salty Dog galloped down the ramp to greet him. After a moment together, Jim rolled and submerged. No amount of whining could entice him to stay. Salty Dog flopped on the dock with a sigh and rested his head on his front paws. "It hurts to lose a special friend," Morgen whispered. "Poor Salty."

Morgen stood beside the mantelpiece under Lydia's portrait, content to watch Angelo's wake from the sidelines. Mia, Joe, Shella, and Fetu were busy serving cioppino brunch to the crowd of well-wishers while John visited with members of the Coast Guard.

Vic crossed the Palace floor to join her, an old, leather satchel hanging from his shoulder. "I want to share with you that many years ago, Angie became deeply depressed after an incident involving him and Carlo but wouldn't confide in me, because he'd been indoctrinated that a Bordacelli never ratted on flesh and blood. You know, *Famiglia per Sempre.* In hindsight, I believe it had something to do with your mother's attack." He dabbed his eyes with a handkerchief. "Years later, he reminded me of the incident and said that a girl he'd tried to rescue ended up saving his life with one penny."

Morgen forced a smile. "I'd asked him about the penny jar on his boat, and he told me that every time he got a new penny, he remembered wanting to get well because a special person, who turned out to be my mom, thought he was worth saving. Makes my heart ache." She rubbed her breastbone. "When his boat beached, we found broken glass and pennies all over his stateroom floor. I hope you don't mind, but I took a few in remembrance."

Vic lowered his voice. "I went through Angie's locker in the harbormaster house and noticed fourteen canisters stored in there had recently been removed, leaving behind clean, circular spaces in years of dust. He always had a penny jar going, so I got curious and went through the rest of the house. Lo and behold, I found fourteen jars full of pennies under Carlo's bed." His expression darkened. "Because Carlo's father was Angie's uncle on his mother's side, he was related, but he was never family." He reached into the satchel and handed her Angelo's missal. "I want you to look at this in private, but I'd like it back, except for one photo that you may keep." He cleared his throat, signifying he was back to business. "On a positive note, I found this under Carlo's mattress." He pulled Morgen's manuscript journal out of his satchel.

"Oh dear Lord. I trusted him because of his singing voice, but in return, he stole my most private voice." Tears flooded her eyes. "And touched my personal things—"

"Is something wrong?" Shella had reappeared.

Vic shook his head. "Do you know Seamus Maloney?"

"Yeah, he's my daddy. Why?"

He reached into his coat pocket and pulled out a gold pocket watch.

"Oh my gosh, that's his watch. Where'd you get it?"

"Carlo had it along with several other things he had no business having." He rubbed his forehead. "My dear, I'd like to thank you for this delicious brunch. Angelo said you make the best cioppino."

"Oh, I don't know, he always told me to add more garlic." Shella stepped closer to Vic. "I keep expecting him to walk through that doorway and give me a hug. Smelling like Old Spice and the ocean and saying 'fetch me a beer and a scoop of spaghetti, per favore, Shella Bella Velella velella.'" She kissed Pearl's forehead. "I miss him so much."

He reached into his pocket. "I thought you'd like to have the taps from Angie's boyhood tap shoes."

Shella's fingers shook as she took the aluminum taps held together with a piece of wire. "He always wanted to be a comedian and a song and dance man, just like Dean Martin."

Vic smiled sadly. "May I please hold her?" He gathered Pearl in his arms. "Next week, we'll discuss a provision of Angelo's estate, because he left you and Pearl a lot of money."

Shella burst into tears, but Morgen smiled because now Shella and Pearl would have a future too. *Grazie, Angelo.*

Blushing and sniffling, Shella took Pearl and returned to the kitchen.

"It seems I'm busy with my executor duties today." Vic closed his eyes for a moment before continuing. "I need to inform you that you've inherited two properties in Seattle."

"What?" Morgen gasped.

"In 1966, Angie's father bought six classic bungalows on Ninth Street near the university. The plan was for Angie to live in one, attend school, and earn ownership of the homes by managing the rentals and doing maintenance, which he did. As the years went by, the properties became very valuable, and at his direction, we sold all but two: the one he'd lived in during prep school and its identical twin across the street that he called the Hippie House. Yesterday, I found a directive dated November 1 adding you as joint tenant on both properties. Simply noted that he wanted you to have a place to live when you began your new job. Now that he's gone, they belong to you free and clear. Depending on which house you choose, I'll help the current tenant relocate."

She remembered that November 1 was the day they'd played catch. She felt lightheaded and grabbed Lydia's mantelpiece to steady herself. She used to think of those twin caramel-colored houses as estranged friends who chanced to meet, each at a loss for words, but unable to move on. Now she knew they had been friends for life. "I know the one you call the Hippie House," she whispered. "That's where Mom lived during college."

Sunday, November 9, 2003

MORGEN COULDN'T SLEEP, SO SHE CURLED UP IN A CLOUD of Old Spice with a mug of cold decaf and Angelo's missal. When she opened the book, several snapshots fell out: a faded black-and-white photo of a teenage Angelo in full catcher's gear standing in front of a backstop, mask tipped back and a smile on his handsome face; Angelo posing with a man and a woman, the names Vincenzo, Gianna, and Angelo Bordacelli written on the back; a dog-eared snapshot of Angelo reclining in a hospital bed with his nurse aka Charlie Marín smiling at his side. "Hi, Mom," Morgen whispered. She set that one aside and dropped an Angelo-penny-of-hope into the sugar bowl.

She turned the page to a narrative handwritten like a confession within the text of the Catholic Mass and heard Angelo's voice. *Bless me, Father, for I have sinned. It has been decades since my last confession, but here's the deal. I was raised with the Ten Commandments, especially the fourth one, honor thy father and thy mother, but obeying that commandment is my greatest sin. My father ordered that I never rat on flesh and blood, so I kept a hideous crime a secret because of perverted family loyalty. For that, I hate my father as much as I hate my cousin, Carlo, who committed the crime. I am heartily sorry for having offended you, and I detest all my sins. I just wish none of this had happened. Thank you. Amen. Dated October 21, 2003.* Evidently, Angelo, too, looked for redemption in the silence between the notes of his faith.

She thought a moment. He wrote this two weeks earlier after learning that Morning Glory was her mother. "Oh dear Lord, I wish it had never happened too, even if it meant I'd never been born." She put the missal beside her mother and Angelo's picture, corrected her posture, and played the Fantasie perfectly on the tabletop, from memory, beginning to end. She began to cry. "I did it, I've finally got it, I can do this—"

She jumped when someone tapped on the windshield. She peered through Fräu Heinrich's curtains and saw Fetu, Joe, and a half dozen young men milling about outside. She scrambled into her sweats and opened the cargo door. "How do you do?" she addressed the crowd. A black pickup came rumbling up the hill with four wheels bouncing in the bed. "Excuse me please, but what's happening?"

"Joe put out a call to the surfing community," Fetu said, "and a guy knew a guy who knew a guy who had a similar bus. Vic paid for everything."

Morgen watched as they jacked up Tutti and, one by one, replaced her ruined wheels. "This was my mother's bus, and I don't know what to say or do, but wait." She reached inside, grabbed a bag of trio mix, and handed it to the individual with the truck. "This is her special recipe, and I hope you like it. Thank you, Joe and everybody, for being so good to us."

Morgen and Fetu, both wearing orange life jackets and Angelo's blue knit beanies, held hands and gazed out *Catchalot*'s windows while the old boat plowed out of the bay and into the Pacific. John sat at the helm munching a sourdough cranberry scone, and Shella rode beside him on the wheelhouse bench with Pearl cradled in her arms and Salty Dog at her feet. Vic stood by the door appearing simultaneously out of his comfort zone and delighted by the novelty of it all.

Chunks of sunlight bounced on the waves. Dolphins leaped and splashed, racing under and ahead of the bow. A lone pelican followed behind them, staring at the wake as though reading the water. After a while, John eased up on the throttle and set the autopilot. Everyone went out on deck, and they drifted in still waters.

Vic held Angelo's catcher's mitt while Shella untangled the string Morgen had used to tie Pearl's umbilical cord.

Morgen threaded the string through Angelo's tap shoe taps and around several of Mia's red roses and tied everything to the mitt's webbing. Shella secured a garlic bulb and one votive candle in the jumbled bouquet, and Fetu lit the wick.

As they said their silent prayers, Vic lowered Angelo's catcher's mitt onto the water where it caught the ocean current and headed toward the sunset and the distant Bering Sea. When the last rays of sunlight kissed Pearl's cheek, the aluminum taps chimed, and a mounting fog bank settled on the horizon looking like the vast lost continent of Atlantis.

Everyone but Morgen returned to the cabin as *Catchalot* headed home. She remained on the aft deck, watching the catcher's mitt bob in the wake. Angelo had said that no matter how big the boat, the wake eventually disappeared. Maybe that wasn't so bad. Maybe the only way she could get rid of the wreckage in her wake was to forgive herself and let it go. "Hey, Angelo," she whispered. "Can you see those *sombreros blancos* out there? You know, white caps? Get it?"

Twenty yards away, a gray whale broke the surface and blew a seawater geyser into the sky. Morgen cried out, and the whale responded with a wave of its magnificent fluke before submerging. She held her breath and scanned the horizon, but the whale was gone. She stared across the blue-black water and was the last to see the candle's distant glow. "Ciao, Angelo."

After everyone had finished all-you-can-eat fried razor clams, French fries, and zucchini frittata, Morgen helped clear the dishes. "I'll never forget that night—the clamming, bonfire, and secrets. Thanks for cleaning and freezing the catch."

"I like having a job to do." John brightened. "Say, I'm still pumping out that, uh, crawlspace. It's flooded twice before in some forty years but never like this. When a wave enters that airshaft just right, it siphons the water in. Since that last storm, much of the ducting's washed away, the shaft is unstable, and the retaining wall is pulling away from the hillside. We got to fill the space with sand and gravel and seal it off."

"I want to preserve the Palace Café at any cost," Vic said, "so get an engineer out there if you have to."

John got up to add another log to the fire, and Salty Dog and One-Eyed Jack sauntered over and flopped down on the floor to warm themselves. "Say, look at that." John gestured at the Weather Channel on his way back to the table. "Cincinnati's getting snow. Kind of makes me hanker for a nice warm slice of pie." He sat again, fork in hand, and waited.

"We have apple-blackberry pie and white chocolate-cranberry cheesecake," Shella said while she and Mia carried desserts to the table. "All the fruit came from the victory garden." Shella cut John a generous slice. "Would you like ice cream too?"

He nodded, Morgen contributed a bowl of trio mix, and they visited and ate while Pearl slept in her crib with Doris purring at her side.

Morgen sat between Mia and Fetu, listened to chitchat as soft as candlelight, and imagined the tall, glowing Palace Café windows as seen from the dark outdoors, but this time *she* was on the inside. This was what having family must be like.

"Family," Mia whispered, as though reading her mind. She studied a page in the dictionary. "This is our big family—"

"Victor?" John cleared his throat. "Me and Joe spent hours on the boat, and sad to say, life's gone out of her, and she'll never sail again. Electronics are fried. Bilge pump's clogged. Mast and radar's gone. Engine's seized up. Prop's bent, rudder's twisted, and the anchor's gone. There's water, fire, and smoke damage, but I had a crazy dream about what to do with her." He took a notebook out from under his chair.

Vic smiled while staring at John's sketches, and everybody crowded around.

"See? We truck it up the hill to the victory garden and set it on blocks. Line the access road with drift logs. Build a deck around the hull that connects to a little white cottage with a widow's walk," John's voice broke, "and a small white lighthouse tower with a cupola."

"You have a fabulous imagination," Fetu said.

John leaned back and smiled.

"I love your idea," Vic said, "and I'll fund it on one condition: that you oversee the work and then live up there and take care of it."

"It's spectacular," Morgen whispered. Just like John's character.

"Speaking of spectacular ideas," Vic said, "Morgen, to celebrate your new job, Angie ordered a gift for you." He went behind the counter and returned with a piece of heavy white rubber.

"For me?" She offered her best smile. "Very nice. What is it?"

Vic laughed. "It's a home plate. He wanted you to have it so that no matter where you went, you'd be safe until you finally got 'home.'" He winked at her. "Get it?"

"Got it, thank you." She remembered pressing her childish nose against the glass brick window at the Hippie House and wondering what it would be like to belong inside a home like that. She smiled as her mother whispered in her mind's ear. *Look who gets to live there now.*

Monday, November 10, 2003

MORGEN HAD JUST FINISHED PLAYING CHOPIN'S BALLADE no. 4 on the tabletop when Fetu flung open the cargo door. Shouldn't he have knocked first?

"Hey." He climbed in waving his notepad. "I finished my song. Want to hear it?"

"Sure." She shrugged.

"Bear with me." He took her mandolin out of its case and flopped down on the opposite bench seat. "I'm not mandolin proficient." He held the instrument in his arms and pointed at the tuning pegs. "See, four pairs of strings tuned alike. G-D-A-E like the four lowest guitar strings but in reverse."

She bit her lip to keep from blurting that Andras had often made her play passages in reverse.

He plucked a pair of strings, and she flinched. "Sorry, I have perfect pitch."

"I don't, but my song kept me up all night, and I had to finish."

She relished the music in his accent as he mumbled and rifled through his notepad. She loved looking at him, at his bittersweet chocolate eyes and full lips. Her body underwent a pleasant but unfamiliar progression of changes, and the word *melting* came to mind. Although she might entertain a little physical intimacy, it wouldn't be fair to either one of them if they made love while Andras hovered backstage in her mind.

After playing a lovely instrumental introduction, Fetu began to sing.

*Hear all the earth's oceans in a single seashell,
hear all the world's voices by listening to
a single heart. Who knew our paths would cross,
if only for a little while? How curious when
you least expect to find love. It's your turn in the
great continuum, so take a leap of faith.
Let them hear your story in this music.
No words. Only love.*

"Wait." Morgen clenched her fists. "Those are my Grandpa Scott's words."

"Just the chorus. What's the problem? I thought you'd like it."

"You should have asked my permission." Because too many times, she'd thought someone was a friend when the person just wanted something from her or to use her.

"Oh, come on." He sat beside her. "You take everything so seriously." He put his arm around her shoulder, but she flinched. "Shit, I thought we were pretty close after everything that's happened, but you're pushing me away again."

She tried to say *please understand me,* but language failed her, and she couldn't access any words. *Damn my autism!* Tears poured down her cheeks. *I'm so scared.*

"I love you for real," Fetu said, "but this isn't working for me." He seemed to be giving her time to reply by slowly putting the mandolin away.

Her brain cried *I want to love you too,* but she remained helplessly mute and unable to move.

"I know you're dealing with a lot, so I'll give you some space." He gave her a long look before kissing her on the lips. "I might visit the Olympic rainforest or Mount St. Helens, so I'll be around. Call me if you want to get together."

Morgen squeezed her eyes shut against her tears, heard the cargo door open and shut, and pounded her fists on the tabletop. *Please don't go.* She picked up the guitar pick, still warm from his touch, and soundlessly wept.

SHE REMAINED FROZEN AT THE TABLETOP TRYING TO ANA-lyze what had happened. Once again, somebody she'd *fiercely* loved left her without warning, just as her mother had, and Gram and Angelo too. She flexed her ice-cold fingers until they began to tingle.

A cat yowled at the door.

"Leave me alone." Her throat burned, and her voice was raspy and dry, but at least it had returned. She grabbed the urn and hugged it to her chest.

Yowl. *Scratch. Scratch.*

She yanked the door open. "What?"

Doris bounded in and perched on the bench seat. She stared at Morgen with those beautiful hazel eyes without blinking as only a sweet Cheshire-like cat could.

Morgen sat down beside the urn and began to cry. "I never dreamed Fetu would leave."

Doris yowled again and began to purr in earnest.

"What?" Morgen sniffled. "Oh. Right." She caught her breath and sang a simple *solfège* to Doris's contented purring until her heart rate lowered to *largo* ($\quad$ = 50, slow and dignified). After devouring a handful of trio mix, she arranged some of the missing pieces of her life and her mother's on the tabletop like a fortune teller might and, for extra measure, in alphabetical order: Angelo's penny purse and pennies-of-hope, blue crystal star, Fetu's guitar/mandolin pick, Gram's storage key, hermit crab shell, Mom's conch shell, photographs, and the wild rose sugar bowl.

She picked up the conch shell and whispered into it. "Fetu? I'm sorry, please don't give up on me."

Her phone lit up, indicating she'd missed a call. *Fetu?*

She ran down the hill, waving at Joe who was cleaning Fetu's vacated trailer but keeping her feet moving until she entered the Palace Café. "Hi, Shella, Hola, Mia. I need to use the phone please."

"This just came." Shella handed her a small package from the frame shop in Aberdeen, and Mia set a mug of decaf on the counter in front of her.

"Thank you," Morgen whispered, but when she heard Violet's voicemail, her spirits fell. Violet chattered that they loved the apartment with the funny beach mural and views of the Sammamish River and that it looked like Morgen had left in a hurry, so they swept up the trail mix and washed her uniform and bath towels. She hadn't opened a letter that had been slipped under the door, addressed to "Chérie" in her father's handwriting. He'd come to the apartment late at night when the lights were off. They could see him through the peephole, carrying a bouquet of roses, but hadn't opened the door because he'd been such a shitty jerk, cutting her off the way he did. By then, Violet was hysterical because the whole thing with Morgen and her father was "so creepy. Whose side are you on anyway?" *Click.*

Morgen hung up and glanced at Lydia's portrait. How awful to be yanked from the wall and flung into a fire while red hot embers, like angry red marigolds, went berserk and threatened to burn everything in their path. Fiery Violet had asked the same question twice, and Morgen needed to answer it.

She sipped her decaf and remembered when she first entered the Palace Café. She looked at the tall windows where she'd draped red and green lights, hoping for Angelo's safe return, and at the leaded glass doors with lacy white curtains that had concealed the access to the conch grotto. What if she stayed? Adopted a jetty cat? Taught piano lessons and general music in the local school? Except, just like when Gram gave Tutti to her when she'd needed it most, Angelo had given her two houses near the U.

The phone rang, and Shella answered it. "Sure, she's right here."

Fetu?

"It's Alberta." Shella put the receiver on the counter.

Morgen swallowed the lump in her throat. "Hello?" As she listened, she learned that Spencer and the Red Cedar Haven residents had prepared a talent show just for her. Highlights? Brady had memorized "Sea Fever" by John Masefield, Charlotte BG would lip-synch Celine Dion's "My Heart Will Go On," and Clifford had prepared a body percussion composition. How soon could she come because spirits were high? Morgen visualized their faces and felt moved. "How about sometime tomorrow afternoon? Would an hour's notice be okay?" She thanked Alberta and hung up.

Then she called Violet because, well, *tempus fugit.* When Violet tried to dominate the conversation, Morgen cut in. "I respect your concerns, but I don't want to discuss them over the phone. Could we meet tomorrow mid-morning for coffee or chowder?" Violet wanted to play the concerto again for her, so they agreed on a diner that had a piano in the back room.

"Sounds like you're leaving too," Shella said when Morgen hung up.

"Tomorrow morning. I have family business to attend to in Seattle and down in Baja before my new job starts. By any chance, do you have Fetu's number?"

Shella shook her head, and Morgen looked away in tears, because Fetu didn't have hers either. She walked over to Lydia's portrait and stared at her own distorted image in the glass. "Come on, face," she whispered. "You can come back. Everything's going to be okay."

When she turned around, Shella and Mia were nowhere in sight, so she returned to Tutti, opened the package from the frame shop, and took out a small photo album she'd had made for Shella. As she turned the pages with Doris looking over her shoulder, the constellation on the headliner began to glow, and she looked up. Her mother had sketched those same seven stars of the Big Dipper beside the piano's final chord in her copy of the concerto. Why? What was the Dipper's job?

Her mother had told her to use the Dipper as a natural compass. According to Gram, her mother's compass and ultimate raison d'être was that no "matter how dark life got, love persevered." That still didn't explain the sketch at the end of the concerto.

She spelled the word *compass* on the tabletop in trio mix and felt compelled to add "ion." *Compassion.* Oh dear Lord, how her heart had grown at Fish Camp. She began to sort and nibble. Angelo had said that Vic had brought him out there as a boy to learn to fish, that *Catchalot* was the first boat he drove. She stared at a photograph she'd taken of John catching razor clams that night. *No matter how dark life got, love persevered.* Who was there for John now while he grieved?

Morgen found John inside *Catchalot*, cleaning a lantern. She sat across from him and caught her breath. Outside, wind and rain began to scrub the old boat's decks and windows. "I brought a bag of gorp for your oatmeal."

"That's real nice." He tied a new mantle to the burner head.

"Remember when I asked you about the history of the Palace Café?"

He set the lantern aside and waited.

She raised her eyebrows. "Did you know about the conch grotto?"

A brief smile crossed his lips. "Why, I built it for Lydia soon after we lost Marty. The cellar with a real door inside the house and all the tiles and mirrors and such. She loved her secret cellar for many years." He stiffened and blinked at her.

"Yes," Morgen whispered. "Lydia saved my mother's life in your cellar."

He sighed as though a hard fight was won. "One afternoon about eight years ago, I found Lydia down there slumped over on that glass bench, and she looked at peace. Must have been waiting for Marty to fetch her and carry her away from her pain." He rubbed his eyes. "Say, a few years after Marty died, Lydia adopted Doris, she being grandmother to the Doris you know. Three generations of 'em as orange and plump as ripe apricots and just as sweet. Now Doris, the granny cat, she come to like that baby, which was you. Cuddle up and lick you, sleep with you while the two women took turns playing the piano for each other."

"Piano?" Morgen smiled as she remembered feeling a piano's vibrations when she first arrived.

"Marty gave a pretty piano to Lydia as a wedding present, and now it's hid behind a false wall in that glass closet. When Lydia passed, it belonged in there," he leaned forward and whispered, "like a secret."

"It was a good secret, but maybe you don't need to hide that piano anymore. Maybe you could bring it out into the light so Pearl can grow up with music in her life. And maybe you could move the Our Lady of Guadalupe statue to the entrance to the marina where she can bless the boats as they pass by." Morgen watched while John frowned through a window at the storm. "Speaking of secrets, I found my mother's cremation urn in the conch grotto."

John's shoulders dropped. "It was me who put it there. See, they was close friends, and Lydia's heart broke when your mother died. When she got so awful sick, she begged me to fetch the urn because she needed your mother's spirit to be with her when she passed." He averted his eyes. "I went and took it from your grandmother's house. Never did anything like that before or since."

Morgen opened the collar on her peacoat and fingered the silver beads on the necklace.

He blushed. "Miss Charlie gave that necklace to Lydia early on, because Lydia found her hiding down there that terrible night and rendered aid. She said that if she was taking the urn away from Miss Charlie's mother, she should leave that special necklace in its place. Which I did."

"My grandfather had given this necklace to my mother, and Gram assumed Mom lost it. The night of the storm when the conch grotto flooded, I noticed that you recognized it. Now I know why." She reached over and patted his hand. "It's okay, John."

He shrugged and spoke so quietly that she thought it

was the wind. "All those years we was together until she took her last breath. I never knew if she loved me back or if it was just because I looked like Marty."

"No, Lydia loved you," she felt her tears rise, "because in many ways, she's still here."

John raised his eyebrows and nodded. "After Lydia passed, I didn't know what to do with that urn. Thought I'd put it up on the ledge for safekeeping, found those pants, rolled the urn up in them to keep it nice and shiny." He shrugged. "Let's have some of that gorp." He took a handful of trio mix out of the bag and ate a few pieces.

She took a yellow M&M out of his hand and popped it in her mouth. "There's a beautiful glass brick bench down in the conch grotto and a second one in the victory garden."

"Glass bricks is special. Lets light pass right on through. The one in your conch grotto is where Lydia liked to sit." He gave her a tired smile. "The one in the garden is where she'd wait for Marty's spirit to visit her from the bottom of the sea. Now it marks her final resting place."

Morgen recalled the glass bricks literally melting into salt water under her touch. "I'm leaving tomorrow, but I'll come back and visit you." They stood, and she hugged him for several moments while heavy rain clattered on *Catchalot*'s roof. "Will you do me a favor?" She pulled her mother's braid out of her jeans pocket. "Please bury this in the victory garden near Lydia. True friends are hard to find, and those two women deserve to be together at long last."

"I'd be honored." John's voice was gravelly. "I miss Skipper."

"I know you do, and I'm very sorry." She tried not to cry as she dug an Angelo-penny-of-hope out of her pocket and slipped it under the wheelhouse bench. "We all do and will remember him forever, sure as the tide."

***

Morgen heard Shella's voice and opened the cargo door.

"My hands are full, but Pearl and I wanted to catch you between squalls." Shella sat, and Salty Dog and Doris leaped in and plopped down side by side in the doorway.

"I'm going to miss all of you more than you know." Morgen closed the door and patted Salty Dog on the head. Doris smiled and began to purr.

"Just so you know, Uncle Vic took care of your bill." Shella gave Morgen a paper bag. "Your flashlight's in there along with a treat for your trip." Her hand trembled while she applied her pale-pink lip gloss.

Morgen looked in the bag. "You're going to make me cry," she said when she saw dozens of raison d'être biscotti.

"What time are you leaving?"

"First light."

Doris yowled and looked from Morgen to Pearl as though considering her options: go with Morgen or remain Pearl's faithful au purr. She hopped on Morgen's lap and lovingly licked her hand. After winking at her with one gorgeous hazel eye, she curled up beside Pearl.

Morgen smiled and winked back. She handed the photo album to Shella. "I made this for you and especially for Pearl. Don't open it now, because we'll both start bawling. And here's the shoelace key to the front door. Thanks for that little privilege." She bit her lip. "You loved Angelo, didn't you?"

"With all my heart." Shella leaned closer. "Let's stay friends, okay?"

"Absolutely. I'll come visit before I start my job." She laughed. "I can't *not* come back to Fish Camp."

"Ciao, Morgen Marín." Shella gave her a hug. "Want to hold her?"

"Sure." Morgen cuddled Pearl in her arms for the first time. "Ciao, sweet baby Pearl." She kissed her forehead and breathed in her baby powder scent. "*Kia ora,* Shella Bella."

Tutti rolled slightly, and they heard scuffling on the roof. Restless roof angels? The pelican-priest? Morgen handed Pearl back to Shella and opened the cargo door to find Joe and Mia tying a surfboard onto the roof rack. They scrambled out to watch.

"Good surfing in Baja but better here," Joe said in well-rehearsed English. "A gift."

"Muchas gracias," Morgen said with a smile.

Mia pulled the English/Spanish *diccionario* out of her back pocket and offered it to Morgen. "I learn many words."

"Then the book belongs to you now, mi amiga. You've more than earned it." Morgen kissed Mia's cheek, and she and Shella watched Mia and Joe walk home hand in hand to Halibut trailer.

Tuesday, November 11, 2003

IN THE DROWSY EASTERN SKY, STARS DISAPPEARED LIKE yellow kites cut free of their tethers. Morgen stood on the dune scarp and watched the surf through her mother's opera glasses. The dramatic surface of the ocean was nature's sensational theater, but a lot more was going on offstage in the depths. That's where life was, where the truth was. She bit her lip. In her life, though, many truths were still under her fingertips where she couldn't grasp them.

She'd been up since four o'clock, and Tutti was packed and ready to go. She'd burned and buried "Coitus Cadenza" in the sand where Joe and Mia's five pillar candles had stood.

Across the water to the west, boat lights peeked out from under the blanket of fog, and the distant foghorn thrummed a G every ten seconds. A lazy string of eighteen pelicans flew overhead. Salty Dog leaned against her leg and yawned, and she reached down and patted him on the head.

First light swelled, and Morgen gazed in awe at countless by-the-wind sailor jellies, brittle as memories, strewn before her on the vast ocean beach. A ship's bell rang in the distance. She closed her eyes and visualized *By-the-Wind Sailor* up in the victory garden with its bow facing west toward the ocean and the setting sun. When night fell, thousands of Lydia Cooper's twinkly white lights would outline and define the boat. In Morgen's mind's eye, the little vessel transformed into a constellation as marvelous as the Big Dipper or the Southern Cross, and she knew that from the beach, it would look like a spirit ship, finally free to sail forever among the stars.

She pulled up the collar on her peacoat and hiked back to Tutti. After taking Salty Dog's picture and giving him a lengthy and heartfelt pat on the head, she checked the straps holding Joe's surfboard on the roof rack and took a long look around Fish Camp. Boats waited in their slips. Gulls dozed on pilings. The weathervane stood as still as a heron. The Jetty Cat Palace Café slept under the pink umbrella of predawn. Fish Camp was going to be a tough friend to leave.

The jetty cats had been out in force during the night, because there were muddy paw prints on Tutti's roof and windshield like a sweet bon voyage card signed by a dozen good friends. How did they get up there? By cat-apulting? She laughed to herself at yet another corny Angelo joke.

She climbed into Tutti and adjusted home plate under her feet. "Ciao, folks," she whispered.

As she departed Fish Camp, she looked in the sideview mirror and saw Tutti's miniature white lights merrily outlining the entrance to the Palace Café. On the boardwalk, One-Eyed Jack watched her with his crooked tail snapping back and forth like the pendulum rod on a metronome while he faithfully guarded the entrance to the harbor.

10.

Morgen stopped at a nursery across the street from the diner to buy a pot of fiery red marigolds as a gift for Violet. She sat in the parking lot and named each flower: young Morgen, Mom, baby Violet, Andras, Margot, Chloe, grown-up Violet, grown-up Morgen. Who had she been protecting all those years, and why? Violet didn't want to be protected anymore, so what would be the best way to reconnect with her in a compassionate way, especially after their previous and unpleasant parting? She considered her options while she pinched off a few withered leaves. Violet had said she wanted to play the Stravinsky concerto for her again, so maybe that would be a good place to start. She looked at the pale scars on her fingers and bit her lip. For better or for worse, the concerto would always be a part of her, and she'd always hold on to her place in the great continuum of pianists who'd performed it before her, like her mother, and after she did, like Violet. Yes, she'd put her trust in the concerto.

She opened her manuscript journal and wrote *AGENDA:*

1. *FOCUS on Violet's progress with the concerto.*
2. *BE PREPARED to answer her questions.*
3. *BE DISCREET: Skip the parts about Andras raping me, sterilizing me, and breaking my fingers.*

4. *BE SENSITIVE: Andras was my abuser, but he's
    still her father.*

Violet rapped on the window, and Morgen opened the driver's side door. They hugged, and Morgen gave her the flowers. "Because I love your dazzling red hair."

"I adore your funky cute cut, and thanks, marigolds are so happy. I'll go put them in my car." She left in a cloud of eucalyptus and lime.

So far, so *bueno*. Morgen corrected her posture, and when Violet returned, they went into the diner and sat at a table by a window.

"I want to play the cadenza for you again, because I think I've nailed it," Violet said, "but first, are you fucking my father?"

Morgen's agenda items blew out the window like withered marigold leaves. "Not anymore. I used to let him do anything he wanted to me, because he said I wouldn't reach my full potential as a pianist without him, and I believed it, because I trusted him."

Violet's eyes narrowed. "You're crazy."

"Hi, Vi," the waitress said. "The usual cherry Coke, or are you here for the piano?"

"Both, and this is my friend, Morgen."

"How do you do? I'd like a bowl of chowder, please, and a cup of decaf."

"Sorry, no chowder, and is Sanka okay?"

Morgen suddenly missed Shella. "Yes, please."

The waitress left, and Morgen looked at Violet. "You just called me crazy."

"I'm sorry," Violet blushed. "I hate name calling."

"I'm *not* crazy. I'm a little different, because I have a form of autism called Asperger's syndrome and *was* vulnerable to manipulation among other things. My therapist said it's because I have unreliable intuition, and I'm not telling you this to excuse anything but to provide some context."

"Holy shit." Violet's jaw dropped. "You're different, I'm different."

"Being different can be cause for celebration." Morgen corrected her posture. "I used to make myself miserable pretending to be somebody else's normal but not anymore."

"That means we're both on the same side." Violet smiled. "Does Daddy know about your autism?"

"Unlikely. I've had it since birth but only got a formal diagnosis last month, which enlightened me about my behavior but not about his."

The waitress delivered a Coke with a deflated maraschino cherry floating in it and a mug of, presumably, Sanka.

"I guess I'm not surprised." Violet's face crumpled. "He had to leave the U because of an affair with a sophomore, and he's on thin ice at East Cape for a similar situation. Pretty creepy, huh? The Fantasie is his last chance to redeem himself. God, I wish you could have had Mr. Ishikawa. He's a perfect prince." Her shoulders dropped and so did her pretenses. "My daddy is a sexual predator. Sorry, name calling again, but if it walks like a duck." She half laughed.

"Salute," Morgen said, and they sipped their beverages. "I wish it had never happened, but it did, and it's in the past. Now you and I both need to face the music, pardon the cliché, and move forward with wisdom. You have Phoebe and the concerto, and I have a new job to look forward to."

Violet started crying. "Daddy loathes that I'm a lesbian—"

"But *you* don't, and that's what's important."

"What's important is that you *heard* what I said at Phoebe's." Violet blushed. "That first crush on you helped me understand what it felt like to be in love even if it wasn't reciprocated, even if I had to keep it a secret. You helped me feel good about being me, about being alive."

"Thank you for telling me, for trusting me. I think we have to believe in love and in our true raisons d'être. Besides, the magic is in the music, not in the title."

Violet stabbed the maraschino cherry and it sank to the bottom of her glass. "The School of Music told me that Daddy is back in town, campaigning for donations to benefit the River Bridge concert."

"I didn't know that, and I don't need to know." Morgen took Violet's hand. "Come on. I want to hear what you've done with Mr. Stravinsky."

MORGEN HUMMED A MELODY FROM THE CONCERTO WHILE warming her hands on a foil-wrapped package of pork lumpia and staring through the windshield at Tutti's reflection in a mirrored glass ball. Autumn was taking its toll on the gardens and rabbit topiaries, but inside Water Street Eldercare, Pauline had been lively and warm. She'd given her a hug, the quilted knitting bag, and a note Gram wrote just days before she'd died. She put the lumpia aside and opened the letter.

> *Well, darling, do you like it? After you release my and your mother's ashes into the great continuum, our urns will make wonderful lamp bases and conversation pieces in your new home. Please give me a call now and then.*

"Bless her offbeat imagination," she whispered. The message was curious, though, because she hadn't found her mother's urn or inherited the Hippie House until after Gram died. In the knitting bag, she found Gram's death certificate and an old photo of Morgen as a child with her mother and grandmother. "Three generations," she whispered, touching the beads on her necklace. "What a treasure." She took out a cremation urn with *Eleanor Rose Marín* engraved on the lid. The dominant color was gold lamé, the base and two decorative handles were hot pink, and it smelled like Chanel No. 5.

She seat-belted both urns and the metronome into the passenger seat. She had a list of places she had to visit before she headed south, but first she needed to stop at the storage unit for two of her mother's precious keepsakes. "Okay, ladies," she whispered. "let's go."

SHE NAVIGATED TUTTI METHODICALLY, DELIBERATELY, AND vigilantly on umpteen rain-washed, one-way streets until she arrived two doors up from the Hippie House on Ninth Street. Rain fell as relentlessly as it had that horrible afternoon thirteen years, five months, and twenty-one days earlier when Charlie Josette Marín, aka Morning Glory, lost her life. The clouds were just as black, and the same unforgiving street and vehicle lights reflected on the same wet, leaf-strewn pavement.

She pulled up to the curb and peered past the whapping windshield wipers at the spot where her mother had left this earth. She rubbed the back of her fingers against the urn like one might touch a child's cheek. The house where Morning Glory had lived was to her right. The wild roses still bloomed even though it was November. Hippie harmonics or another quirky housewarming gift? Directly across the street stood its twin where Angelo had lived. Two hand-some, classic bungalows in a well-tended neighborhood, and now both of them belonged to her. *If only the walls could talk.* She returned her attention to the Hippie House. She would probably sleep in that upstairs room with the curious dormer windows; invite John to do some creative tile work; make a collage with those old photos from the sixties; hang her great-great-grandmother Therese's nude Rubenesque self-portrait; get both urns transformed into the most beautifully bizarre lamps in the whole wide world; plant morning glories; track down C. D. Hayes, adopt her mother's piano, and fill her home with music.

But she would never be able to live in the Hippie House until she found the courage to forgive herself and get out of the bus. She put Tutti in gear, glanced at her sideview mirror for approaching traffic, and saw something glitter in the middle of the street. She shifted back into neutral, set the brake, and got out to investigate. On closer inspection, she found a shiny penny and remembered the thousands of pennies strewn with shattered glass all over Angelo's stateroom. For the rest of her life, whenever she saw a penny, she'd remember that first penny her mother had given him. *Hope. Future.* She picked it up, shoved it into her pocket, and returned to Tutti.

She shifted back into first gear and inched the bus for-ward until she was directly in front of the Hippie House. There, parked at the curb with the engine running, she tucked the photo of the three couples smiling on the porch behind Dashboard Guadalupe. As she ate pork lumpia with her fingers and watched rain trickle down the windshield, warm, yellow light began to flow like wet paint out of the front porch windows and across the lawn in her direction, presumably coming from lamps burning somewhere deep within the house. She pressed the conch shell against her ear and listened as Morning Glory Marín played "To a Wild Rose" by Edward MacDowell on Grandpa Scott's mahogany piano. She was probably wearing her tie-dyed dress with two beautiful golden-brown braids cascading down her back.

AFTER MORGEN SIGNED HER CONTRACT IN THE SCHOOL of Music office and accepted a hefty stack of music to learn, Hannah, still smelling like lavender and vanilla, asked if she'd like to see her new studio.

Morgen followed Hannah down the hall, and as they started up the stairway, her mouth went dry, and her heart raced *accelerando* in her chest. She followed the sound of Hannah's stiletto heels *tick, tick, tick* up the stairs and across the hallway where she unlocked the door to Andras Bacon's former studio 212. "This spacious studio is the most coveted in the building, and Dr. Byrd felt it would be perfect for you."

"Of course he would." Morgen involuntarily clenched her jaw.

"Mr. Ishikawa taught in here since Andras Bacon left but offered to relocate."

Hannah stepped inside and turned on the lights, and Morgen followed, leaving the door unlocked and wide open for once. She only partially heard Hannah's comments: "Such a lovely campus…watch the seasons change…beautiful corner studio with tall windows…floor-to-ceiling mirrors, shelves packed with music and books…this gorgeous rosewood Steinway baby grand…"

"Yes, thank you. I've been in here before." She glanced around the room. She'd slept on the floor like a submissive pet, sat blindfolded and naked on the piano bench, and under that chandelier of blue crystal stars and music symbols…

"About that kitschy, old dust-catcher up there? Some of the bulbs burned out, and I can try to match them, or we can take it down altogether if you like."

"Oh no, thank you. The chandelier belongs here, and yes, new bulbs would be, well, enlightening." Morgen took the blue crystal star out of her pocket and set it on the piano. "My mother's star may have fallen, but mine's still rising, and please don't ask, because it's a thirty-five-year-long story." She took off her coat, red sneakers, and socks, stepped up on the piano bench, and returned the star to its rightful place. The other pieces chimed together, a light and cheerful tinkling as though singing "welcome home." Then she crossed the room, pulled thirteen music books off the shelf (Bach through Bartok), and found that her drawing of a falling star was still scribbled on the wall in black felt-tipped pen. With a smile, she replaced the books and sat on the bench. "May I please have a few minutes?"

"Of course, Dr. Marín. Take as much time as you like." Hannah stepped back, *tick, tick, tick,* and was forgotten.

If Frédéric Chopin's music couldn't exorcise the evil presence in that studio, nothing would. Morgen brushed her fingers across the closed keyboard lid that nine years, seven months, and six days earlier had crushed her hands. *No words. Only love. Only music.* She opened the lid, placed her fingers on the keys and bare toes on the pedals, corrected her posture, and began to play Ballade no. 1 with rich parallel octaves resonating up from deep below middle C as though filling the room with purifying incense. Music flowed from her memory as naturally as breath from her lungs, and for thirty-six perfect minutes, she played all four ballades, one right after the other, her fingers flying like hot light across the piano keys.

When she finished, sweating and satiated, she folded her hands on her lap and felt a peaceful smile warm her face. *Inevitably, music transcends the personal drama of those of us who profess to make it.*

Cheers and applause erupted behind her, and she turned to see that dozens of individuals, including Dr. Byrd, had slipped into the studio to hear her play—or rather to hear the ballades. She blushed, stood, and curtsied to her enthusiastic audience.

Dr. Byrd extended his hand, and Morgen shook it. "As director of the School of Music, I am beyond delighted to welcome you back to Northwest Coast University and to finally have you on my staff."

"Thank you." She bent down to put on her socks and shoes. "By the way, the A-flat below middle C is a little *too* flat."

"We'll have the grand tuned for you." He turned to his secretary. "Hannah, please schedule Ed."

As the room emptied, she noticed a full-size, touch-sensitive Yamaha keyboard on a shelf. "May I please borrow that? I'll be traveling for a while and really could use it." She gestured at the stack of music she had to learn.

"Of course. Take anything you need, and please drop by my office before you go."

"Thank you."

After everyone left, she put the shiny penny she'd found on Ninth Street on the top bookshelf. "Now we have hope," she whispered. "Now we have a future."

Morgen and Dr. Byrd enjoyed a peaceful moment watching the songbirds in the trees outside his office window. He crossed his arms over his chest. "First, I'd like to express my condolences on the passing of your grandmother." He pressed his fingertips against his lips as though trying to filter his words. "Eleanor and I kept in touch over the years because of you. In fact, she last phoned me when you learned about the attack on your mother, and she was concerned about you. You see, I loved Charlie like a sister. She'd been my soul mate, and we planned to teach here at the U together." He shrugged. "She gave me courage to be true to myself when I came out as gay to my housemates."

Soul mate? Housemates? Morgen felt lightheaded, and her hands began to flap. It hit her, songbirds-bird-Birdie-Bertie-Byrd—"You're Bertie, aren't you?"

He bowed slightly. "That's what they called me back in the days of peace and love but never again after those days ended."

"You helped rescue my mom that night." She rummaged through her backpack and showed him her mother's torn cadenza pages with colored-pencil doodles.

He studied the sketches and squeezed his eyes shut as though in pain. "It all happened so fast, a fabulous party, music and skinny-dipping, then a violent mêlée and a sneaker wave. When it was over, Riff was gravely injured and Charlie barely conscious. We never knew who assaulted her, but it could have been any one of a hundred people there that night. I tried to lift her but couldn't. Our gardener, of all people, appeared out of the mob, helped me carry her toward a house he was familiar with, said she'd be safe with the woman who lived there, but as soon as Charlie saw the lights, she pushed us away and took off running."

"Wait, if you're Bertie as in Bertie-the-gardener, who was the gardener?"

"A good-looking kid named Angie, son of the owner. Lived across the street. No idea why he was there or what happened to him. Funny…he, Riff, and I used to play catch—"

"Angelo Bordacelli?" Morgen felt lightheaded again. Vic had told her that a girl Angelo rescued ended up saving him with one penny. She leaned on Dr. Byrd's desk for support.

"Do you know him?"

"I did, but he was recently lost at sea." She caught a sob before it cracked the surface. "Oh dear Lord. May I please sit down?"

"Yes, I'm sorry for forgetting my manners." He picked up the phone. "Hannah, may we please have a couple bottles of water? Thank you." He hung up. "As a postscript, Angie came from a very rich family, and his foundation has paid for Riff's care all these years."

Riff, the bloody blue note under a jumble of drift logs? She rubbed her breastbone to quiet her heart. "Why didn't anybody ever tell me?"

"Because we promised each other that we'd never discuss it, that we'd close that door forever to protect ourselves and again later to protect you. Tragically, after that day and until her death, my only communication with your mother was in preparing you to perform the Stravinsky concerto."

She handed him the Polaroid of the three college-aged barefooted couples. "You likely saved Mom's life and, in turn, mine."

"Oh my God, look at us. We were so young. That's your mother, of course, and Riff, percussion specialist, drum major, and my dear friend. That's me and your Headmistress Nancy Collier, who never married. She was and still is very uptight and barely fit in with our group but worshipped Charlie's talent. She was absolutely horrified when I came out." He shook his head. "That's Hannah, who later married Spencer who was taking the photo, and finally, Carlo, the misfit."

"Who? Carlo? Carlo Russo Ricci?" Morgen snatched the photo out of his hands. "Which one is he?" *Restraint is my friend, restraint is my—*

"Do you know him too? Small world." He pointed to a long-haired individual doing a squinty thing with his left eye.

"Yes, I do." *Well, crap.* Some afternoon that winter, she would tell Dr. Byrd the truth about Carlo Russo Ricci. As for Headmistress? She knew all along who Morgen was and only changed her tune when she realized that the charade was ending. She stared at the photo. Why hadn't she recognized Dr. Byrd, Headmistress, or Carlo? Because, according to her therapist, she was a rigid literal thinker and very analytical but, sadly, only in context. Because she didn't expect to see them, she couldn't comprehend that they were standing right in front of her like an optical illusion.

When Hannah arrived with two bottles of water, Dr. Byrd showed her the photo.

"Oh for heaven's sake. What a treasure." She smiled at Morgen, handed her a bottle, and left, closing the door behind her.

Morgen guzzled the water, but Dr. Byrd carried on, energized by his memories.

"Carlo competed as an opera tenor in the baccalaureate competition that year but lost to Charlie and finished near the bottom of his class. He was our housemate only because he was related to the owner. Afterward, we all went our separate ways but got together later, hoping music would heal us. We chose Mozart's Quintet for Piano, Oboe, Clarinet, Horn, and Bassoon in E Flat. Piano, Charlie; oboe, Hannah; clarinet, Nancy; horn, Spencer; and bassoon, yours truly. You know, the sweet third movement melody, so-so-so-do-mi-so-fa-re-mi-do—"

"Yes, I know it well because it was one of Mom's favorite pieces, and it's also in the repertoire you assigned me, thank you very much."

He nodded. "During our first rehearsal, Charlie abruptly stopped playing, her face went white, and she said, 'I can't do this anymore.' She walked away from us and away from music. We didn't know she was pregnant at the time, but she must have." He brightened a little. "Years have gone by, but the four of us keep in touch, because in a way, we're still family. If you're willing, we could finally bring the Mozart to fruition on the NCU stage." He raised his eyebrows at her. "Get the band back together, so to speak."

"For Mom and all of you?" She fought her tears and won. "Yes, Dr. Byrd, I'd be honored."

As she left the building, she heard Dr. Byrd sing in her mind's ear, *so-so-so-do-mi-so-fa-re-mi-do.* A goofy little girl's voice replaced his. *When I grow up, I will find my daddy out beyond the deep blue sea and bring him to my mom so we will be a fam-i-ly.* Imagine, her mother and her housemate-friends had rehearsed that same beloved piece, and now she'd get to perform it with them. Just imagine.

Morgen returned to Tutti with new music in one arm and the Yamaha keyboard cradled in the other. She wrapped the keyboard in the eiderdown, stacked the music under the bench seat with the mandolin, and tucked Dr. Byrd's business card under the metronome. *Tempus fugit.*

Fatigue rolled over her like Fish Camp fog, and she climbed onto the platform bed for a nap. She should call Alberta and postpone attending the talent show until after Todos Santos. Alberta would understand. After all, she'd been her mother's friend. Morgen chewed her lips. The Red Cedar residents had been so happy to see her. She couldn't recall *not* knowing many of them. The North Star sticker on the headliner winked at her. *Compass. Compassion. Because blood alone does not a family make.* She sighed and reached for her phone.

MORGEN CURLED UP IN AN ARMCHAIR AND ENJOYED THE talent show of poetry recitation, singing, dancing, and playing instruments, and her hands were sore from applauding.

Alberta stood and spoke to the audience of residents, staff, and family members. "We will have a grand finale presentation, and it's dedicated to our friend, Morgen Marín. First, as is his habit, Clifford DuPree needs to warm up, so let's give him a few minutes."

When Spencer sat two seats over from Morgen, she remembered an Angelo-penny-of-hope in her pocket. "So by having a performance goal," she whispered, "each resident has a future."

"Well said." Spencer nodded.

Dr. Byrd's words niggled her memory about Hannah-the-palindrome who later married housemate-Spencer. "By any chance, do you know Hannah?"

He smiled and pressed a finger to his lips as Clifford shuffled in with his walker and sat in a wicker chair about twelve feet in front of them. Clifford wore a short-sleeved Oxford shirt and paisley necktie with slacks. Gray had softened his longish blond hair, but his face lacked emotion. He blinked several times, raised his hands like a conductor before cuing an ensemble of musicians, and began to flail. Alarmed, Morgen looked around, but nobody made a move to intervene. He paused and rested his hands in his lap.

Alberta scurried over to Morgen. "Just a little context," she whispered. "Clifford suffered a massive head injury as a young man. The damage to his brain was severe and permanent, resulting in complete hearing loss among other things, but he still enjoys and *feels* music. Just watch." She patted Morgen on the hand.

Clifford patted a lengthy drum roll on his thighs while rhythmically nodding his head. He paused, raised his arms again, and began a body percussion composition with sounds and textures, alternating *accelerando* with *ritardando* while bouncing across changing time signatures like light rippling off ocean waves. His head marked tempo, and his hands slapped his legs, subdividing the beat. Fingers snapped, hands clapped, lips popped, and heels scuffed varying the degree of intensity. His toes joined in, tapping syncopated rhythms and accenting the off beats, *sforzando*.

His sense of rhythm was beyond extraordinary. Morgen laced her fingers like a bouquet of white knuckles and leaned forward. Her hands warmed, and her feet began searching for the pedals on a piano. She caught her breath, and the first movement of the Stravinsky concerto rushed into her mind, heart, hands, and fingers like an aural tsunami. "I know this music," she cried. She jumped up and dragged her armchair closer to Clifford. "I had to learn every part backward and forward!"

She began to mime playing the piano part on an ottoman, shamelessly pounding her way through energetic rhythms and melodies. Five more frenzied minutes of slapping and scat-singing music shook the solarium, and they briefly paused, as is customary, between the first and second movements. As she began to play the ottoman again, *largo,* she noticed that he was reading her hands, and she knew without a doubt that he would join her in the tenth measure. Sure enough, he was there to meet her. When she reached the first of two piano solo cadenzas, the one that had crushed her spirit as well as her hands, terror choked her heart, but he pushed and gave her the strength to perform the passage just like Stravinsky would have played it, *tick-tick-tick-tick—Birdie-Bertie-Byrd-Clifford-RIFF—*

"Riff?" She cried out but continued to play with him as he began the third movement of the concerto, fiercely complicated with a rapid tempo. He watched her hands and filled in with woodwind, brass, and double bass rhythms precisely as written until the timpani part returned like a pounding heartbeat in the thirtieth measure. Her voice joined his as he uttered sounds and muffled tones with perfect pitch even though he could no longer hear himself. As they approached the end of the composition, the opening rhythm reprised, *long, long, short, long, Char-lie Ma-rín, Mor-gen Ma-rín, Clif-ford Du-Pree,* over and over, *Ma-rín, Ma-rín, Du-Pree,* until the tick of her mother's metronome raced deep in her core, *stringendo* ($\textrm{\small ♩} = 132$, accelerate and grow louder) and Riff, sweating with effort, pushed the rhythmic tension to a rousing climax. "Bravo!" Morgen cheered all by herself. She broke down and wept.

Riff's head remained bowed, his lips parted. He stared at the floor and rocked while rapidly rubbing the pads of his fingers against his thumbs.

"Maybe we have to let go of the dissonance *before* we can find resolution," she whispered to him. "Maybe we have to take that leap of faith, so let's take it together."

He continued to sway as she listened to the *hush, hush, hush* of skin against fragile skin.

"Mom believed that no matter how dark life gets, love perseveres. She's never given up on either one of us, and she loved you to the last chord in that concerto and to the last moment of her life."

He stopped rocking and, for the first time, looked directly at her with lapis-blue eyes flecked with gold.

"Oh, what the crap." She stuck out and rolled her tongue.

As though on cue, he rolled his tongue before gently kissing her on her cheek. He bowed to the audience, took his walker, and shuffled unescorted through the archway into a long passageway that presumably led back to his room.

Morgen remained frozen. Nobody moved or made a sound. *It's a portrait of my family. I have no words. I have only love.* She leaped to her feet. "Alberta, thank you for inviting me. Lovely program, but I must fly." Tears poured down her cheeks as she hurried out of the solarium and ran back to Tutti.

SHE COLLAPSED ON THE BENCH SEAT AND HUGGED THE aquamarine urn to her chest. Her mother had tried so hard to tell her what had happened that night by drawing colorful doodles on the cadenza pages beginning eight months and twenty-six days aka 267 days before she was born. Average gestation was closer to forty weeks aka 280 days. *That's two*

fricking weeks! What if her mother had been pregnant *before* Carlo raped her?

In their last conversation, her mother said that secrets were locked in the piano concerto and that they would come around and bite her on the derrière. Morgen's wish had finally come true, because that "secret" just kissed her very sweetly on the cheek. Her mother must have known that if she truly was Riff's daughter, the concerto would eventually lead them to each other.

She jumped when someone knocked on Tutti's cargo door. She peeked between the curtains and saw Alberta and another woman standing beside her, holding a tea tray. She took a deep breath and opened the door.

"This looked like Charlie's beloved old bus, so we took a chance that you were in here," Alberta said. "May we come in?"

"Yes, of course." Morgen wiped her eyes with a tissue and cleared clutter off the other bench seat, and they sat. "How do you do?"

The other woman smiled at her and set a teapot and cups on the tabletop. "You left before we could serve refreshments. Hello, I'm Connie DuPree, Clifford's mother. You know me as C. D. Hayes for Connie DuPree Hayes. Two surnames because I'm twice widowed. Remember? A couple of weeks ago, I wrote to you that I have Charlie's piano and that I want you to have—"

"You're *who*?" Morgen felt faint.

"Connie is my mother," Alberta said quietly. "Clifford, or Riff, is my brother, and he and your mother were supposed to get—"

"Oh dear Lord, I have an auntie and a new grandmother?" Morgen's voice shook.

Connie served the tea with trembling hands. "May I please have some sugar?" She gestured at the wild rose sugar bowl.

"Sorry. That's beach sand. For my new garden." She rubbed her breastbone. "Out of breath."

Alberta looked at her mother. "Where to begin?"

"Let's begin with now." Connie sipped her tea. "Often the brain doesn't mature or grow beyond the age at injury, but I learned today that the heart does. What astonishes me is that Riff seems to understand on some level who you are."

Morgen leaned forward. "I don't understand how we got to now."

Connie looked happy and sad at the same time, if that was possible. "Years ago, I was astonished to learn that Charlie's daughter, you, who I didn't know existed, was presenting her baccalaureate concert, so I did the math and figured that she'd gotten pregnant in 1968. Oh, my heart swelled, and I hoped against hope that you were his daughter. I attended a rehearsal, and when I saw you play, I was convinced that you were my granddaughter but didn't know what to do. I helped myself to a study score from a stack near the stage. Only thing I've ever stolen in my life." She quietly laughed. "On the night of your concert, I took a snapshot of you in your elegant black dress with your hands on the keyboard, Rylan Byrd conducting, and the ensemble in the background. I sat in the audience and waited for your mother to arrive, but of course she didn't." She paused to sip her tea. "On a whim, I left the study score and that photo on a shelf in Riff's room. In the solarium a couple months ago, he acted out a lengthy and frenetic body percussion creation. I was taken aback, but my fear turned to wonder, because he was performing something he'd consciously rehearsed. Afterward, I learned that the entire event had been recorded on surveillance camera. I requested and was given a videotaped copy. I wrote a detailed account and marched over to the School of Music to ask for help. Before long, I received a phone call from Andras Bacon in New Jersey. As I remember, he was your teacher."

Morgen shrugged. "Go on."

Connie pursed her lips and nodded as only a tactful grandmother would. "He confirmed that Riff had created a remarkable arrangement of the Stravinsky concerto, that his rendition was genius, and he overnighted a second score to me with Riff's part highlighted." She took a study score out of her bag and handed it to Morgen. "He commented that Stravinsky had showcased the piano as the magnificent percussion instrument that it is. I felt comforted by the piano/percussion connection."

Morgen opened the score. Andras's broad, yellow line revealed that Riff started at the beginning and ended at the end but followed a nonlinear trail through the concerto, often performing several instrumental parts simultaneously by using different parts of his body. He may have been deaf, but he lived an extraordinary life in the silence between the notes. "I always felt that the Stravinsky concerto was a portrait of my family, and now I know why."

"What has moved and inspired me most is that for thirteen years, Riff committed to memory every single note written for all twenty-five instruments out of love for Charlie." Connie ran a finger around the rim of her teacup. "I'm sad that you grew up not knowing who your father was and that we never knew about you, but I believe that Charlie likely thought you were his daughter and kept it to herself to keep that hope alive."

"Why not live with hope rather than accept a nightmare as reality?" Morgen rubbed her temples. *My dad kissed me.* "May I please borrow this score for a while?"

As they chitchatted and sipped their tea, Morgen heard her mother's voice in her mind's ear. *Sometimes we don't understand certain things, and all we can do is give life our best and keep moving forward. Maybe someday we'll look back, and it'll all make sense.*

After Alberta and Connie left, Morgen remained at the tabletop, chewing her lips. Connie, her brand-new grandmother, said that Andras did the highlighted analysis of Riff's video performance a couple months earlier. That's when he was struggling to finish the Fantasie for his doctorate. It was rather out of his self-absorbed character to take time to help Connie. She poured a mountain of trio mix onto the tabletop and began to sort and munch. Maybe he'd needed inspiration. Maybe Riff's videotape had arrived just in the nick of time. God knows Riff's performance had inspired the socks off of her.

She put the highlighted concerto score on the tabletop and studied Riff's trail as it meandered back and forth, up and down, and hopscotched through the music. Anything but random, it maintained a high level of musicianship and made sense in her mind's ear. It also recalled a variety of Andras's teaching techniques that he'd claimed would make her "one with the music." Like when he'd make her play her part while singing one of the instrumental parts, play a memorized piece in another key or another meter, or play a phrase upside down or backward like Hannah's name, or in music, like Bach's Crab Canon.

She popped a handful of trio mix into her mouth and placed the two scores side by side. As she chewed, her eyes darted back and forth from the concerto to the Fantasie. *Something's going on, but I don't get it.* Her fingers spasmed, and her eyes played tricks on her causing a phrase in the concerto to morph like an optical illusion into a phrase from the Fantasie.

A violent shock surged through her hands and arms like when the string exploded inside her piano. *What the crap?* She rubbed her eyes and flipped through Riff's highlighted concerto score again, familiar to her because Andras had made her memorize every one of the twenty-four parts from piccolo to double bass in addition to her solo piano. Then she started to read through the Fantasie with the same scrutiny. "That's it, I got it!" She jumped and hit her head on Tutti's ceiling. "Andras didn't write this phrase. It's from the trombone part in the Stravinsky concerto but written backward." She continued searching and found phrase after phrase that Andras lifted note for note from the oboes, clarinets, and horns, and slyly integrated into his Fantasie for Piano. He even had the audacity to lift an entire passage from the piano part and shuffle the measures like playing cards. No wonder her hands had rebelled. Okay, so Riff had bounced like a rabbit through the concerto out of love for her mother, but Andras had deliberately stolen material, manipulated it, and written it down as his own without attributing it to Stravinsky. That was plagiarism of Riff's creative concept as well as Stravinsky's published phrases. Like an optical illusion, Andras's Fantasie was rife with deception. *Well, crap.*

By the time she finished analyzing Andras's Fantasie, she had proof that he'd composed only twenty-three percent of his doctoral composition versus the seventy-seven percent originally written by Igor Stravinsky in 1924, which meant Andras didn't deserve to even park at the curb in front of Carnegie Hall.

She'd spent hours and hours working on his Fantasie. Why hadn't she noticed what he'd done? Probably for the same reason she hadn't recognized the individuals in the Hippie House photo. Because she rarely saw the forest for the trees. Because Stravinsky's phrases didn't belong in the Fantasie, she couldn't comprehend that they were right in front of her. Until now. "Like Fetu promised, he'll get his," she whispered.

She moved M&M's into rows by color and sorted dried cranberries and almonds into heaps while she considered her options. She'd promised Headmistress that she'd perform the Fantasie for the River Bridge fundraiser. If she backed out now, her students would lose revenue, and she'd destroy her reputation in the performance world. If she went ahead, she'd be complicit in Andras's fraud and perpetuate "pretending," a behavior that she'd battled all her life. If she exposed him, she knew from experience that he would retaliate. However, down in the conch grotto, she'd vowed to use the Fantasie to beat him at his own demented game. *Tempus fugit.*

She rearranged the trio mix pieces into a different path forward. "I feel rather energized." She grabbed her cell phone and called Gram's attorney. Next she called Rylan Byrd to request that he arrange a meeting with Andras (who was in town) ASAP—a meeting, she alerted him, that she would interrupt with a vengeance.

Morgen pulled into the NCU parking lot, parked under her familiar cedar tree, and got out. Dr. Byrd told her that he and Andras Bacon would meet for dinner at the Faculty Club, which was a short walk away.

As soon as she entered the dining room, Dr. Byrd waved her over to the table he shared with Andras. She corrected her posture and remembered her mother's pithy advice: *No matter what, SMILE!* "Good evening, gentlemen. Thank you for letting me join you."

Dr. Byrd held her chair while she sat.

"You've done something different with your hair." Andras's signature scent had soured. "You've been rude, and you owe me an apology."

"No, I don't. And actually, *you* need to apologize to your students in New Jersey because, evidently, you prefer stalking me to teaching them." She turned to Dr. Byrd. "Have you ordered yet?"

"Yes, an abundant variety of appetizers. We can share—"

"What is wrong with you?" Andras said without a trace of his seductive Welsh accent. "Demanding privacy like a spoiled diva. We have an understanding, Chérie, and I trusted you with my magnum opus."

"Excuse me, but I've mastered your magnum opus beyond your wildest dreams. It helped that I'm exceptionally analytical, because sometimes I have to stop trying to understand or like something and just do the work." She pulled the Fantasie and concerto scores out of her backpack and put them on the table.

Andras paled.

A waiter arrived with a tray. "Antipasto, potstickers, garlic shrimp, artichoke dip, and sourdough toast, and an extra plate for the lady. Would you like a beverage, Miss?"

"Yes, please, a glass of chardonnay."

The waiter nodded and excused himself.

"This looks delicious, thank you." She put a piece of sourdough toast and a garlic shrimp on her plate. "You never can have too much garlic." She opened the compositions on the table and offered Andras her best smile. "I know what you did."

He appeared to stop breathing.

"It took a while. My hands tried to tell me that something screwy was going on, you know, stubborn muscle memory? It never occurred to me that you would pull a stupid sophomoric stunt like plagiarizing Igor Stravinsky."

"Clifford DuPree inspired my work with his whimsical exploration—"

"He did *not* inspire this!" She slammed her hand on the Fantasie. "You made a conscious and arrogant decision to steal Riff's organic joy and Stravinsky's exquisite phrases and bend them to your will. What you've done is unforgivable." She corrected her posture. "And what you've done to me since I was thirteen years old is also unforgivable."

"What do you want?" Andras downed his beverage, presumably vodka.

"For you to cancel the gala and release me in writing from the performance and recording contracts. For you to make a ten thousand dollar donation to the River Bridge Scholarship Fund by the end of December. For you to immediately destroy every page of the Fantasie. If you don't, or if you attempt to discredit or contact me again or are *ever* accused of sexual misconduct with another student, I will expose you." She grabbed the scores and stuffed them into her backpack. "You brought this on yourself, and I'm not owning any of—"

"Hi everybody." Violet appeared at the table, eyes blazing and a fiery red marigold tucked over her ear. She grabbed a chair and sat down. "May I join you?"

Andras grumbled, and Dr. Byrd scrambled for words. "Perhaps another time would be better."

"I'm sorry, but I followed Daddy because I wanted to see what he was up to." She clucked her tongue. "Everybody looks pissed. What'd he do now?"

"Parlor tricks." Morgen shrugged. "Have a shrimp. You can share my plate." She hadn't planned on Violet's showing up and stalled for time by sipping her wine and eating appetizers. How to make this a teachable moment? "I recently told you that the magic was in the music, not in the title. In the context of recent events, I've extended that to *a greater truth* is in the music, not in the title. Think about that for a minute while I remind your father that you are just two months younger tonight than I was the night of my baccalaureate concert." Morgen rubbed her eyebrows. "There must have been caffeine in the tea I drank earlier with my new family, because I'm feeling agitated. Speaking of family, let's talk about you and Phoebe. I'm thrilled that you've found a soul mate who adores you and treats you with respect, and FYI, I found you a permanent place to live, and it's across the street from my new house and only three blocks from the concert hall. All you and Phoebe have to do is take care of the gardens. Maybe I'll grab a potsticker. I'm famished and positively giddy." She handed a paper to Andras. "This is a copy of my attorney's business card. She wants those documents from you by Friday. *Tempus fugit.*"

She hugged Violet and nodded at Dr. Byrd, who was smiling at her.

"Thanks for the snacks, but I have to fly." She popped the potsticker into her mouth and left.

Morgen parked Tutti at the curb in front of the Hippie House and turned off the engine. *All my life I've felt like an outsider looking in. Now, not really.* Illuminated by a streetlight, the glass brick sidelight windows gleamed like mirrors. A smile softened her face. She had likely been conceived inside that house, and now it was going to be her home. She tapped her toes on Angelo's home plate and climbed over the seat to the back of the bus.

After she closed Fräu Heinrich's curtains, she put on her mother's tie-dyed dress and started to make a peanut butter and trio mix sandwich on stale sourdough when she heard her mother's voice in her mind's ear.

My star is waiting, Sweet Baby. Are you ready to let me go?

"Yes, I guess we're both finally ready," she whispered. "I love you, Mom. Always have, always will."

Me too.

She climbed back into the driver's seat, crushed the dried morning glory from the victory garden in the palm of her hand, and brushed the purple fragments into a heap at Dashboard Guadalupe's feet. She added sprinkles of sand from the wild rose sugar bowl and Todos Santos paper star. She took her mother's urn out of the backpack and unscrewed the lid. Attached inside was a gold filigree box that contained a patchouli-scented wax cube. She reached in with thumb and forefinger and took a pinch of the powdery grit. After securing the lid, she blended the ashes with the mixture on the dashboard and felt her hands tremble like caged birds excited by the promise of impending flight. She put on her mother's Victorian touring hat, opened the door, and turned back to sweep the luminous potpourri into her palms.

She stepped outside onto Ninth Street and glanced around. The rain had stopped, and the curtain of clouds parted, revealing the Big Dipper and North Star. The hushed neighborhood became a watercolor backdrop for this grand finale performance. She took a deep breath, corrected her posture, and walked barefoot to the exact spot where her mother had died.

"Mom, you promised that someday we would be able to look back and that it would all make sense. Well, it finally happened, and to celebrate our mutual enlightenment, may I please have one last dance?" She curtsied and began a wild dance with pirouettes and ballet leaps while singing "Gypsy," their favorite Fleetwood Mac song, harmonizing with the memory of her mother's voice as the floor of her childhood fell away from beneath her feet. As her clenched hands began to flap with unfettered joy, she raised both arms and spread her fingers to the night sky, finally giving her mother the wings she needed to fly away like electric blue stardust above the moon-gray lawn.

Wednesday, November 12, 2003
Interstate 5–Southbound

AT FIRST LIGHT, MORGEN SEAT-BELTED BOTH URNS, THE conch shell, and the metronome into the passenger seat. She sat in the driver's seat, called Vic, and left a message relaying that she'd just met her biological father. She would have phoned Fetu, but she had only regrets and no phone number. Next, she phoned Dr. Byrd and left a message that she would like to develop a partnership between the School of Music and Red Cedar Haven and that she'd treat the Hippie House-mates to a champagne brunch when she got home.

"Home," she whispered. *Right where I finally belong.* She touched her foremothers necklace and tapped rhythms with her toes on home plate while imagining dancing up the wood steps to sit in a chair on that porch where she'd always feel safe. Luckily, the individuals who'd ended up meaning the most to her had never been far away, always waiting patiently offstage, just out of the daily limelight, there and at Fish Camp.

She placed Fetu's plectrum and hermit crab shell at Dashboard Guadalupe's feet and turned on the engine. When she hung the penny purse from the rearview mirror, she was startled to see her undistorted reflection gazing back at her, complete with a fancy, modern, college professor haircut, lapis-blue eyes with flecks of gold, and a slight overbite. "Thanks, face, for finally showing up again," she cheered. "Okay, ladies, we're headed to Todos Santos."

Tick, tick the metronome on the passenger seat reminded her.

"Right, seatbelt, thanks." She buckled up, bit into a raison d'être biscotti, and headed for the freeway, the roof angels chitchatting and spreading their wings overhead. She turned up Fleetwood Mac's *Greatest Hits*, kept time by rocking, and for hundreds of miles, *tempus fugit.*

She drove on for hours, always in the slow lane, the window rolled down just enough so she could enjoy the smell of the rain. Tutti's four new tires harmonized with the wet pavement: "*kia ora, kia ora.*" Fetu came to mind with his curious scent of petrichor and lemon grass, and she touched his hermit crab shell in remembrance. The windshield wipers struggled against the wind and incessant applauding rain. *Jet-ty-Cat-Pal-ace-Ca-fé (rest),* they thumped (*andante,* ♩ = 68), *Jet-ty-Cat-Pal-ace-Ca-fé (rest).* Past the exit to Mount St. Helens. Across the long bridge over the Columbia River into Oregon. On and on. Mountains, forest, ranchland, and towns.

Long ago, her mother had written *Where does music go when it fades away?* Trick question, because it *never* faded away. Music, and evidently love too, reawakened itself over and over. As a result, her star-crossed parents had taught her all she'd ever need to know about love in the only way they could, and that was by living it. Maybe she needed to take a cue from them and be brave and strong about love too.

Just north of Salem, Oregon, near mile marker 260, she noticed an interesting sign that read:

45TH PARALLEL

HALF WAY BETWEEN THE EQUATOR

AND NORTH POLE.

As she motored on at about fifty miles per hour, she monitored the traffic merging onto the freeway. A sea-green Geo Tracker caught her attention. She glanced in the rearview mirror and watched as the Tracker approached from behind. As though on cue, the driver flashed his headlights and waved at her through his window as he passed.

"Oh dear Lord, it's Fetu." How long had he been waiting for her? She rolled down the window and waved back through the rain. He pulled in front of her, and she saw that he'd painted a blue ocean swirl and bright red heart on the Gooey's spare tire cover. However, instead of the Big Dipper and North Star design that was engraved on her mother's urn and had inspired Morgen's remembrance tattoo, Fetu had superimposed the four stars of his Southern Cross over the entire design. *Well crap, he tweaked Mom's doodle, and didn't even ask my...* The foremothers necklace grew pleasantly warm against her throat. *No worries, I rather love it!* He sped up. Should she accompany him or let him go on his merry way? He answered by singing in her mind's ear, "*Who knew our paths would cross, if only for a little while? How curious when you least expect to find love.*" A scrumptious glad feeling washed over her. She smiled, pressed the accelerator, and the bus's fifty-three horses began to gallop *stringendo* (♩ = 132, accelerate and grow louder).

A strong wind gust broadsided Tutti, and Morgen tightened her grip on the steering wheel, maintaining her southerly course. When seen from the stars overhead, Joe's surfboard with its upright fin on the dove-blue roof resembled a by-the-wind sailor jellyfish gliding free and bravely bound for distant shores.

Book Club Questions and Topics for Discussion

Theme

1. What themes does the author explore? Of these, which do you feel is the dominant theme and why?

2. *Jetty Cat Palace Café* isn't a ghost story per se, but some form of the words "ghost," "spirit," and "haunt" are mentioned fifty-four times. What ghosts (literal or metaphorical) are present in the story? And in relation to which character?

Setting

3. Are the settings realistic? What was your first impression of Fish Camp. Was it intriguing, quaint, or dreary? The Jetty Cat Palace Café? The conch grotto? The drift logs beach? Tutti? Did your feelings about these places change as the story progressed?

4. Would Fish Camp be an appealing destination for you? Why or why not?

Morgen

5. As you know, Morgen has Asperger's syndrome, a mild form of autism, and the story is told from her point of view. How would the story be different if it were told from a "normal" point of view?

6. Because of her Asperger's syndrome, Morgen will always have a hard time reading social cues, interacting with others, and understanding innuendo, subtext, and humor. That said, how does she change and grow throughout the story? Did a particular incident help you empathize with her difficulties? With her triumphs?

7. Morgen seems to have more of an affinity for things (pianos, the old house on Ninth Street, Tutti, the jetty cats) than for other people. Why might she feel this way? Can you relate?

8. As much as Morgen struggles socially and feels disconnected, she generally views life with joy and with an inventive sense of wonder. What is your most memorable image, phrase, or moment concerning Morgen? Why did it resonate with you?

9. Have you ever struggled to communicate with someone you care about only to be misunderstood? Share an example.

10. At what moment does Morgen feel empowered to take responsibility for her future? Have you experienced a similar turning point?

11. Morgen is introspective and often in tune with her mind's eye and mind's ear. What images and songs get stuck in your head?

12. How important is music in your daily life?

Characters in General

13. Do the characters seem believable to you? Which ones do you like best, like least, and why? Which one would you enjoy talking to? Taking a walk on the beach with? Having dinner with? Inviting into your world? What do you have in common with this character?

14. Comment on the relationship between power, love, and sex in the story.

15. Why do some women tolerate psychological and physical domination or abuse?

General

16. What emotions did the story evoke for you and when did your strongest emotions occur?

17. In general, what did you like best about the story? What did you like least?

18. If you were making a movie of *Jetty Cat Palace Café*, who would you cast for each character?

19. Comment on the use of symbolism, magical realism, and Morgen's peculiar perceptions in the story. Do you find these elements enjoyable? Why or why not?

20. Does the story come full circle in the end? In what way? Is the ending satisfying? If not, how would you change it? What issues are left unresolved?

Takeaway

Every character in this story has a secret! For example, Grandma Eleanor says, "Daughters never know everything about their mothers." Later, Morgen reflects, Mothers never know everything about their daughters, either.

What makes us keep secrets from those we hold dear?

Have you ever kept a secret from someone you love?

Why? And how did it affect your relationship?

How did you feel when the truth emerged?

Is there a story there?

The author would love to read your answers to these questions.

Please contact her at jettycatpalacecafe.com or on Twitter @jettycatsanta